CRISTINA

By
Jake Parent

First Printing, 2016

ISBN: 978-0-9909036-0-4

Modern Minimalist Press
www.jakedparent.com

Author: jake@jakedparent.com
Press: press@jakedparent.com
Bulk ordering: info@jakedparent.com

Cover art and design by Riley James Milhem

For all the single mothers in the world.

PLEASURE POINT

1

It had been four years since the little girl's body was found, mutilated and buried in a quarry near her home in Pleasure Point, California.

The same home Cristina Rodriguez now wanted to buy.

Elbows propped on a towel, lying on her back, Cristina wiggled her feet into the warm sand. The sun toasted her light-brown skin. She closed her eyes, inhaled a deep breath of salty air, and listened to the waves crash onto shore.

Thankfully, she'd remembered to grab her bathing suit before leaving her grandmother's place that morning. A bikini, red with white polka dots, the tight material stretched around her youthful curves like a second sheet of skin.

After going by to see the house, she pulled over at the first beach she could find. It turned out to be a secluded paradise. Of the few people there, most were surfers, either going into or coming out of the water.

Cristina's thick, black hair, normally hanging in waves down to her breasts, was now tied up in a red bandanna. Her almond eyes hid behind sunglasses set on high cheekbones. She dug a tube of Carmex from a canvas bag and rubbed it onto plump lips.

One hand protected a file folder against the breeze. She used the other to put away her lip balm, and then to light a cigarette.

The folder held a stack of photocopied news articles the real estate agent had given her. Each clipping told a part of the gruesome story.

But the beach is only ten minutes away, Cristina reminded herself. *You can literally see the water from the front yard.*

The agent had tried to be brief about what happened. Actually, all she would really say was that a "tragedy" occurred in the home, and that Cristina could get all the details by reading the collection of articles. That, of course, seemed more like the lady's tactful way of not discussing it any more than she had to.

From what Cristina was reading, the official account was that the stepfather basically went crazy one day, secretly kidnapping his wife's daughter, Annie. He then hid her away somewhere for several weeks, before murdering her and burying her body in a quarry up in the mountains.

Police only discovered he was the one who did it because he wrote out a confession letter before taking his own life. Prior to that, he'd successfully fooled everyone into thinking he had nothing to do with the crime.

Things only got worse from there. Annie's mother was so grief-stricken by her loss, she too took her own life, hanging herself in the home's downstairs closet.

The story touched a particularly strong nerve with Cristina, who herself had a young daughter. At five, Anise was only a year older than the murdered girl had been at the time of her death.

Even their names are similar.

With all that had happened to Cristina over the past year, Anise was now everything. Her entire world. She couldn't imagine what it would be like to lose her.

She smothered her Lucky Strike in the sand and slid

another one from the package. She was supposed to be quitting, but lit up anyway before going back to the articles.

Skimming, but unable to really bring herself to read closely, most of what she saw concerned events immediately surrounding the girl's disappearance. There was surprisingly little about what, if any, evidence had been uncovered later on.

One article talked about the initial massive search of the woods around the house, and even included a quote from the stepfather.

"We're so worried and just pray every day that our little girl comes home."

What a scumbag.

Cristina flipped onto her stomach, hot with anger.

She flicked an ash and kept reading, still not putting full effort into it. Not wanting to. Somehow her mind couldn't bring itself to believe that something so awful could ever have happened in such a perfect house.

There was, however, one headline that caught her attention, just before she closed the folder.

FBI Questions PPPD Findings in Killing of Local Girl

But she couldn't read anymore. No matter what had happened, it was in the past. It had nothing to do with her. And none of it changed the fact that Pleasure Point was an absolute paradise.

Finishing her second smoke, she unceremoniously removed her bikini bottom from her butt crack, examining her backside and legs as she did.

Cristina had always thought of her thick, round

booty as her best physical feature. And still did, despite the numerous scars now covering it – part of a dense network of healed wounds that ranged from her knees to the small of her back.

She then peeked down at her chest. It wasn't too bad either. Big for her small frame. Full. And despite having had a baby, her breasts still managed to defy the will of gravity, even when she was naked.

Rubbing lotion onto her arms, she fingered the slightly raised edges of her tattoos. A thick bush of red roses completely covered her left arm, beginning at the wrist and extending just past the curve of her shoulder. The flowers popped so vibrantly, sometimes she could almost smell them. The spaces in between the blooms were filled with dark-green leaves and thorned stems.

Her right arm was a mix of individual pieces she'd been compiling since she was a teenager. A music note on her shoulder. The California flag on her forearm. A calligraphy of her daughter's name on her inner bicep. And a few other more random ones that had seemed like good ideas at the time.

Her chest, stomach, back, and legs were all inkless. Many times in the past year, she'd thought about getting something done to cover her scars, but could never decide on anything in particular. And, lately, she'd come to accept them as a part of who she was. A visible reminder of her journey.

Continuing to rub in the lotion, she smiled at the spongy elasticity of her skin. It felt so alive and vibrant, and she remembered a time, not so long ago, when that hadn't been the case.

She slipped the bottle of Banana Boat back into her bag, watching as two blond surfers with dark tans walked by carrying boards. Each wore shades, and open wetsuits pulled down to the waist, showing off ridged abs.

Cristina watched them and smiled.

Both returned smooth grins.

One of them lost track of where he was going. His foot caught on a mound of sand, lurching him forward. But he managed to hang onto his board and recover impressively.

She held in a laugh.

Staring off toward the blue horizon, her mind continued contemplating the beauty of the house and the area, allowing the perfectness of it all to cancel out her uncertainty about the disturbing events that had taken place there.

Ten minutes from the beach, she told herself again. *Ten minutes.*

2

Cristina wanted to hit a 12-step meeting while she was in town.

She'd recently collected her one-year sobriety chip. To commemorate the occasion, her sponsor, Michelle, suggested she renew a commitment to recovery by going to 90 meeting in 90 days.

It seemed kind of ridiculous. Like something only a person fresh-on-the-wagon should have to do. But Cristina had learned to trust Michelle – a feisty, black lesbian, ex-crackhead, originally from South Central LA, whom Cristina credited with having saved her life.

For that reason, if nothing else, she dutifully drove her 12-year-old red Honda Civic around the big white church's neighborhood, looking for a place to park.

Her hometown was only about 50 miles away, but its vast urban sprawl, filled with more than a million residents, was a separate universe from Pleasure Point.

The beach town had a little more than 50,000 people living in it. Big enough that a person could more-or-less stay anonymous if she wanted to, but small enough to find a sense of community, too. A perfect balance. At least, that's what Cristina hoped.

As disturbing as the story behind the house might have been, every second she was in Pleasure Point, the town strengthened its pull, beckoning her toward paradise with its carefree vibe and quaint, tree-lined streets.

She finally found a place to park and walked into the meeting five minutes late. Everyone in the room looked up at her. With an apologetic smile, she found a seat in the back of the musty room that smelled like her grandmother's closet.

Just as she sat down, the guy running the meeting asked if anyone was new to the group.

She hesitated, but then said, "Hi, I'm Cristina. I'm an alcoholic and an addict. First time at this meeting. Thinking of moving to the area. Thanks for having me."

"Hi Cristina," came the well-practiced response.

Sitting again, she scanned her surroundings.

Most of the people there were around her age. Mid- to late-twenties. Some a little older. A lot of them were white, but not all. There were a few other brown faces in the room, too. One lady kept mean-mugging her, presumably because of the interruption. But the overall vibe was pretty casual. Everyone seemed to know each other and acted comfortable in the space they occupied.

Cristina felt completely out of place.

About halfway through, all she wanted to do was get up and leave. But when she started to stand, Michelle's loving, forceful, voice popped into her head, repeating annoying 12-step sayings.

"Meeting makers make it, honey."

"It only works if you work it."

Cristina pulled her lips into a grin. She glanced at the woman who'd been staring, and who was now visibly frustrated with the fact that the stranger in the room was happy. Cristina smiled wider.

The clock ticked slowly away, reminding her of junior high. The way time slowed down near the end of a period. She even once had class in a room where she swore the minute hand sometimes moved backward.

Mercifully, the meeting eventually ended.

The group stood, joined hands, and said the Lord's Prayer.

"Keep coming back, it works!" they collectively added in semi-unison.

Cristina almost tripped over someone's dog as she rushed toward the door. Without stopping, she apologized to no one in particular, moving out into the sunlight and the fresh, salty air.

The minute she was outside, she lit a cigarette, trying to remember which direction her car was in.

Before she could be on her way, she felt a tap on her shoulder. She glanced in that direction. No one was there. She turned the other way. Nothing. So she continued in a complete circle, until her eyes caught someone crouching, trying to quickly move around her.

His presence revealed, the man straightened his legs and jumped into the air.

"Hi!" he let out, kicking his legs out like a hair-metal guitarist.

Judging from his smell, he was obviously homeless, but appeared to be sober.

He extended his hand.

"I'm Danny Dee," he said. "Just want to welcome a fellow traveler to town."

"Hi," she responded, taking his hand out of politeness.

When she tried to let go, he pulled her hand toward his mouth, where he gently pressed his lips into her soft skin.

His scruffy beard felt coated in grease.

She was about to reach for the knife she kept in the back pocket of her jeans, when he finally released his grip.

He bowed like some kind of knight and then backed away, at which point she got a better look at him. He was a lot taller than her, but that wasn't unusual. Most people were. Other than that, she thought he looked like your typical burnout. A skinny white dude sporting a Pearl Jam shirt with a red and grey flannel tied around his waist. Gross, old blue jeans. Long, oily hair. And, of course, the beard.

His smell – sour sweat with a slight hint of dried piss – made Cristina want to throw up.

"Hey, Danny, leave the newbie alone," a flat voice said from behind her. "Didn't you hear the lady? She's thinking about moving here. You want to scare away such an attractive woman?"

Oh God, another one, Cristina thought.

When she turned around, Cristina was surprised to see how much the ambiguity of the voice's tone matched that of the speaker's gender. The person standing before her was wearing a plain, buttoned-up shirt that completely masked any curves (or lack thereof). The hair was cropped and combed neatly forward. Thick eyeglasses magnified a pair of eyes that looked like tiny olives.

The person smiled and said plainly, "Hi."

"Hi," Cristina returned.

All she got back was a blank stare.

Cristina tossed her finished cigarette into the gutter. The guy with the beard dove toward it, actually throwing himself onto the ground. When he bounced up again, the smoldering butt was hanging from his nose. He puffed it that way, as casually as if it were in his mouth.

Cristina looked at him, then back at the other person. She laughed and walked toward her car, waving to the duo behind her without looking back.

3

After a weekend of consideration, and a couple of deep conversations with Michelle, Cristina decided to take the place in Pleasure Point.

Since she had the entire purchase price in cash, she was allowed to move in as soon as she wanted.

The decision meant that, for the first time during her sobriety, she would be away from Michelle and the support network of strong women she'd built up over the past year. But, thankfully, it also meant she would be a lot farther away from her ex-husband. And, best of all, she and Anise would, for the first time, have their very own place.

Cristina would be forever grateful to her grandmother and uncle, who'd taken turns letting she and Anise stay in their respective one-bedroom apartments over the past year. But neither of those places felt like home. After all, it's hard to settle in when you have to sleep curled up on the couch together, even for someone as petite as Cristina.

So she couldn't help but let out a whoop of joy and relief as she drove her Civic up the steep, gravel driveway and into the dirt courtyard, parking in front of their new home.

From the backseat, Anise tried to make the same sound, ending up instead with a shrieky wail that made Cristina laugh.

"You tell 'em, chica," she said, reaching her hand back so they could high-five.

"Ok, baby," Cristina added, watching in the rear-view mirror as her daughter undid herself from the car seat. "You ready to see our new house?"

Anise's forehead creased.

"Mamma, why do we have to live by ourselves? Why can't Aba come stay with us?"

"Don't worry, she'll come visit. We can't sleep on her couch forever though."

Anise didn't seem convinced. "I think it's fun."

Outside the car, Cristina bent down and kissed her daughter's forehead. She felt washed over by a warm feeling of contentment, one she'd only ever known in Anise's presence. It felt like they were the only two people in the world, together in search of all life had to offer.

Their house sat atop a foothill overlooking the ocean, among two other similar places, the collection of which was spread out in a triangle around a dusty courtyard. A sort of dirt cul-de-sac.

Of the three houses, theirs was the smallest. It wasn't much, actually. Not compared to some of the giant Victorian homes Cristina had seen while driving through downtown Pleasure Point. Their new house was simple. Two stories. Plain wood. Light-brown with dark-brown trim. Some of the paint peeling at the corners. A dense rose bush under the front window, one that made Cristina unconsciously run her fingers along her tattooed arm.

Unlike the other two houses, theirs had no garage. Not that it was really an issue. There was plenty of space to park in front of the small crabgrass lawn. Space was something they had in abundance. The shared property was a bit outside of town, and the only thing around for a couple of miles.

The area behind the house was forested. Mostly a mix of Redwoods and coastal pines. The earthy smells of green needles, dirt, and tree bark nicely complemented the brine of the sea.

From the front yard they could see a dirt path worn down the hill, leading to a stretch of coast below where the sea butted heads with a rocky cliffside.

Further out, the sparkling water of the Pacific Ocean filled Pleasure Bay.

"Momma look," Anise said, pointing and giggling. "It's a bunny rabbit!"

Cristina returned from her thoughts to see that a small brown rabbit with a white stomach had indeed come out of hiding to greet them. His little nose wiggled as he looked up, cautious but seemingly unafraid.

"She's so cute! Can I pet her?"

"Let's leave her alone for right now, baby. I'm not sure if she's really that friendly. If she is, I'm sure we'll have a chance to pet her later. How about . . . we go see your new room?"

"Yaaaaaay!"

Anise had spent most of the drive talking about having her own room.

"How big is it?"

"Is there a bed?"

"Where will my stuffed animals sleep?"

"Can I put pictures on the wall?"

Cristina had smiled at that one.

"Of course you can," she'd told her. "Just no boys."

"Eww," Anise responded.

"Good girl."

Cristina had laughed, but she knew it was only a matter of time before her little girl wasn't so little anymore. That fact made her even more determined to get busy building their new life.

She pulled the key to the front door from her bag,

inserted it, and turned the knob. As soon as the two stepped inside, a horrible stench blasted them in the face.

"Gross!" Cristina coughed and covered her face. "What *is* that?!"

"It's yucky, mamma!"

"I know, baby. Let's cover our noses and try to open some windows, OK?"

They made their way down the hall and into the kitchen, where the smell was even worse. Cristina opened the window over the sink with one hand while she continued to hold her nose. A gush of fresh, salty air rushed in.

Locating the source of the smell, she opened the refrigerator and shrieked.

Inside was a possum mother and her litter of babies. All dead.

Before a curious Anise could wiggle around her mom to see what was inside, Cristina shut the door. With a gentle touch, she guided her daughter's face up to her own. Anise was plugging her nose and breathing loudly through her mouth.

"What is it, mamma?" she asked nasally.

"It's, OK. It's just some yucky stuff someone forgot to clean up. We'll get it out of here in no time."

Cristina slid open the glass door leading from the kitchen, out into a small backyard overgrown with weeds and bushes. The jungle of growth was surrounded by a short fence. A gate opened more-or-less directly into the forest.

The worst of the gamey stink was soon carried away by the draft.

Cristina took Anise by the hand. Together they walked back through the kitchen and down the hallway, toward the front of the house.

Cristina glanced at the closet door, remembering

the newspaper article describing how the previous tenant had taken her own life. A vision of a lifeless young woman flashed into Cristina's mind, one end of a rope tied to the closet's wooden hanger rod, the other looped around the woman's neck.

She shook the thought away and led Anise up the stairs, down another hallway, toward a closed bedroom door.

"OK, chica," Cristina said. "Shut your eyes."

Anise used both her hands to cover the top half of her face.

"Alright, mamma," she said seriously. "I'm ready."

Cristina had barely touched the doorknob when another scene projected itself across her mind: a young girl being pulled from bed, held quiet by an adult's gloved hand over her mouth.

The vision disappeared as quickly as it had arrived. All that remained when the door swung inward was a completely empty bedroom.

"Open your eyes, baby!"

Anise did as she was told. Her face beamed with wonder. Yet, she hesitated at the threshold, as if unable to believe the reality of what was before her. Glowing with anticipation, her gaze slowly turned toward her mother.

"Go ahead," Cristina said. "It's all yours."

With that, Anise dashed into the room, filling the space with a rapid sequence of squeaky giggles. She ran toward each corner and touched the seams where the walls met. Then to the room's center, where she spun around in circles several times before slowly coming to a stop.

With a confused look, she asked, "Mamma?"

"Yes, chica?"

"Where am I going to sleep?"

Cristina laughed hard. The joyful sound echoed

against the room's bare walls. She fell to her knees and grabbed Anise with both arms.

"Don't worry. Your bed will be here with the rest of our stuff very soon."

A few guys Cristina knew from her hometown 12-step scene had kindly volunteered to drive a truck down with all of their belongings. One of them had the hots for Cristina. She suspected he was the one who talked the others into joining the effort. She had zero interest in him – in any guy at the moment – but she'd certainly been grateful for the offer of help. It's not like they were going to fit it all in the Civic.

Lost in thought, Cristina didn't notice that Anise had found a piece of paper, which the girl now dangled in the air with two fingers.

"What's this, mamma?"

"I don't know, baby. Let's see."

It was a picture of a young girl, and appeared to have been cut from a newspaper clipping. It hadn't been in the collection of articles the real estate agent had given Cristina, but somehow she knew it was the girl who'd been killed.

Annie.

"Oh," Cristina said. "That must be the little girl who lived here before. Maybe she left the picture because she liked her room so much."

"Can I keep it?"

Cristina didn't know what to say.

Where did the picture even come from?

It most likely fell out of the folder of clippings the agent lady gave me. Or from someone else's. She probably handed that same folder out to every person who saw the place.

Part of Cristina wanted to rip the piece of paper into tiny pieces right there, just to be rid of it. But she could tell by Anise's face that doing so would result in an instant tantrum, putting a damper on an otherwise perfect day.

So she said, "Um, sure. But how about we go see what else this house has in store for us, huh?"

"OK!"

When Anise turned away, Cristina crumpled the piece of paper into a ball and slid it into her pocket.

4

There were no more surprises to be found in the rest of the house.

Cristina called the real estate agent, who, thankfully, was able to get someone out right away to remove the unlucky possum family from the fridge.

Cristina was sure she would never forget the sight of those poor dead little creatures, but by the time everything was disinfected and cleaned, the refrigerator looked and smelled brand new.

The exterminator was nice about it all. A little too nice, actually.

He wouldn't stop staring at her cleavage as he explained that a cleaning person probably left the fridge open. His guess was that the possums climbed in and made a home, then the wind slammed the door closed, causing them to eventually either suffocate or starve.

"Happens all time."

He gave her his card and told her to call him if she ever needed "anything at all."

She half-expected him to add a big, cartoon wink.

"OK, great," she said, holding the business card up as he packed his things. "You're the best. I'll definitely let you know when I need you."

She wiggled her fingers in the air as he pulled his van away from the house, adding a bubbly smile for good measure.

Anise pointed to the picture on the side of the van. "It's a giant bug!"

"Yes," Cristina said, chuckling. "It certainly is. How about some lunch, chica?"

The two went inside and opened a small blue cooler. Most of the food was gone, eaten on the drive. But there were still a few of Aba's tamales left, tightly covered in Saran Wrap. After Cristina warmed them using the built-in microwave over the counter, they sat on the floor to eat.

As usual, Anise was quiet the entire time, sitting straight-backed and proper, even without a table. Cristina had no idea where she'd learned the habit of silent eating, but she wasn't about to question it.

Just as they finished lunch, Cristina heard the sound of a big vehicle crunching gravel under its tires as it came up the driveway and parked in front of the house.

"That must be our stuff," she said.

"Yaaaaay!"

The two disposed of their lunch trash in an empty plastic shopping bag. Cristina casually added the crumpled up piece of newspaper from her pocket as well.

In the courtyard, they found three men doing their best to quickly pile out of a U-Haul truck's crowded cab.

"Good lord, Rich," one said. "Maybe burritos weren't the best idea before a road trip, huh?"

Rich was the one with a crush on Cristina.

The guy giving him a hard time was Brian, his 12-step sponsor. A large man, both in body and personality, Brian was in his fifties and had more than 25 years of sobriety. He'd seen just about everything in his time, and had an endless number of crazy stories to prove it.

She ran toward him and threw her arms around his hefty frame.

"Hey!" she said.

"Oh, hello," Brian deadpanned. "And you are?"

She smiled and socked him in the arm.

He then added, seriously, "How the hell are ya, sweetie? You guys manage your way down here OK? You need anything . . ." He scanned the surroundings and held up his arms. ". . . like a freakin' roommate? Good lord, this place is sweet."

He was purposely ignoring Anise, who now stood patiently looking up at him with bright, round eyes.

"Helloooo, Uncle Brian!" she finally said with feigned annoyance.

He acted surprised.

"Oh, well hello little lady. Where'd you come from?"

"I was right here the whole time, silly goose!"

"You were?" he took off his glasses and examined them. "Wow, I need to get these things checked. Well, what's your name?"

She laughed at their familiar game. "It's Anise! You know it! Where's my candy, mister?"

"Chica!" Cristina said. "Be polite."

"No, no, no," Brian said, absentmindedly searching through his pockets. "I admire a woman who knows what she wants. Oh, here we go."

He produced a green-apple Jolly Rancher. Anise's favorite. She reached out with a mischievous look, snatching the candy from his hand and immediately unwrapping it.

"Hey, what do we say?" Cristina asked.

Using two fingers, Anise carefully placed the candy onto her tongue.

"Thanks, Uncle Brian!" she garbled through a full mouth, lunging forward to hug his leg.

He patted her on the head.

"Where'd the other guys go?" Cristina asked when she noticed they'd disappeared.

"I don't know," Brian said to her, before shouting like a foreman. "HEY! Knuckleheads! Where you be?"

From the other side of the truck walked two guys who were Cristina's age. One was Rich. He seemed to be looking around at everything *except* Cristina. The other was his friend, Pete, who Cristina hadn't heard say more than a few words the entire time she'd known him.

"You guys forget how to say hi to a lady?" Brian scolded.

"Hi, Cristina," Rich said, finally looking at her just long enough to offer a shy smile.

Pete waved.

"Hi guys!" she said. "How was the ride?"

"OK," Rich answered. "Long. But, um, not too bad. It was OK. I really didn't mind it."

Pete shrugged.

As much as Cristina had no problem messing with overly-aggressive males, she hated to see the nice ones squirm. She hugged them both in turn with all the enthusiasm she could manage.

"Well, thanks for coming," she said. "I really appreciate you driving down here with our stuf—"

"HEY!!!" a deep, powerful voice screamed from the other side of the truck.

All of them jumped, except Brian. Cristina instinctively grabbed Anise by the shoulders and moved in front of her.

"HEY!!!" The voice barked again. "Whose fucking truck is this?! Whose FUCKING truck is this?! WHOSE FUCKING TRUCK IS THIS?!"

A beast of a man appeared from around the edge of the truck, his face a reddened nest of rage. He was well over six feet tall. White with a shaved head. Bulging muscles bursting from under a white tank top. Tattoos covering his chest, arms, and neck. He even had a couple on his face, but the ink was old and faded, making it impossible to tell what any of it depicted.

After a moment of shock, Cristina told Anise to go inside.

Then she snapped.

"Look, motherfucker!" she yelled at the man, standing on her toes and still needing to reach so she could point a finger in his face. "I don't know who the fuck you think you are, but I've got a little girl and you just scared the crap out of her."

At first, he seemed stunned. But after a moment, he crossed his arms and cackled a dismissive laugh.

"Oh, a tough little beaner bitch, huh? I ought to show you what I do with women who have too much lip on them."

He dropped his clenched fists and stared hard, his face now almost purple with anger.

She didn't back down or look away.

With slow patience, she said, "Get. The fuck. Away. From. My house."

He snickered out his nose, but broke eye contact.

"Look, bitch," he said, still not meeting her eyes. He pointed to the house next door. "You see *that*? That's *my* house. And your shithead friends here are blocking my path to the driveway with their fucking truck. So, unless you move it, I'm going to move it for you."

Cristina continued to stare him down.

After a deep breath, she responded, "I said get the fuck away from my house. I'm not afraid of you, you pussy-ass motherfucker. And if you come back here like this again, you'll wish you hadn't."

He finally looked at her again, trying to scoff and remain hard, but his fierceness had mostly evaporated. Now he seemed lost for something to say.

He stuck his finger about three inches from Cristina's face.

Part of her was tempted to bite it.

"Move it," he said, before turning around to head back the way he'd come. As he walked around the truck, he punched its sliding back door, leaving a sizeable dent.

The crash of metal echoed in the courtyard.

A few seconds later, they heard his front door slam.

"Aw, man . . ." Brian said after a few moments of tense silence. "The fine folks at U-Haul aren't going to appreciate *that*."

The other two guys chuckled uneasily.

Cristina was still too upset to do anything but scowl.

"Ugggggh," she said, pacing the lawn. Her light-brown cheeks were flushed with hot blood. She was on the edge of tears. "Ugggggggggggggggh. I'm so pissed."

"I would have never guessed," Brian said.

She looked at him with a flash of anger. He distorted his face in mock fear and she couldn't help but laugh.

He put his arm around her, drawing her small frame into his girth.

"Can I just say one thing?" he asked.

"What?" she said, still trying her best to be angry.

"You're a bad ass."

Blood again rushed into her cheeks, although this time in slight embarrassment.

"I was so ready to kick that guy's ass."

"I know, kid. I know."

"What am I supposed to do with a neighbor like that?"

"Don't worry about it, OK? In my experience, most bullies won't bother you once you pop them a good one in the mouth, and I think you accomplished that with your words, if not with your fists."

"Is everything, OK, mamma?"

Cristina turned around and saw Anise staring up at her, clutching her favorite blue teddy bear to her chest.

Cristina squatted so she was at eyelevel with her daughter and said, "Yes, chica."

"We're still going to stay here, right? I still get my own room?"

Cristina took a breath, projecting strength outward, a trick she'd learned at a meditation retreat Michelle once dragged her to.

"We're going to be just fine," she said. "Mommy told that mean man to go away, and he won't bother us anymore, OK?"

"OK, mamma. Can we go to the beach now?"

Cristina chuckled uneasily, a mix of emotions still buzzing in her chest.

"Not yet, baby. We have to unload our stuff first."

With that, the crew first moved the truck a few feet closer to the house, then got to work.

Despite the incident, the mood was light as they unloaded the U-Haul, a levity fueled in no small part by Brian's jokes and mock-criticisms of their collective efforts. But Cristina couldn't go more than a few minutes without glancing at the house next door, wondering if this really was the last she would hear from her delightful new neighbor.

5

The last few boxes were coming off the U-Haul when a car puttered up the gravel road – an old red Hyundai that looked remarkably similar to Cristina's car.

Given what happened earlier with Mr. Psycho, she wasn't sure what to expect.

But the man behind the wheel was definitely no crazy skinhead. His puffy, grey beard and thick glasses made him look more like someone who might work at a library. He waved cheerfully before continuing on to park in front of the house across the courtyard, the one nearest the ocean.

The short, portly man made his way toward the tired group of movers, an enthusiastic smile on his face.

"Oh, boy," he said as he approached. "I can't tell you how happy it makes me to see someone moving in after all this time."

When no one spoke, he continued, "You must be the new young lady of the house. Cristina, right? That's what the real estate agent told me. I'm Jack Benning. I teach at the community college. History mostly. But I also teach remedial civics in the fall. And I used to have a few more classes too, but the bureaucracy of it all got me so frustrated I had to take a step back a few years ago. Sorry, I'm rambling. I do that sometimes when I get excited. How are you?"

He offered his hand. His mouth bent into a grin. The friendly sparkle in his eyes dented Cristina's cautiousness. She couldn't help but return a smile of her own as she shook his hand.

"Hi, sir," she said.

"Oh, no, no, no, no. No sirs. That makes me feel as old as I look. How about Jack?"

"OK, Jack. Nice to meet you. I'm Cristina."

She introduced her friends and told Jack about their earlier confrontation.

"That would be Rick," he said, shaking his head. "I wish I was surprised. Needless to say, he's a jerk. Thinks he's some kind of survivalist getting ready for the end of the world or something. Sometimes he spends weeks out in the woods rolling around like an animal. If it was up to me, he'd have been out of here a long time ago. The truth is though, from what I've seen at least, he isn't as tough as he acts. Sounds like you really put him in his place, though. I wish I could've seen it." He paused and then continued. "But if you want to know more about him, I'll tell you once you get settled. I don't want to do anything to dampen what should be a momentous occasion. I know it sure is for me."

Cristina thought for a moment and then said, "You know what? You're right. It *is* a big day for us. We can't let one jerk ruin it. That would be like letting him win."

Jack's face lit up. "Exactly." He spread his arms and added, "Hey, you guys look pretty beat, can I make you all dinner tonight? It would be my pleasure."

Cristina thought about it for a moment. She considered asking for a rain check, but instead said, "Well, since our fridge is completely empty, I think we might just have to take you up on that. You can meet my daughter, too. Her name's Anise. She's conked out at the moment, poor baby. It's been a long day for her."

Brian stepped in and said, "Well, Jack, me and the boys here would love to join you all, but unfortunately I have to get them back into their cages before the zookeeper realizes they're missing. Next time?"

"Sure," said Jack. "So, two for dinner then? I'll make your reservations for around six, if that's OK."

Cristina agreed.

After saying his farewells, her new neighbor walked back to his place, whistling a happy tune.

Halfway across the courtyard, he started to skip.

6

Anise and Cristina were busy eating edamame at Jack's kitchen table. They greedily slid soy beans into their mouths as their host stood at the countertop chopping ginger and green onions on a cutting board.

"These are delicious, Jack," Cristina said, covering her mouth as she chewed. "What is it you're cooking?"

"I hope you like fish. I found some great fresh-caught salmon at the farmer's market today. This guy was probably swimming this morning."

Anise looked at her mom with some doubt but didn't comment.

The fish turned out to indeed be amazing. The best Cristina had ever tasted.

Everything about the meal was wonderful.

To go along with the fish, Jack prepared green beans and some kind of squash. The fish sat atop a scoop of perfectly-cooked brown rice, something Cristina normally didn't care for. But somehow Jack managed to make it taste more like popcorn than the soggy lump she usually produced. For dessert, fresh local strawberries with a bowl of melted chocolate to dip them in.

Cristina smiled at the way her stout, scholarly-looking neighbor seemed a bit guilty as he took his fourth and fifth strawberries. She loved that he went for it anyway.

The whole dinner experience made her feel like a mature, responsible adult.

During dinner, Jack told Cristina a bit about himself and the history of the town. As he spoke about these things, his voice changed noticeably into that of a teacher, though it wasn't unpleasant in the slightest.

He said he'd lived in Pleasure Point since he was a boy. His parents both worked at the cement factory their entire lives.

"Although it's become a tourist town in recent years, Pleasure Point was built on the business of extracting limestone and clay from the earth, and then processing it into cement. For almost fifty years, in fact, that was the lifeblood of the whole area. But when the factory and its quarry closed ten years ago – or, I should say, when the greedy owners moved the whole operation to China – the entire town was devastated. What was once a thriving enclave of working-class people soon saw its unemployment rate rise to nearly fifty percent, almost overnight. When that happened, Pleasure Point was transformed, for a time, from paradise into a desperate shadow of itself."

He stopped there. They put the dishes in the sink and moved outside to sit on the back porch.

Their timing was perfect.

As the three of them each claimed a place to sit under a standup propane heater, the blood-orange sun was ending its day by painting the sky with a full palette of brilliant colors.

Despite the fact the beach beyond the cliffs was still a good distance away, Cristina could clearly see the waves as they folded over themselves. Offshore, the wind diced the water full of whitecaps.

A number of sailboats traced a path across the glowing horizon. Above them, seagulls and pelicans soared, gliding more than flapping. Every so often, one dipped down into the sea, coming up a few moments later with a mouthful of water, and presumably dinner.

"We're lucky," Jack said. "There's no fog tonight. The ocean must like you guys."

Anise curled into a ball on an oversized beanbag chair and fell asleep almost instantly.

Jack had brought out a bottle of port, which he said he'd been saving for a special occasion. He poured some into two small glasses.

"None for me, thanks," Cristina said, sounding harsher than she'd intended.

"Oh, OK, very good. Not a fan of port, huh? I suppose it's not for everyone."

"No, it's not that. I just don't drink."

Jack studied her. "Well, you can tell me *that* story another day."

He smiled and held up one of the glasses.

"To new neighbors," he declared.

"Yes!" Cristina answered cheerfully, raising her glass of water into the air.

Jack sipped his wine.

"You want to hear more about the town?" he asked, leaning in conspiratorially. "I have to warn you, it gets a little ugly from here. We should make sure Anise is asleep. I wouldn't want her to hear what I'm about to tell you."

As he paused, they could hear her gently snoring.

"I guess that answers that," Jack declared.

He downed the first glass and went to work on the second as he returned himself to teaching mode.

He said that after the factory closed, homelessness skyrocketed. Then the drugs came in. And for about five years, there was a whole lot of destitution and not a lot of hope.

"It got so bad, there was even a weird cult that became pretty prominent, made up of speed-freaks and junky types. The guy who led it was sort of this Manson type. I mean, I don't know how much of it's true, but people say he tried to make doing drugs into a kind of religion. Apparently, they even had their own little bible and everything."

Cristina tried to listen without reacting. It was hard. She felt sick to her stomach, and could feel the color rushing out of her face.

Jack told her, "I'm not telling you this to scare you or anything. I can stop if you want me to. In fact, I should do that. I'm not sure what I'm doing, anyhow. Filling your head with all this nonsense on your first day here."

"No, it's OK," Cristina assured him. "I'm fine. It's just hard to believe something so ugly could exist in a place that's so perfect and beautiful. But go on. How did the town recover?"

"Well, I'm not sure I would go so far as to say that Pleasure Point has really 'recovered,' per se." He curled his fingers into quotes as he said the word recovered. "But it does seem like things have started to turn around. At least in some ways. Probably the biggest factor is tourism. Once the town got so bad, property values plummeted, and eventually a group of developers and businessmen saw it as an opportunity to make some bucks. A few years ago, after the feds arrested that cult-leader scumbag, these developers started reopening stores down by the amusement park. A lot of us locals were pretty skeptical at first, and to be honest still are, to a degree. These business guys definitely seem to have their own ideas about what's best for the future of Pleasure Point. But I have to admit, *that* part of town looks a whole lot better than it did. And a lot more people around here have jobs now, even if the work pays significantly less than those same people made working at the quarry."

Cristina nodded and said, "I'm surprised I've never heard about that cult. It sounds crazy. What was the guy's name?"

"Charles Walters. I'll never forget that. Sounds kind of like the name of a TV weatherman or something."

Cristina snickered, holding her hand against her lips as it morphed into a yawn. She closed her eyes for a moment and then rubbed them.

"Well," Jack said. "Looks like it's time for mom to hit the hay, too."

Cristina tried to make herself alert. "Oh, no. I have to help you clean up, Jack. It's the least I can d—"

"Fagettabout it!" he said in a fake Italian accent. "Get that little girl and yourself to bed. Although, normally I'd take you up on it. I cook. You clean. That's a deal I'm always game for."

Jack walked Cristina, Anise snuggled in her arms, across the now dark courtyard.

Above them, a blanket of stars twinkled with a brilliance Cristina had seldom witnessed growing up in a light-polluted city. She was distracted enough by the sky's beauty that she only casually glanced in the direction of Mr. Psycho's house. His lights were all out, anyway, making the place barely visible in the shadow of several towering redwoods.

They paused in the middle of the courtyard to gaze down at the shoreline. The crickets hummed a steady stream of chirps around them. The property suddenly felt quite remote. And at the same time, so beautiful.

As if highlighting the thought, the rising moon, almost full, reflected a brilliant silver light onto the fingers of rock below. Even from a distance, Cristina could hear the water thunder against the cliff, each rumbling wave sounding louder than the one before it.

"Wow," she said, almost to herself.

"Yep, south swell. That's when we get the big ones

down in The Cove."

He turned to her, obviously trying to hold in a laugh.

He asked, "Did anyone tell you about Pirate's Cove?"

She shifted Anise in her arms and raised an eyebrow.

"No. Is there a treasure or something?"

Jack answered her with a hearty belly-laugh that showed no concern for the fact they were outside.

He said, "You *could* say that. Actually, it's one of the prettiest stretches of coast in all of California, and probably the world, if I do say so myself. When the current is like it is tonight, it has some of the biggest waves around, too. And when it's coming from any other direction, the break goes out a bit and it's actually a pretty nice place to swim. But . . ."

He started laughing again.

"What?" Cristina asked, now genuinely curious. "What is it?"

"Oh gosh. You'd think I'm eight years old. I tell you what though, sometimes I feel like it." He turned and pointed down toward the water. "You see that stretch of sand? Out past where the water comes right up to the cliffs."

"OK," she answered, squinting to show her enthusiasm for the task. "Sure."

"Well, when the tide's down, you can walk along the rocks under the cliff and over to the beach. And, well, uh . . . just be fair-warned that some people . . . OK, I'll say it, old-fogies like me, sometimes swim or just walk around in their birthday suits down there." He held his hands in the air. "Now, it's not nearly as exciting as it sounds. Like I said, it's mostly just a few of us old fatties who've been swimming, "in the skin," since the seventies. We even have a name for ourselves."

It had to be one of the weirdest conversations Cristina could ever remember having, but she somehow felt nothing but positive about it. It was nice to see older people enjoying themselves and being free about who they are.

Plus, although life had made her a cautious person, she already felt totally at ease around Jack. He had something warm and fatherly about him that she'd instantly connected with.

What an opposite pair of neighbors, she thought to herself as they stood there, both having drifted their attention back up to the stars.

"You didn't tell me the name," she said, still staring into the sky.

"Well, maybe I had one too many ports, but the name of what?"

"Of the . . . uh, the club."

"Oh! Well, there are technically two groups. One for men and one for women."

"OK," Cristina said, rocking Anise in her arms.

"The men are called the Polar Bareskins."

"OK, nice. And the women?"

"Uh, their name is a bit more colorful."

"What is it?"

"The Shriveled Titties."

"Oh, damn!" Cristina said. "Who came up with that?"

"An ornery biker-dyke named Cassie. She's one of my oldest friends. Maybe you'll meet her sometime."

"I'd like that." She yawned as she opened the front door. "I know one thing already, Jack. Pleasure Point sure is an interesting place. I can't wait to explore it some more. Where do you think Anise and I should check out first?"

He thought for a moment.

"Definitely hit *The Wharf*. It's a great amusement

park right on the beach. Eat a fried Twinkie, or ten, for me."

"Yah, we saw it when we drove into town. They have rides for this little one?"

"Oh, of course. Lots. And definitely get kettle corn, too. Other than that, head to the beach and run your toes through the sand. Walk out on the pier and get some fried clams. Anise can get an animal balloon, too. There's always something interesting going on down in that area. My advice, and I'll let you get inside finally, is to explore, explore, explore."

He used his hands to mimic someone staring into a smartphone and then continued, "You know, what? We do way too much of *this* these days. People have lost their sense of adventure. And, well, I'm rambling again, so I'll stop. But you seem like a bright young woman. I hope you'll really get to know the area and give it a chance. I feel like, after all the stuff I told you, maybe you might be apprehensive about Pleasure Point, but it really is a great place, for the most part."

They said goodbye and Cristina closed the door. She flipped on the light switch and was confronted by three stacks of cardboard boxes filled with their stuff. The living room was by no means large, but it was big enough to make their few belongings seem like hardly anything at all.

She spoke to the still-sleeping Anise as she carried her up the stairs, "Who needs *things* when you've got a nice place in a nice town with nice people? And, most importantly . . ."

With great care, she lowered her daughter down into bed.

For a moment, she was sure Anise would stir and wake up, wanting to sleep with mommy. But after a few squirming stretches, she settled. Her head fell to the side and her mouth gaped opened.

Cristina walked back downstairs and slid open the glass door to the backyard, her cigarettes and lighter in hand.

Facing away from the ocean, hidden from starlight by the redwoods overhead, the backyard was quiet, dark, and more than a bit creepy.

The dense forest beyond the fence appeared as a wall of blackness. Her eyes strained for a source of input.

Away from the sound of the waves, her ears felt muffled. The only noise now was the wind moving through the trees, and an occasional small animal rustling its way from branch to branch. The crickets had all but disappeared.

She lit a cigarette, and was half-tempted to stand there with the lighter on. Realizing what a ridiculous idea that was, she lifted her thumb, letting the flame flicker out.

The burning tip of her Lucky Strike pulled the darkness closer. She stared into the emptiness, her eyes producing waves of color. At first, she wanted to look away, then embraced it. It reminded her of being a kid, when she would rub her eyes as hard as she could to "make stars."

Somehow, that memory made the night feel less scary. She spent the rest of her last smoke before bed making a game out of turning darkness into brightness.

"Woah, heavy," she joked to herself as she stomped out the butt on the single concrete step.

She hardly even glanced at the hallway door when she walked by it on her way back upstairs. The history of the house and the town didn't scare her. Cristina felt a sense of pride in that.

She checked on Anise once more before getting into bed herself.

Cristina fell asleep smiling.

Outside, the trees rustled and the wind blew. In the distance, waves crashed against the rock, again and again.

7

When Cristina awoke, she had a pair of five-year-old eyes staring her in the face from only a few inches away.

"Hi," Anise said, stone-faced.

"Good morning, beautiful."

Cristina stroked her daughter's hair away from her face.

"Mama," Anise began. "I think it would be a good idea if we went to the beach today. You know, just to see what it's like."

Even in her sleepy state, Cristina struggled not to giggle.

"Yah? Is that what you think, chica?"

"Uh-huh."

"Hmm . . . well, let me think about it."

Cristina put a finger to her chin, pretending to deeply consider the idea.

No longer able to contain her excitement, Anise burst with a surge of energy, breaking out in squeals as she jumped on the bed.

"Pleeeeeeeease!?"

After a few more moments of torture, Cristina finally gave up the act.

"OK," she said, as if relenting to some brilliant argument.

Anise jumped into her arms.

"YAY!!!"

"But first," Cristina said, yawning. "We gotta eat."

They went downstairs and into the kitchen. Cristina moved around a few boxes, until she found one marked FOOD. From it she removed a bag of Peet's Coffee and her little French press. She also dug out a box of Bisquick pancake mix and poured some into a metal bowl.

After cooking breakfast and sitting down for the first time at their small kitchen table, Cristina noticed the sliding glass door was cracked open.

"Anise, did you go outside this morning without asking?"

She shook her head.

"Are you sure?" Cristina asked again, pointing toward the door. "It's OK if you did. Mommy just wants to know."

Anise forked her pancakes in silence.

Cristina stuck her head outside. All seemed as it should be. If anything, the backyard and its overgrown weeds appeared pleasantly normal compared to the way it had looked in the dark.

Still, she was *sure* she'd closed and locked the door. *It had to be Anise.*

But Cristina wasn't about to get the day off to a bad start with an argument over something so trivial. Besides, even if Anise did go out, it was important to cut her some slack. In a new house in a new town, a little strange behavior was to be expected.

Cristina just wanted to know.

They finished breakfast and started putting together their beach gear. While Cristina wanted to shove everything into a canvass shopping bag and go, Anise insisted they neatly fold the towels and extra clothes before stacking them inside the bag. She gently placed her plastic bucket and shovel on top.

It was past 10 AM when they finally pulled the Civic down the gravel driveway. As they turned onto the road, a lifted pickup – the kind Cristina had always referred to as a "tiny-dick truck" – pulled around them and up the driveway. She was too low to see who was inside, but Cristina thought she only needed one guess.

Trying not to let Mr. Psycho bother her, Cristina rolled down the window, letting in a gust of fresh ocean air. She turned on the stereo. The smooth sound of *Buena Vista Social Club* came pouring out of the speakers. The pop of conga drums made her wish she could sway her hips. Instead, she gently wobbled the steering wheel back and forth, rocking the frontend of the Civic.

"Car dancing!" Anise said from the backseat, waving her arms off-rhythm.

"You bet, chica. Time to move those dance muscles!"

Although not really all that far from town, their new place was on a two-lane road that could have been in the middle-of-nowhere. Cristina saw green in every direction. The grass and brush grew thick, right up to the edge of the forest. The only indication they weren't deep in the backwoods was the scent of the brine-soaked air.

Cristina let her mind wander as they made their way along the scenic road.

She felt immensely grateful and happy to be where she was. After what she'd been through over the past twelve months, and for so many years before that, this moment of freedom was priceless.

Of course, she was glad just to be alive.

After almost being killed by Anise's father, Anthony, (and not for the first time) Cristina had been forced to take out a restraining order against him while they went through their divorce and he faced criminal charges.

They were no longer married, but the bastard only did six months. And *that* wasn't even in real prison. Because his family had money and connections, Anthony was able to turn what should have been *at least* a five-year sentence in San Quentin into a relatively easy six-month stint fighting fires in one of the state's "conservation camps."

That's just how it was for him, too. A rich kid who'd gone through his whole life always getting what he wanted.

In the beginning of their relationship, he'd convinced Cristina that what he wanted was her. And not just her body, which just about every male she'd come in contact with since Jr. High seemed to go crazy for. No, Anthony had told her he wanted to get her off the streets. Help her make a new life following her dreams of being an artist. A life worth living. Even if she hadn't really believed in happiness, not then at least.

It turned out what he *really* wanted was someone to boss around. To take care of him. To baby him when he went into one of his moods. And, of course, someone to take out his anger on.

For almost eight years, she was that person. All the while hoping, somewhere just around the corner, they would find happiness together.

Truth be told, Anise was an accident. And it wasn't until her daughter was four that Cristina finally worked up the courage to leave. Not that she'd had much of a choice by then. If she hadn't gotten the hell out of there when she did, he would have killed her. She was sure of it.

God knows he'd come close.

One night, Anthony had been doing his usual thing.

Getting drunk in his favorite chair watching the ball-game. After Cristina put Anise to bed, he told her to sit on the ground in front of him. He made her drink whiskey and do lines of coke while she rubbed his feet. Shot after shot she took. Line after line. She wasn't allowed to talk. Only to listen as he threatened over and over again to punish her if she stopped, even for a second. She never doubted his sincerity. He'd proven it plenty of times before. But after what seemed like hours, she could hardly keep her eyes open, much less continue massaging. Her hands were cramping. Her head spinning.

Without warning, he pulled down his pants, forced her head forward, and shoved his half-hard piece of meat down her throat. She gagged and choked. Her cheeks flushed red as the oxygen was cut off. She turned her eyes toward his face and saw, not the anger she'd expected, but a cold, blank stare. A look of pure evil. One she'd seen before.

In that moment, her whole existence seemed like one giant nightmare.

Sitting there on the floor, drunk and choking to death on his now rock-hard cock, she'd felt half-tempted to simply let go. Allow death to take over. Drift off into nothingness. Just to make the pain of life finally stop.

Then Anise's smile flashed into her mind. The innocence of a life not yet tarnished by the evils of humanity. An angel on earth.

The vision had given Cristina the strength she needed.

With what felt like her last ounce of energy before succumbing to unconsciousness, she reached up with her right hand and grabbed that son-of-a-bitch's balls. She squeezed so hard, she thought they might pop like two swollen grapes.

When he screamed and let go, her lungs wheezed in a frantic search for oxygen.

The king of assholes sat writhing in his favorite chair.

At least for a few seconds.

Before she could recover enough to run, his eyes were again locked on to hers. First with hurt. Then with the hateful rage of a spoiled child who has failed to get his way.

Luckily, they were near the fireplace. She reached over and grabbed the black iron grip of a two-pronged poker, warning him she would bust his head open with it if he stood up.

He hadn't believed her.

And that's when she finally did something she'd been trying to find the courage to do since the first time he ever hit her.

She fought back.

When he lunged forward, she slammed the cold steel poker downward.

The feeling of hard metal hitting his skull was strange. On the one hand, it was disgusting and awful how she could actually feel the bone crack. Yet, she'd also never felt more pleased with herself. It took all her self-control not to hit him again.

Although she would never say it out loud, she knew in her heart that she'd been trying to kill him – a feat she likely would have accomplished if he hadn't ducked to his left at the last instant. As it was, he immediately went unconscious and began twitching and pulsating on the ground. Spittle and foam frothed from his mouth.

She called 9-1-1, told them to send an ambulance, and then grabbed Anise and bolted out of there.

Cristina wasn't sure how much, if any, her daughter remembered about her father. She never mentioned him, and hadn't seen him since that night.

In court, Anthony hadn't looked Cristina's way during the entire proceeding. Not once. Hadn't looked at much of anything, actually. He sort of just stared off into nothingness. Cristina thought (and partially hoped) that she'd given him permanent brain damage.

After a couple weeks, the female judge handed Anthony a measly six-months at the fire camp. She'd been on Cristina's side throughout the hearing, but ultimately said it was the maximum sentence allowed, due to some obscure legal loophole Anthony's expensive attorney had managed to dig up.

As part of their divorce, he also had to pay Cristina a settlement of a million dollars, which in reality was hardly anything for a guy who'd been given a five-million-dollar trust fund when he graduated from high school.

That money was the only reason she could afford to buy the house in Pleasure Point. But even at a deeply discounted price because of the murder, the purchase basically ate up most of her half of the settlement. The lawyer had taken the other half.

Anthony had to make alimony and child support payments, too. That money covered basic expenses. But it didn't come anywhere close to making up for the nightmares Cristina still suffered from most nights. Though, for someone who grew up in poverty, it was at least nice not to worry about how she and her daughter were going to eat, or where they were going to sleep.

All she wanted to do now was start over.

After a lifetime of selfishness and self-centeredness, Cristina now lived to make her daughter happy. Her road through life had produced a lot of regrets, but one thing she never second-guessed for a minute was Anise. She was determined to be the good mom she herself never had. Even if it was hard sometimes to look at her precious baby and not get at least a little mad at herself for having stayed so long with such a horrible man.

As much as she hated to admit it, she saw his face in Anise. Although brown in color, she had his eyes. Big and round. Quite different from Cristina's own distinctive almonds. And Anise didn't look at all like she was half-Mexican. Her skin was an almost pasty white, like her father's. Her shoulder-length brown hair was light enough that in bright sunlight it appeared dark-blond.

Almost as if she'd heard her mother's thoughts, Anise spoke, snapping Cristina out of her daze.

"I love you, mamma."

"I love you too, chica."

They came around a bend in the road and the trees suddenly disappeared, revealing one of the most stunning views Cristina had ever seen. She instinctively turned off the music, as if its presence hindered her ability to fully appreciate what was before her.

She'd driven this way before, but somehow she'd failed to realize just how beautiful her surroundings really were until now. Cristina could see all the way across the half-circle of shimmering blue water that was Pleasure Bay, twenty miles to the upscale town of Presidio Grove on the other side – a ritzy getaway village for the wealthy, including her ex-husband's parents.

On the Pleasure Point side of the bay, the beach town stretched from the ocean to the mountain foothills. She could see a Ferris wheel and several twisting roller coasters standing near the water. On the far end of the amusement park, a long row of luxurious houses lined the coastal cliffs, some of them so close to the edge of the rocks, they appeared to lean out over the water. On the other end, a wooden pier extended out into the ocean for at least half a mile.

Further down the coast, she saw the abandoned factory Jack had told her about, its grey, cylindrical buildings reaching up from the ground like ashy fingers. Between the factory and the pier stood what looked like a small, self-contained town set apart from the rest of Pleasure Point.

The whole landscape belonged on a postcard.

Cristina wiped a single tear from her cheek with the palm of her hand.

"Why you crying, mamma?" Anise asked.

"It's OK, chica. Mommy's just really happy. Isn't our new home gorgeous?"

"Uh-huh," Anise answered dutifully.

The road dropped down the hill in a long, sweeping curve. Single-family homes began to appear, at first some distance apart from one another, but bunching together the closer the road got to sea level. At the bottom of the incline stood an old house that Cristina imagined had seen better days.

Creepy, she thought.

The place was five stories, surrounded by a high iron fence, and belonged in a horror movie. The decrepit gray wood looked ready to buckle under a soft sea breeze.

In front of the house was a stop sign and a T-junction. There were no other cars around.

Cristina and Anise were headed left toward the amusement park. But before pushing down the turn signal, Cristina paused for a moment, engine idling, looking to her right. She decided to take a little detour and explore a bit.

Quickly, she realized that the old mansion was not the only rundown home on this side of town.

Houses lined the street, but all of them had obviously been sitting vacant for some time. The windows were boarded. The lawns dead. Once vibrant paint now peeled under an assault by the salty air.

The neighborhood was dead.

It wasn't until she neared the end of the street that she thought she saw movement from the corner of her eye. But when she turned her head in that direction, she saw nothing but another formerly beautiful home.

On top of the general eeriness of having no one around, she could have sworn that the sky actually started to darken as she drove deeper into the neighborhood. She craned her neck to peer out the windshield, sure she would find clouds or a bank of fog. To her surprise, there was nothing but clear blue.

"Mamma, where are we?" Anise asked.

"Don't worry, chica. Everything's OK."

Suddenly though, Cristina didn't believe her own words. Not one bit. Without looking, she spun the steering wheel to the left so she could pull into a driveway and turn around.

She had to stomp her foot on the brake as a man suddenly appeared in front of her. The Civic stalled. Its engine puttered and died.

Her mind froze as she made eye contact.

At first, she thought he must be some kind of creature risen from the dead. His face was as thin as the Nazi concentration camp victims she once saw on a History Channel documentary. The few chunks of stringy hair remaining on his head looked as though they'd been singed by fire. His mouth gaped open, showing rotted teeth the color of a school bus. The filthy white t-shirt hanging off his gaunt shoulders was tattered, his blue jeans completely ripped down one side, revealing a bare leg covered in red sores. He was not wearing underwear.

But none of those things were as frightening as his black eyes. Set deep in a high forehead covered with the same raging pustules as his legs, the man's oversized pupils were motionless. Cristina felt, for a moment, like the dark, lifeless orbs were calling to her.

She only became certain he wasn't a ghost when the corners of his lips curled into a salivating grin, the way a starving wolf might admire a steak.

"Mamma?" Anise said.

Cristina snapped out of her hypnotized stare and looked over her shoulder, heart hammering against her chest when she saw a second man only a few feet away from the car, a similarly hungry expression on his face. He was nearly as skinny and just as dirty as his companion. The same ugly sores covering his face.

Soon he was fumbling with the door handle. Cristina had never felt so grateful for her grandmother's overly-cautious insistence on locking the doors every time they were in the car. A habit that had worn off on her.

She started the Honda and threw it into reverse, slamming her foot down on the gas pedal. In her rush, she let the aging clutch out a bit too fast. The car again sputtered and died.

Her hands shook as she tried to turn the key in the ignition one more time.

"Mamma?" Anise repeated.

The first man stepped toward Cristina's wide-open window. His legs moved faster than she would have expected, as if with a newfound sense of purpose.

The key turned, but nothing happened.

He'd already reached the front of the car.

Overgrown fingernails shrieked against metal as he slid his sore-covered hand across the hood.

"Mamma?" Anise repeated.

"It's OK, chica. Just hold on a second."

Cristina tried once more to start the car. Again nothing happened.

It wasn't until the man's filthy hands were nearly sliding up onto the windshield that she realized the problem. In her panic, she'd forgotten to push in the clutch. As soon as she did, the reliable old Civic fired to life.

Cristina took one last look at the man's eyes. Despite his now fearsome grin, there still appeared to be no light in his pupils whatsoever. Together with the rotting scent of his body odor, he might as well have been a walking corpse.

She backed out of the driveway and then quickly took off down the street, watching as the two men grew smaller in the rearview mirror.

Wiping her hair from her face, she realized her forehead was covered with sweat, despite the fact it couldn't have been more than 65 degrees out.

"You OK, Anise?"

"Yes," came the plain answer. "Who were those men, mamma?"

"Don't worry about them. We shouldn't have gone down this road. Mommy made a mistake."

"OK. Can we go to the amusement park now?"

"Yes, chica. That sounds like a great idea."

8

Cristina used some slick parallel parking skills to slip into a tight space between two cars on her first try.

"Aww, yah," she said as she pulled the e-brake.

Anise quickly unbuckled herself from her car seat, and would have burst out the door with excitement had it not been for the Civic's childproof safety locks.

Cristina still couldn't quite shake the image of the two meth-zombies from her mind. But the warm sun on her face as she stood near the car went a long way toward brightening her spirits.

The lingering chill under her skin vanished almost completely when she saw her daughter smile ear to ear, awestruck by the countless rides darting and dashing and diving in every direction. Hand-in-hand, they walked toward the front entrance, listening to screams of joyful terror fill the air.

Cristina couldn't help but feel like a kid, too.

"Where do we go first?" she asked.

Without looking at her mother or uttering a single word, Anise simply pointed, jaw dropped open, toward a beautiful antique carousel. Under the umbrella-shaped roof, a herd of wooden horses bobbed up and down, circling their well-worn path. A whimsical melody chimed from the automated pipe organ, calling forth potential riders.

"Which horse are you going to ride?" Cristina asked

as they waited in line.

The question and all its prospects made Anise's eyes bulge even wider than they already were. She seemed almost paralyzed by the immensity of choosing.

Then she caught site of a bright-pink mare with a blue bow in its mane.

"I'm riding Pinky!" she declared.

Cristina thought it was certainly one of the more eccentric horses of the bunch.

"Good choice."

They were second in line behind a little blond girl about Anise's age, who stood with her father – a large, mean-looking white guy with a swollen, rosy nose. He tried to be nonchalant as he twisted his pudgy neck to check Cristina out. He wasn't looking at her face, but at the firm roundness of cleavage bulging from her tank top. The sight distracted him so badly that he didn't even react when the pimply-faced kid running the ride signaled for the next group to take their places. Not until his daughter silently tugged on his pant leg did they finally move along.

Cristina tried to ignore him.

She walked Anise over to the pink horse and lifted her up onto its saddle, gently strapping on the safety belt, against Anise's strong insistence that she was a big girl and didn't need it.

Cristina hopped onto the horse next to Pinky, and away they went. The organ music came to life. The lights on the inside of the roof flashed in harmony.

Cristina sat back, admiring the innocence of her daughter's joy and wonder. Her giggles and squeals as the ride whirled around and around. And, more than anything, her bright smile. It was everything good in the world.

At the same time, Cristina was consciously trying to avoid the continued stares coming from Red Nose. But even when she didn't look his way, she could still *feel* his cheap, car-salesman grin from across the carousel.

As the ride came to a stop, the dismounting children all begged their parents for another turn.

Red Nose approached Cristina as she and Anise walked toward the exit turnstile.

"Hey, baby."

Oh, for fuck's sake, Cristina thought. *Is that the best you can do?*

There was a time when she probably would have just called the guy out. Made him feel stupid. But, for one, she didn't want to embarrass his daughter. No matter how much of a scummy douchebag *he* was, the poor girl didn't deserve to feel awkward. Her life was probably hard enough already. And, secondly, Cristina was just tired of it. Tired of the way men slobbered and gawked and tried to casually rub against her in crowded places. How they touched her ass when she went to concerts. She was just done.

So, instead of saying anything, she simply tried to walk around him, holding Anise's hand, responding to his words with nothing more than a nod and a polite smile.

But, of course, that wasn't good enough. It never was for these kinds of guys.

"I said hello to you," he insisted, moving his wide body to block her path. "Don't you think it would be polite to say something back?"

"That was sooo much fun," Anise said next to her, ignorant of the man's presence. "Can we ride again? Can we?"

"Of course, baby."

Once more, Cristina smiled and tried again to walk around him, this time toward the wall. He stepped in front of her, straightening his arms so one palm was on either side of her body, trapping her in place.

"You're a little short on manners," he lectured. "I think you owe me a few words."

Now she picked up the yeasty scent of beer on his breath. In fact, he smelled like he hadn't taken a shower in at least a couple of days. She also noticed for the first time that his eyes were as red as his nose.

"No thanks," she said. "Come on, chica. Let's go."

Anise protested. "But I want to ride Pinky again!"

"No. We're going."

"Aw, c'mon," Red Nose said, keeping his arms locked in place when Cristina tried to move.

He was short. Only a few inches taller than her. Which didn't give her much room to maneuver without being forceful. She looked past him. The little blond girl was just standing there in silence, staring off into the distance in some kind of trance.

Her defense mechanism, Cristina thought.

Red Nose continued, "How about we let the girls ride again? You and me can sit and talk a little about how mean you've been."

Cristina had had enough. Adjusting herself ever-so-slightly, she lined her knee up with the center of his crotch, hoping to give herself enough room to build up the force she needed to make sure he would never have the chance to breed again.

She offered a coy smile, to which he returned a prideful look of victory. She leaned toward his ear, so neither of the kids could hear. He moved toward her too, grinning like he just won the lottery.

"Look, asshole," she whispered. "If you don't get away from me, I'm going to knee you so hard you're going to bleed out of your eyeballs."

He jerked back his head a bit. His eyebrows crooked and his beery lips opened in surprise. He took in his surroundings. First looking at Anise. Then seeming to notice his own daughter for the first time, her stare still stuck on something far off that only she could see. His eyes returned to Cristina's unflinching glare. What he didn't see was her hand creeping toward the back pocket of her jeans. In her mind, she pictured pulling out her knife, flipping it open, and shoving it right into his dirty face.

"Yah," the man said, considering his situation one last time before spitting on the ground. "Well, it's not like you're all that pretty anyway."

With that, he stepped back from Cristina, grabbed his daughter roughly by the arm, and dragged her away. The blank look on the girl's face barely shifted as her tiny legs stumbled to keep up.

Suddenly, all Cristina wanted to do was cry. Not so much for herself. It wasn't the first time she'd been harassed by some creep, and she was positive it wouldn't be the last. But her heart ached for that innocent little girl.

Why do people have to be so horrible to children?

Cristina bit down hard on her bottom lip.

She took a deep breath.

Squatting, she brushed Anise's hair out of her eyes and kissed her forehead.

"Is everything OK?" Anise asked.

"Yes, chica. Mommy's fine."

"I love you, mamma."

Anise leaned forward and smacked a kiss onto her mother's lips.

Then, leaning back, she put on her most angelic face.

"Can we ride Pinky again?"

Cristina let go a cathartic laugh. Along with it came a single tear, which she wiped away with the back of her hand.

"Yes, baby. We can ride Pinky as many times as you want."

9

Anise kept Cristina to her word. They rode the carousel another seven times.

Then they had giant corn dogs at an outside table overlooking the beach. The number of people crammed onto the sand was a sharp contrast to the wide-open space Cristina experienced at the beach she'd found when first visiting Pleasure Point. And most of the people here were pale tourists, sitting under umbrellas, staring at screens.

Why even come to the beach?

Cristina had never been a computer person. Probably due to the fact she was more interested in drugs for most of her life, and maybe because her ex was a bigshot tech entrepreneur with his own startup. Well, it wasn't like it was *really* his, given that he'd started it with money from his father, who was himself some kind of computer bajillionaire.

All that aside, the world of technology was so damn impersonal. Cristina had spent most of her childhood being raised by her grandmother – an old-school woman who believed a person gains respect by looking other people in the eye, telling them exactly what's on her mind.

Sometimes it seemed to Cristina as if her own generation had been transformed into a bunch of robots. Everyone loved to stare into their smartphones, to the point they would walk right into you on the sidewalk and not even apologize.

She snapped out of her thoughts when a seagull landed at the end of the table. The brave bird stared at them while it inched toward their basket of french fries.

"It's a birdy!" Anise declared. "Can we feed him?"

Before Cristina had time to answer, her daughter had already thrown one of the fries.

"Anise!" Cristina said, more harshly than she meant it.

Anise froze in the shock of a kid being scolded for something they don't understand to be wrong.

"Sorry, mamma." She turned toward the seagull. "Go away, Mr. Bird!"

He didn't listen. Instead, he waddled his webbed feet forward, helping himself to another fry, this one straight out of the basket, before retreating back to the far end of the table.

Cristina put a playful tone back into her voice.

"Do you think he likes ketchup?"

Anise considered the question carefully.

"Yes, I think he does."

Cristina coated one of the fries with red goop, then lobbed it toward the bird's end of the table. The gull inspected the offering, flipped it over once with his beak, and tossed it into the air before gulping it down his throat.

"See!" Anise said. "I told you, mamma."

At that point the word was out. Two more seagulls landed on the table. Then a few more. There were soon seven of them vying for space on the table. As the size of the group increased, so did the intensity of their squawks. Anise threw another fry and the birds loudly argued over who it belonged to.

About a minute later, the flock decided the game

was over. They moved forward with the unity of a disciplined military unit. Cristina and Anise were forced to retreat, leaving behind the last of their food and a trail of shared laughter.

After lunch, they continued exploring the park. First, Anise rode on a green-tracked kiddie-coaster. Then, together they boarded a slow-moving cave train on a trip back through time, all the way to the land of dinosaurs. That was followed by shooting water guns into a plastic clown's mouth, in a race to fill the balloon extending from the top of his head. Cristina won, beating a guy who seemed genuinely annoyed at having lost to a woman. His frustration made victory that much sweeter. At another booth, she knocked down a stack of bowling pins with a softball. She let Anise pick out the prize: a stuffed, blue octopus.

Once they had their fill of rides and games, the two walked hand-in-hand out onto the beach. They moved slowly over the uneven sand. Through the mass of bodies.

It was the warmest part of the day. After finally finding a spot with a bit of distance between themselves and anyone else, they spread out towels and stripped down to their bathing suits. Cristina's bikini and Anise's one-piece were matching black-and-white cheetah print.

Then they headed for the water.

Cristina hadn't even put a toe in when she went to the other beach, so the icy coldness came as a bit of a shock. She yelped when the water first washed over her feet and ankles.

Anise, however, was unaffected. It was her first time in the ocean, but she took to it as if she'd grown up a block away.

Cristina had a vague recollection of coming to the beach once or twice with her cousins when she was

younger, and somehow she remembered the water being *a lot* warmer.

Eventually, however, she worked up the courage to
wade into the shallows near the pier, Anise in her
arms.

It's not that bad once you're in for a few minutes,
she kept trying to tell herself.

They floated and laughed and smiled as the surf
tossed them about.

From the water, she could see the amusement park
stretch down the beach. It looked a lot bigger than it
had earlier from up on the hill.

Reality is always a lot bigger up close.

That felt like something Michelle would probably
say.

It had only been a couple days, but Cristina already
missed their daily conversations over coffee.

Floating at the mercy of the ocean, she suddenly felt
a bit isolated and alone. She promised herself she
would call Michelle that evening, and would try to
make it to a 12-step meeting as soon as possible. Even
if the first attempt at connecting with the local recovery community had been a little bit . . . well, weird.

Cristina refused to stop doing what had brought her
so far.

Despite having somewhat adjusted to the frigid
temperature of the water, she still shivered when she
and Anise finally plopped their wet bodies face-first
onto a towel. Cristina lay on her belly, elbows tucked
close to her body, soaking the warm sun into her skin.
Anise copied her mother precisely, glancing over every
few seconds to make sure she was doing it right.

10

Cristina must have fallen asleep.

Before she could even manage to blink her eyes all the way open, her mind slammed into full-alert. Anise was no longer beside her.

She jumped to her feet, looking up and down the beach.

Nothing.

There were so many bodies occupying the space around her, lying, sitting, digging, standing, running, jumping, it was almost impossible to see through them all. The only clue she had was the fact Anise's plastic bucket and shovel were gone, too.

OK, she must be down by the water.

But when Cristina came running up to the shoreline, she saw no sign of her daughter anywhere. She asked several people if they'd seen her: two long-haired stoners throwing a frisbee, a young couple holding hands, and an older guy with a big, round belly wearing nothing but a cowboy hat and a pair of red speedos.

None of them had seen anything.

She couldn't have gone far.

But which way?

The beach suddenly seemed to stretch on forever. In one direction was the pier, and past that more beach. In the other was the amusement park, and then the cliffs and the fancy homes Cristina had seen earlier from above.

She decided to go toward the pier.

Her bare feet kicked chunks of dirt into the air as she sprinted across the hard-packed sand near the water. The beachgoers gave strange looks to the short, brown-skinned girl with the tattoos weaving in between the crowd.

She hardly noticed.

After what seemed like half an hour – and in reality was no more than a minute – Cristina finally arrived at the pier, her smoker's lungs woefully out of breath.

The tall wooden structure blocked out most of the sun, making the air underneath much cooler. The sudden change from bright to dark also made it hard to see.

Cristina rubbed her eyes into focus.

After the blur cleared, she felt a wave of relief. There was Anise, kneeling in the wet sand, digging with her shovel.

Next to her was a man Cristina had never seen before. A white guy with a shaved head, wetsuit pulled down to his waist, the top half of his body completely covered in tattoos. He was bent over and pointing, saying something to Anise.

Filled with frightened rage, Cristina yelled, "Get away from her!"

He immediately stood and put his palms in the air as he opened his mouth to speak. She didn't give him the chance, instead turning to her daughter.

"Anise, what are you doing!? You know you aren't supposed to go away from mommy without asking. What were you thinking?"

Anise continued shoveling dirt into her bucket. She spoke softly and without looking up.

"Sorry, mamma."

"Look at me."

After some hesitation, Anise did as she was told.

"You scared me," Cristina said. "Don't you ever do that again, OK?"

"OK."

Anise went back to digging and said, "This nice man showed me how to find the sand crabs."

Cristina glared at him, a bit surprised he remained standing there, looking almost comical with his hands still in the air. Though by then he'd added a disarming smile. She checked him out a bit closer and noticed that his body was not only covered with tattoos – one of the more prominent a large triangle with a circle around it on his stomach – but he was also quite muscular. Not like a body builder. More like a well-honed athlete. Actually, his ridged abs seemed carved from stone. The sleek lines of muscle dove toward the confines of his wetsuit.

When she finally looked at his face again, she found his square jaw and full lips still grinning.

"Hi there," he said, sticking out his hand with confidence. "I'm Casey."

Cristina said nothing.

After an awkward moment, he shrugged, turned, and walked toward a surfboard he'd propped against one of the pier's support pillars. He put the board under his arm. Before heading off, he turned back toward her, his face assertive but not unkind.

"I promise I'm not a bad guy," he said. "I just saw your girl playing under here by herself and wanted to make sure she was OK. I run a surf shop just across the way, so I kind of think of this beach as like my second home. I try to look out for the people who use it. Sorry if I scared you, but I was just showing . . . Anise was it? I was just showing Anise how to hunt for sand crabs. The key is to let the water wash up, and then you have to dig where you see bubbles when it retreats."

"Bubbles!" Anise shouted to herself as she continued her excavation.

Still skeptical, Cristina took in the scene.

Him. The board. Him. Anise. Him.

Suddenly, it all made sense. She felt kind of horrible. With an effort, she loosened her scowl, replacing it with a sincerely apologetic smile and an extended hand.

"I'm sorry, Casey. I'm Cristina. I didn't mean to get so pissed. It's just, well, I hope you can understand how scary it is to doze off on the beach and wake up to have your only little girl in the whole wide world gone. It kind of scared the crap out of me."

"I can imagine. I mean, I don't have any kids, but I have a lot of young people I teach, and they're kind of like my kids. Anyway, like I said, sorry I scared you. I guess I'll catch you later."

As he turned, Cristina took a step toward him.

"Wait . . ." she started, but was unsure what should come next.

He planted his feet in the sand but didn't turn.

"Yah?" he asked over his shoulder.

"Well, I'm new in town and I noticed your tatt."

"Which one?"

"The triangle. You're sober."

He spun on his heels like a person well at home in the shifting sand. The move struck Cristina as graceful for someone with a frame towering a couple of inches above six feet.

She casually checked out his body again, moving her eyes over the ridges of his stomach, his carved chest, his broad shoulders, his statuesque arms. The tattoos were intense. Besides the triangle symbol, most of the art covering his body was dark: skulls, a grim reaper, spider webs, a couple of sultry-looking

women. He also had two interlocking roses at the top
of his throat. Their stems wrapped around his neck in
a way that made it look like he was being strangled by
the sharp, bloodied thorns. The sight made Cristina instinctively touch her own rose-covered arm.

"Uh, yah," he said. "I've always felt weird calling it
'sober' though. Makes me feel like I'm some cancer patient in remission. But, yah, I've got a few years clean.
I still go to meetings sometimes, too. It saved my life.
But these days I get my biggest fix of spirituality helping young men get on the straight path. And, of course,
out there."

He pointed toward the ocean.

Cristina's gaze followed the hard profile of his arm,
out to the tips of his fingers, toward the breaking surf.
She felt an unexpected surge of excitement in her
chest.

"Wow, surfing is really that intense, huh?"

"You can't even imagine until you do it. It's the best
feeling in the entire world."

"Really? Because I've had some pretty amazing feelings."

She didn't mean for it to sound quite so dirty. Well,
maybe a little. Either way, she kind of enjoyed making
a big, tough surfer-dude blush, if only for a moment.

"Is that right?" he asked, recovering his coolness.

She responded, "I've been around the block a few
times. I've got a year clean myself."

"I wouldn't have guessed it. You look so, um,
healthy."

Cristina tried hard not to look down at herself, but
she couldn't help adjusting her bikini top to make sure
her chest was at maximum fullness.

When she looked up again, she could see Casey was
definitely checking her out.

"Well," he said, looking away and then back at her.

"You want to hang out sometime?"

Instinctively, she looked at Anise.

He quickly added, "Oh, I mean, if you've got time, and are, uh, available. Oh man, that sounds bad. All I meant was, I know it's probably pretty crazy with the little one. And I'm not sure if you're looking or what. OK, I'm just going to shut up before I say something stupid."

"You mean something else?"

He laughed. "Yah, exactly."

She let him squirm for a minute more.

"Well?" he asked finally.

"Well what?"

"Well, do you want to go out sometime?"

"Yah, I guess we can make that happen. Anise is staying at my grandmother's during the week until school's out. So maybe sometime then. If that's cool with you."

"Sure, yah. I'm teaching ocean swimming to some junior lifeguards on Thursday nights before summer starts. That usually ends around six. You want to meet me down here around six-thirty?"

"Under the pier?" she asked, looking around sarcastically.

Sometimes she couldn't help herself.

"Nah, how about at my shop? It's called *Bula's*."

"What the hell is a bula?"

"It's a Fijian word. It means, well, it means a lot of things, but it mostly means like 'have a good day,' or 'positive vibrations.' That kind of thing. People there say it all the time."

"Nice. Well then, Mr. Casey. Until Thursday, bula bula I guess."

He laughed.

"Sweet. I'll be seeing you then, Ms. Cristina."

11

That evening, back at her new home, Cristina felt elated.

She put Anise to bed and went out front to smoke her first cigarette of the day. The rush of nicotine lifted her head higher into the clouds than it already was. Everything, the house, the starry sky, the moonlit courtyard, the ocean below, it all felt magical. The crickets chirped louder. The crisp, briny air felt even more refreshing and full of life.

Besides her ex, she couldn't remember ever meeting anyone who excited her so much. But even Anthony – who in the beginning had seemed like everything Cristina ever wanted – hadn't left her feeling quite *this* giddy.

Long gone were any thoughts of the ghost town and its dead-eyed inhabitants. So too was the rage from being harassed at the carousel. And from the previous day's run-in with Mr. Psycho.

It had turned out to be one of the best 24 hours she'd had in a long time.

Maybe ever.

Meeting Casey was great, and she looked forward to Thursday so much she wished she could snap her fingers and speed up time, but the best part of the day *by far* had been watching Anise's smile as she went around the carousel. Seeing that happy, carefree love for life on her daughter's face was *exactly* the reason Cristina had decided to pack up and move to Pleasure Point in the first place.

Standing there alone in the dark made her want to share the happiness with someone else. She pulled out her phone and started to call Michelle. It would be great to hear her friend's voice.

Before she could send the call, Cristina heard the sound of a car coming up the driveway. It was Jack. She paused for a moment, looking down at the phone.

I really should call her. It's been a few days. I bet she's worried.

Instead, she returned the phone to her pocket and stood where Jack could see her as he drove by. She waved into his headlights until they flashed. He left the car idling as he pulled beside her and rolled down the passenger window.

"Hey there!" he said. "You look like you're enjoying this gorgeous evening."

"I am. What a great day."

He looked at her with interested curiosity.

"You met someone!" he said. "I can tell. Let me go park the car. I want to hear all about it."

The two met in the middle of the courtyard.

"So," he said immediately. "Who's the lucky guy?"

"Is it *that* obvious?"

She'd spent so much energy over the years trying to hide her emotions. Even now, it made her feel a bit vulnerable that someone could read her so easily.

"You're glowing is all," Jack said with his sharp grin. "What's his name?"

"Casey. He's a surfer."

Jack raised a bushy eyebrow.

"Not Casey Peters, is it?"

"I don't know. He didn't tell me his last name. Tall guy. Shaved head. Lots of tattoos. Pretty dreamy."

"That's him," Jack said, sounding genuinely amazed. "Sweetheart, he's not just a surfer, he was once the top pro in the whole world. Until, from what I understand, he got more interested in doing drugs. That was a few years ago now, of course. I've heard he's been doing much better lately. Has a little surf shop near the pier. And he's even successfully avoided getting pushed out by the developers, who'd probably rather see that prime piece of real estate turned into a Target or an Applebee's, or some other such monstrosity. Wow, that's really who you met, huh?"

"Yah, sounds like it. He seems really cool." She thought about the words coming out of her mouth and couldn't help but laugh. "God, I sound like a teenager."

"You practically are one, so I wouldn't worry all that much."

"True. Sometimes I feel like I've lived enough life to be an old lady, though. I mean, until earlier today, I wasn't even sure I *wanted* to try dating. To be honest, I still don't know."

"Well, as they say, age is but a number," Jack said. "Trust me, though. You get old quick. Don't be in such a hurry that you let your life go by without taking some time to enjoy it a bit. I say go for it. What's the worst that could happen?"

That was the question Cristina had been trying to avoid.

12

It was a bittersweet moment when Cristina's grandmother and uncle picked up Anise on Sunday afternoon.

As independent as she was trying to be, Cristina had to admit that she was more than a bit happy to see them. The presence of what was her closest family reminded her that, although things felt a bit isolated in her new home, she at least still had two people who were out there thinking of her.

Despite the fact her grandmother was undergoing chemotherapy for breast cancer, she still somehow found the energy to cook a big batch of tamales. And after carrying them into the kitchen herself, she proceeded to stand in front of the refrigerator giving a slow, thorough explanation on how to properly freeze them.

(As if Cristina hadn't helped her do it a hundred times before.)

Her uncle hauled in a couple bags of groceries, filled with some essential Mexican staples he must have feared she wouldn't buy on her own. Rice. Beans. Corn tortillas. Tapatío. And, of course, her all-time favorite: a bag of pinwheel *duros* from the ice cream man. When she was a little girl, every time a *paletero* pushed a cart through the neighborhood, ringing his high-pitched bell, Cristina would pester her uncle to buy her some of the fried snack.

Tío Alberto had also bought her a candle of the Virgen de Guadalupe, along with instructions to light it every evening when Cristina said her prayers.

She hadn't prayed since her First Communion. Even in her recovery work with Michelle, she'd always thought the idea of talking to God was kind of silly. But she would never tell her uncle that. He was about as religious as one could get without being an actual priest. So she solemnly promised to do as he said, and then hugged him as hard as she could.

All the family love made it difficult to watch her grandmother's Ford Taurus disappear down the driveway. Her eyes started to burn. But before any tears could come, she lit a cigarette and put on her tough face.

Anise will only be gone for a week, she told herself. *School will be out in a month, and then she'll be here full-time.*

Of course, in the moment, a month seemed like a year. And the perfect house ten minutes from the beach again felt like it was about a million miles from anything that mattered.

Suddenly not wanting to be there, Cristina decided to hop in the car and go for a drive.

***

Rolling around Pleasure Point in her car, exploring but not paying attention to much of anything in particular, Cristina eventually ended up on a stretch of road about two miles long that slowly meandered its way along the scenic ocean cliffs.

Next to the road was a busy walkway full of joggers, old couples holding hands, and way too many loud-talking women with double-wide strollers and no sense of the fact other people existed in the world.

Apparently, she wasn't the only one who had the idea of watching the sunset. Just about every parking spot along the road was taken. Eventually she did manage to find one between a yellow Volkswagen Bus and a chromed-out Harley.

While there were benches along the pathway, most people seemed into hanging out on the hoods of their cars, staring out across the ocean.

Cristina did the same, firing up a smoke.

Through the scent of the cigarette, she also smelled something else. Something skunky. Over her shoulder, she saw it was coming from the bus. The couple inside appeared to be about Cristina's age, maybe a little younger. And when the guy holding the joint saw her looking their way, he gestured for her to join them.

Cristina shook her head with a sternness that made her feel like an old hag. The man didn't seem to care much. He shrugged and continued to puff away.

She sat on the hood of her car a minute longer, but soon felt awkward and kind of annoyed. Although she wasn't quite sure at what. She supposed herself, more than anything.

Restless, she scooched off the Civic's hood and started down the path.

A middle-aged woman with a fanny pack speed-walked by and said, "Some of us are trying to breathe here."

"Oh, sorry," Cristina said, stamping out the butt and tossing it in a nearby trashcan.

She flipped the lady off behind her back. Then caught herself and tried to calm down. An effort that wasn't working well at all. There were so many thoughts racing through her head. Most prominent among them was the fact that she was all by herself in a new place, surrounded by new people, all of whom seemed to be so much different from her. Either they were way too normal, like the ladies with the strollers and Mrs. Speedwalker. Or they were fucking out-there in a way that seemed to Cristina like they were *trying* to be weird.

Turning the corner, the walkway temporarily departed from its path alongside the road, curving around a small park built where the land jutted out toward the sea. In the middle of the park was an old lighthouse. According to the sign on the door, it had been turned into a museum dedicated to the history of surfing in Pleasure Point. She wanted to go inside but it was closed.

In front of the building was a healthy-sized plot of green grass.

Part of her felt like the universe had read her mind about the strange people she'd been encountering, and now it was messing with her. In a misshaped circle on the grass, a large group of people sat pounding away on various drums and other instruments.

Oh my god, for real? she thought. *This can't be happening.*

The whole scene reminded her too much of being on the street, surrounded by dirty homeless people who preached some kind of pseudo-hippy "love-thy-neighbor" crap, but then would steal your wallet and your drugs the first chance they got.

Still, despite Cristina's best attempts to stay mad at the world, she had to admit, whether it was the drums, the fresh air coming off the ocean, or the increasingly beautiful sunset, there was something about it all that made her feel at peace.

Instead of storming away, she stood at a distance and took everything in.

Upon further inspection, the people in the drum

circle weren't really *that* weird. There was certainly a fair share of hippy types – white guys with dreadlocks were a huge pet peeve of Cristina's. And a few folks with that uneasy homeless-person vibe she herself had no-doubt let off once upon a time.

But there were also plenty of regular, working-class people who seemed to be there just to smoke a joint and relax. Guys wearing Ben Davis pants and short-sleeve collared shirts. Women in hoodies and jeans.

Cristina half-consciously inched closer.

It wasn't just drums either. Someone strummed chords on an acoustic guitar. Another bleeped a silver trumpet. One hippy-chick with no shoes was busting out a pretty decent solo on a harmonica. And there was a guy with a Jesus beard blowing through a weird-looking piece of tubing Cristina had never seen before. The sound it made reminded her of the way a lightsabers warbled in the Star Wars movies.

Somehow, Cristina had to admit, it all worked.

Out of nowhere, one of the dreadlocked white dudes handed her a pipe. She almost took it without thinking, drawn in by the scene and her memories of getting high in groups of less-than-fresh-smelling humans. But she caught herself and instead shook her head.

"No thanks," she told him.

He grinned from ear to ear, squinting his eyes as he threw up a peace sign and walked away.

Then the sunset drew her attention. An orange light blazed across low clouds, making the horizon look like it had burst into flames.

But when the sun finally passed the edge of the world, the color vanished. There was a sudden steep drop in temperature. Cristina shivered as she thought of her sweatshirt, which she'd left on the passenger seat of her car.

She decided to head back, feeling surprisingly better as she walked away from the drum circle, listening to a steady barrage of thumps fade into the evening.

She hadn't gotten too far when she felt a tap on her shoulder, and thought it might be Dreadlocks again, maybe this time wanting her to meditate with him or something. But when she turned around, it only took her a moment to recognize the person standing before her.

Cristina still couldn't quite tell if she was looking at a man or a woman. Regardless, the person smirked and slightly bowed, but didn't offer any words, seeming instead to be waiting for her to speak first.

"The 12-step meeting," Cristina said. "You were at the 12-step meeting."

The bow dipped a little further.

"That's correct. My name's Jordan, but you never got the chance to learn that, I'm afraid, having run off before we could exchange pleasantries. However, you seem like a nice person, so I'd like to give you a second chance."

What the fuck? Who does this person thing he (or she) is?

"Excuse me?" Cristina asked.

"Hey, I understand what it's like to be seen as an outsider. I know what it's like to feel judged and to be pushed into a lonely corner of shameful existence. Trust me, I do. And I'm here to tell you, it's OK. I'm not here to judge you."

Huh?

Cristina had to force herself not to drop her jaw open in amazement. The person she was talking to had to be either an egomaniac or a lunatic. Maybe both. Either way, it seemed like a good idea to get going as soon as possible.

At the same time, Cristina had always been a magnet for the eccentric people of the world – something she supposed could be attributed to the fact she herself had always preferred, through thick and thin, to live life her own way. And, if she was honest with herself, Jordan wasn't exactly wrong. While Cristina didn't quite feel *shameful* about herself – at least not anymore, not really – she *did* feel like an outsider. She *did* feel lonely, especially without Anise.

"What's your deal?" Cristina finally asked. "What are you about?"

"About?"

"Yah, twice now you've approached me like you're testing me or something. What's up with that?"

For the first time, Jordan seemed flustered.

"Um, well, I assure you that's not what I intended. I simply wanted to make sure you weren't the kind of person who was quick to judge."

"So, what you're saying is that you were judging me as to whether or not I would judge you?"

"Uh, I guess when you put it that way it seems like kind of a silly exercise, doesn't it?"

"Yes, actually. Yes it does."

"Well, how about we start over?"

Jordan stuck out a hand and, after a short pause, Cristina grabbed it.

"Hi, Jordan. I'm Cristina."

"Hi Cristina. I'm Jordan. It's a pleasure to welcome you to Pleasure Point. Can I make up for my past indiscretions by asking you to dine with me this evening at the Venus Café – it's all vegetarian, all the time."

"Hmm . . . well, I'm pretty partial to a good burger, but I guess I could be convinced."

"They have great milkshakes too."

"OK, sold. Hey, Jordan?"

"Yah?"

"Is this a date?"

"Um, no. You aren't really my type. Let's just keep it friendly."

"Deal."

13

Jordan and Cristina walked into the Venus Café and found a seat right away, though the place seemed surprisingly popular for a Sunday night.

Cristina knew she was going to like the restaurant as soon as they walked in. The ceiling and walls were covered by a painted night sky, complete with planets and stars and quasars and black holes, along with a few cartoon-looking UFOs piloted by little green spacemen.

Spread around the room were other eccentric, some actually pretty impressive, pieces of art. Impressionistic paintings of cows flying spaceships. Sculptures of oversized forks, spoons, and knives intertwined in ways that made them look both elegant and disruptive. Her favorite, though, was the working jukebox set up near the cash register, made to look like the kind of far-out rocket ship one might expect David Bowie to pilot.

The booths fit right in with the theme, too. Bright-red bench seats covered with little alien-looking symbols that appeared meticulously hand drawn. The table was shaped and painted to look like a set of cockpit controls.

"This place is hella cool," Cristina said.

"Yes," Jordan said. "It's one of my favorite establishments as well."

"Are you a vegetarian?"

"Not strictly speaking, but I do believe in defending the rights of all lifeforms, including those of the non-hominid variety."

"Non-hominids?"

"Yes. A hominid is an ape."

"I knew that." It sounded familiar at least. She added, "But some of those lifeforms taste pretty freakin' good."

"I must admit that's true."

A waitress came to their table – a young woman a couple of years younger than Cristina. She had blue hair to match her eye makeup, a spiked bar through her septum, and about a dozen or so small, hooped earrings in each ear.

Cristina ordered Galactic Vegan Nachos and a chocolate Moonshake.

Jordan asked for french fries.

"That's it?" Cristina asked.

"Indeed. My eating habits are somewhat irregular. My system can only handle certain things."

"OK."

Cristina thought Jordan was totally weird, but was quickly coming to enjoy the company. On the ride over – Jordan didn't have a car so they both came in her Civic – the two had really clicked.

She learned Jordan was a writer (an "artist of the starving variety" as Jordan put it) who, for the past year and a half, had been working on documenting the stories of addicts from Pleasure Point, with the goal of eventually releasing them as "a tool for humanizing an issue that has, for far too long, been relegated to discussion only within a regime of criminality."

The project sounded fascinating to Cristina, but she sure hoped the writing would be a lot less preachy than the way Jordan talked.

Cristina had also learned that Jordan once spent an extended period of time as a sex worker.

"Mostly out of crack motels and in back alleys."

The way Jordan described the experience was incredibly candid. Cristina didn't really know what to say, except that she could very much relate. But she stopped there, not ready to talk about her past in any greater detail than that, at least not until they knew each other better. Thankfully, Jordan hadn't pushed the subject.

But the two apparently had more in common than Cristina first suspected. And now she felt a bit guilty for being so quick to judge.

"Wow, this shake is amazing," she said.

"I imagine it is," Jordan responded, moving hand to belly. "I've never actually tried one. I'm lactose intolerant."

"Aw, that sucks."

"Indeed."

"So, Jordan. Tell me about the recovery scene here. So far all I've been to is that one meeting with you and the homeless guy."

"Danny Dee?" Jordan chuckled. "He's far from homeless. He actually comes from one of the richest families in Pleasure Point. His grandfather invented the wetsuit, or some such thing. Whatever it was, they have lots of money. No, Dan is more of what you might call a traveler. At least, that's the way *he* puts it. In other words, a person who has disavowed his worldly possessions in order to live life raw and unencumbered by material needs."

After a pause to chew a fry, Jordan continued. "I don't know . . . I think about a decade doing hard drugs might have caused him to develop a bit of a mental disorder, but he really is one of the more fascinating people you'll meet in Pleasure Point, or anywhere else for that matter. He doesn't speak much about his past, but I've pieced together a few things over the two years I've known him. Like the fact he went to Harvard, including law school. Then he worked for some investment bank and was a bigshot in the New York City social scene. But I guess all of a sudden, after a week-long binge on high-end booze, cocaine, and heroin, he decided to get sober. So he quit his job, moved back to Pleasure Point, and gave away a fair amount of his sizeable bank account."

"Wait, and now he smokes cigarette butts off the ground?"

"Well, sort of. And I believe he calls them 'stumpies,' by the way. In all seriousness, he does a lot for people, but always totally in as secretive a way as possible. The whole *One Flew Over the Cuckoo's Nest* thing is partly an act. I think he does it to test people. You know, see how they do when they're outside their comfort zone."

"Wow, I suppose I failed that one."

"Maybe. But he isn't the kind of guy to hold a grudge. He pretty much loves everyone. When I first got sober, he really helped me out a lot. I've always been thought of by most people as, well, a little strange. But not by Dan."

"Is he your sponsor?"

"No. I've never been all that into the whole steps thing. I mean, I get the principles involved, and I think they're helpful and all, but only in as much as they lead to action toward living a better life. And I think that's what I like about Dan. He's isn't just about the talk. He truly believes in the idea of service to others, not just as a means to an end, but as an entire end in itself."

"I guess that's pretty real," Cristina responded. "My sponsor Michelle has this program to get people off the street. She's helped like a thousand women find homes over the past twenty years. It's pretty crazy actually. But, she's also kind of obsessed with the 12 steps. I don't know, to each their own, I guess."

"Surely. I didn't mean to sound like I was being hostile. The 12-step community saved my life, and I'm forever grateful. I guess I'm just jaded."

Jordan smiled at that, dipping a hand down to finish off the last fry.

"These nachos need real cheese," Cristina said as she finished her own plate. "But I guess they were alright."

"I suppose you can't please everyone."

"Truth. Well, Jordan, I'm glad we ran into each other. And I'm sorry again that I was kind of a bitch the first time."

"Ancient history. It's always nice to make a new friend. I find so many humans are less than ideal candidates for the role."

"Truth again."

14

Arriving back at home, Cristina was ready to settle in for her first night alone in the new place.

She walked through the front door and was met with a living room full of cardboard boxes marked with big black letters.

CLOTHES.

SCHOOL STUFF.

DISHES.

"Can't you all just unpack yourself?" she asked out loud.

She spotted a box marked BATH and sliced open the taped edges with her knife. Digging through it, she found the bottle of her favorite bubble bath. She also came across a familiar black bag.

Smiling, Cristina unzipped the fake-leather case and carefully pulled out her Lucky Rabbit's Foot waterproof personal massager. She rotated the bottom of the sleek, black-plastic device and it buzzed to life. Her eyes brightened. She set the Rabbit's Foot back into the bag, the bag back into the box, and then lifted the whole thing and carried it all into the bathroom for some much needed relaxation.

The tub seemed to take forever to fill. When it finally did, the water was wonderfully hot and topped with a mound of fluffy, vanilla-scented bubbles.

Cristina slipped off her robe and dipped a foot in.

She closed her eyes and forced herself to take the sting while her body adjusted to the heat.

She'd always loved that feeling.

Before getting all the way in, she fished a couple candles out of the box, set them in the corners of the tub, and used the lighter from her cigarette pack to ignite them. While she was at it, and even though she didn't really want the place smelling like an ashtray, she lit a Lucky Strike, almost giddy at the fact it was *her* house and no one could tell her otherwise.

With the lights off and candles burning, Cristina slowly crouched down into the tub, bracing herself again as the almost-too-hot water came right to the edge of burning her skin. She winced when it slipped around the scars covering her legs and the fleshy curves of her ass. She rested there for a moment, closing her eyes, feeling the lively skin between her legs tingle.

Dipping further down, the scalding water rounded the slight thickness of her tummy, caressing its way toward her full, plump breasts. Her lungs inhaled a sharp, involuntary breath when the heat pinched her dark nipples. She rubbed them as she settled fully into the tub, again feeling grateful for how firm and elastic her body remained after having a baby, and after so many years of abusing it.

Enjoy it while it lasts, she thought. *And thank God for Victoria's Secret after that.*

Not that she was too worried. She'd always understood that the sexiest part of any woman – or man for that matter – was the brain. If someone didn't *feel* sexy, it was likely that no one else would think they were either.

And being sexy was one thing Cristina had always been good at. Even through her darkest days, when she hated her existence so much she thought often of taking her own life.

She tossed her finished cigarette into the toilet and began to massage her breasts in earnest, squeezing them gently around the nipples at first, feeling them stiffen, and then with more strength as they started to buzz with pleasure.

An image of Casey came into her mind. Shirtless and covered in dark tattoos. The sharp cuts of his muscles practically glowing. She imagined what it would feel like to have him hold her, pressing her naked body into his hard chest. The fullness of her lips kissing his neck and chest and stomach, and then finally taking him into her mouth.

Her hand slipped between her legs and began rubbing tiny circles as she thought of him on top of her. Slipping inside. Sliding. In and out.

With one hand, she reached outside the tub and felt for the vibrator.

It soon whirred to life.

She imagined riding him. Rolling her hips back and forth. Holding down his hands.

Then he was behind her, slapping her thick backside, scars-be-damned, as he pounded her hard. She would tell him to go harder still. Faster. Give it all to her. Until they both screamed out in a shared explosion of pleasure.

Which is exactly what she did there in the tub, kicking her legs out, groaning, spilling enough of the bathwater to extinguish the candles, leaving herself in the dark while her body pulsated. The spasms continued until she finally pulled the vibrator away, clicking it off and blanketing the room in silence.

Her skin was left saturated with a warm, relaxed energy.

A perfect calm.

Luckily, she'd left her cigarettes on the sink instead

of the now soaked floor. She lit one in the dark, holding it high in the air as she slid down into the water, far enough to submerge the top of her head. The warmth sank into her thick hair.

When she finally came up for air, she felt like some kind of sea goddess rising up from the water.

Wow, that was exactly what I needed.

The cherry of her cigarette was the only light in the bathroom. She inhaled and blew smoke through its glowing aura.

Cristina looked toward the open door and the hallway filled with blackness.

She'd never been one to be afraid of the dark, not even as a kid. But in that moment, her new place felt eerily quiet — the only sound a trickle of water slowly escaping through the bath's imperfect drain plug.

Before her cigarette was done, she tried to light the candles again. The wicks wouldn't catch, so she lit another Lucky Strike.

The thickening layers of smoke mesmerized her. She watched the clouds morph into shapes before disappearing into the black depths of the hall. Her eyes strained to follow it.

Then, in a flash that disappeared so quickly Cristina wasn't sure it had ever actually been there, she swore she could see the outline of something in the hallway.

It was nothing, she immediately tried to tell herself.

Yet, it seemed real enough that she'd instinctively jerked away. Even now, she felt like she could still almost see a ghostly imprint, like the remnants of a picture flashed in front of her eyes.

A little girl.

No . . . she tried to tell herself. *That's ridiculous, Cristina. Stop letting your mind get the best of you. There was nothing there. You're just tired.*

But she couldn't get it out of her head.

As she sat naked in the now lukewarm bathwater, the image became clearer. A girl, in her nightgown, close to Anise's age, holding some kind of stuffed animal in one hand, staring into the bathroom.

Cristina shivered, trying to think of something else, anything else, while she wrapped her body in a robe and her hair in a towel.

After drying off and climbing into bed, she could hardly bring herself to close her eyes. The news articles she'd read about the murder kept flowing into her mind. But only in small, incomplete snippets.

She couldn't help thinking there was a lot she didn't know.

15

It was well past midnight when Cristina came downstairs after being unable to sleep.

She walked through the house turning on every light.

On top of one of the packing boxes, she set the folder filled with everything related to the house. She sat on the floor, feet stretched out in front of her. She separated out the legal documents and moved them as far away as she could reach. Their officey smell reminded her too much of court.

Cristina had been in front of a judge more times than she cared to remember. Most recently, of course, for her divorce. But she'd also been caught stealing three times as a minor. Twice she was given probation, and on the other occasion she spent three months in The Camp – a juvenile rehabilitation center for girls located somewhere high in the Sierra Nevada mountains. During her time there, she was beat up by a group of cholas who decided they didn't like her, sexually violated by a fat guard, and imprinted with a lifelong distrust of the criminal justice system.

She spread the news clippings onto the hardwood floor and lit a cigarette, using an empty Coke can from the recycling bin as an ashtray.

Police Search for Missing Girl

May 7 – A local four-year-old girl, Annie Stewart, was reported missing by her mother.

According to Pleasure Point Police Chief Walt Blunderberg, the girl was last seen by her stepfather playing in the woods near her backyard.

Police say evidence found at the scene leads them to believe foul play may have been a factor. Anyone with information is urged to contact the Pleasure Point Police Department immediately.

Family Pleads for Return of Daughter

May 8 – A day after young four-year-old local Annie Stewart was reported missing, the girl's stepfather, Thomas Walker, gave a brief press conference on the steps of the Pleasure Point Police Department's headquarters.

He offered a tearful plea for her safe return.

"We're so worried and just pray every day that our little girl comes home," Mr. Walker said.

The girl's mother, Amanda Stewart-Walker, stood near her husband during the press conference, sobbing at times, but did not speak.

The family did not take questions from reporters.

While police, joined by volunteers, have launched an all-out search of the area near the girl's home, they have yet to say publically whether or not they are treating the case as a kidnapping.

Girl's Neighbor Questioned in Disappearance

May 11 – A local man, Rick Atkins, has been questioned and released without charges in the disappearance of missing four-year-old Annie Stewart, according to a spokesperson for the Pleasure Point Police Department.

The spokesperson declined to elaborate on what prompted the formal questioning, saying only that the man lives next door to the girl's family.

Mr. Atkins did not return repeated requests for comment.

Search for Missing Girl Called Off

May 14 – The day and night search for young local Annie Stewart has been suspended, Police Chief Walt Blunderberg said today. The announcement comes just one week after she was reported missing by her parents.

The investigation is still ongoing, he told reporters at a news conference, but due to insufficient progress, police and volunteers will no longer continue combing the area around the girl's home, at least not on a continuous basis.

Blunderberg hinted to members of the press that police were now looking into the possibility that the girl's disappearance could have been the result of some sort of accident. He did not elaborate further, except to say it was his assessment that whatever has happened to the girl is almost certainly an isolated incident and should not be cause for alarm to visitors and residents of Pleasure Point.

FBI Joins Hunt for Annie Stewart

May 17 – In a controversial move, prompted by what it said was a lack of action by local police officials on an active case, The Federal Bureau of Investigation has opened its own inquiry into the disappearance of Annie Stewart, a four-year-old local girl who vanished earlier this month while playing near her home.

A visibly frustrated Police Chief Walt Blunderberg told reporters at a press conference following the announcement that he believed the FBI's involvement in the case was premature, given that there are no clear suspects or motives in the case.

He added that he worried federal involvement in the case might spur unnecessary panic in the community. Blunderberg stressed that residents of Pleasure Point, as well as visitors to the area, had no reason to think that the case represents any broader danger to the general public.

Mother of Missing Girl Pleads for Her Return

May 21 – A distraught Amanda Stewart-Walker, mother of missing four-year-old Annie Stewart, made a fresh plea today for the safe return of her daughter.

Joined by her husband at a special press conference

with the FBI, Ms. Stewart-Walker burst into tears as she asked for anyone with information to come forward.

For five full minutes, she spoke on camera about the little girl, repeating numerous times that her daughter loved the ocean and animals. The broadcast also featured pictures of Annie, presumably in an attempt to humanize her in the mind of an abductor – a common tactic used by the FBI.

The agency joined the investigation earlier this week.

Special Agent in Charge for the Pleasure Point area, Kevin J. McPherson, added to reporters that the FBI was re-interviewing key witnesses and hoped to announce a break in the case soon.

Possible Suspect in Girl's Disappearance

May 27 – A source inside the FBI, speaking on a condition of anonymity, told this newspaper that the agency was closing in on a possible suspect in the case of missing four-year-old Annie Stewart.

The source declined to name the possible suspect, or give any further information as to why authorities believe this person may have been involved in the girl's disappearance.

Field agents for the FBI, as well as the Pleasure Point Chief of Police, both declined to comment further on the case.

According to additional sources, however, no one has been brought in for questioning since a man was briefly detained shortly after the girl disappeared. That man, neighbor Rick Atkins, was released without being charged with any crime.

Missing Girl's Stepfather Confesses to Crime, Kills Self

May 31 – In a startling turn of events, Thomas Walker, the stepfather of missing four-year-old Annie Stewart was found dead in the woods near his home, apparently the victim of a self-inflicted gunshot wound to the head.

Local police say he left behind a typed note indicating that he abducted the young girl and killed her. They said the note also revealed the location of the missing girl's body, but added that authorities have not yet recovered any remains.

This confession comes despite weeks of tearful pleas by Mr. Walker in local and national media, in which he repeatedly begged for Annie's safe return.

Missing Girl's Body Recovered, Still No Motive

April 1 – After learning of its location from an apparent suicide confession by her late stepfather, police today recovered the body of four-year-old Annie Stewart.

Authorities found the girl buried in a shallow grave near an abandoned rock quarry, less than two miles from the family's home.

Police say Mr. Walker admitted in his note to having abducted his stepdaughter before murdering her and burying her body in the quarry.

No explanation has been made available as to why police and volunteers were previously unable to locate the body, despite days of intense searches in the area surrounding the girl's home, including the quarry.

Additionally, neither Police Chief Walt Blunderberg nor local FBI agents would offer comment on Mr. Walker's motive for committing this horrible crime.

Annie Stewart's Mother Found Dead

April 3 – Adding to an already horrendous tragedy, Amanda Stewart-Walker, mother of murdered four-year-old Annie Stewart, and wife to the man police say confessed to killing the girl before taking his own life, was herself found dead in her Pleasure Point home, the victim of an apparent suicide.

A neighbor reported hearing screams and sobs coming from the home through most of the night. When he went by to check on Ms. Stewart-Walker in the morning, he discovered she had hanged herself in the downstairs closet.

The neighbor, who requested anonymity, said he did not see a note of any kind, and police have so far refused to comment on the incident.

FBI Questions PPPD's Findings in Killing of Local Girl

April 10 – Special Agent in Charge Kevin J. McPherson, who has himself headed the FBI's investigation into local four-year-old Annie Stewart's disappearance and murder, today lodged an official complaint with state officials against the Pleasure Point Police Department.

Although exact details as to the nature of the complaint remain sealed, McPherson indicated to reporters in a press conference that the FBI was dissatisfied with the lack of evidence supporting the PPPD's conclusion that Annie Stewart's stepfather, Thomas Walker, committed the murder.

McPherson added that, although he believes the case should remain open, because of jurisdictional interests, the FBI would be forced to discontinue its active pursuit of leads, until such time as the PPPD files an official request for assistance.

16

That was the last news clipping in the folder.

Still sitting on the floor, Cristina set the stack of photocopied articles down in front of her and lit a cigarette. She could tell by the grey glow seeping through the window that the sun would be coming up soon.

She shifted her body to look at the hall closet, which she'd yet to open since moving in. Her hand shook as she flicked ashes into the soda can. The sense of loss the mother had felt was thick in the air.

Who could do such a horrible thing to a child?

The sadness overcame Cristina. She leaned forward and wept. Tears gushed down the sides of her face, dripping onto the paper.

This kind of horror was *exactly* why she was absolutely certain there was no such thing as God. There's no way a divine, all-powerful being would ever allow something so bad to happen to someone so innocent.

Reading those articles left her feeling ill for even taking the house in the first place. She tried to figure out how she'd ever convinced herself it was a good idea.

Should she just get the hell out of there and never come back?

What would I do? Go back to sleeping on the couch in Aba's tiny apartment?

The truth was, she had nowhere else to go. There

was nothing she could do but suck it up and be strong. For herself, and for Anise.

"You can't keep runnin' your whole life," Michelle had told her when they discussed Cristina moving to Pleasure Point. *"You've got to find a place to call home. Then stick with it. Build a life."*

Cristina wished her friend and sponsor was there right now. She knew the big, strong woman would take her into her beautifully flabby black arms and comfort her, tell her things would be alright, like she'd done so many times before.

She probably thinks I'm dead.

Cristina wasn't exactly sure what time it was, but she knew Michelle would be awake. She always got up at around 4 AM every day, in order to hit the 5 o'clock 'Sunrisers' meeting she'd been going to for the past twenty years. Cristina had gotten dragged to it once when she first got sober. It was great. Full of positive women who all had way too much energy for so early in the morning. But she just wasn't much of an early bird, and firmly believed she never would be. So she hadn't been back.

Regardless of the time, Cristina figured this would be the perfect opportunity to call and catch up. Maybe vent a little. And, hopefully, find some comfort and sanity.

She was halfway up the stairs to go grab her phone when a sharp knock came at the door. The suddenness of the sound brought her young body about as close to a heart attack as it could get. Every muscle tightened. Her chest vibrated like a ringing bell. The first thought through her head was that it had to be Mr. Psycho coming to finish their discussion from a week ago.

But through the smoked-glass window in the front door, she could see a figure with a bushy beard and a belly.

Jack.

He stood on the small front porch, reaching up for something. She almost didn't answer the door, really wanting to make her phone call, and hopefully get some sleep after that. But she realized ignoring him wouldn't exactly make her a very good neighbor.

So she shuffled back down the stairs, chastising herself for being so on edge. With her fingertips, she fixed her hair. Then remembered she was still wearing the comfortable but well-worn white t-shirt she almost always slept in. And no bra. Her dark, perky nipples stood out clearly as her breasts pressed against the threadbare fabric. She casually covered them with her forearms after opening the door.

"Good morning!" she said with enough enthusiasm that Jack jumped backward. His sunhat fell from his head, kept from hitting the ground only by a brown leather strap wrapped around his neck. He had on shorts, high black socks, and a dark-blue athletic shirt.

"You OK?" he asked without looking at her. "I was, um, on my way to take a little hike, and uh, I heard you crying. I just wanted to see if you were OK. Sorry to pry. You can tell me to go away if you want to."

Cristina could feel her cheeks flush with heat and redness.

"Oh, wow, how embarrassing," she said. "I feel so touched you would come check on me, though. I'm fine. It's just that time of the month, I guess."

She felt bad lying to such a nice guy, but she was also certain that if she told him the real reason she'd been crying, the tears would just start right back up again.

"Like I said," he told her seriously, holding up his hands and finally making eye contact. "I didn't mean to intrude. I just know how it feels to be sad. I've certainly had times when I've wished someone would come see how I was doing. So I always try to make the effort." He peeked past her into the house. "But I have the perfect cure for the blues if you guys are up for a hike."

"Oh, Anise is with my grandmother during the week until she finishes school. Another month or so."

"Ah, I see," he said. "Well, the two of us then?"

Cristina *really* wanted to call Michelle. She *needed* to call. But the feeling of warm sun on her face as she stood in the doorway told her it was going to be a beautiful morning – the kind Michelle would probably tell her to make the most of.

Cristina decided she would call when she got back to the house.

She told Jack, "OK. I need to change though."

"Take your time. I'm going to go get a screwdriver and fix this light for you." He jiggled the bracket to show how loose it was. "It's bugging me."

"Thanks," she said, already feeling a bit better. "To be honest, I hadn't even noticed."

She hurried upstairs to put on a sports bra, shorts, and a tank top. She still had the pair of running shoes from when she'd been jogging regularly about six months earlier. Well, regularly for about two weeks before she gave it up. So the shoes were still in great shape.

By the time she returned to the front door, Jack had already fixed the light and had moved on to tightening the brass knocker.

"You're too sweet," she told him.

He saw she was emptyhanded and suggested grabbing some water.

"We'll probably do about five miles," he added.

That worried her. She honestly wasn't sure she could do it. On the other hand, she wasn't about to get schooled by a guy in his sixties, especially one with a belly as big as Jack's.

"Shall we cut through the house?" he suggested. "The trail starts just on the other side of your backyard.

They walked through the living room, into the kitchen, out the sliding glass door.

Cristina hadn't spent any time in the backyard since she'd been spooked that first night, a fear that seemed silly in the light of day. There were even a few spring flowers blooming between the weeds and the other bushes. Their sweet scent floated in the grassy air.

Jack walked over to one area of the yard as if he'd been there before. He moved aside a bush and pinched off a branch of rosemary, setting it on the wooden fence.

"Remind me to grab that when we get back," he said. "I'm making a pork roast tonight, and it would do well with some fresh herb. There should be some thyme around here too. But, you know what? I can never find the time."

He looked at her and waited until she finally provided a sympathy laugh.

"You're ridiculous," she added.

They had to lift a few branches at the tree line to find the hiking trail. But once through, the way forward was clearly worn.

Overhead, thick trees blocked the sun, making the air a bit chilly. Cristina rubbed her bare, tattooed arms to stay warm, wondering if she should go back and get something to wear over her tank top.

"Don't worry," Jack told her before she could say anything. "You won't need a sweatshirt. We'll start going uphill pretty soon, and I promise you'll be warm after that."

As they made their way along through the cool air, Cristina's tiredness faded away. She tried to focus on the beauty of her surroundings, pushing aside what she'd read in those articles.

Jack wasn't kidding about the hill. They started up the sharp incline, and Cristina's heart soon felt like it was going to explode in her chest. She looked over and saw Jack casually checking out the scenery, barely breathing heavy at all.

I need to quit smoking, she told herself.

"Beautiful isn't it?" Jack asked with a bit of childlike wonder in his voice. "I've been doing this walk for thirty years now, and I never get tired of it."

"Yah . . . it's . . . great."

The hill seemed to keep going and going and going. Until finally she saw a break in the pine trees ahead. The sun poked through the foliage, promising a sanctuary of relief from the burning in her lungs. But in a cruel joke of nature, when they finally reached what looked like the top, the pathway kicked sharply to the right and became even steeper.

Cristina hoped Jack would call for a break. He didn't. Instead, he turned to her, smiled kindly from underneath his hat, and continued pushing up the path.

He's enjoying seeing the youngster suffer. I definitely can't quit now.

She dug deep.

In reality, it wasn't much farther to the top, but the severity of the grade made the effort incredibly difficult. For a few moments, she thought there was no way she could make it without stopping. But the sight of flatter ground about fifty yards ahead brought a new surge of energy.

It felt amazing to finally reach the top and step without strained effort.

Cristina immediately bent over to catch her breath.

"Hijole!" she said as she stood and deeply gulped

water from her bottle, already wishing she'd brought more. "That's a bitch."

"You're supposed to be the young, vibrant one," Jack teased. "I'm just an old fat guy."

"You've definitely got my respect." She offered her hand for a high-five and he slapped it. She asked, "Where does this go anyway? You know, it's not every day I wander into the woods with a man I've only known a few days. Consider it a compliment."

"I'm pretty scary and all." He rolled his eyes. "So, this trail actually splits a couple of ways. One path goes up and through the quarry, then back down to the ocean. That's the way we're going. The other goes deeper into the mountains. I actually have a piece of property up that way. I'll have to take you there some time. It's a great walk."

"Oh, Anise would love that. I would, too."

"It's not much, but it's my little sanctuary."

"Wow, sounds great. These mountains are so beautiful."

He nodded and put a hand on her shoulder. "Shall we continue?"

The next leg of the hike wasn't nearly as bad as the first. It was still uphill, but nowhere near as steep. And now that they were warmed up, Cristina found she was actually enjoying herself. She tried to remember the last time she'd gone into the wilderness voluntarily and couldn't.

After her experience as a teenager at The Camp, she'd sort of always been turned off by nature. The mulchy smell of fallen leaves and dirt reminded her too much of being thrown into what had felt to her teenage mind like some kind of psychotic nightmare.

When the girls incarcerated at The Camp weren't being forced to sew clothes for ten or twelve hours a day, many of the guards – euphemistically referred to as "counselors" – made it a point to try and get them alone.

One afternoon, a fat male guard followed her into an otherwise empty bathroom. He started talking to Cristina through the stall door while she peed. Dirty stuff about how he could smell her womanhood, and other similarly weird shit. He told her he would taste it soon enough, and then walked out.

She was so afraid to leave the stall, she missed check-in and got herself thrown in a "time-out room" for 24 hours. All alone, locked inside a dark room no bigger than a closet, she sat curled up in the corner, shaking, fearful that at any moment the fat guard was going to open the door and make good on his promise.

He didn't.

At least not then.

But about two weeks later, he again followed her into that same bathroom. She was alone, sitting in the stall. When the clack of his boots echoed against the tile floor, an icy fear chilled her spine. She tried to hide by pulling her feet up onto the toilet. It didn't work.

He rattled the door, but of course she'd locked it.

In a quiet voice, he told her to open it or she would be sorry.

She continued to ignore him.

Suddenly, his face appeared underneath the stall door, complete with a hungry-looking grin. He even licked his lips in sick anticipation of what was to come.

"I'm going to get what I want," he said. "One way or another. For your sake, you might as well make it easy."

She started to cry and he laughed.

"Open the door, you little bitch." His face snarled. "If I have to pull myself under, I'm going to make you feel so much pain, you'll never walk straight again."

Cristina knew he wouldn't be able to make it under

the door. He had to have weighed at least 300 pounds. But she was so afraid. With a quivering hand, she unlatched the lock and let him in.

He forced her to sit on the toilet while he stuck his pudgy lips in between her legs, smacking them like he was eating his favorite burger. Then he made her give him a blowjob, laughing when she gagged and finally vomited into the toilet.

Every time he saw her after that, if no one was paying attention, he quietly mimicked her retching.

"Well, do you?" Jack repeated his question for the second time.

"What?" Cristina responded, coming back from the memory. "Do I what? I'm sorry, I guess I'm a little out of it. I didn't sleep much last night."

"Quite alright. I asked if you want to know more about the history of the quarry. We'll be coming up on it in just a moment."

On cue, they came to the gated opening of a concrete wall. A thicket of red manzanita and other bushes had done a good job reclaiming the terrain, reducing what was once a vehicle road to a path now wide enough only for people.

The gate was rusted open. On the wall next to it, a black metal sign with worn-out white letters remained attached to the concrete, barely visible from under the dense growth.

Perkins & Co. Quarry and Cement Company

Underneath was a smaller white sign with red letters.

AUTHORIZED PERSONNEL ONLY

"Don't worry about that," Jack said, sounding like he was getting ready to make one of his speeches. "It's all public land now." He pointed at the black sign. "That guy Perkins owns all kinds of stuff, but mostly mining and oil interests around California and elsewhere. He came to town in the sixties as a young man, looking to spend a rather large inheritance. Before that, the only thing in Pleasure Point was a few cheap motels near the beach and a couple of hamburger stands. Perkins opened the concrete plant and made this whole area boom. That is, until the bastard and his partners decided to up and move the whole operation."

They passed through the gate. The path widened into something that looked more like a proper dirt road. After about a quarter mile, they came to the quarry itself.

Cristina could still see where a vehicle path spiraled down the giant hole in the ground, ending at a pool of surprisingly clear-looking water.

"People swim in it," Jack told her. "I just wish they'd pick up after themselves."

The ground was littered with trash. Mostly empty beer bottles, cans, and boxes. But plenty of other stuff, too. Styrofoam fast-food containers. Cigarette butts. More used condoms than Cristina cared to count.

"People are so disgusting," she said.

"Never have truer words been spoken."

Jack kicked a few pieces of debris, looking like he wanted to pick them up, while at the same time realizing the effort would be useless. He instead squatted, forearms resting on his knees.

He said, "Everywhere you go on this entire planet, you'll find this kind of crap. Trash, everywhere. It's like humans as a species just can't get our heads out of our collective backends long enough to realize we actually need to take care of the world around us. It's sad."

He pondered that for a few moments, continuing to survey the area.

The longer they stood there, the more the quarry took on an ominous feel. Cristina's mind drifted back to the articles. There were so many things about it all that didn't make sense. The least of which was why the stepfather would do something so horrible in the first place. She supposed he could have been plain crazy, but somehow that didn't seem to fit. And why bury the body here in the quarry? And how come no one found it earlier?

Running her hand along a square of quarried limestone, she tried to imagine what had happened. Was poor Annie afraid when her life ended? Did her stepfather hurt her? Torture her? Do things to her? Or did he make it quick?

Cristina thought Jack might be able to shed some light on what had happened, but she was afraid to ask. The last thing she wanted to do was traumatize her poor neighbor any more than he'd likely already been.

"As I was saying," Jack said, gathering himself back into teaching mode. "Perkins and his developer buddies sold the plant and the quarry, but before that it was the lifeblood of Pleasure Point. Anyhow, I told you about most of this I think, right?"

"Yah, you basically said that the plant closing really hurt the area, and that afterward a lot of drugs started coming in. Which reminds me, I wanted to ask you about something. When I drove into town the other day, I took a wrong turn and ended up in this really creepy area. It was like totally abandoned."

"Perkins Town."

"What?"

"Perkins Town. That's what we call it." He waved his arms to indicate the quarry. "As in Perkins, the man himself. He built that housing for the original workers of the concrete factory. And for three generations, many of the people who mined this quarry and worked in the factory lived there."

"I see," Cristina said, remembering the men she saw. Their haunting black eyes. "And now?"

"Now it's a genuine slum. The only people who ever go there are the homeless, and people trying to score dope."

Jack pulled back his wandering stare and looked at her seriously.

He added, "I wouldn't go there again if I were you. That place is dangerous. The people who frequent it have no reason to live, and no reason to care about anyone but themselves."

Cristina didn't have much to say. She had no plans to spend any more time in that place.

Jack added, "I'm sorry. I sound like I'm trying to be your father or something. Let's keep walking, shall we? Sometimes this place gives me the willies, especially after what happened to poor Annie."

He turned quickly and began walking toward another footpath. Cristina again felt driven to ask him about the little girl, but still couldn't find a way to do it.

Oh hey, can you tell me all about the time your next-door neighbor killed his stepdaughter and buried her here?

Yet, the more she thought about the events, the harder it was to shake the feeling there was something important left out of the newspaper clippings. Something she needed to know if she was ever going to have any peace of mind living in her new house.

"Jack?" she asked timidly.

"Yes." His voice sounded distant, as if he knew what was coming and hoped that it wasn't.

"Would you be willing to tell me more about what happened at my house? With Annie, I mean." After a moment of silence, she added, "I understand if you don't want to talk about it. But if you feel like you can, I'd really like to hear what you have to say."

He was quiet for long enough that she thought he might not speak at all. She started to wish she hadn't said anything.

Probably the worst thing he's ever been through, Cristina, and you feel the need to bring it up out of the blue, ruining a perfect hike and a perfect day. Nice work, girl.

"Sure," he said suddenly. "Sure. What do you know?"

"Well, only what I read in the newspaper articles the real estate agent gave me."

"Hmm . . . unfortunately, you probably know about the same as the rest of us. Honestly, there isn't all that much more to tell. I wish there was. I knew them, but not well. Not really. I do know that Annie was a lovely, lovely little girl. And Amanda seemed to be a great mom." He smiled fondly. "You should have seen the two together, Cristina. It was a thing of beauty, watching them walk hand-in-hand together. Not unlike you and Anise, I'd say." His smile faded. "Even Tom, that sick son-of-a-bitch, was, from everything I ever witnessed, a good guy. He always showed so much love for his stepdaughter. Everyone who knew them was shocked by what happened. Just devastated. Me included."

"So there really was no sign that something like that was going to happen? No abuse? Fights? Nothing? It all just seems so strange to me."

"There was nothing. They were what most people would describe as a perfect, happy family. I suppose everyone has their issues. But I certainly never saw anything that would've even hinted at what was to come." He paused thoughtfully. "You know, as happy as I was to see him kick the bucket, I do wish they could have put Tom under the hot lights and interrogated him. Figured out why he did it. The rumor was, at the time, it had something to do with that drug cult I was telling you about your first night here. I think maybe he was wrapped up in it somehow. But, of course, it's hard to tell where facts end and town gossip begins. Not that knowing would bring back her sweet, innocent face."

He turned away from her. When he looked back, his eyes were dry, but she could see that talking about the subject had choked him up.

"I'm sorry, Jack."

"Don't be. If I were in your shoes, I'd want to know, too. I just wish there was more I could tell you."

They kept walking, staying silent for a long time, the only sound the coastal breeze blowing through the trees.

Jack stared down the path, lost in thought.

The beautiful day seemed a little less so after such a heavy topic. Cristina tried to think of a way to lighten the mood.

"I'm definitely excited about my date this Thursday," she said finally.

"With Mr. Dreamy?" Jack turned to her and smiled, though it obviously took some effort.

"Yep. I'm sure I'm setting myself up for a big disappointment. But hey, what can you do?"

Jack didn't answer. He only shrugged and kept walking.

Another long stretch of silence.

Cristina kept expecting to eventually reach some peak in the trail, complete with a great scenic view like the one she saw driving into town. But it never came.

At some point, one she failed to recognize, they simply began to trek downhill, back toward the coast.

About half a mile from the sea, the path broke from under the trees, cutting through a field of wild grass and other vegetation that grew from hard-packed dirt. Deep ridges had been dug into the trail by rainwater on its way back to the ocean.

The closer they came to the shoreline, the louder and deeper the waves boomed. The sound echoed as the path took them into a small, sandy canyon.

Jack removed his shoes and socks. Cristina followed his lead, listening as she did to the increasing intensity of the waves.

"I can't believe how much bigger they are down here than at the beach by the amusement park," she said in a voice that was close to shouting.

"Yes," Jack responded calmly. "It's the south swell I was telling you about. I think we should hurry along. The tide's coming up. We should have plenty of time, but if we're not careful, the water could come up on us." He saw her wince a bit. "Don't worry. I've been through here a million times. We'll be alright. Let's go."

They exited the canyon, coming out on a small ridge overlooking the ocean. To the right, Cristina saw a gentle stretch of beach covered in driftwood and golden sand.

Jack pointed and said, "That's the naked hippy beach I was telling you about." He strained his eyes. "In fact, I think the little human-shaped dot you can just barely make out in the distance is my friend Cassie. She and her girlfriend have a house about a mile down that way." He swung an arm in the other direction. "And *that's* where we need to go."

The path to their left looked as ominous as the sandy beach looked inviting. Over many thousands of years, the water had carved a trough-like canal through the rock, big enough for a person to walk in. The path was flanked on one side by a fifty-foot cliff pocked with dark caves, and on the other by a natural outcropping rising out from the sea. This wall of rock shielded the path, turning it into a bunker against the constant onslaught of waves.

But Cristina could easily see how, once the tide rose to a certain height, there would be no stopping the water. The entire path would be flooded and washed out, along with anything or anyone stupid enough to be there at the time.

She felt motivated to hurry. With a sense of purpose, she slid her socks and shoes back on. Following Jack, she gingerly took her first steps across the uneven rock.

The only obvious sign of life around them was a flock of seagulls perched on the cliffs above. They seemed to be watching. Everything else appeared barren at first. But as they made their way along, Cristina noticed more than a few crabs and other creatures scurrying away. She couldn't help but think they knew what was coming and were making for higher ground.

She and Jack didn't speak as they moved forward. The unbalanced terrain forced concentration with every step. Progress was painfully slow.

When they'd made it about halfway, Jack said he wanted to show her something. He grabbed her hand and pulled her up onto a flat outcropping that extended into the sea like a mushroom-shaped platform.

"This is my favorite place in the entire world," he said.

Away from the protection of the path, they were now face-to-face with the full fury of the sea. The rocks shook every fifteen seconds or so from the force of another wave. Jack hardly seemed to notice as he bent over and poked around in a tide pool. He was almost giddy, splashing around like a little kid.

Cristina bent down and offered a distracted glance at a bright sea anemone as it grasped onto a snail Jack had set into its sticky tentacles.

She hoped they were going to be on their way soon, and said as much after a particularly large breaker sent a surge of water over the rocks and down the back of her shirt.

"Oh, OK," Jack said, sounding disappointed. "I could play here for hours though. It makes me feel young again."

Back in the canal, Cristina tried to ignore the way the intensity of the waves kept increasing. And the growing size of the salty spray.

The seaweed and algae covered rocks were getting slick.

Water soaked Cristina's shoes and socks, almost knocking her off-balance in the process. She regained her footing, but a sense of panic washed over her as she stumbled forward.

Jack continued moving with calm ease, now a good distance ahead.

Feeling the need to catch up, Cristina put less concentration into finding perfect footholds, increasing her pace, but making each step a little less stable.

Finally, she was only about twenty feet from the safety of a set of wooden stairs built into the cliffside.

Jack had already begun his ascent.

She managed to make short work of the final stretch. As she skipped from rock to rock, closing the last bit of distance between herself and the stairs, another powerful wave hit. Its deep boom rolled like thunder, shaking the rock beneath her. Water shot high into the air and then rained down, hitting her with a jarring force, drenching her entire body.

She was relieved to still be standing.

The bottom of the stairs was only a single step away now. As she plunged her front foot forward, the back one slipped on a patch of algae, sliding out from under her.

She yelped.

The rocks below rushed upward. Luckily, she managed to bring her hands up before she bashed the side of her head against them.

She tried to reach her feet.

Jack was yelling at her, but she couldn't make out what he was saying.

By the time she realized he was telling her to hurry, the next wave hit. It covered her in water cold enough to suck the air from her chest.

In that moment, a horrible picture came into her mind: Anise, frightened and crying above a grave with her mother in it.

Then, almost completely by instinct, she gathered her strength and jumped out of the water, pulling herself onto the steps.

Cristina couldn't breathe. Her long, thick hair was plastered over her face, covering her eyes and mouth.

Panicked lungs gasped as they searched for oxygen.

"Woah there," Jack said.

He wiped the hair away with his hand. Her breathing started to settle. He looked at her with serious worry, until suddenly her panting turned into a giggle, and then a full-on laugh.

Jack probably thought she'd hit her head.

"I'm fine," she said, repeating it with relief. "I'm fine. I'm fine. I'm fine."

"I'm so sorry," Jack said, shaking his head. "I shouldn't have brought you this way, I don't know what I was thinking."

Cristina stood, offering a hand for him to slap.

"Don't be sorry. That was pretty damn awesome!"

He looked a bit shocked, but softly tapped her hand with his own.

Together, they made their way up the stairs.

Behind them, another waved crashed over the outcropping, this time completely filling the pathway with water.

17

Cristina finally pulled up in front of the library, after getting lost only about a dozen times.

Pleasure Point's small downtown area was no more than six blocks long, but somehow she kept ending up at the same stone statue of a surfer. She only found the small, grey building after accidentally driving in the wrong direction down a poorly marked one-way street.

It was Thursday. The day of her date with Casey. She was almost as excited about it as she was about seeing Anise in just 24 hours.

A blanket of fog had come in early and hadn't yet burned off. In the damp mist, the entire town seemed more withdrawn and cautious. And definitely a lot colder. She stood next to the Civic, pulling on a hoodie with the California flag emblazoned across the chest, identical to the one she had tattooed on her forearm.

A small spiral notebook in hand, she made her way into the building.

Since Cristina was embarrassingly bad with technology, Jordan had agreed to help her look some stuff up about what had happened in her house.

She just knew there had to be something she was missing. Especially given what Jack had said about the possible connection to this cult, something that wasn't mentioned in any of the articles.

And then there were the dreams.

For the past three nights, ever since going through the news clippings more thoroughly, Cristina had been visited by a series of vivid nightmares.

Each was similar, beginning with her lying in bed. The room dark. A faint knock coming from downstairs. Not the door. Something else. Quiet, hollow, but steady as a metronome. She stood, trying to turn on the lights, but none of the switches did anything.

The knock grew louder as she crept down the stairs in the dark, feeling strangely like she had little or no control over her body. By the time she reached the living room, the sound reminded her of a fleshy fist pounding against the top of a table.

It was coming from the hall closet.

She watched as her hand reached out on its own. Her fingers gripped the metal doorknob. Touching it was painful, like holding a handful of ice cubes.

The door felt impossibly heavy. The hinges creaked like they hadn't moved in a thousand years. Inside, swinging from the end of a short rope, rhythmically bumping into the closet's back wall, was the body of Amanda Stewart-Walker.

Cristina was again drawn forward, unwillingly inched toward the putrid stench of death. The smell washed over her, soaking her hair and skin with the rotten-fruit-and-cinnamon fragrance of decaying flesh.

She'd been pulled almost half-way into the closet when the corpse's eyes opened.

Black pupils dug into her. Questioning. Accusing.

Blood-crusted lips parted, revealing a swollen, purple tongue. Out poured a gurgling wail, so horrible and so close to Cristina's ear that she awoke, herself screaming as the image of the hanging woman faded away.

The next night was eerily similar.

She was pulled down the stairs. Toward the closet door. Willed to open it by some force she didn't understand. Only, this time, it wasn't Amanda hanging by the neck, body rapping against the wall. It was Cristina herself. Not decayed yet, but blue and bloated and definitely dead. And not hanging from a rope, but from the end of a familiar belt with shiny silver studs. One that had been the source of so much pain.

The third night was the worst.

This time there were two rhythmic knocks. One after the other. Tap, tap. Tap, tap. Tap, tap. And two belts in the closet. One for Cristina, and the other slightly shorter. Hanging from the end of the second belt, wearing her favorite polka dot pajamas, was Anise. Her eyes, so vibrant and filled with wonder in life, now no more alive than dull pieces of sea glass.

Everything about the dreams had frightened Cristina. Coming to the library was her way of turning fear into action. She knew the nightmares were probably just her mind trying to solve the mystery of what had happened in her home. It was natural to want to know.

Walking into the building, Cristina immediately felt lost. She hadn't been in a library since before she'd dropped out of high school. In fact, she was kind of surprised they even existed anymore.

"I thought everything was online now," she said after she found Jordan sitting at a computer terminal.

Annoyed, Jordan said, "It's one of the biggest problems with research nowadays. Everyone thinks the fine people at Google have all the answers."

They grabbed a free computer and quickly found the same articles Cristina had already seen. Then she saw the photo of Annie standing in front of the house, a stuffed hippo clutched in one hand. The same picture Anise had found. The one Cristina had for some reason felt compelled to dump in the trash.

"Can we print this?" she asked Jordan.

"Yah, of course. Just put in your library card and it will charge the printing fee to your account."

"Uh, yah, I don't have one of those."

"OK," Jordan said with disapproving eyebrows.

Cristina shrugged, slightly embarrassed.

Jordan sighed. "We can use mine. What exactly do you want to print?"

"Just the picture for now."

With a click, the printer next to the bank of computers whirred to life. A few moments later, it shot out a black and white copy of the photo.

Cristina stared at the image, drawn to the little girl's eyes. They were sweet, but at the same time infinitely sad. Almost as if she could sense fate barreling toward her like a ghostly, runaway freight train.

Shaking off her own feeling of impending doom, Cristina went back to peering over Jordan's shoulder. In addition to the local paper's coverage, several national articles appeared in the search results as well.

Most of the big newspapers focused their coverage similarly to the local ones, filling articles with lots of vague speculation and few specific details. But these bigger publications added a dash of sensationalism for extra flavor. Cristina thought most of the headlines read a bit like something you would see in the checkout line at the supermarket. And when she scanned through a few, there really wasn't much, if any, new information.

After clicking on a couple more, she started to get discouraged.

"OK," she said. "All this seems pretty familiar. What else can we search for? What do you know about that crazy drug cult that used to be active around here? What was the name of it again?"

"Hmm," Jordan looked at her, seeming puzzled but

intrigued. "That's interesting. The group was called *New Horizon*. I remember coming across some information about them and the founder for my book research. *His* name is Charles Walters, I believe. But what makes you think he or his group had anything to do with the girl? I'm pretty sure he was arrested before she was killed."

"My neighbor Jack mentioned it. I don't know, maybe something he picked up that wasn't public. He's lived in Pleasure Point his whole life, so he probably has a lot of connections."

Jordan nodded and then typed in a new set of search terms.

The results page had about a dozen hits.

"Anything specifically about Annie?" Cristina asked.

Jordan tried including her name in the search, but the query came back blank.

Cristina said, "Hmm . . . OK, go back to what we had." She nudged Jordan out of the seat and sat down herself. "I'm going to hang here for a bit and go through these. If you have something to do, don't let me keep you."

"I'm at your disposal until the noon meeting. I'll be over in the non-fiction stacks if you need me. But it would appear that you have things figured out."

Jordan offered an encouraging smile and walked around the corner.

Cristina began reading.

She soon discovered that Walters wasn't actually the one who founded *New Horizon* after all. He actually took over the organization following the original founder's death.

The best source of information Cristina found was an investigative report on *New Horizon*, written by a journalist named Duke Thompson.

Thompson first outlined the group's philosophy, as he'd seen it laid out in a short book written by the original founder. The organization believed that humanity had gone too far down a destructive path. The only solution left now was to enlighten the human race, both through the use of mind-altering substances, and also by cleansing it with blood.

Thompson called the text – known within *New Horizon* as "The Handbook" – a "winding diatribe against modernity" and "a pseudo-religious doctrine designed to lure in the vulnerable, depraved, and forgotten citizens of our society."

After gaining membership and spending more than a year undercover, Thompson concluded that, "Although the group may have started as a genuine attempt to make sense of a Nixonian world hell-bent on rejecting the counterculture of the 1960's and 70's, *New Horizon* has since become primarily a minor drug cartel run by members of California's most notorious motorcycle gang."

"Like most cults," the article continued, "this group is full of rituals, from secret handshakes, to orgies, to the sacrificial killing of animals. However, most of the more extreme activities are practiced only by a few of the group's most hardcore adherents. The majority of those involved in the organization seem interested solely in taking over abandoned buildings within the scenic beach town of Pleasure Point and its surrounding areas, the end goal being the establishment of drug manufacturing and distribution facilities for profit.

"Lower ranked members are tasked with activities that include enlisting new members, getting recruits high for the first time, and then making sure the fresh meat consistently buys product only from the group."

Cristina had spent her fair share of time snorting, smoking, and shooting dope in abandoned buildings, and had never heard of any organization like that, much less some crazy end-of-the-world philosophy.

Shit, she thought. *I probably would've jumped on that bandwagon when I was at my worst.*

The other interesting article she found was written a year later by the same author. A follow up to the first report, this one was published after Charles Walters had been arrested for a laundry list of crimes: murder, drug dealing, kidnapping, rape, lewd behavior with a minor, arson, theft, and arms trafficking.

Cristina was baffled.

How does a guy like that get away with doing dirt for so long?

It turned out Walters had been playing both sides of the fence. While running *New Horizon,* he also worked for the federal government as an informant. In exchange for the Feds turning a blind eye to his drug dealing activity, Walters ratted out arms dealers who were selling weapons to terrorist organizations in South America and the Middle East.

He was apparently well-protected until he decided to burn three ATF agents alive in their Suburban. A national manhunt followed, one that lasted almost six months, eventually leading to Walters being arrested while trying to cross the border into Mexico.

After a quick trial, he was found guilty of almost everything they put on him.

During sentencing, he took the stand and gave a lengthy speech about how the end of days was coming, saying there was nothing the federal government or any other earthly power could do to stop it.

Cristina was a bit surprised at the passion with which the guy seemed to actually believe all the crap he was spewing. Then again, she probably shouldn't have been. She'd never been religious at all, but growing up watching the 9/11 attacks happen on TV – as well as a steady stream of other violent events around the world – it never ceased to amaze her how dangerous a person was when they were willing to trade their own life for the lives of others, especially in the name of a particular belief.

Personally, Cristina thought all organized religions were primarily just ways of controlling people. Even the 12-step program that had saved her life could get that way in the wrong hands. Sometimes, instead of using the recovery philosophy to empower people, there were those who liked to twist it around in ways that made others fearful. And, as Cristina knew all too well, a scared person is the easiest to manipulate.

The article finished by saying that Walters's trial and conviction forced the group's leadership into hiding. And when Cristina scrolled through the search results, the last news article mentioning Walters or *New Horizon* was dated more than a year before Annie had disappeared. That made it seem highly unlikely there was any link between the organization and the murder.

Cristina rubbed her eyes.

Staring at a computer screen had made her mind go numb.

There were still so many questions floating around in her head, maybe even more than when she'd started, but at least she'd filled in a few blanks.

She wondered if it would be enough to stop the nightmares.

18

Cristina wandered the library until she found Jordan near a shelf full of books on philosophy.

"Are you sure you don't want to attend the noon meeting with me?" Jordan asked without looking up from *Human, All Too Human.*

Cristina thought about it. She really *wanted* to. But she also felt like she had a ton of stuff to do before her date. So she said her goodbyes and made the drive back home.

Out of town. Up the winding hill. Under the canopy of trees.

Parked in front of the mailbox at the bottom of the driveway, she discovered she already had some junk mail: a menu for a pizza place, a credit card application, and a coupon for Bed Bath & Beyond. There was also a thick, beige envelope.

She grabbed it all, drove up to the house, and headed inside, glancing as she did toward Mr. Psycho's place. It was quiet, looking exactly as it had for the past week. She'd yet to hear so much as a sneeze come from that direction.

Standing in the hallway, away from the closet door, she used her knife to slice open the envelope.

"Mother fucker!" she yelled at the tri-folded stack of paper inside.

On a piece of stationery that included a finely mon-
ogramed "WCIII" in a box at the top, the following letter was typed:

Ms. Rodriguez,

*Contained in this package is a summons
to appear in court at 9 AM on Friday,
May 31. At that time, an evaluation will
be conducted as to the custody status of
your daughter Anise.*

*Prior to these proceedings, you have
been ordered by Judge Angelo Peterson,
Family Court Division 1, to undergo
urine and hair analyses using one of the
certified laboratories listed in the attached directory.*

*Failure to obtain these tests and/or to
appear at the assigned date and time
will result in your being found in con-
tempt of court, a charge punishable by
fine, jail time, or both. It could also af-
fect your custody standing.*

*Thank you for your thorough and
prompt cooperation in this matter.*

*Any questions can be directed either to
the clerk for Family Court Division 1, or
to my office. Contact information for
both can be found below.*

Sincerely,
Walden Chester III, Esq.
Attorney for Mr. Anthony Stevens

May 31st.

Next Friday.

As in a week from tomorrow.

Cristina wanted to laugh. And cry. And take her knife and stab Walden Chester III, Esq in the goddamn heart. Anthony, too. Along with whoever this stupid asshole judge was that would even entertain her ex making a claim for custody after what he'd done.

"This is fucking bullshit!" she yelled, throwing the papers into the air. "A fucking drug test? What, Anthony? Did you tell them I was getting high when you met me? Did you tell them how you found me in a bar one day selling myself for dope? How you made me your little brown-skin slave? Huh?! HUH!?"

She slammed the blade of her knife into the wood-paneled wall. Unsatisfied, she wiggled it out, cracking the thin wood as she did. She stabbed the wall several more times, grunting a little louder with each thrust.

Then came the tears.

With the knife's silver handle still protruding from the wall, she collapsed to the floor, eyes dripping like a broken pipe.

"Why?!" she asked the world, her voice cracking. "What did I do to deserve this? I've been doing everything right. Why can't I just move on? Why can't he leave me alone?"

All the worst possible scenarios flashed through her mind. She just knew that, somehow, someway, Walden Chester III, high-price-scumbag-attorney was going to find some legal trick he could use to take her baby away.

The system was rigged for it.

Cristina had seen it before. When she was sent to the girl's detention camp for stealing. Forced to give a blow job to a fat guard. All while her friend Marcy — the one who actually stole the stupid makeup from

Target in the first place – only had to do three days of community service. *Her* family had money and hired a lawyer. Probably Walden Chester III for all Cristina knew.

The entire fucking world is so corrupt. Why do I even try?

She lit a cigarette, but it wasn't enough.

Cristina felt a sudden and distinct desire to get high.

Her old self spoke with a gentle assertiveness.

Do something to take the pain away, Cristina. Anything. You deserve it. Just a beer, Cristina. Maybe a little weed. A bump of crystal. A few pills. And why not, Cristina? These rich assholes are going to take away everything you have anyway. Why not go out in a blaze of glory?

Then she heard another voice in her head.

Michelle's.

"Resentments are like drinking poison and hoping the other person dies."

Cristina hated 12-step sayings with a passion. People in those rooms were always rattling them off in this stupid, cheerful way. As if they just invented them. As if they hadn't already been said ten-thousand-million times before. She would have hated them even more if some of them didn't make so much sense.

Her tears weakened. A swell of resolve rose up inside her.

She wasn't going to let that asshole win. Not now. Not ever. If he wanted to waste his money trying to screw her over, that was fine. She would annihilate him.

19

Cristina was putting on makeup, something she hadn't done since leaving Anthony. He'd always demanded that she get dolled up. Every day. Even if they weren't going anywhere. Because of him, she'd come to hate the whole ritual with a passion.

Now she was doing it to spite him. Every dab of foundation, every stroke of lipstick, every pin slipped into her hair.

She was putting on the finishing touches when Anise called.

"Hi, my beautiful," Cristina said, switching the phone to speaker and setting it on the back of the toilet while she brushed her eyelashes. "How's Aba's?"

Anise told her about going to the park with Tío Alberto, where she jumped off the swings and played princesses with a girl named Carolina. She was six. And then Cristina learned that Anise's teacher, Mrs. Dulce, had given her the "Citizen of the Week" award because she helped other kids practice drawing.

"That's my smart, talented girl. I'm so proud of you!"

Without comment about the praise, Anise continued, recalling several adventures she had with Rico, Aba's pet chihuahua. The dog had been alive as long as Cristina could remember. He hated everyone. Even Aba herself. But he loved Anise. To the point he even let her dress him up in doll's clothing, sitting patiently on his side panting while she painted his toenails.

At the end of the call, which, as always, came too soon, Cristina told her daughter that she loved her and would see her tomorrow.

"Mamma, I wish I could be with you right now."

"Me too, chica. Me too. But we'll be together after you sleep tonight and go to school one more time. And pretty soon, you'll get to stay here in your new room all the time, OK?"

There was a pause. The longer it went on, the closer Cristina's freshly-applied mascara came to running down her face.

"OK, mamma," Anise finally said. "I love you."

"I love you too, baby,"

After two air-kisses toward the phone, Cristina ended the call.

Holding her chin high, she stared into the mirror, determined to be happy.

***

Cristina took one last look at her reflection in the Civic's window.

It had taken her half the afternoon to decide what to wear.

Despite the fact she'd sported nothing but t-shirts and jeans for the past year, she did own a rather extensive wardrobe. In addition to full-makeup every day, Anthony had also insisted she dress sexy, and he provided her the clothes to do it.

He was an asshole, but a rich one.

After pulling out most of what she'd crammed unceremoniously into her new closet, she finally decided to go with a black leather miniskirt on the bottom. It would show her scars to the whole world, but she didn't care. Not anymore. Like the rest of her past, she was ready to own it.

To complement the skirt, she chose a white halter-top that tightly wrapped around what little of her boobs it actually covered, lifting and squeezing together the rest.

Running perfectly between the halter and the skirt was a pencil-thin strip of light-brown skin.

Not knowing what they would be doing, she wore a pair of cute black-leather flats, with straps that criss-crossed up her ankles.

Her thick, long hair was curled and up, tied with a red bandanna that matched the color of the roses on her arm and shoulder.

Standing next to the car, admiring how her own body curved from head to toe, smelling the spicy musk of her perfume, she felt nothing but fierce confidence.

It was still too warm for the black leather jacket, so she held it over her shoulder with two fingers. With a flick of her wrist, she opened a pair of white-rimmed sunglasses and slid them onto her face. They sat perfectly on her high cheekbones.

Last but not least, she smacked her plump, crimson-coated lips in a kiss to her own reflection.

Having parked near the amusement park, she had a few blocks to walk to get to Casey's shop. She strolled casually down the sidewalk, hips swaying back and forth under the tight black leather.

The late sun cast a golden hue across the world.

There seemed to be a lot of people out and about for a Thursday afternoon, and all of them looked happy. A number of teams played volleyball on the beach across the street, near where Cristina and Anise had been the previous weekend. Other people floated frisbees or kicked soccer balls. Some were just kicking back, soaking in the last sunshine of the day. A group of hoodie-clad guys and gals hauling boxes of wood had arrived to claim one of the fire pits poking out from the sand at regular intervals along the beach. There were even a few brave souls still surfing the frigid water. Down the block, couples and families made their way out onto the pier to grab dinner and catch the sunset.

Every guy Cristina passed on the sidewalk – and some of the girls, too – had nearly identical reactions. First, eyes locked on. Then, as she got closer, necks craned and twisted, as if trying to see something off in the distance behind her. Finally, as she passed, heads swung back over shoulders to savor every moment in the presence of the short Latina bombshell confidently making her way down the street.

Nobody so much as glanced at her scars.

Cristina couldn't help but smile.

Still got it, mamma. Still got it.

Bula's Surf Shop was across the street from the entrance to the pier. The store was one of many establishments in a long line of places leading down the block toward the amusement park. Many of these shops looked almost identical, selling similar types of beach-related items, everything from sunscreen to towels. And just about all of them had the same, somewhat cheesy, Pleasure Point branded merchandise in the windows: sweatshirts, t-shirts, hats, magnets, coffee mugs. Scattered into the mix was an occasional hamburger joint, ice cream place, and even a taquería Cristina thought looked like it could be pretty good.

She arrived at the store a few minutes before 6:30.

Bula's seemed to be one of the more popular spots on the block. A steady stream of locals and tourists, young and old, streamed in and out of its door.

Instead of Pleasure Point swag, the windows of

Bula's were full of surfboards, wetsuits, and something called "Sex Wax," which made Cristina's sculpted eyebrows curl.

A chalkboard sign on the sidewalk advertised surfing lessons. All Ages Welcome!!!

Three long-haired teenage boys, all wearing *Bula's* hoodies, awkwardly bumped into one another as they exited the store, their brains seeming to malfunction in the presence of Cristina's bulging cleavage and short skirt.

She smiled patiently as they fought over the privilege of holding the door for her.

The store had a warm, positive feel to it. Reggae played over the loudspeaker, and there was no shortage of happy conversation between customers browsing racks of clothes and equipment.

Working the register behind the counter were two good-looking young women. One blond and one brunette. Their flow of customers was steady, but neither of them seemed rushed.

Not seeing Casey anywhere, Cristina walked around the store looking at clothes. Most of the merchandise was for men, but there were a few cute *Bula's Surf Shop* tank tops she thought she could see herself wearing.

After a few minutes, she made her way to the counter and waited.

Eventually the brunette came casually walking over.

"Hi there," she said. "What can I do for you?"

"Hi, I'm here to see Casey."

The girl's face lit up. She stuck out a hand.

"You must be Cristina. I'm Katlyn. I have strict orders to treat you well when you arrive. Glad to meet you."

The two shook hands.

Katlyn then turned over her shoulder and shouted, "Yo, boss! Your hot-ass date's here!"

Cristina was glad she'd put on enough makeup to keep anyone from seeing her blush.

"Thanks," she said.

"Oh, no problem. We like to embarrass him whenever we can. You need anything? Glass of water? Soda? Kombucha?"

"I'm cool. Thanks though."

"Sweet. Well, go easy on the poor guy tonight. Catch ya later."

Katlyn put two thumbs in the air and went back to helping customers.

Cristina was bobbing her head to a mellow Bob Marley jam about being loved when Casey popped out from behind a black curtain. Stacked in his tattooed arms was a tower of shoe boxes. In his mouth, he carried a sheet of paper.

He raised his eyebrows toward her in greeting as he walked by.

She parted her lips, eyes twinkling with excitement.

After dumping the boxes and handing the paper to Katlyn, Casey walked back to where Cristina stood. He put both of his palms on the counter and leaned forward, slightly grinning from under a mesh *Bula's Surf Shop* hat.

Cristina felt a tingle bubble up in the pit of her stomach as she tried to play it cool.

"Uh, hello there, dude," she said in her best surfer voice. "I'm here to buy some of your Sex Wax."

He straightened his back, chest swelling under a black *Bula's* t-shirt.

"Whatever you need, ma'am," he said, grabbing a bar of the stuff from a display rack. He held it in the air like a spokesmodel. "*Bula's Surf Shop* is the official store for all your sex-waxing needs."

They both laughed.

A good start, she thought.

He walked around the counter and they hugged. He smelled like coconut sunscreen. The top of her head came perfectly to the center of his chest. It wasn't a long embrace, and part of Cristina thought she wouldn't mind being in those powerful arms a bit longer.

When he pulled away, Casey's face broke slightly from the stoicism that seemed to be its default setting. He rubbed the stubble on his cheeks with one hand as he admired her for a moment, seeming genuinely impressed.

"Wow, you look amazing," he said. Tugging on his shirt, he added, "I feel a bit underdressed."

"It's cool," she answered. "I'll make us both look good."

"No doubt," he agreed. "Well, I feel kinda bad, but I don't have much planned. I was hoping we could grab some food, and then walk down to *The Wharf.* Go on some rides. Walk around. Nothing too crazy."

"I'm down. As long as we can hit up that taquería on the way."

"Done deal."

He grabbed his own leather jacket from behind the counter, checked for keys and wallet. They were about to leave the store when he stopped.

"I almost forgot . . ." He went back around the counter, reached underneath it, and produced a single long-stem rose. Minus the bloody thorns, it looked remarkably like the two that were permanently inked onto his neck, and the ones on Cristina's arm.

"Aww," she said, cheeks again warming underneath her makeup. "It's beautiful. You're so sweet. Thanks."

She slipped the flower from his fingers.

Standing on the tips of her toes, she kissed him

softly on the cheek, leaving behind a light crimson imprint of her lips.

"Oh whoops," she said, wiping it away with her wrist. "Sorry about that."

"Hey," he said, somewhat seriously. "I make it a personal policy never to be offended when a beautiful woman kisses me."

"Good. Now, can we go get a burrito?"

Before they left, she threaded the rose through the bandana holding her hair in place.

Casey shot a peace sign to his staff.

"Be good," he told them as he slid on a sleek pair of dark Oakley sunglasses.

Together, he and Cristina walked into the light of the setting California sun.

20

Cristina felt like a celebrity from the moment they hit the sidewalk.

Every other person they passed offered a casual, "What's up, Casey?"

Or whispered to their friends, "Is that who I think it is?"

To his credit, her date handled it all in stride. He acknowledged each person with a wave and a smile, or simply a cool jerk of his chin.

"Wow," Cristina said after about half a block. "You're kind of a big deal."

He shrugged.

"I've lived here my whole life. It's a small town."

She was tempted to hold his arm as they walked, but decided to wait, play things cool. She was satisfied to stroll beside him. His strapping body made her feel small but safe.

The setting sun had obliterated the blue sky, replacing it with reds and pinks and oranges. The breeze coming off the water was cold enough that Cristina put on her jacket, at the same time feeling a surge of energy from the crisp air hitting her cheeks.

Dinner was delicious.

They both ordered al pastor burritos and horchata. Everyone behind the counter knew Casey and stopped what they were doing to say hi. The woman working the register said something to Cristina in Spanish. She didn't understand. Besides a few slang words here and there, her Spanish skills were basically nonexistent.

But she definitely knew good Mexican food. And her initial instinct about the taquería was confirmed. She was especially impressed with the fact they didn't have any Corona signs hanging on the wall.

"Real Mexicans drink Bud Light," she declared proudly while dripping Tapatío onto a huge burrito. "This place is legit."

Conversation with Casey was easy, despite the fact they didn't really talk about much of anything in particular. She teased him about being so popular, and he teased her about being in a gang because of her bandana. She said he was a gringo when he didn't put any hot sauce on his burrito, and he pretended like he was going to get up and leave when she let out a small burp.

After dinner, the two walked the rest of the way to the amusement park.

The sky was now purple-grey, on its way toward night.

Coming through the gates, they passed by the carousel. Cristina barely even thought of the red-nosed creep she'd encountered there, remembering instead Anise's smile atop her pink horse.

Inside the park, there were fewer people who acknowledged Casey. More tourists, Cristina figured. Although he still had to stop every so often to sign a hat or high-five a shaggy teenager holding a skateboard.

Without Anise in tow, Cristina and Casey were able to go on all the rides she'd previously skipped. They started with a front-row seat on a wooden roller coaster called The Big Dip. Riding with hands high in the air, Cristina screamed her head off each time they hit another drop.

They both cracked up when they saw the TV monitor outside the exit turnstile. Next to Casey's calm grin, Cristina's face was twisted in joyful horror. Although she playfully pleaded with him not to, he bought a copy of the photo and slid it into his back pocket.

"That's a keeper," he said with a wink.

Next, they hit the bumper cars.

"You want to ride together?" he asked.

"No thanks. I don't need a chauffeur."

She proved it by slamming him into the wall, spinning his car around, leaving him facing the wrong way. She laughed a bit evilly and flipped him off.

After bumper cars, Cristina almost lost her burrito on the Pirate Ship.

"Oh wow," she said as they walked down the exit ramp. "I could taste pork on that one. How about a break?"

To mellow out, they took a ride in the Sky Buckets.

Snuggled into a two-person chairlift, casually cruising above the length of the park, they watched the sandy beach glow in the moonlight, all the way down to the pier where they'd met.

Cristina heard strange noises coming from that direction, something like a pack of hungry dogs barking.

"What the hell is that?" Cristina asked.

"Calm down, killer. It's just the sea lions."

"Yah? Sounds like someone getting freakin' murdered."

"Have you been out there yet?"

"No. Is it safe? That thing kind of looks like it's going to fall down."

He stared at her like she was crazy. "That pier is so sturdy. It'll probably be here long after you and I are both dead."

She looked at him skeptically and then said, "Alright, I'm down."

Cristina was having so much fun, she probably would have gone just about anywhere.

They spent the rest of the Sky Bucket ride in silence. At one point, Cristina got the chills and shivered. Without looking, Casey put his arm around her shoulders and pulled her close.

21

A small crowd, mostly couples, stood gathered around a wooden guardrail near the end of the pier.

Cristina and Casey made their way forward to look down through a square cutout at the sea lions. Almost all the burly creatures lay sleeping, sprawled out on platforms built especially for them. A few were awake, barking for the others to make room, or at the strange, hairless apes above.

"They kind of stink," Cristina said, removing the rose from her hair and holding it to her nose.

Casey sniffed the air.

"Oh, I thought that was you."

She chuckled sarcastically and smacked him in the chest.

"Seriously though," she said. "I think I'm going to throw up."

He offered his arm and she took it, continuing to twirl the rose in her fingers as they strolled the short distance to the end of the pier.

There was a stench there, too. Leftover from the guts of fish caught earlier in the day. But it was faint in the salty breeze, and still better than the sharp body odor of the sea lions.

The only other people nearby were an elderly man and woman silently holding hands on a bench. A few moments later, the old couple got up and walked toward wherever their lives were going, leaving Cristina and Casey alone, staring into the dark endless expanse of the Pacific Ocean.

The sea teemed with the energy of a living being.

Casey leaned his hands onto the rail, while Cristina turned to stand against it, her back to the water. She grinned in distant thought, trying to remember a time when she'd been so at ease with a guy, whether on the first date or the twentieth.

It sounded almost cheesy, but just then it felt like nothing in the world could hurt her. And not just because, given his impressive physique, Casey could probably take on just about anyone physically. There was something more. Something deeper. Beneath his tough exterior – the tattoos, the muscles, the hard-to-read face – he seemed to possess an aura of tranquility that calmed the world around him as he passed through it.

After a long but not uncomfortable silence, she asked, "So what's your story, Mr. Casey Peters?"

He didn't respond right away, not even with the playful little smirk he'd had on his face most of the evening. He only stared into the distance, as if the answer to her question lay submerged somewhere in the water.

"I'm not sure you want know," he said finally.

Cristina was no stranger to how much effort a person could put into pushing other people away.

"Yes," she said, admiring the profile of his strong jaw in the moonlight. "I really do."

He turned toward her.

There was the grin.

"Why do I feel like I know you?" he asked.

The question caught her off-guard, but she knew exactly what he meant.

"I don't know. Past life maybe?"

"Maybe . . ."

"Seriously, though." She put a hand on his dense forearm. "Tell me about yourself. I promise I won't judge. Trust me, I've got enough of my own story to fill a book. Ten books, probably."

"What do you want to know?"

"Tell me how you ended up with that tattoo on your stomach."

He laughed. "The demon throwing fireballs out of his eyeballs? Wild, drunken night in Indonesia. Woke up the next morning and there it was." He turned and gave her a sarcastic look.

"No, dumb ass," she said. "The triangle."

"Oh, *that* one. Well, the short version is that I did a lot of dope, and basically sabotaged a surfing career. Then I got clean about five years ago."

For all his kidding, he actually seemed a bit stand-offish when he told her this. His words had a bite to them that made her wish she hadn't asked.

"I'm sorry," he said after a while, taking off his mesh hat and rubbing a hand across the stubble on his head. "I guess I'm still a little sensitive when it comes to talking about my past. Where I come from, people deal with what they need to deal with and they move on."

She took him by the hand and led him to the bench that the old couple had been using. She sat, pulling at him to join her. He hesitated, looking almost afraid, but then allowed himself to be drawn down.

"Look," she said, staring into his eyes and choosing her words carefully. "From what little I already know about you, I think we have a lot in common."

She paused, debating whether she should say what she wanted to say.

She continued, "All the flirty bullshit aside . . . I'm not really a chick who's interested in playing games.

Even if we only become friends, and that really would be cool with me, I just want you to know that, with me, what you see is what you get. I've been through a lot in life too, so I try my hardest not to judge people."

He snickered.

"What's so funny?" she asked.

"That's *hella* real."

He looked a little overwhelmed. Maybe even intimidated.

Good, Cristina thought. *He should be.*

Suddenly, she had a gut-instinct she decided to follow. A theory that needed testing. She leaned toward him and kissed his lips. A deep, passionate embrace. But not lusty. There was no tongue. That wasn't part of the experiment, at least not yet.

She pulled back and shared her results.

"Yep, I was right. Our lips fit together perfectly."

For a moment, the face of this hard-cut man transformed into one that more resembled an awkward little boy with no idea of what to do. The look didn't stay there for long. She thought he might go in for another kiss. But he surprised her by instead taking her hand into his, squeezing her fingers tight.

Then, in a calm, matter-of-fact tone, he began to tell his story.

22

Casey Peters was born in the mountains above Pleasure Point, in the back of an old van his mom was living in at the time.

It wasn't that she wanted to give birth to her first and only child that way, but the van's rear axle had cracked in half when her high-ass boyfriend drove over a boulder on the way to the hospital.

Luckily, her companion happened to be a nurse — the kind who liked to raid the morphine supply at work, which was probably why Mom liked him in the first place.

But this man was *not* Casey's father. The man with *that* distinction had long since left for god-only-knows where. Casey had never met him, and would be damned pleased if the arrangement stayed that way.

Eventually his mom did get the baby to a hospital, where the doctor declared the little boy to be in perfect health, except for the fact he was suffering from opiate withdrawals.

His mother was a junky through and through. Casey never got the chance to know her. She ended up dying a few years after he was born, from a heroin overdose in the back of that same van.

After she died, the county wanted to put Casey into foster care. But they couldn't find anyone to take him. So he ended up going to live with his mom's sister.

It was his aunt who eventually told him the story of how he was born. And she did what she could to welcome him into her dirty, two-bedroom trailer in the backwoods. But she was married to an alcoholic who hit her on a regular basis. If Casey was around, he got beat, too.

Casey became quite adept at seeing the rage coming. When it started to boil up, he would camp out in the woods. Sometimes for days at a time. Creeping back in only when his uncle finally passed out.

The violence eventually became too much. Casey ran away at 13 and lived on the streets, mostly sleeping under bushes along the concrete levees around Pleasure Point. It was during this time he discovered two things that would change his life forever: punk rock and surfing.

Punk gave him a philosophy to live by. Surfing gave him a reason to live.

He found a political and social consciousness in California punk bands like Bad Religion and Pennywise, one that helped provide a framework for understanding the chaotic, unfair world he'd grown up in. He snuck into every show he could. And, while most of the homeless people around Pleasure Point panhandled for booze, Casey usually spent any cash he managed to get on CDs.

As for surfing, he was a natural from the very beginning, able to stand up on the first wave he ever attempted. But he never would have even tried if it hadn't been for a Pleasure Point local-legend named Jerry "Hound Dog" Parker. Feeling sorry for the wide-eyed kid he saw standing on the beach one day, Hound Dog let Casey try out one of his boards, and would continue letting the young man use it as he learned the ropes. And when Jerry found out Casey was homeless, he also let him crash on his couch.

Within months – working hard every day, sometimes from dawn until dusk – Casey became the talk of the local scene. Everyone wanted to see the new phenom who was giving even seasoned vets in the area a run for their money.

Before he knew it, brands like O'Neil and Quicksilver were scouting him.

Pretty soon they were paying for him to enter contests.

He officially dropped out of high school after his sophomore year to focus on surfing full-time. It wasn't like he'd really been going anyway. Besides, school had never done much good for him. He seemed to learn a lot more about life by actually going out and living it.

At 16, he was featured on the cover of *Surfer* magazine. The following year, he was consistently winning major tournaments on the pro-circuit, bringing in big bucks, attracting attention from beautiful young women, and basking in all the glory a teenage boy could dream of.

In short, he was on top of the world.

Just after his 18th birthday, he fell surfing a 40-foot monster at Mavericks in Half Moon Bay. When the jet ski finally pulled him from the rumble and tumble, x-rays revealed fractures in both legs.

He recovered fine, but the process introduced him to the world of opioid pain pills.

Before getting hurt, Casey had practically been straight-edge. Like everyone else in the surfing world, he smoked a little weed here and there, drank a few beers, and sometimes more than a few. But riding waves was really the only high he'd ever needed.

Those painkillers, though. It was insane just how fast they crawled into the pores of his being and refused to let go.

And with the network of connections he'd built

around California and the world, there seemed to always be an endless supply. Even when he felt an urge to stop, he could easily flush a whole bottle of pills in a morning rage, only to have a refill in his hands by noon.

Despite the pills, Casey continued to dominate surfing. The way he rode was so intense, so innovative, that by 20-years-old people were calling him "the Michael Jordan of the sport." They said he'd completely changed surfing forever.

Heavy pressure for a young kid to handle.

With all the fame and glory came the parasites. The hangers-on. The gold-diggers. Some of them women, sure, but the men were just as bad, if not worse. It seemed like everyone wanted something, and nobody really gave a shit about who Casey was anymore, much less what was in his best interests. And *nobody* dared say a thing about his growing drug habit.

Without any family to fall back on, he became more and more absorbed in the surfer's quest for an endless summer. He and his cohort of top-pros traveled the globe, in search of perfect waves and never-ending fun.

For a while that was enough. Especially the surfing. As long as he could get on a board, he felt like he had a purpose in the world, even when he found himself scratching his arms bloody after taking ten pills full of poison.

But one night things finally went over the edge.

Casey and his boys had a two-day layover in Amsterdam on their way to South Africa for one of the most important big wave competitions of the year.

The plan was to hang out in the city the first day, and then check out a punk festival that was happening the following afternoon. Casey had scored VIP passes from Fat Mike of NOFX, and was stoked for the chance to meet some of his other favorite performers.

He never made it.

The first night in town, he found himself in the red-light district, smoking lots of pot and taking bumps of cocaine that were as pure and white as Tahoe snow.

At some point, one of several ladies Casey was paying to be his friend brought out a small black bag that looked like a shaving kit.

It wasn't.

By some dark instinct, Casey knew exactly what the bag contained, even before the long-haired blond with the big chest sensually dragged open the metal zipper like a practiced pro. Inside was a number of disposable syringes, a couple spoons, and a big bag of amber-white powder that would change his life forever.

He missed the tournament in South Africa. In fact, no one heard from him for more than a week. He just disappeared. And to this day, he still couldn't remember much about where he'd been or what he'd done.

When he emerged from the fog long enough to catch his breath, he discovered he'd gotten a pair of roses tattooed on his neck. He also had an armful of track marks, and the feeling that his soul had been ripped from his body.

After that, surfing no longer mattered. Neither did music.

The only thing that had any meaning now, the only thing that gave him purpose, was a substance called heroin.

It didn't take long for the rumor mill to start churning.

Within days, representatives from his biggest sponsors were calling. They acted casually concerned at first, but as he failed to show up at other tournaments, the calls quickly turned into demands for answers. And he didn't have any. Not for his sponsors. Not for his agent. Not for his surfing buddies. And especially not for the kids who chased him around everywhere he went, begging for autographs.

There really wasn't much to say. He didn't answer to them. He answered to heroin. And it stole everything from him, more quickly than he could have ever imagined.

Unable to handle the pressure being put on him, Casey took a hiatus from the circuit and locked himself away in his expensive Pleasure Point bungalow. Ironically, the place was not all that far from where, just a few years earlier, he'd spent his nights sleeping outside, a death grip around a bundle of meager possessions, hoping that the sun came up before he got robbed.

He taped dark blankets over the windows, so he didn't have to see the sunlight. The only people allowed over were his dealer and those few people who could keep up with his increasingly insatiable need to get high.

Anyone who gave him shit about the bruises on his arms, or about anything else, was promptly told to fuck off. Eventually, he covered himself in tattoos to hide it all away.

But no one could miss the emptiness in his eyes.

Not even himself.

It took less than a year to drain his sizable bank account. He then sold his surfboards, the BMW, his boat, and eventually even his trophies. He took pennies on the dollar for it all, but he didn't care as long as the money came fast and in cash.

Next, he sold his house.

Flush again with funds, he figured he ought to try and make it last. He decided to start dealing and bought a big brick from a biker who was part of an organization called *New Horizon*. Not only did the guy have tons of dope to sell, but he also had a whole philosophy to go along with it. These were the end of days, he told Casey. And in order to get on the right side of the universal revolution – the one that would wipe out the bullshit materialism of modern times – a person had to open new doors in their mind.

At that point in his life, Casey really didn't care about anything philosophical. Heroin was the only god he prayed to, and the only guiding force he needed. But the great thing was, this pseudo-religion was based on exactly that. Doing drugs wasn't selfish, they said. It was a path to enlightenment.

Looking back, it was all batshit crazy. But, at the time, he was so disillusioned with the world around him, it seemed to make sense. In the same way punk had done, *New Horizon* offered a way to make some sense out of a world filled with chaos.

Casey went so far as to take up residence in one of the many abandoned buildings the organization had taken over in the rundown area of Pleasure Point people call Perkins Town. It became Casey's job to help make sure the increasing number of new junkies in the area were getting their dope from the group.

Of course, the whole illusion imploded one day when the DEA raided a squat Casey was holed up in. They caught him with a gun and a half-kilo of pure heroin.

He thought he was looking at 20 years.

The only thing that saved him was the fact that the feds screwed up something to do with the chain of evidence – a minor technicality Casey still didn't fully understand – and a lot of the case got dropped. The only thing that stuck were state charges.

He still got five years, but only ended up doing 18 months.

It was in prison that he began going to 12-step

meetings. He became close friends with the other men in the group. It was amazing how so many of their stories, while at times wildly different, were so similar to his own. Their support gave him courage. An internal fire he'd only ever felt on a surfboard.

He did his time without much incident.

While locked up, he worked with a sponsor to take on the ominous task of figuring out how to live life without heroin. It wasn't easy, and he admittedly fought the process most of the way.

But, in the end, it worked.

He also got his G.E.D. inside, and an A.A. degree in business management.

Thankfully, Jerry "Hound Dog" Parker — who remained, through it all, one of Casey's only real friends — had seen the writing on the wall before the shit really hit the fan. He'd managed to somehow snag $25,000 of Casey's earnings, and had stashed it for the younger man to fall back on.

When Casey got out, he used that money to open *Bula*'s. He couldn't afford rent for both the store and an apartment, so he set up a cot in the back. It wasn't much, but it was a lot better than some of the places he'd stayed over the years.

The store was doing alright, too. He started off with just himself as the sole employee, but now there were three other people working there — the two girls Cristina had seen earlier, and a kid who stocked shelves and folded clothes part-time.

The store didn't bring in anywhere near the money Casey pulled as a pro surfer. Not even close. It never would. But he was getting by, trying to live a frugal, simple life as he saved up. And it's not like he'd taken some vow of poverty. He even recently splurged on a nice used Harley as a present to himself, in celebration of *Bula's* third anniversary.

Nowadays, most of his free time was spent either surfing, going to shows, helping out with the Junior Lifeguards, or mentoring young addicts at the Pleasure Point Youth Center.

All-in-all, he felt pretty proud of himself, given the distance he'd traveled. For a long time, he thought he wouldn't live to see 25. Now he was coming up on 30.

It had been a wild ride, and he regretted plenty of things he'd done along the way. But if he had it to do all over again, he probably wouldn't change a thing. His journey had made him who he was. It had shown him a strength inside himself he never thought possible.

For that, he would be forever grateful.

23

Cristina smiled, fighting off a yawn. It was well past midnight. The wind had grown cold. She snuggled closer to Casey, pulling her jacket over the exposed skin of her chest. Her bare legs were numb.

After he finished his story, they sat in silence for a long time. There wasn't a hint of awkwardness. Nor did either of them seem in any hurry to go.

Like with so many other stories Cristina had heard about overcoming addiction and adversity, there was a lot of her own journey in his words. Many differences, too, of course. But she definitely felt the familiar bond between two people who've shared similar hardships.

She wanted to ask him about *New Horizon*, but decided that could wait for another time. Right now, she was simply in awe of his bravery and tenacity.

"I don't even know what to say," she finally admitted. "Thanks for sharing all that with me." She leaned in and kissed the rough stubble of his cheek. "You have an amazing story, have you ever thought about writing it down? I bet it would make a great book."

He laughed. "Thanks. But this high school dropout can barely even spell, much less write a whole book worth reading."

"I don't know about all that. I'd buy it."

She again tried not to yawn, but this time couldn't

resist the urge.

"You getting tired?" he asked.

"Yah, mind if we walk back?"

She hadn't said where "back" was, and found it pleasantly surprising to hear him ask where she'd parked her car.

Not only is he a big, strong, sexy man with a huge heart, he's also a gentleman.

The happy tingle inside her stomach, the one that hadn't left her the entire night, now blossomed into a full-blown explosion of happiness, resonating in waves, all the way to the tips of her fingers and toes.

The two didn't talk much on the walk back. There didn't seem to be a need. Neither did they rush. They simply held hands, watching the stars and the moon disappear behind an encroaching bank of fog.

They stood for a few long moments on the curb in front of her car, eyes locked together. His face seemed somehow different now. More open and inviting. There was a happiness in his eyes that made Cristina realize how much of a wall between himself and the world he was able to put up.

Oh, how she could relate.

"I hate to go," she said.

"I hate to see you go."

Her hands came down gently behind his ears and pulled him forward. They kissed, deeply and passionately. This time with plenty of tongue. Her lips soon moved to his neck. Her hands caressed the hardness of his chest through his shirt. She suddenly wanted nothing more than for him to throw her onto the backseat of the car and do everything she'd imagined that night in the bathtub.

Perhaps he knew. Perhaps not. Whatever the case, with a level of self-control she'd never known any man to have, he softly pushed her away from his body.

The sly smile returned.

"Goodnight, Cristina."

There was one more kiss, a short one through the window after she started the car.

Then he turned and walked into the night.

***

Cristina checked her phone when she came in the door. She was a bit disappointed by the fact Casey hadn't sent her a goodnight text.

But, by the time she brushed her teeth and climbed into bed, it was there.

> *Hope you made it home safe. Thx for an amazing night. One of the best ever. Let's do it again soon. Next time it will be your turn to tell some stories. Sweet dreams. —Casey*

She held her phone to her chest and threw her head back onto the pillow, giggling like a teenager.

There were no bad dreams that night.

24

Cristina spent most of the next day trying to get things organized and put away.

Her goal was to have the place looking like something resembling an actual house by the time her grandmother and uncle arrived to drop off Anise that afternoon.

The task of unpacking seemed monumental, but between her amazing date and getting her first good night's sleep in a week, she buzzed with energy. Even before sipping on her first cup of coffee.

After breakfast, she found the small speaker box she'd somehow ended up with and hooked it to her old laptop. She made a quick YouTube playlist. A little Prince. A little Radiohead. Some Mac Dre. And Tito Puente to add a bit of extra spice to the mix

Wearing a tight, white NorCal t-shirt, boy shorts, and her hair up in the same red bandana she'd worn the night before, she set about finally getting moved in.

As she unpacked, she tried hard not to think about Anthony and Walden Chester III. It proved difficult. She wished she could call the lawyer she used for the divorce settlement. Unfortunately, he charged $750 an hour. She was only ever able to afford him in the first place because, knowing that a big divorce settlement was almost certain, he didn't make her pay anything up front.

This time around, it looked like she had no other choice but to represent herself.

It's not like there's anything all that complicated about it, she told herself as she carried the BEDROOM boxes upstairs. *Besides, if he wants to waste his energy trying to say I'm not clean, he's going to have a tough time proving it.*

Good luck, Anthony. Maybe after it's said and done I can sue your punk ass for another million.

Still, there was something about the whole thing that didn't sit right. Her ex was a lot of things, but stupid wasn't one of them. There had to be more to all this. She needed to be careful.

It at least felt good to be thinking clearly, something she reminded herself as she examined the knife wounds in the wall. The wood looked like someone had mistaken it for the girl from the shower scene in *Psycho*. She decided to hang one of her sketches over the damage – a chalk drawing of a woman sitting on a park bench smoking a cigarette.

With the upstairs basically done – *Anise will be so happy to see all her little stuffed animals perched on the dresser* – Cristina was ready to move on to the downstairs.

But first she took a quick sandwich-and-cigarette break in the backyard. She realized it was her first smoke in 24 hours, and was more than a little annoyed with herself for not giving up the habit altogether.

Nonetheless, she absorbed what had turned into another perfect sunny day. Warm, but with the usual cool sea breeze that kept it from getting hot.

Sitting on the single concrete step, she looked around at her patch of overgrown weeds. Their green, earthy smells mixed in the air with the tuna from her sandwich. Despite her knowledge of plants being limited to the fact they need water, she felt inspired to start a garden.

How hard can it be?

She made a mental note to ask her uncle about it. A landscaper for more than twenty years, if anyone would know what to do it was him.

Just the thought of Tío Alberto made her smile.

Cristina finished her lunch, and then went back to setting up the living room.

The thrift store couch got a blanket thrown across it.

On top of the end table, which barely fit between the couch and the wall, she set a picture of Anise. A coned hat poked up from the girl's head as she laughed hysterically at her third birthday party, right before blowing out the candles on her Finding Nemo cake.

On the coffee table – another thrift store find – she stacked a few random drink coasters. They didn't have a TV yet, and honestly Cristina didn't really care if they ever got one. She'd always been more of a music person anyway.

That thought brought with it a picture of Casey. The cute way he got all starry-eyed when he talked about his love for punk. Her chest buzzed.

"Oh my god, who are you?" she asked herself out loud and laughed

Working through one of the last boxes, she found Anise's baby book. It was hard not to tear up a little flipping through it, especially at the picture taken five minutes after Anise was born. Cristina had almost forgotten how small her baby girl was when she held her for the first time.

Near the end of the scrapbook was a photo of Anthony. At first glance, holding Anise in his arms, he actually looked something close to human. But Cristina knew better. Behind the thin smile, his hollow eyes betrayed an evil lurking just below the surface.

She tried to remember back, wondering if she'd been able to see that coldness in his soul when they first met. She supposed she might have, but couldn't be sure. It wasn't like her mind had been in the best place at the time.

Without much emotion, she removed his picture from the photo album, ripped it in half, folded it, and then ripped it again.

She wished she could do the same to the man himself.

There were a few boxes left, mostly filled with clothes Cristina hadn't yet worked up the heart to donate. She needed a place to stash them and turned to the downstairs closet. The same place where she'd dreamed of finding the previous tenant swinging at the end of a rope. Dreamed of finding *herself* swinging. And, worst of all, Anise, too.

Since moving in, she'd yet to even open the closet door. Had barely noticed it. Like her mind was actively working to ignore its presence.

Come on, girl, she told herself. *After all the craziness you've seen in your life, you're going to be afraid of a damn closet?*

Besides, in the middle of the day, away from the confusing world of dreams, with the bright California sun glowing through the window, the door seemed like, well . . . a door. It was as plain and unremarkable as any other rectangular piece of wood she'd ever laid eyes on.

Feeling a surge of strength, she walked over and stood in front of it.

She wasn't sure what she expected to be there. Some kind of demonic pulsation coming from the other side? Whatever it was, all she felt at that particular moment was an ocean breeze flowing in through the window, cooling the beads of sweat collected between her shoulders.

Yet, she still couldn't seem to find the will to reach out and turn the doorknob.

As hard as she tried to block the image from her mind, it was impossible not to picture the rotted face of Amanda Stewart-Walker. Teeth visible through a hole in her blackened cheek. Orbital cavities sunken in, revealing the decayed remnants of what had once been a living brain. And Cristina would never, *ever* be able to forget that fruity, cinnamon smell of death. The way it oozed from the woman's body like some disgusting perfume. Just the thought of it made her gag.

She knew that if she didn't open the door right then, she likely wouldn't.

At least not that day.

So, after a deep breath, Cristina grabbed the knob and turned.

What she saw inside was far from terrifying. Just like the door, the closet itself had an unremarkable aura of plainness. The tall space was empty, except for a bit of accumulated dust. The wooden hanger rod from which Amanda hanged herself had been removed and never replaced.

Cristina laughed a bit uneasily, not quite able to let go of the tense nervousness inside her. The door and the closet and everything else looked normal now, but there was still some lingering sense of strangeness to it all. Something out of place that she couldn't quite put words to.

It reminded her of an old abandoned house in the neighborhood she grew up in. Kids would stand outside its door, daring one another to go inside. The emptiness of the house, or maybe something else, always made being there seem like a really bad idea.

Before she lost her nerve, Cristina quickly stacked the boxes into the closet and shut the door, making sure to double-check that it was securely closed.

The experience made her want to take a shower.

She looked at the time, and saw it was only an hour before her uncle and grandmother were to arrive with Anise. One whiff of her armpits told her that she definitely needed to wash off more than just some creepy closet vibes.

Upstairs, she took off her sweaty clothes in the bathroom and turned on the shower. While the water warmed, she walked naked down the hallway to do one more check of Anise's room. She wanted everything to be perfect, and it was. Cristina glowed with anticipation as she pictured the joy on Anise's face when she saw her toys and animals all in their own little places.

From the corner of her eye, a flash of something caught her attention. Subtle enough that she didn't even turn her head. Until she saw it again, right at the edge of her vision. But when she finally turned, nothing was there.

Suddenly her naked body felt exposed, like someone was watching her. She covered her nipples with her forearms, squeezing her breasts against her body.

Her first thought was the window. But the blinds were down. And when she peeked through them, all she saw was the glow of the afternoon sun, shaded slightly by a big redwood.

You're going crazy, girl.

But she *had* felt something, and still did. Enough that she walked around to check the other side of Anise's bed, even bending down to look underneath.

A mouse maybe?

"Hey, Mr. Mousey," she said into the air, "You better not be sneaking in here messing with my baby at night. I'll cut your cute little tail off."

Before leaving the room, Cristina looked at herself in the Minnie Mouse mirror she'd spent an hour connecting to the top of Anise's dresser. Holding her hands to her side, she smiled with her eyes and stuck out the fullness of her chest. She ran her hands down the sweeping, streamlined curves of her body. Then she turned, stopping for just a moment to look over her shoulder at the intricate web of scars.

Happy with what she saw, she headed back into the bathroom and took a shower.

25

Cristina heard the car door open, followed by the sound of tiny feet running toward the house.

"Momma! We're heeere!"

"Chica!" Cristina said, opening the front door and stepping into the yard.

At least two full steps away, Anise leaped forward, trusting fully that she would be caught. Cristina whirled around, swinging her daughter into the air.

"Eeeeeeeeeee!" Anise squealed, settling onto her mom's hip.

"Oh my baby, I think you got even bigger than you already were!"

Following behind was Cristina's uncle, who held the door for her grandmother.

Aba, as she was known to her grandchildren and great grandchildren, was not yet 70. But after six children, more than three decades working double-shifts in a cannery, and her current battle with cancer, she looked much older. Her small frame was hunched over from painful arthritis in her back. Her spine twisted to the right side. She constantly flexed her hands to prevent them from seizing up.

Despite the pain, she rarely grimaced, and almost never complained.

She'd lived a hard life. As a teenager, she journeyed alone to the U.S. from the dusty Mexican village she grew up in – a place so poor, she once told Cristina, that even the *burros* were without work.

When Aba first arrived in the States, there had been much abuse. From men who wanted to make her do things, and from Americans who treated her like she was stupid and useless.

She eventually married a mean-tempered *borracho*, a drunk from the same town as her. A man who was angry at the whole world. He died at fifty of a heart attack. But before leaving the earth, he beat his wife almost every day of their marriage.

None of this adversity ever broke Aba. Instead of allowing what she'd faced over the years to defeat her, she was stubbornly proud of her ability to withstand hardship. Sometimes to a fault.

Growing up in Aba's house, Cristina had always been loved and taken care of, but there was little sympathy for the difficulties of life. Aba's primary advice – be it for a skinned knee or a broken heart – was almost always the same. Some version of, "quit crying and do what you need to do, because the only two choices you have in life are to fight or to give up."

Tío Alberto was, in many ways, the complete opposite. He had the kindest heart Cristina had ever known. With no kids of his own – he'd never even had a girlfriend that Cristina could remember – his entire adult life had been spent living in the apartment next door to his mother.

A deeply religious man, he awoke early, sometimes hours before dawn, to pray and meditate. For the past twenty years, he'd worked every day but Sunday mowing people's lawns, cutting their trees, and putting up with their righteous pettiness and anger. All with a smile. And he'd never worked for anyone but himself, something he proudly reminded Cristina of many times. He built his business client by client. Job by job.

Day by day. He was a man of honesty and integrity, and there was nothing he wouldn't do for his family and his church.

"Hi, Aba," Cristina said, respectfully kissing her grandmother on the cheek.

The older woman returned the gesture. She then held her granddaughter at arm's length, examining her thoroughly. There was no smile, but her eyes held a sparkle of love.

"Mija, you are a truly beautiful woman."

"Aww," Cristina said, feeling herself blush.

She turned to her uncle, who was still standing in the doorway holding Anise's bags, along with a couple of extra ones that looked to be groceries. She kissed him on the cheek as well, albeit less formally. "Hi, Tío. How was the drive?"

"Oh, very good, sweetie." As always, his voice came out slow and thoughtful. "I brought you some stuff from the market. Wasn't sure what you might need, so I had to guess a little."

"Thanks, Tío." She took the shopping bags from his hands and gave him another kiss on the cheek. "I'm going to go put this stuff in the kitchen."

She said to Anise, "Chica, you should show Tío and Aba your room. I think you're going to be pretty happy with how it looks."

Anise's little feet ran in place like a cartoon character, then quickly zoomed up the stairs. A few seconds later, there came a joyous shriek. Then more footsteps, back to the top of the stairs.

"I have my own room! Aba, come see! Come see!"

Cristina's grandmother took one doubtful look at the steps and said back, "Maybe later, mija. Aba needs to rest a bit from the car ride before she walks up them stairs."

Anise said next, "Tío! Tío!"

Without question, Tío Alberto hoisted Anise's bags and hurried his way up to see the room.

After taking the groceries to the kitchen and receiving a silent blessing from Aba in the form of a waved hand, Cristina followed her uncle up the stairs.

She found Anise already jumping on the bed. Part of Cristina wanted to tell her to stop, but she couldn't bring herself to do anything that would dim the brightness on her daughter's face.

Except when she saw that Anise had thrown the entire collection of stuffed animals off of the dresser and onto the floor.

In her best patient-mom-voice, Cristina asked, "Chica, didn't you like your pets up there?"

Bounce. Bounce.

"Up where, mamma?"

"On the dresser. You threw them on the floor."

Bounce.

"No I didn't."

Cristina rarely got mad at her daughter. But when Anise lied – blatantly lied – it was hard not to. Even in those instances though, she always tried to give Anise at least a couple of chances to do the right thing.

"Anise, tell mommy the truth. Why did you throw the animals on the ground?"

Bounce. Bounce. Bounce.

"I didn't."

"Anise, get down and come over here. Right now."

Hearing the unusual seriousness in her mother's tone, Anise immediately stopped jumping. She meekly stepped down onto the floor and walked across the room, looking like a scolded puppy.

"Young lady, I'm going to give you one more chance. I don't want to put you on timeout, since Tío and Aba are here. But I will if you don't act like a big girl."

First, Anise's lips started to quiver. Then she burst

into tears.

Like most kids, she was pretty good at turning on the waterworks when it suited her purposes. But Cristina had developed a strong sense for when her daughter was faking it. This bout seemed genuine.

"Who's crying up there?" Aba yelled from downstairs.

"Everything's OK," Cristina returned. Then said to Anise, "You're *sure* you didn't throw the animals on the ground? Mommy spent a long time putting them up there and getting your room just right."

"I didn't m-m-mamma, I p-promise."

"Tío, did you see anything?"

Tío Alberto came alert for the first time since the argument had started, as if he'd been minding his own business in another world. He said, "By the time I got in here, sweetie, the animals were already on the floor."

More frustrated and confused than ever, Cristina raised an eyebrow at Anise.

The girl squinted with a tentative hope for reprieve.

"OK, I believe you," Cristina finally said, although she hardly did. There really was no other plausible explanation for how the toys would have moved. They sure as hell didn't jump off on their own.

Then Cristina remembered her earlier feeling of being watched.

She turned toward the dresser. Propped against the center of the mirror was the same photocopied picture of the little girl – Annie – that Cristina had thrown in the garbage.

Her heart jumped into her throat.

No . . . she told herself. *Anise had to have snuck it out of the trash. Stop it, Cristina. That's enough.*

Cristina put her full effort into pushing the fear and

doubt from her mind, to the point she was mad at herself for getting lost in fantasy.

The fact was, her daughter lied sometimes. Just like every other child who had ever been born. Cristina needed to deal with it, make her point, and move on.

Anise was already picking up the stuffed animals off the floor, a serious look on her face as she carefully set them back on the dresser. Tío Alberto helped, and together the three of them quickly had the job done.

A little shaken, but still feeling excited to spend the evening with family, Cristina picked up Anise and set her on her hip.

They walked downstairs and sat on the couch next to Aba.

"Shall we order a pizza?" Cristina asked.

"PIZZA!" Anise shrieked.

"I guess that's a yes," Tío Alberto said. "And I'm buying."

26

Cristina tried to pay the kid who delivered the pizza. But her uncle insisted, casually moving around his niece so he could slip a neatly folded stack of bills into the young man's front pocket, including a more-than-generous tip.

As they stuffed themselves with slices of Hawaiian pizza, Cristina watched her uncle's face, again admiring him for being such a wonderful example of how to be a good human. His combination of humility and strength was something she'd discovered to be sadly rare in the world.

Growing up, she always knew she could depend on him to make her feel safe. If anything ever scared her – be it a monster in the closet, or mean, ugly Stacy Sanchez on the playground – she always knew she could go to her Tío. His calm eyes and slow, sympathetic way of speaking could magically make the frightening parts of life seem almost silly.

Unfortunately, things changed as soon as she hit her teenage years, and fast. Tío Alberto was still his same, kind self, but Cristina morphed into a terror almost overnight.

She began actively blocking him and Aba out of her life.

His only fault had been trying to inspire her to be a good person. But she lived in a world that left her with no parents. Sleeping on the couch in her grand-mother's one-bedroom apartment. Wearing hand-me-down clothes from her cousins that were way too big. Hearing kids make fun of her for it every single day.

"Tee-nee Cristee-nee" they called her.

All she wanted to do was act out. Control *something*.

To this day, she knew Tío Alberto partially (and per-haps fully) blamed himself for the fact Cristina had started hanging out with the cholo-kids on the block at the ripe young age of 13. He once told her, just after she got sober, that he was sorry he hadn't loved her enough, a comment that made her want to crawl under the nearest rock and die.

The truth was, no one in her life had ever loved her so deeply and consistently. Certainly not her own fa-ther, wherever he'd decided to go. And not her mother, Tío Alberto's sister, who, despite her best efforts, was cut from a cloth that made her more suited for robbing liquor stores than taking care of a child.

Not even Aba. It had only taken two instances of finding Cristina getting hickies from a boy on the couch for her grandmother to boot her out into the street.

"It's for your own good," Aba had said, without so much as a tear.

No, it was Tío Alberto who drove his white Nissan truck around the neighborhood looking for Cristina when she stormed off. *He* was the one who took her in when Aba wouldn't speak to her. The one who made sure she got up in the morning and went to school.

At least until . . . it still pained her to think about it . . . at least until she stole the money he'd stashed in an envelope under his mattress. His entire meager life-savings. She could still remember the look on his face when he asked her about it. It wasn't anger, or even disappointment. Just a deep sadness.

Cristina hadn't stuck around long enough for him to kick her out. Although, looking back, she was pretty sure he wouldn't have.

Regardless, that's when she started hooking up with just about any guy who would give her even the least bit of attention. Cristina had matured early and quickly, so there was never any shortage of willing, mostly older, suitors. As long as she was willing, too. Willing to do whatever they wanted. Willing to let them treat her like some kind of object. A toy that existed for their pleasure.

It was an identity she started to believe herself. One she eventually embraced as her true self. Learned to use to her advantage, realizing she could get a lot more than just a place to stay out of the deal. Guys gave her money, jewelry, clothes, drugs. Anything she wanted.

Except respect.

And, all the while, she would hear from people in her neighborhood that Tío Alberto was asking about her here or there, wondering if she was OK. Telling so-and-so to deliver a message from him that it was alright for Cristina to come home.

Unable to face her own guilt, she never even called.

There were certainly moments she considered it. Nights when whatever guy she was with at the time would take the games too far. Choke her a little too hard maybe. Or, when one of her boyfriends had been up smoking meth for so long that he locked her in the closet for two whole days without food or water, claiming she was some kind of snitch, threatening the entire time to set the tiny space on fire so he could laugh as he watched her burn alive.

She spent those 48 hours in the closet crying and screaming and thinking about the sad, sad look on her uncle's face as he stood there with the empty envelope in his hands, surely hoping beyond hope that it some-how hadn't been his favorite niece who took the money, but knowing in his heart that it had been.

Even a year sober, the fact that he still loved her as if she'd never done anything wrong made Cristina feel simultaneously blessed with love, and also completely inadequate as a human being.

He definitely made her want to be a better person every day.

As the two of them cleaned up the kitchen from dinner, they could hear Aba snoring in the living room. Cristina peeked in and saw that Anise had curled up next to her, eyes closed, the slightest hint of a smile on her little lips.

The sun was finishing its work for the day when Cristina led her uncle out into the backyard.

"Ah, mija," he said as she lit a cigarette. "You're still smoking those cancer sticks? You're going to end up looking like an old squash, like your Aunt Carla." He puckered his lips and sucked in his face in a comical impression of his older sister, a two-pack-a-day smoker for as long as Cristina could remember.

"I know. I know. I honestly only smoke a few a day now though."

He smiled without judgment, then went about examining the overgrown plants in the twilight.

"Looks like you've got some nice stuff here. Rosemary. Thyme. Lemongrass. You just need to clear out some of these here weeds." He bent down and smelled the rosemary bush. "Boy, would I love to have a little piece of dirt like this to play in."

Cristina responded, "I'm too afraid of spiders I think."

"Ah, they never hurt no one," he said, waving his hand. "Not on purpose anyway. Like a lot of dangers in life, I guess you've just got to learn to stay out of the way." He sat on the concrete step and kissed the cross around his neck before tucking it into his shirt. "How is everything else in life going, sweetheart?"

He let the words hang in the air while he stared into the weeds.

"Pretty good," she answered after a while. "Getting settled in, but I'm having a bit of a hard time."

"Oh?"

"Yah. I know it's kind of silly, but I feel like there's something about this place that's a little weird."

He spread his arms.

"It sure seems lovely to me. Like a piece of paradise."

"That's why I said it's probably silly, bu—"

"—No concern of yours is silly," he said, pointing a finger at her.

"I know, Tío. It's just, well . . ."

She proceeded to tell him the story of Annie and her family. What she knew, at least. When she began, she really only planned to describe what was in the newspaper. But that part by itself felt empty. So she ended up recounting her dreams, the image she may or may not have seen in her hallway, and what she'd found out about the cult.

He sat for a moment, hands on his knees. Before speaking, he pulled the crucifix from under his shirt and once again kissed it. This time he left it dangling in the air.

"It sounds to me like the souls of that woman and her child are stuck here." His face was quite serious, but still warm. "Perhaps there's something more to the story of what happened to them. Something that needs to be known before they can rest." He nodded, more to himself than to her, then removed the crucifix from his neck, kissed it, and clasped the chain around Cristina's neck. "I want you to wear this and to burn the candle of the Virgen each night while saying ten Our Fathers and ten Hail Mary's."

Cristina's face betrayed her apprehension.

"I'm serious, mija." He looked at her, again pointing. "Don't underestimate the power of the devil. He's a master of illusion, and he always does the most damage when disguised as those things which makes us put our guard down."

The backyard was now in complete darkness, lit only by the glow of the kitchen light from the other side of the sliding glass door.

Cristina held the crucifix in her hand. She had, of course, seen the symbol many times before. But it was only there in the backyard with her uncle that she realized one did not have to be a Christian to see what tragedy and sadness there was in the way Jesus – a man who cast away everything he had in order to serve others – was given such a horrible fate.

When she said nothing, Tío Alberto continued, "It may be that the spirits themselves won't directly do anything to you. To my knowledge, they're more often good than bad. That's not how it is in the movies, of course. But in reality, the devil tends to work through real people. Often those we love and trust. He uses them to make us do things we otherwise wouldn't, and to hurt us when we allow ourselves to be vulnerable."

He said he wanted to have the priest from his parish, Father Antonio, come to the house and do a cleansing ritual, which he hoped would allow any souls trapped there to leave in peace.

"There's a chance it might not work, though," he added. "As I said before, if there's some other piece of business these poor souls have here on Earth, they must finish it. Do you have any idea what something like that might be?"

Cristina was not really a believer.

"How many people have been killed in the name of god?" she'd always asked her uncle when he tried to take her to church as a teenager.

But, on the other hand, Tío Alberto was not a man prone to fits of emotional indulgence. For that reason, if nothing else, she was willing to humor him.

Cristina lit another cigarette and tried to put everything together.

She said, "There does seem to be a lot of unanswered questions about the murder. The police seemed pretty sure it was the stepfather. But I never came across a reason why. And it seemed like the FBI had a lot of questions about the case, stuff they didn't feel got answered."

He nodded and said, "There's a man whose yard I've been doing every Tuesday for twelve years. He's an FBI agent. We're on pretty good terms. If I ask him nicely, maybe he can talk to you. Help fill in the gaps."

"Wow, thanks Tío. That would be great. I think a big part of what has me kind of cuckoo over all this is just not knowing."

He nodded again without looking convinced.

"Maybe, mija," he said. "Maybe. But I want you to promise one thing."

"Of course, anything. What?"

"No matter what you do. No matter where you go. Don't take that cross off your neck." He stood, stretched, and kissed her on the forehead. "OK? You promise?"

"Yes, Tío. I promise."

"Good then." He slid open the glass door. "I think we better get Aba home so she can make it to her Friday night bingo with the rest of the old crows."

"Tío!"

"What? That's what they sound like when they get together." He turned his arms into wings. "Caw! Caw!"

27

After her uncle and grandmother had gone, Cristina tucked Anise into bed.

She kissed her on the forehead and turned to go. Before flipping off the light switch, she stopped to examine the stuffed animals, all still on the dresser, right where they belonged. Leaning against the foot of Anise's blue teddy bear was the picture of Annie. As much as Cristina wanted to, once again, crumple the piece of paper into a little ball and dump it into the trashcan, part of her felt afraid to even go near it.

***

Sometime in the middle of the night, the Virgen de Guadalupe candle flickered a soft-yellow glow across the walls.

Cristina was dreaming. Not a nightmare, though. Not this time.

This dream was almost the exact opposite of those from earlier in the week. She and Casey and Anise were all sitting on the beach in front of *The Wharf* building a sandcastle. The sand was empty except for a group of sea lions barking near the water.

The three of them laughed in the sunshine. They dug their hands into wet sand. Felt the cool wind caress their skin.

In this world of endless happiness, Cristina experienced a deep contentment she'd been searching for her entire life.

The sense of wholeness stuck with her when she opened her eyes back in her bedroom. Her cheeks buzzed with joy as she walked down the hallway toward the bathroom.

The cheer vanished as soon as she peeked into her daughter's room and saw the blankets pulled neatly aside.

Anise was gone.

Cristina called out her daughter's name. Checked under the bed. The closet. The bathroom.

Nothing.

She ran downstairs and was both relieved and terrified at what she found.

Anise stood in front of the hall closet door, head tilted to one side, staring straight ahead. Cristina watched as her daughter's lips pulled back in a mischievous grin. Cristina's stomach tied itself into a knot. For a moment, she was sure she would vomit.

Her brain screamed at her to shake Anise awake. Slap her if she had to. Anything to break the spell of whatever had taken hold of her. She also remembered once hearing something about not waking a person who's sleepwalking, although she wasn't sure if that was even true.

And is that what this is? Sleepwalking?

No. There was something more going on. Some force in the room with them. Anise's body pulsated with an unseen electricity, making Cristina think of the high-powered electric fence that had surrounded the girl's detention camp. The buzzing energy was so palpable, she couldn't bring herself to reach out and touch Anise, fearful that doing so might mean both of them receiving a powerful shock.

The fear and uncertainty paralyzed Cristina.

She had no idea what to do.

Anise turned toward her, still with that wicked smile. The lids of her eyes were closed but shaking, as if in the middle of an intense dream. Then they opened, and for a moment, Cristina thought *she* must be the one dreaming. The eyes she was looking at weren't the soft brown of her daughter's. Not even close. They were now an electric red, like a picture taken with bad lighting.

Their glow intensified. The heating coils of an electric stove.

Along with the light came a vision.

As if a projector had penetrated into Cristina's mind, she saw Annie being lifted from her bed in the room that now belonged to Anise. The little girl was afraid, not wanting to go. As hard as Cristina strained, she couldn't see who was taking her. Everything but the girl was soaked in the same red glow that filled the living room.

Annie's face morphed into Anise's and then back again

Reality and hallucination – if that's what it was – were fully meshed, to the point Cristina could no longer tell what was real and what was imagined.

These parallel worlds felt like two scenes from a movie spliced together, with some unseen person on a set of controls fading them in and out. At one moment, she was staring into Anise's hypnotic red eyes. In the next, she saw Annie wearing a pretty white nightgown with polka dots, holding her stuffed hippo in one hand, being carried down the stairs, the hallway, and out the backdoor by someone whose face Cristina still couldn't see. The little girl looked too afraid to cry. But even if she'd been able to find the will, producing any sound would have been impossible. Her mouth was sealed tight by her abductor's leather-gloved hand.

At a total loss for what to do, Cristina suddenly remembered the crucifix.

She heard Michelle's voice.

"There ain't no atheists in a foxhole, honey."

Grabbing the cross from under her shirt, she kissed it and began to say the only prayer she knew.

"Our Father, who art in heaven. Hallowed be thy name . . ."

The red glow of Anise's eyes began to pulsate, brightening and dimming like a lighthouse beacon.

". . . Thy kingdom come. Thy will be done. On Earth, as it is in heaven . . ."

The pulse quickened, reminding Cristina now of the spinning lights on a dance floor.

". . . Give us this day our daily bread. And forgive us our trespasses. As we forgive those who trespass against us . . ."

"NO!" Anise suddenly said in a deep voice that wasn't quite human.

"NO!" This time in the voice of a child, though not her own.

"NO!" A woman who sounded both scared and angry.

Cristina squeezed the crucifix in her hand, hard enough that she thought the metal might snap.

Tears ran down her face.

". . . Lead us not into temptation. But deliver us from evil . . ."

Anise reached into the pocket of her nightgown and pulled something from it. Cristina couldn't tell what.

Anise touched the object to the closet door.

" . . . For thine is the kingdom. The power. And the glory forever. Amen."

The light stopped.

Anise collapsed to the floor.

Cristina ran to her daughter and held her tiny, limp body close to her own. At first, she was sure Anise was dead.

Tears became intense sobs.

Then, she felt the subtle pressure of the girl's chest moving up and down. She grabbed the back of her daughter's wrist and found a slow but steady pulse, as if Anise had fallen into the deepest, dreamless sleep imaginable.

"Oh, thank God," she said, a phrase she'd probably used a million times in her life, but had never meant it sincerely until now.

"There ain't no atheists in a foxhole, honey."

Fear and sadness combined inside her with an intense sense of relief, leaving her mind exhausted and numb.

Anise shivered.

Cristina rubbed her daughter's cold, bare arms.

"Owie, mamma," Anise said in her familiar voice, blinking sleep from her eyes as she spoke. "Why are we downstairs?"

A new wave of tears made it hard for Cristina to speak.

She managed to say, "Chica, I love you so much. You scared mommy."

"Why?"

"You don't remember anything, baby?"

Anise looked up into her mom's eyes and said, "I was dreaming that a little girl who used to live in my room wanted to play with me. Her name is Annie. She couldn't talk because someone bad did something to her. But she showed me pictures in my head, and it was kind of like talking. She told me that she didn't want to scare us. She thinks we're nice people and that's why she wants to help us."

"Help us do what?" Cristina was trying her best not

to freak out any more than she already was. "Tell mommy, right now."

"I don't know, mamma. We were playing with my animals and then I woke up. I'm really tired. I want to go back to sleep now."

"OK, baby. OK."

Although the rational side of Cristina's brain said to immediately walk out the front door, get in the car, and drive as far away from the house as possible, there was a deeper, primal instinct inside her that said they needed to stay.

She picked Anise up from the floor and held her in her arms.

As she turned to walk toward the stairs, Cristina saw what Anise had been doing with the object in her hand. There were three chilling words written on the door in the bubblegum-pink kid's lipstick Anise had received as a present for her birthday.

DON'T TRUST HIM.

TRUST

28

"Michelle, it's Cristina. Hey, girl. Sorry I haven't called lately. I've just been really busy getting moved in and all. But I've been thinking about you and the ladies a lot. I miss you guys. Anyway, I promise not to wait so long before I call again. But give me a ring when you get a chance. It would be nice to hear your voice. OK. Love you. Bye."

It was 6 AM.

The sun had finally started to come up. The cheap wax of the Virgen de Guadalupe candle from Walgreens had burned almost completely down to the bottom of its glass cylinder. Yet, Cristina remained hesitant to blow out the flame. She knew the candle was nothing special, but for some reason it still seemed so comforting. Even in the grey light of morning, the red, yellow, and blue-green of the praying woman's clothes warmed her bedroom with a sense of security.

Cristina sat up in bed, trying to remember the story of the Virgen de Guadalupe. She could only recall bits and pieces. Something about an Aztec boy who saw a vision of the Virgin Mary. That was all that came to mind. And the fact that the image of the Virgen, along with that of St. Christopher, was prominently displayed in just about every Mexican household she'd ever been in. Both were supposed to protect you. She was never sure from what. Evil, she guessed.

But was that even possible?

The more she thought about it, the more she began to believe what her uncle had said about the way evil most often works through subtle deception. She didn't necessarily believe in some red devil with a pitchfork (any more than she did a bearded white-guy in the sky), but Cristina did feel like she'd seen "real" evil before. And whether that evil came in the form of her ex (a person she once very much saw as a savior), or in a stranger (like the charming serial killers she'd seen on TV documentaries), their deception was almost always revealed only after a mask of goodness had been removed.

Fingering the crucifix between the tips of her fingers, she couldn't help but snicker at her new found interest in spirituality.

"There ain't no atheists in a foxhole, honey."

Since Michelle hadn't answered the phone, Cristina decided to call Tío Alberto, who she figured would be awake even so early on a Saturday. He answered after the first ring.

"Cristina? Is everything OK?"

"Tío, um . . . yah. Everything's fine." She didn't know why she felt the need to lie, or even exactly why she'd called him in the first place. Maybe just to hear his voice. "Why aren't you working? You're always working."

"I am working, sweetheart. But I stopped by church to speak with Father Antonio about your situation." The way he said the last word reminded her of when she got her first period and he found someone to talk with her about how to use a tampon.

When she didn't say anything, he continued.

"Father Antonio says he can come by on Friday. Does that work for you?"

She was about to say yes, before she remembered the stupid family court summons. Which then reminded her she was still supposed to get a drug test. And *that* flared her intense hatred of Anthony.

She had to fake a smile to make sure the anger didn't come across over the phone.

"Tío, Friday's bad for me."

"OK, well he told me if Friday didn't work for you that he could do Thursday, but he'd have to cancel some things to make it happen."

That made her feel bad. Did she really even want to bug this guy? What had actually happened last night anyway? She was still unsure it hadn't all been a dream. Or at least parts of it. Who knows. Everything was so confused. Her brain felt like a car engine that had been running too hot for too long. She kind of wished she could just turn it all off for a while.

And, like that, out of nowhere, for the second time in a week, she felt like getting high.

"Mija? Are you there?"

"Yah, Tío. I'm here. Thursday's fine."

"Alright. You're sure everything's OK? You sound a little distant."

"I'm just tired is all."

"More dreams?"

It was on the tip of her tongue to tell him.

"Just girl stuff, Tío."

"OK. OK. I'll let you go."

She could almost hear him blushing.

"Oh," he said. "I also called my client last night, the FBI agent. I asked him about the case of that little girl. He said he didn't work on the investigation. But he knows about it, and he said he'd talk to a few people who had. I gave him your number. I also told him about that cult."

As happy as she was about possibly getting some

answers, she hated the idea of dealing with cops. And, at a time when one of her main goals in life was to create some space for herself, she really didn't like the fact that there were more and more people getting involved in her business.

"Thanks, Tío," she said, trying to sound as sincere as possible.

"Anything for you, sweetheart. You know that. Now, I have some trees I have to go try not to fall out of. You get some rest."

Cristina said goodbye and ended the call.

Rest sounded like a wonderful idea. The adrenaline of last night had dissipated, leaving her feeling simply exhausted.

She sank into her bed and fell asleep.

29

The phone buzzed on the nightstand, but Cristina wasn't able to shake herself awake in time to answer it.

Before she could look to see who had called, a series of loud banging noises rang out from the kitchen. She slipped out from under the covers and crept downstairs, hand wrapped around the knife in her robe pocket.

She was surprised, shocked, and then confused when she looked at the closet door on her way down the hallway. Completely blank. Not even a hint of the words that had been so clearly written there the night before.

An image flashed into her mind like a video clip. Annie being carried through the sliding glass door, out into the dark, some unknown person's gloved hand over her mouth.

The ghostly memory burst like a balloon as soon as Cristina turned the corner into the kitchen. She had to bite her bottom lip and cross her arms to stop from breaking into laughter.

There was Anise, making her way across the kitchen, an intense look of concentration on her face as she carried the large metal mixing bowl filled with what must have been half a box of Cheerios floating in a deep pool of milk. The concoction slopped over the sides as her little hands fought a losing battle to keep the liquid in balance. It didn't help that her fingers were also attempting to keep hold of a giant serving spoon.

Cristina stood watching until Anise finally noticed her. The girl stopped. A bit of milk flopped over the edge of the bowl, adding to the trail of white spots on the floor leading from the refrigerator.

Anise's focused face morphed into a bright-eyed, angelic smile.

"Hi, mamma. I was hungry and you looked really tired. So I figured I'd just get my own Cheerios today."

"That's what you figured, huh?" Cristina held her hand in front of her face to hide a smile. "Looks like you did quite a job there, chica."

Anise considered her mother's words for a moment. Deciding they were a compliment, she offered a thankful nod before sitting at the table to begin her breakfast.

Does she remember anything? Cristina wondered as she replaced the serving spoon with something more suitable.

Kids were certainly resilient, and hers perhaps more so than most. But Cristina thought there was no possible way Anise could have zero memory of the ordeal.

Yet, there she was. Looking as peaceful and happy as could be.

"Chica?"

No answer at first. Only a far-off stare as spoonfuls of Cheerios went from bowl to lips.

"Do you remember what happened last night?"

Still no answer. She was in her silent eating mode.

"Anise, I need you to talk to mommy for a minute. Do you remember what happened last night?"

"Yah."

Cristina sat next to her.

"Tell me what you remember, sweetie."

After a moment of thoughtful recollection, Anise answered, "We ate pizza! And Aba was here. And Tío, too. Mommy, I wish they could have dinner with us every night."

"Me too, baby. Me too. What else happened?"

"Um . . ." Anise's face searched for a piece of information she was sure she was supposed to know. "I went to sleep with Aba on the couch and she was snoring."

That memory brought a round of giggles.

"That's it?"

"Yah."

Anise leaned forward, placed her small palm on her mother's forehead, and asked, "Are you feeling OK, young lady?"

It was a halfway-decent impression of Cristina.

"Yes, Dr. Anise. Mommy feels fine. You're *sure* you don't remember anything else? Not even a dream you had? About the little girl who used to live here?"

Anise contemplated the question and then shook her head.

"I don't remember any dreams."

It was possible she was lying, but Cristina didn't think that was the case.

"OK, sweetie. You eat your cereal. Mommy is going to go outside for a sec."

Anise's only response was the sound of cereal crunching between teeth.

In the backyard, tightening her robe and making sure she was out of Anise's line of sight, Cristina lit a cigarette.

Her phone showed that the missed call was from Michelle, but she hadn't left a message. There was a text, though.

Hey girl. Love you too. Call back when you can.

Day or night. Stay right.

Cristina was about to call her again when another text came through. This one from Casey.

Can I take you two beautiful ladies to lunch?

As hard as Cristina tried to fight it, as much as she sat there and hated herself for thinking it, some part of her now doubted Casey.

DON'T TRUST HIM.

The "him" couldn't be *him*, could it?

No. She refused to believe that. There was no way Casey was a bad person. She'd known plenty of awful – *horrible* – men in her lifetime. He wasn't one of them.

Besides, she couldn't just throw away a chance to connect with the best guy she'd met in years, maybe ever, just because of some message she probably dreamed up.

The further she got into the sunny morning, the more she was convinced that's exactly what it had been.

A dream.

Had to be.

Done with her cigarette, she texted back.

We'd love to. Just tell us when and where.

His reply came quickly.

Meet at the end of the pier. Noon. Bring swimsuits.

30

It turned out to be another gorgeous day in Pleasure Point. The California sun was shining. The breeze light. The beach in front of the amusement park was again crammed with people.

Cristina and Anise looked out over the sea of bodies as they walked hand-in-hand up the pier's entrance ramp. Underneath them, sand turned to water. The empty spaces between the pier's wooden planks provided a clear view of the choppy ocean below. Anise squeezed her mother's hand and stared downward, using great caution not to bring either of her feet anywhere near the gaps.

On the car ride down, and as they circled for twenty minutes looking for parking, Anise hadn't stopped talking about jumping in the water. She was disappointed they weren't going directly there, and she was letting Cristina know about it.

"Why did I put my bathing suit on?" she asked with attitude.

"We'll go in the water. But first we have to go meet Casey and eat some food."

"Who's Casey, mamma?"

A good question, Cristina thought.

"He's the nice man who was playing with you under the pier the last time we came to beach."

"Oh."

Cristina wasn't sure what to make of that answer. There seemed to be some kind of apprehension in Anise's voice, but it could have just as easily been simple distraction.

"We're going to see the sea lions, too," Cristina added.

Anise's face tensed.

"Lions mamma? Are they scary like on TV?"

Cristina managed a smile.

"No, baby. These ones are like doggies who swim in the ocean. They can't jump all the way up here either."

"Oh."

Anise returned her attention to the important task of not falling through the gaps.

The pier was almost as packed with bodies as the beach. Most of the people meandered about, aimless and happy. Some stood staring off into the water. Others took pictures of themselves with the backdrop of the amusement park. Almost everyone seemed relaxed and just glad to be alive on such a spectacular day.

Cristina wished she could say the same. She was exhausted. And she had the creeping feeling Anise was headed toward a tantrum at any moment.

Along the length of the pier were numerous shops. Most of them tourist traps selling the same kind of junky merchandise Cristina had seen in the windows near *Bula's*.

Anise came out of her focused, downward gaze when she saw a sign in front of one of the stores. TWO SCOOPS FOR $2. She couldn't read yet, but it didn't take a literary genius to recognize the pictures.

"Ice cream cone! Mamma, can we get one? Please!? Please!? Please!?"

Anise stopped dead in her tracks.

Cristina tried unsuccessfully to pull her along by the hand.

"Please!? Please!? Please!?"

"Maybe later, after we have lunch."

The tears were almost instant. A puffy bottom lip and red face, too.

Cristina was finding it hard to stay patient. People were staring. Some with disapproving looks on their faces, judging the young, brown-skinned mom with the tattoos.

"Anise Rodriguez," she said, tugging her daughter's arm a bit more forcefully, without any movement. "You better get moving right now, or we won't get any ice cream at all. *And* we can just go back home instead."

Anise rubbed her eyes with the back of her hands. Peeking through the tears, she saw that the sincerity in her mother's voice matched the look on her face. Reluctantly, Anise stumbled forward, continuing to whimper, albeit at a lower decibel level than before.

She was no longer worried about the gaps.

They passed a group of fisherman. Older Mexican men, whose calm-looking faces reminded Cristina of Tío Alberto. She could smell the stink of chopped bait, as well as the faint, brassy scent leftover from the beers some of them had for breakfast.

One of the men turned to smile at her. She'd just started to politely return the gesture when someone going in the other direction bumped into her. He seemed to be in a hurry and was wearing a trench coat, like a cop in a bad movie. It seemed odd, but Cristina had already become used to seeing weird things and people in Pleasure Point. It was an endearing part of what made the town unique.

She didn't like how this particular guy looked at her, though. It wasn't the kind of impatient glare a person gives someone they just ran into. And he wasn't checking her out, even though she was wearing only a blue bikini-top and a short white wrap. He seemed to be studying her. For what purpose, she didn't know. And by the time she thought about confronting him, he'd already vanished into the crowd.

Before she could think too much about it, they found Casey sitting in front of a place called *Arthur's Fish Shack*. Cristina tried to gather herself and put a smile on her face, but the effort felt just short of impossible.

"Hey ladies!" Casey said, standing as they approached. He curled an eyebrow when he saw that neither of them looked very happy. "Everything, OK?"

"Hey," she said with a polite hug. "Yes, everything's OK. This little one just wanted to eat ice cream before lunch. And big, mean mommy had to say no."

He leaned down so he was at eyelevel with Anise. "Hi there."

She tucked her head behind her mom's leg, in part out of shyness, but mostly to hide a sprouting grin.

He added, "I like Rocky Road, personally. And I'll buy the scoops after we have lunch, if that's cool with you."

"OK," Anise answered, revealing part of her face. "Can we look for sand crabs too? I brought my bucket."

"You do remember me."

"Duh."

Cristina felt some of her tired tension and wariness ease as they all shared a platter of fish and chips. She enjoyed watching Casey with Anise. Especially the way they bantered back and forth. By the end of their meal, the two seemed on their way to becoming best buddies.

After lunch, they went to look at the sea lions.

"Do they fetch?" Anise asked Casey as he held her up on the railing so she could peer down. "My Aba's doggy has a squeaky toy, and he brings it back to you when you throw it."

"Oh yah," Casey said. "They sure do. They like fishies though. And little girls."

He held her out over the opening. She shrieked and he brought her quickly back. Her lip puffed out but she didn't cry.

He said, "Sorry. Sorry. Just kidding. They don't like kids. Only fishies, OK?"

"OK. Can we have ice cream now?"

They both looked at Cristina, her eyes halfway-closed, mind off in the distance.

"Mamma?"

"Uh, yah. Ice cream? OK . . ."

"Yay!" Anise and Casey both said, slapping hands.

They walked back toward the ice cream shop. Anise's fear of falling through the boards had completely evaporated. She skipped happily ahead.

Casey put an arm around Cristina's shoulders. She didn't tighten or cringe, but she didn't exactly make him feel welcome either.

"You OK?" he asked. "For real, you can tell me if something's wrong."

"No, really. I'm fine. I'm just tired. I barely slept last night." She made sure Anise was out of earshot. "Her dad, my stupid ex, is dragging me back into court and making me do a drug test."

She expected to see Casey cringe, or at least offer a look that said he would rather not hear about it. Instead, his blue eyes sparkled with genuine sympathy.

He said, "I'm not sure of your situation. I'm guessing you'll tell me soon. At least, I'm hoping you will. But in your own time, and in your own way." He stopped, spun her toward him, looked into her eyes. "I only have two things to say about it. One, I've got *zero* doubt that you're an amazing mom. That little girl loves you, and anyone, be it me, your ex, or any judge, should be able to tell that just by the way she looks at you. Second, I don't know who this guy is, but the whole thing sounds pretty messed up on his part. He's not even in her life, is he?"

"No," she said, looking away. "And you're right. I'll tell you about it. Just not right now. It's a long story. But yah, he isn't in her life. For good reasons. Like he's an abusive, manipulative psycho. But he's also rich, and he knows how to be dangerous with his money."

He lifted her chin up with one finger so their eyes met. "I told you what my experience was with seeing abuse firsthand. If you feel like you're in danger, there are people who can help."

"No, it's not that. It's just—"

"Just what? There's no justifiable reason for him to make you feel this way."

"I know. But—"

"No buts, either. You deserve to be treated like the strong, intelligent, capable woman that you are."

She again turned from him, wanting to keep her face stern. Strong. But as hard as she tried, she couldn't prevent the corners of her lips from curling into a smile.

"See," he said. "Like mother, like daughter. You two are both so beautiful, Cristina. Don't let him or anyone else make you believe otherwise."

Her eyes drifted back to his.

She kissed him, gently on the lips.

It felt wonderful. Safe.

How could she have thought for even a second that he was any kind of a threat?

The more distance she put between herself and whatever had happened in her living room the night before, the dumber the whole thing seemed.

This isn't a movie, Cristina. This is real life. Look around you. You own (OWN!) a house in one of the most beautiful places in the world. One of the nicest and sexiest guys on the planet is obviously gaga over you. Your daughter is in perfect health, and so are you. You've got everything you've ever dreamed of.

There were a lot of people in 12-step meetings who talked about self-sabotage, and it had always been one of the concepts Cristina most related to. She'd also been given plenty of opportunities in life to learn that happiness wasn't some far-off destination. It was something right there in front of her. Always had been, and always would be.

She decided to accept whatever craziness might be going on in her life – be it her ex, her haunted dreams, or whatever else might come. Otherwise, she was going to miss out on what she'd already been blessed with.

Holding hands, Casey and Cristina caught up with Anise, who'd come to a stop in front of a man making animal balloons. He was already in the process of twisting one into shape for her. An octopus.

When the balloon-man was done, he handed over his creation. Anise beamed with joy, holding it close as Casey slipped the guy a couple bucks.

They spent the rest of the afternoon eating ice cream and playing on the beach. The three of them waded out into the shallows together, holding hands in a circle as they splashed and laughed. Then they caught sand crabs, letting the harmless little creatures wiggle between their fingers before returning them to their burrowing. They even built a sandcastle.

Besides the fact the beach was crowded with people, the scene could have been the one Cristina dreamed of, down to the barking sea lions echoing in the background.

31

Later that night, Cristina and Casey were in her bedroom. He sat on the edge of the bed, leaning back on his strong, tattooed arms. She lit candles and put on her favorite TLC album, the one she stole from her older cousin years ago and had loved listening to as a boy-crazy preteen.

The room filled with a song about scrubs.

Cristina swayed her hips to the smooth beat as she flipped off the light, continuing to rock them back-and-forth on her way toward the bed.

She stood in front of Casey as he tried to hide his nervousness.

"What's the matter," she teased, pushing him back onto the bed. "Big tough guy like you isn't scared are you?"

"Nah." The grin creeped onto his face as he rested his head in clasped hands.

Cristina's stomach buzzed with anticipation.

She crawled on top of him, legs straddling his body, lips kissing his neck.

"Anise is OK?" he asked.

Cristina had put her to bed an hour ago.

"If she hasn't gotten up yet, she won't. One thing about that girl, she can definitely sleep." She added in a whisper, "Relax."

"Alright."

"You need to take this off, though," she said, pulling his *Bula's* t-shirt over his head and throwing it to the ground.

His muscular body felt almost magical as she caressed it with her soft hands. Somehow that glowing strength lightened the fury and terror of some of his darker tattoos. Skulls eating the world, a skeleton riding a motorcycle, a dead-eyed demon choking a beautiful woman caught in a spider's web.

She gently traced a finger along the roses on his neck. He did the same to those on her arm.

Her eyes tightened into seductive slits. She scooted back so she could rub her tongue along the ridges of his chest, and then slowly around the metal bars he had through his nipples.

Pulling her own shirt off, she threw it aside and undid her bra. Her breasts floated in the air without falling. She pushed them together, softly pinching her own nipples.

***

The sex was amazing, although not quite as crazy as she'd imagined when she was in the bathtub. After all, they had to be somewhat quiet to keep from waking Anise.

From the moment she reached back and slipped him inside of her, there was a surprising gentleness to it all. An almost nervous desire on both their parts to make it last.

It was unlike any first time she'd ever experienced. Their two bodies felt made for one another. His cut muscles and her just-thick-enough curves clicked together like perfectly matched puzzle pieces.

And it wasn't *all* gentle.

There were a few – more than a few – times when she had to bite down on the pillow to keep from screaming. Especially when he took her from behind. That had always been her favorite position, but it didn't always work right. The guy had to be just the right height. She didn't know exactly what that ideal measurement was, but Casey was it.

She came at least five times. Maybe more. She lost count as the intense pulses crashed against one another, like waves on the beach.

"That was wonderful," she told him when she crawled back into bed after going to the bathroom and ducking her head into Anise's room, where she found her daughter sound asleep on her stomach, one leg pulled out from under the covers, snoring ever-so-slightly.

Casey lay in her bed smiling, looking almost boyish. Cristina thought vulnerability was cute on him, but didn't say so. Instead, she told him he was amazing. He said she was amazing. In the end, they agreed they were both amazing.

"You aren't going to leave are you?" Cristina asked, feeling needy and lame as soon as the words came out.

"Nope," he said plainly. "Not unless you want me to."

Her only response was to curl up against his bare chest, one leg draped over him, the top of her head nuzzled underneath his chin.

That night there were no dreams at all.

32

Before Cristina knew it, her uncle was driving Aba's little Ford Taurus up the driveway and buckling Anise into her car seat.

Casey was already long gone by then. He hadn't even stayed for breakfast. A big Sunday sale, he said as he snuck out just after dawn.

Her uncle was tired and they didn't talk all that much, though he made sure to remind her about Father Antonio's plans to visit on Thursday. She thanked him for everything and said her goodbyes, feeling an ache in her heart as she kissed Anise.

Cristina was again left with a lonely house all to herself.

It was still relatively early in the afternoon. The sun blazed high in the sky. A bank of fog sat just offshore.

The last thing she wanted was to be alone.

She walked across the courtyard toward Jack's place, realizing she hadn't seen him all week. There was a note taped to his door.

Gone camping. Hold all calls. —J

He'd added a smiley face for emphasis, which made Cristina miss his hearty belly-laugh.

She walked back across the courtyard, watching Mr. Psycho's place as she did. Still no sign of him.

Is he dead, or what?

She was surprised at the bitterness she felt.

I hope so.

With a sigh, she sat on the front porch and smoked without enjoying it. Cigarettes were starting to taste worse every day. They hardly even did anything for her anymore.

Her hands went into her pocket and pulled out her phone. There was a text from Jordan.

Dinner with myself and Dan at Venus Cafe tonight??

Yes, she wrote back immediately and went inside to get dressed.

***

With time to kill, Cristina decided to check out the drum circle again. She didn't really know why. Mostly, she supposed, because she really wanted to be around other human beings.

Plus, as much as she kind of hated to admit it, she really liked being there the first time. For one, she just loved music. But that wasn't the only reason. She'd also been pleasantly taken in by the overall vibe.

When she was getting high, her favorite thing in the world – probably the most fun she ever had – was getting trashed and going out dancing. The way the sound moved her body. Touched her soul. Being at the drum circle kind of felt like some mellow version of the same thing.

There were no open parking spaces along the scenic cliffside road. She ended up pulling the Civic between two cars on a side street. After walking about a block, she realized she'd once again forgotten her sweatshirt and had to go back for it.

By the time she walked up to the lighthouse park,

wispy tendrils of fog were creeping onshore. The more the shroud of mist thickened, the more the sound of the drums seemed to exist in its own little enclosed world.

Cristina didn't stand at a distance this time. Instead, she plopped herself down onto the grass, sitting between a white hippy wearing a somewhat ridiculous Rastafarian hat, and a college kid hiding behind dark glasses. The latter shifted nervously when she sat next to him. Even through the glasses, Cristina could see him glancing at her chest.

Dude, I'm wearing a damn sweatshirt.

When he saw that she'd noticed, his cheeks turned bright red.

The rhythm he was tapping out fell apart.

Eventually, he gave up the effort and leaned toward her, as if working up the will to say something. His nervous energy was thick. Finally, he tilted his well-worn bongos forward and said a few words she couldn't quite hear over the other noise.

"Do you play?" she heard him ask when he leaned in further.

She swiped a hand in the air to say, "who me?"

He handed her the drums.

Now it was *her* turn to blush.

Unsure of what to do, she tried her best to copy the other people in the circle. At first, her attempts sounded about as random as popcorn in a kettle. But once she settled down and stopped trying, she actually had some fun with it. Poncho Sanchez wouldn't be asking her to join his All-Star Band anytime soon, but she enjoyed herself, swaying back and forth, weaving her energy together with the rest of the players.

After about 15 minutes, she decided to quit while she was ahead.

As soon as she handed the drums back, someone

passed her a joint. She took the tube of smoking, white paper without thinking, barely even looking at it, but clearly smelling the skunky aroma drifting up into her face. Having always preferred booze and harder drugs, she'd never been a huge pothead, but she'd always loved the smell.

For a moment, she imagined holding the crinkly paper to her lips, sipping smoke into her lungs, feeling her body float weightless like a balloon.

The thought died when she noticed a man wearing a trench coat and dark glasses staring at her from across the circle. He wasn't standing among the crowd, but just at the edge of where the fog became too thick to see past.

He had a camera and it was pointed directly at her.

When he saw her looking his way, he turned and took off speed-walking in the other direction. She could have sworn she knew him from somewhere.

After passing the joint along to someone who would actually use it, she went to see if she could get another look at the guy.

No luck. He'd slipped into the mist.

Then she realized where she'd seen him.

33

The Venus Café was packed.

Through the window, Cristina could see that all the tables were full. Several groups of people stood outside the front door, lining the wall along the cigarette-covered sidewalk. Everyone seemed patient, laughing and taking pictures with their phones.

Jordan and Dan were there waiting when Cristina walked up.

"Wow, what a difference a week makes, huh?" she said, trying to deflect attention away from her frustration.

"Tourist season is just about full-blown now," Jordan agreed, watching her. "The wait shouldn't be long, though. You OK? You look rather flustered."

Dan hadn't as much as glanced her way. He rubbed his bearded chin like he was contemplating some deep universal truth. He seemed a lot cleaner than the last time Cristina saw him, but she was pretty sure he still wasn't wearing deodorant.

"Oh, it's nothing," she said. "Just some creeper taking pictures of me at the drum circle right now."

"Eww," Jordan said. "Do you know him?"

"No, but I think I saw him yesterday too, on the pier."

"Private detective," Dan said out of nowhere, not breaking his thoughtful stare.

"Huh?" Cristina asked.

Dan dropped his hand from his chin and slowly turned toward her.

"Private detective, I said."

"Yah, I heard you. I just don't understand what you mean. What would a private detective be doing following me, of all people?"

"I don't know," Dan said. He spoke fast and didn't move his lips much when he did. Still, he was surprisingly articulate. "Back when I worked civil litigation cases, we always hired private dicks to follow around people when we were planning to sue them. Sometimes to find out specific things – like if they were having an affair with their secretary, or maybe any drug habits. Sometimes just to monitor them and build up a psychological profile, so we would know how to rattle them in court."

"Oh shit," she said, putting it all together.

"I assume you know who might have hired this guy?" Jordan asked, trying to sound sympathetic, but still coming off as condescending as ever.

"Uh, yah," Cristina said. Then she screamed, "FUCK!"

Jordan jumped back. Most of the people standing outside the restaurant stopped what they were doing and cautiously stared. Everyone except Dan. He looked a bit like a child after discovering a fascinating insect.

"Who?" he asked with a combination of curiosity and kindness.

The last thing Cristina wanted to do was sit there and yap about her problems with two people she hardly knew, one of whom she didn't know at all.

But Dan's eyes were warm. Behind the silly homeless act, Cristina could see something else. A sparkle of genuine empathy. The kind she'd only ever seen in people like Tío Alberto and Michelle. Those saints of the world who have dedicated their lives to helping others.

"My ex," she said. "It has to be him. And the guy likely got a picture of me holding a joint, too."

"What were you doing holding a joint?" Jordan asked with more accusation than Cristina was in the mood for.

"It was nothing, alright?" she snapped, firing up a Lucky Strike. "Some dude at the drum circle put it in my hand. I didn't hit it or anything. I passed it on to the person beside me. But Trenchcoat had a goddamn camera on me right at that moment."

"Well, what can he really do with it?" Jordan asked. Dan watched.

Cristina said, "I have to go to court this Friday for a stupid custody hearing. My ex has an expensive lawyer and I have shit. He's obviously trying to set me up to look like some horrible mother." She felt a tingle in her eyes. "I've worked hella hard to get away from that life, and now he's trying to make me look like I've fallen back so he can take my baby away from me. I even have to take a drug test."

"That's good!" Dan declared.

"Good?" Cristina asked, trying not to sniffle. "How can that possibly be good?"

"Well, did you smoke the joint?"

"I said I didn't, OK?"

"That's what I thought I heard. So, like I said, that's good. You're going to do the drug test, and it will show that you haven't smoked pot."

"I guess I didn't think about it like that . . ."

"That's OK." Dan's face remained soft and patient. He glanced down at his clothes, running his hands through his beard. "Hey, I know I might not be dressed for the part at the moment, but I *am* a member of the

California Bar. I'd be happy to represent you."

She looked at him skeptically. "Are you serious? I can't really pay much." That wasn't totally true, of course. She did have *some* money. But after seeing what her divorce attorney had charged, if things got complicated at all, she knew that the relatively small bit of cash she'd stashed from the settlement would be burned up in no time.

Maybe that's what Anthony wants, she thought. *Maybe he thinks he can bleed me dry until I have nothing left.*

"I'm serious as a heart attack," Dan said. "Free of charge, too. Or, *pro bono* as we say in the legal world. It sounds more important that way. Actually, I think it would be fun." There continued to be an almost spiritual empathy in his eyes, but now there was something else there, too. The look of a lawyer who smells blood. He continued, "If your ex has an expensive attorney, you're going to want *someone* in your corner when you walk in there. I'm telling you . . . no, I'm *begging* you, because from what Jordan has said you sound like a great person, if you don't want my help, then at least let me make a few calls and find you someone else."

It didn't feel like she had much choice.

"Alright, you're hired." She extended her hand and he took it.

"Thanks!" he said, making it sound like she was the one doing him a favor. "You won't regret it."

"Somehow I don't think I will."

The hostess — a young woman with a fake green parakeet tied into her hair — stuck her head out the door and called Jordan's name.

As they made their way to the table, Dan put his arm on Cristina's shoulder.

"Let's meet this week to talk," he said seriously. "I

really do think I can help, or I wouldn't have offered. I hope you know that. I'm not kidding around here. I may not look like much, but I've got it where it counts."

34

Cristina forgot to leave the porchlight on.

With the dense fog, it was almost pitch black when she parked the Civic in front of the lawn.

Her foot kicked a package on the doorstep as she fumbled the keys into the lock.

Once inside, she turned on the hall light, trying not to look at the closet, but nonetheless finding her eyes locked onto the spot where three ominous words had been written in pink lipstick. Well, at least part of her still thought they had been. Maybe.

DON'T TRUST HIM.

She willed her feet forward. But froze in front of the door, trying to understand what had happened, and if any of it had been real.

Her hand twisted the knob and pulled.

Still just a closet, now filled with cardboard boxes.

She shook her head and closed the door.

The package that had been left on the porch was small and circular, wrapped in nice-looking white paper without any postage.

Must have been dropped off.

Flipping open her knife, she carefully cut open one side of the paper. Inside was a box of chocolates. Not the cheap, mass-produced ones you get at the super-market, either. These were high-end. The kind you spend twenty minutes picking out at a shop while chatting with a nice old-lady who works behind the counter.

There was a small notecard attached.

Hope you enjoy every bite as much as I enjoy you.

There was no signature, but she knew it had to be from Casey.

She smiled, her cheekbones buzzing with joy.

The box was thick and heavy. She shimmied the top off and pulled the matted cover away, revealing twenty of the most beautiful chocolates she'd ever seen. There were dark-brown truffles rolled in cocoa-powder. Smooth, velvety ones with white pinstripes. Some with nuts sprinkled on the outside. And, in the middle, Cristina's absolute all-time favorite: dark-chocolate-covered cherries.

Delicately, between two fingers, she grabbed one of the cherries and bit into it. A bit of the oozing center dripped onto her chin. She wiped the dark-red liquid away with a finger and then licked it with her tongue, imagining for a moment that it was Casey.

Oh, he's going to get his. Guaranteed.

She pulled out her phone and sent him a picture of her finger in her mouth, the edge of her bottom lip pulled ever-so-slightly open.

Along with the picture, she wrote: *This is going to be you the next time I see you.*

Her heart raced a little as she finished that first morsel of chocolatey goodness. It felt wonderful. She grabbed another and went to take a shower.

***

Despite the long week, Cristina felt completely ener-gized after slipping into her comfy clothes. She'd planned on just chilling and doing nothing, but in-stead decided to clean the kitchen. Then the living room. And then her room, too.

Every so often, she grabbed another chocolate and felt a new surge of warm affection for Casey as she gob-bled it down.

It wasn't until around 1 AM that he finally texted back.

I think I can handle that action. Haha. You're prob-ably in bed. Wish I was there. Sweet dreams. XOXO

She finished cleaning and was smoking cigarettes in her bed while drawing – something she hadn't done much of since getting clean.

Her sketch of the coastline was coming along nicely.

Not bad for being out of practice for a year.

It made her wonder why she'd ever stopped. Not that it had been a conscious decision. She just never seemed able to focus like she could on this particular evening. Her body didn't even feel like it needed sleep. Which was nice. She really didn't want to know where she would end up if she closed her eyes.

35

Cristina got her wish and didn't have to discover what dreams were waiting for her. She didn't sleep at all.

Surprisingly, staying up all night didn't make her feel all that bad. She still felt so full of energy when the sun started coming up, she skipped breakfast and walked down to the cliffs.

Having zero desire to climb down the stairs to where the water had almost carried her away, she instead found a flat boulder to sit on. From there, she smoked cigarettes and gazed out over the ocean, watching the sunrise, listening to the rhythmic pounding of waves below. It kind of reminded her of the drum circle, the way the sound connected her to the rest of the universe.

She thought about all the other people across the world who might be sitting on beaches at that very moment, hearing the same body of water crash against their particular piece of coast. The way it had since long before any of them were born, and as it would continue to do for long after they were all dead.

Thinking that way made the whole world feel vibrant. Alive.

Despite the challenges in front of her, Cristina promised herself she would do her best to meet them head-on.

***

The next couple of days weren't so bad. There were no nightmares. No crazy visions. Actually, Cristina hardly slept much at all until Wednesday, when she crashed for almost 12 hours straight.

It had been the strangest thing, staying up two nights in a row. But being no stranger to insomnia, Cristina decided to make the most of it.

So she spent much of those two days and nights going back over the case documents from her divorce. Reading them made her feel a lot better about what was going on. In her anxiety about it all, she'd almost forgotten just how supportive Judge Samantha Redding had been.

Cristina's lawyer was ecstatic when he'd discovered that a woman would preside over the case.

"They tend to be about a thousand times more sympathetic," he'd said.

And sympathetic she was. Throughout the entire trial – though Cristina remembered it hadn't actually been called that. During the proceeding, or hearing, or whatever it was, Judge Redding blasted Anthony again and again.

For being an abuser, a liar, a cheater, and once even for dozing off.

There was no sympathy at all for the fact his head was bandaged like an escaped mummy. At one point, she even called him, "a conniving rat bastard." Anthony didn't react. He only sat there with the same blank stare he carried with him the entire time they were in court. But even the seasoned Walden Chester III had been taken aback by the viciousness of the judge's comments.

Cristina's own lawyer had been kind of an asshole –

definitely in it only for the money – but he was also very good. Now, she found herself grateful to him for keeping such meticulous notes. She thought they would serve her well in this sham of a hearing coming up.

So did Dan.

"Call me Daniel in any legal setting," he told her when he came by to go over everything. "Daniel Davidson."

"And you really went to Harvard?" Cristina asked, curiosity winning out over her feeling of being impolite.

"Top of my class," he told her without so much as a smile. "But it's honestly not all it's cracked up to be. I mean, there are some smart people there, don't get me wrong. But there are a lot of jackasses, too. Rich kids who're there for the wrong reasons, like making money or impressing their overbearing parents."

"Was that you?" she blurted out.

"Yep," he answered plainly. "But I'm my own man now, and I certainly hope to stay that way. I wouldn't change a thing about my journey either. Not school. Not the drugs. It all made me who I am."

"Absolutely," she agreed. "I just hope we can get this whole thing over with as quickly as possible."

He nodded and said, "I'm not a family attorney. I studied corporate law, like most of the other people in my class. But this stuff isn't all that complicated when it comes down to it. I've gone over your documents, as well as some of the related case law around these sorts of decisions." He was getting more excited as he went on. "We won't know *exactly* what Anthony's claiming, as far as his rights to custody or that kind of thing, until Friday. But from what we *do* know, it seems obvious he's trying to make the case that you've relapsed. So that makes our biggest asset the fact you're *not* actively using any longer, which the drug test will show. Secondly, we have these case files, which clearly indicate a strong pattern of abuse on his part, as well as the previous Judge's very, um, clear feelings about him."

Dan sounded like he not only knew his stuff, but that he was taking her situation seriously. And he'd obviously been doing his homework.

Before leaving, he told her to dress conservatively, and to answer every question the judge asked her with absolute honesty.

36

According to the list that came with the summons, there were several drug testing places in Pleasure Point. Cristina called one of them and was told to come in any time. No appointment necessary.

When she showed up, she discovered the testing center was really no more than a small office in an out-of-the-way strip mall on the edge of town.

Walking inside was a lot different experience than getting tested after being released from The Camp when she was a teenager. Back then, Cristina had to check in with a probation officer, which required going through a metal detector, getting searched, and almost always being given an "additional pat down for security" by some greedy-eyed male guard. There never failed to be a great amount of concern for what she might smuggle into the building between, around, and under her sizable young breasts.

As far as she could tell, the strip mall place had only two employees. One man and one woman, both of whom wore blue hospital scrubs and sat behind a counter looking bored to death.

The woman walked Cristina back to a small bathroom with a doorless stall. She handed over a cup and watched Cristina pee into it. She also took a hair sample. Then made Cristina sign documents verifying, under penalty of perjury, that she was, in fact, Cristina

Rodriguez. That she was female. Her address was correct. And so on and so forth. All pretty standard stuff. The whole thing was over and done in about twenty minutes.

Cristina got out of there as fast as her feet would carry her.

On the way home, she stopped at a coffee shop. Besides having a bit of a tired, achy body, she was feeling pretty good about things. There were a lot of unknowns about the case, but at least she no longer felt totally alone. She had her secret weapon. The most unusual attorney she'd ever met: Mr. Danny Dee.

Sitting outside, drinking black coffee and smoking, a hoodie covering her head in the foggy afternoon, Cristina felt her phone buzz in her pocket.

"Hello?"

"Cristina Rodriguez."

"Speaking."

"Hello, Ms. Rodriguez. This is Jim Canfield with the FBI. Is this a good time?"

He sounded like he was trying hard not to be heard. Cristina imagined him huddled in a car, alone in some dark parking garage, holding an envelope full of documents he wasn't supposed to have.

Or maybe she'd seen too many movies.

He began with a few pleasantries, saying how her uncle was not only the kind of admirable businessman who made up the backbone of this country, but he was also a friend. He then went on to completely shock Cristina with a story she'd never heard. Agent Canfield said he owed her uncle an eternal debt of gratitude for saving one of his little girls when she ran into the street.

"Lucy would have been crushed by a garbage truck if Al hadn't reached out and grabbed her right at the last moment. My wife and I thank God every day that he was there."

Canfield wanted to make it clear to Cristina that this debt was the *only* reason he'd even agreed to speak with her about the case, an act he said could probably cost him his job.

"Needless to say, I'd appreciate it if you keep what we talk about off the record. Your uncle tells me that you want to set your mind at ease. That's all this is for."

Cristina agreed.

He said it was his understanding that she had two points of interest. The first being the criminal drug distribution network known as *New Horizon*. He told her that he himself had worked on a multi-year operation to apprehend the fugitive leader of the organization, and in that time he saw their brutality firsthand.

"My brother-in-law was one of the ATF agents who Charles Walters – AKA 'The High Priest' – burned alive. Mr. Walters became the de-facto head of the organization after taking over from the original founder. A man by the name of Jonathan Krauser, who himself disappeared sometime in the 1980's. It was believed that he died, but that was never confirmed.

"It was Walters who transformed the organization from its original incarnation as a relatively harmless, anti-society, hippy-cult that encouraged people to use LSD and smoke marijuana. Walters turned it into something much more dangerous. Something designed specifically to suck up disenchanted youth and get them hooked on hard drugs like heroin and meth. All for profit."

He added that the organization seemed to be experiencing a resurgence.

"They recently published a new version of their propaganda manual, although from what I've seen it mostly consists of the same malarkey about a coming collapse of society, and the need to embrace some kind of spiritual awakening through the use of drugs. The same basic garbage the group has been using for decades to lure in new recruits."

He ended that part of his speech with a stern warning.

"*New Horizon* is very dangerous and so are drugs. You don't want to live the life of a drug addict, Ms. Rodriguez. Trust me, I've seen what it does to people."

Cristina had to bite her cheek to suppress a laugh.

Canfield moved on to the next part of his presentation.

"Now, secondly, you also want to know about the disappearance and murder of Annie Stewart, correct?"

Cristina had been so deep in listening mode that she didn't answer right away.

"Hello?" he asked. "Are you still there, Ms. Rodriguez?"

"Yes, sorry. That's right about the case. I recently moved into the home the family lived in. Any information you can give me about what happened to them would really help give us some peace of mind."

Another pause.

He seemed momentarily lost for words.

It didn't last.

"Here's the thing. This one's a bit more delicate. Although I didn't work the case myself, like most people in the area I followed the events while it was going on. And the fact I have a couple of daughters myself made it that much more personal. Anyhow, I talked to a colleague of mine who *has* been actively working the case since the beginning."

Actively?

Canfield continued unprompted, "He says, and again I have to be careful with what I say here, he says there are still some ongoing concerns about what happened."

Cristina had, of course, read the article about the FBI questioning the police findings. But since she wanted to hear what Canfield was willing to volunteer, she decided not to mention it.

Instead she asked, "As in, what? The person who did it wasn't caught?"

"Perhaps. The conclusion drawn by the local PD was that the stepfather committed the murder, but there's always been some doubt as to whether or not that was the whole story. My colleague says that once the stepfather ended up dead too, there was significant pressure from the local business and political communities to push that story, despite there being a number of holes in it. Such as the fact no one was ever able to nail down a motive.

"As a matter of fact, everything seemed to point to the conclusion that Thomas Walker loved his stepdaughter very much. He treated her like his own child. Local police might have bought him as the culprit, perhaps helped along by the fact that having some kind of drug-cult killer on the loose is probably not the best thing business-wise for a town that brings in most of its revenue from family tourism . . ."

So there was a connection to the cult.

He added with pride, ". . . But we here at the FBI are a little harder to convince. We require a clear and provable motive. And our profiler basically said flat-out that there was no way Mr. Walker could have done something so horrible to this little girl. It just wasn't in him. So it's possible that the he didn't have anything to do with it, and was only set up to look like he did."

Cristina's heart raced. Her mind filled with a sudden sense of vulnerability.

"What can I do?" she asked, almost pleading. "I need to keep my baby girl safe."

A pause again.

"I didn't know you had a daughter, Ms. Rodriguez. Like I said before, I've got two, so I can understand your concern. Well . . . I'm not sure how much more I can tell you, but our profiler also says that whoever did this is likely either dead, or in jail for something else. Because people who do these kinds of crimes don't usually stop. In fact, they often only get more aggressive in their efforts. That being said, I'd be careful about who you trust."

DON'T TRUST HIM.

The scrawled words flashed into her mind.

Canfield continued, "Ms. Rodriguez, Pleasure Point, for all its beauty as a tourist destination, is a well-known gathering place for lowlifes and deviants, especially in its more rundown areas. And for your own safety, I don't want to give you the impression that the person, or people, who hurt that little girl aren't still out there. They could be simply biding their time. There *is* such a thing as a patient criminal. And if it's the case that the perpetrator is still on the loose, it's likely to be someone who's had a traumatic past. To the point that, despite what they might show on the outside, they're unable to feel empathy toward other human beings."

Cristina said, "You mentioned the killer might have had a cult connection. Any more you could add to that would be appreciated. Off the record, of course."

The longest pause yet. A full thirty seconds. She realized that maybe he hadn't intended to divulge that part of the case. Cristina was about to speak again when Canfield's voice finally returned.

"Ms. Rodriguez, I wish I could go into greater detail.

Like I said, I owe your uncle a lot. But I've already given you more than I should have . . . though I will say one last thing. And again, I shouldn't be doing this. But certain details about the crime scene were not publicly released, including items found near the body, and communications made by the killer, both of which would seem to indicate some kind of connection to the *New Horizon* cult." His voice suddenly became more lecturing and authoritative. "Now, I'll remind you, that if you ever tell anyone what we've discussed here to-day, I'll not only deny it, but I'll be forced to bring a great deal of difficulty into your life."

She wasn't sure what *that* meant. Except, she did. Same cop intimidation crap as every other law enforcement officer she'd ever dealt with. But she also realized he was probably just trying to cover his own ass. He'd given her a lot and didn't have to. For that, she was grateful.

Cristina told him so before ending the call.

She set her phone on the coffee shop's metal table, closed her eyes, and rubbed at the dull pain in her temples. There was so much to process. Caufield had given her some interesting new information, but she again felt like she had more questions than when she started.

37

That night, Cristina stood in her kitchen, staring blankly at the last few chocolates. She wanted to eat them but her stomach said no. So into the trash they went.

Her whole body had felt progressively worse ever since waking up from her sleep-a-thon. Now her skin itched. Her forearms and back felt like little worms were hatching underneath her skin, trying to wiggle their way to the surface.

Great, all I need is to get the flu right as I have to appear in court.

The only thing she could bring herself to do was curl up in bed with every blanket she could find. She lay there sweating and freezing at the same time. It eerily reminded her of the first encounter she had with shooting meth and heroin together.

She'd been hanging out with a skinny (but psychotically ruthless) gangbanger people called Muerto. By then, she'd already shot smack a couple times and loved it, but the idea of combining it with meth scared the shit out of her.

When Muerto suggested they do just that, Cristina at first tried to play it off like some purist connoisseur. He kept insisting, telling her how good it would make her feel.

"Like angels kissing your whole body, baby," he

said, standing there in his living room wearing only a pair of boxers, body covered with tattoos, waving a dripping needle in the air.

After a few more coy refusals, he started to get angry. Then quiet. At that point, she knew he was going to start hitting her if she didn't go along. So she reluctantly stuck out her arm, trying not to show how scared she was as he pricked her skin with the needle and slowly pumped a stream of liquid into her vein.

The concoction traveled through her bloodstream toward her heart, gently warming her at first. An explosion of bliss shot out from her chest, moving quickly throughout her body, all the way to the tips of her fingers and toes. That was the heroin. Then, just as she thought she was going to go blurry and pass out, the speed hit. Her entire being, all the way down to what Tío Alberto would call her soul, took off like a rocket ship. She felt so beautiful. Completely at peace. And confident. Like she could do anything.

For the next several hours, she had the strange feeling of being distant from her own body. She barely even noticed when Muerto flipped up the short, yellow sundress she was wearing and slipped aside her panties. He sat there humping her like some rabid dog for what seemed like hours. It probably was. She couldn't feel a thing. Her body and mind and soul were entirely somewhere else.

Of course, when she came down the next day, her whole universe swung like a pendulum back toward the opposite extreme. She went from absolute joy to feeling like the essence of life itself was being sucked out of her by an evil vacuum, leaving nothing behind but pain and ugliness.

Then there was the vomiting and diarrhea. And clogged sinuses filled with a dark-green mucous that drained down her throat like someone had turned on a faucet, gagging her to the point that she threw up even more.

That was the price of the needle, though. Ultimate high and ultimate lows.

Whatever it was she was feeling now – the flu or food poisoning or whatever – wasn't half as bad as coming down off shooting dope. She did her best to comfort herself by remembering that fact. It wasn't working particularly well.

All her body wanted to do was sleep.

She called Anise and wished her goodnight. Then, hoping to keep away the nightmares, she lit a new candle she'd bought earlier in the day at Walgreens – a duplicate of the one her uncle had given her.

Seeing the image of the Virgen de Guadalupe etched onto the glass reminded her that Father Antonio was supposed to come by in the morning. She wanted to call and cancel. There hadn't been anymore bad dreams, anyway. Not since the one with Anise. It kind of felt like the whole exercise would be a waste of both their time. And if it really was the flu she was coming down with, she certainly didn't look forward to trying to remember all the little intricacies of interacting with a Catholic priest, especially while trying not to throw up all over him.

But she fell asleep before she could pick up her phone.

38

That night, she did dream.

Drawn by the unseen force, she found herself standing in front of the hall closet. Only, this time there was nothing there when she opened the door. At least, no bodies. No boxes either.

She rubbed her eyes, and when she again looked at the back wall of the closet, a small door had appeared. One that seemed built for a child.

Cristina got down on her hands and knees to crawl through the door and into the small tunnel beyond. In the distance, she could see a bright light. She was frightened, but continued making her way through the cramped space, unable to stop. The light became so intense that she had to shield her eyes with one hand, forcing her to limp along like a three-legged dog.

After inching forward, she finally reached the threshold of the dazzling aura and crawled through. She was immediately overcome by a feeling of peace and tranquility. For a moment, the purest form of happiness she'd ever known. More than any drug could have ever possibly offered.

Then came the sensation of falling down the side of a steep incline. It wasn't frightening or painful, though. It was joyous, reminding her of when she and her childhood friend Nick used to roll down the grassy hill at the park in their neighborhood.

The falling stopped and the light vanished. She was left sitting by herself in the dark. Compared to the happy contentment she'd felt a moment earlier, the world now seemed hollow and empty. A part of her was angry for having that sense of bliss taken away.

Then the landscape around her slowly brightened, like the stage in a play. She found herself somewhere in the mountains above Pleasure Point. She recognized the trees, and the smell of the ocean as it mixed with the clean earthiness of dust and rocks.

She found a path through a thicket of trees. On the other side was an unfamiliar house. Its exterior was painted red, but the color had faded like an old shirt. Two giant redwood trees stood over the house. The gutters were full of dried needles. The roof covered in them. The porch and front yard, too.

The entire scene felt both familiar and unfamiliar at the same time.

She walked closer, toward an old car parked in the yard. A model with big fins that looked like it hadn't been driven in decades. The front grille was rusted and detached on one side, like a set of dead, decaying lips.

Cristina entered the yard and felt cold. Unwelcome.

That's when she awoke to the sound of someone knocking on the door.

39

The blocky red numbers on her digital clock said it was exactly 9 AM.

Did I really sleep for 12 hours again?

The knocking continued, growing louder. She ran to the bathroom and threw on her robe. At least she felt about a thousand times better than she had when she crawled into bed. Her head still hurt a little, but her stomach felt stable. And her skin didn't itch anymore.

When she answered the door, Father Antonio stood waiting, his dark eyes smooth and patient behind square glasses. He wore jeans and the priest's traditional black shirt and white collar.

She remembered him, of course. He'd been at Tío Alberto's church – which she supposed was technically her church as well – since Cristina was a little girl. He oversaw her First Communion.

But that Father Antonio had been a much younger man.

He still wasn't elderly by any stretch of the imagination. Maybe five years older than Cristina's uncle. But he'd certainly aged since the last time she saw him. His well-trimmed hair had turned almost entirely grey, and was slightly disappearing at the hairline. The black mustache she vaguely remembered him having was now a full beard. The hair on his face still held onto a few solid patches of black, but it was well on its way to being the same color as the hair on his head.

"Hello, Cristina," he said warmly. "Are you feeling, OK? If this is a bad time, I can come back another day."

She tightened her robe and pulled back her hair, still trying to blink sleep from her eyes.

"No, I'm sorry. I wasn't feeling well last night and overslept. Come on in."

She stepped out of the way and he entered.

"Please, have a seat," she added. "Just give me two minutes and I'll be right back."

She ran upstairs and changed, throwing on jeans, a bra, and a plain black t-shirt.

The rush of blood from moving so fast made her head throb.

"Can I offer you something to drink?" she asked, coming down the stairs, pulling her hair into a ponytail. "I was going to have coffee."

"Sure. That would be great. If it's not too much trouble. A little cream. A little sugar."

She put water on to boil and came back into the living room.

"Thanks for coming by," she said, even if she still wasn't entirely sure why he was there.

"You're welcome, Cristina. It's quite nice to see you after all these years."

It felt like there might be a slight coating of judgement in his voice – the kind a dentist has when talking to a patient about flossing. But it could have just been her lingering headache making her sensitive.

"You too, Father. I'm sure you're a busy man, so I'm grateful for your time."

"Ah, well, we all must make time to do God's work, my child." He smiled. A polite, well-practiced look. They exchanged a few more pleasantries and then, with coffee cup in hand, Father Antonio removed his glasses. His eyes looked oddly small without them.

"So, tell me, what's been happening with you. Your uncle says you've been experiencing some . . . disturbances since you moved into this lovely home."

For about 15 minutes, she told him the history of the house, and about her dreams. She was certain that's all they were, she said. They had to be. She didn't think there was anything supernatural about it. It was just that they seemed so real. And with what happened to Annie and her family, it was maybe better to be safe than sorry.

"If there is some kind of spirit," she started and then made a correction, "or soul, I just want them to be at peace."

Father Antonio nodded along, sipping his coffee and occasionally pursing his lips while Cristina spoke.

For some reason that she didn't quite understand, the act of telling him about what had happened was already making her feel better. She said as much.

He didn't show a reaction, except to fold his hands and sit back in his chair with one foot propped on the other leg.

"Well, yes. Perhaps. Perhaps. Tell me though, Cristina, what is your relationship with God like right now?"

Somehow she knew a question like that was coming.

"Well, I think over the course of the past year I've been as spiritually sound as I've ever been in my life. I haven't been to church lately, but I do regularly attend what I would consider spiritual gatherings."

"12-step meetings, I presume you mean?"

"Yes," she said, a little surprised he knew. "It's really changed my life, too. And taught me a lot about how not to be the selfish person I was in the past."

She meant those things, of course. But as the words came out, she couldn't help feeling as though they were a bit rehearsed. Like at least part of her was saying what she thought he wanted to hear, and not necessarily what she fully believed. In reality, she had learned a lot. Had grown so much. But she felt like she still had a long, long way to go.

"Your uncle told me of your recent successes. I'm glad to hear it. We were worried about you for many years. Unfortunately, far too many of our young people have left the flock, searching for answers in places I'm afraid we can't reach."

The openness and understanding in his words sounded strange to Cristina's ears. She'd always seen church – and religion generally – as being made up mostly of people who sat around judging others, all while committing sins of their own without a second thought. Her addiction recovery work had taught her, however, that the relationship people have with God (or a "higher power" as they liked to say in the 12-step rooms) was really a personal choice.

"The only thing you need to realize about your higher power is that you ain't it," Michelle told her when they first met. "You need to stop trying to control everything in the world. When you learn how to do that, then you can start working on the things that you do have power over, like your own actions."

Cristina said, "Thanks, Father. I feel lucky to have found a path to follow."

"Good. Good. I know you haven't had the easiest upbringing. Are you aware that I knew your mother?"

Her eyes perked up. That was definitely a surprise.

"No, I didn't know that."

He looked away, staring upward, searching for a distant memory.

He found it and said, "Yes, indeed. We were schoolmates. I was a shy young boy sitting in the front row of class, and she was the feisty young beauty in the back, always passing notes and getting into trouble. But we were actually quite close for a couple of years. Both of us walked the same route to school, you see."

Cristina tried to imagine her mother as a child, but couldn't. She'd barely ever even seen her as an adult. All she could picture in her mind was Anise, walking alongside a little boy who was an exact miniature version of the man sitting in front of her now, all the way down to the greying beard.

"She even saved my life once," he continued, still gazing off toward the past. "We were on our way to school one day, when a van drove up and parked next to us. A strange man said he needed help finding a lost dog. I, filled to the brim with trustful naiveté, nearly jumped into his vehicle without thinking twice." He laughed distantly. "Your mother, however, would have none of it. 'What's the dog's name?' she asked. 'What color is he?' 'How old?' She berated the man with these questions until he simply closed the door and drove off."

Father Antonio returned his hard-to-read eyes back to Cristina.

He added, "I see a lot of that fire in you, too, Cristina. The heart of the lion, some might say. Personally, I would call it the strength of God." He ran his fingers over his beard for a moment. "This may sound strange coming from a priest, but I think God wants us to question His universe. I think when Jesus came to live here on Earth, His message was that we should never take what we are given. He told us that we should always be free to seek out the 'why.' And that doing so will never make God love us any less. For His love is eternal and unconditional."

He finished the last sip of coffee and set his mug down on the thrift-store table.

"Anyhow, I'm rambling I suppose. I do that from

time to time. My point is, despite the fact you've been away from the church for a number of years, that doesn't mean you've been forgotten, or even necessarily that you've gone astray. I want to encourage you to keep doing what you're doing. And, hopefully, when you're ready, you'll come back to see us."

He smiled again, and this time Cristina felt sincere warmth. Perhaps it was the mention of her mother, but she couldn't help thinking Father Antonio had the look of a proud father – a look Cristina had always dreamed of receiving.

"Thanks," she said, holding back a sudden strong wave of emotion. "Thanks for your kindness, and for what you do to make the world a better place."

"It's God who makes the world a better place, Cristina. I only try my best to listen to His will. That's all any of us can do. Now, shall we have a look around? See if we can't chase away some ghosts?"

He stood and pulled three things from his bag. A rosary, which he wrapped around the fingers of his right hand. A small, plastic bottle of clear liquid, which Cristina assumed to be holy water. And, lastly, a long piece of white cloth that she couldn't remember the name of. He draped it over his shoulders.

Together, they walked through the house. In each room, Father Antonio squirted a bit of holy water in the corners and in the doorway, saying something in Latin as he did.

Nothing spectacular happened.

Finally, he performed the same rite on the hallway closet.

"Remember Cristina, never take the world at face value. The will of God is not always obvious, and sometimes it takes asking questions to understand what He wants from us." Father Antonio looked away thoughtfully and then back at her. "But never forget, as well, that God helps those who help themselves." He touched the rosary to her forehead. "Be blessed child, and may you find peace in service to your fellow man, and in the glory and grace of Almighty God." He lowered the rosary and smiled. "Do you know the Lord's Prayer?"

"Of course!"

They said it together, holding hands in the living room.

If the teenage Cristina had been watching, there would have been plenty of snide remarks and laughter.

It's not like she was about to hang a picture of the Pope in her bedroom any time soon, but she did feel a surprising sense of security in the fact that she had access to a community of people who, at least judging by Father Antonio and Tío Alberto, were deeply aware of what it means to be a good human being.

The priest said his goodbyes, giving her his card and telling her to call anytime, even if she just needed someone to talk to. He waved and smiled through tight lips as he drove his Toyota Camry away from the house and down the driveway.

The morning fog had burned off and the sun was out. Cristina decided to walk down to the cliffs and think. The tide was rising and the size of the waves had become fearsome. The rocky pathway she'd taken with Jack was wet, but not yet flooded. From the safety of the cliff's edge, she watched the water and listened to the waves thunder.

40

Cristina was picking out her outfit for court the next day. Then she planned to go to bed early. She still didn't feel all that great and wanted to make sure she got plenty of sleep.

The phone buzzed on the dresser.

She thought it might be Casey, but when she picked it up the display said UNKNOWN.

"Hello?"

Nothing.

Someone was there. She could hear them breathing.

"Hello?" She repeated.

"Cristina."

Her heart rushed into her throat so fast she could barely speak.

"Anthony? What the fuck? What are you doing calling me? How the hell did you even get my number?"

"You should know by now that I have my ways. I'll always be able to find you."

"I'm going to hang up and call the cops." He snickered his familiar dismissive laugh and said, "Yah, OK, well I'm on an untraceable line. So I guess it would be your word against mine, wouldn't it?"

"Fuck you. What do you want?"

"I just want you to know that I'm going to win, Cristina. No matter what I have to do, I'm going to take Anise away from you. And then you'll know what it feels like to be alone. The same way you made me feel."

"You'll never get her. You're going to look stupid tomorrow. And if you ever come near us, I swear to god I'll fucking kill you, you piece of shit. I'm not afraid of you anymore."

"You should be, Cristina. You really should be."

He ended the call before she could say anything else.

As hard as she tried to stay strong, she couldn't keep from crying.

41

Cristina expected the hearing to take place in a formal court setting. But the room the clerk's assistant led them to looked more like the kind of place a corporate board would meet. The grey-walled space was empty except for a long, black table surrounded by office chairs.

They were told to sit on one side. Dan set his brief-case on the table before pulling Cristina's chair out for her.

Her jaw had dropped that morning when he picked her up at her house in a sparkling-clean, blue BMW.

"Wow," she'd said. "I thought you gave up all your money."

"Most of it. But it's amazing how far a little can go."

She really couldn't imagine, actually. Aside from what she'd received in the settlement, which almost all went to the house and expenses, Cristina's bank account had never had more than a hundred bucks in it. Ever. But she knew what he meant. Sort of.

After the shock of his new look had worn off, she realized Dan looked quite handsome in his freshly pressed suit. Armani, she recognized. His hair was washed and brushed. Face shaved clean, letting off the faint hint of an expensive aftershave.

Cristina dressed in a grey skirt and black blouse – the most professional outfit she could put together from her collection of clothes, which, as nice as they were, had mostly been purchased for their sex appeal. Her hair was parted down the middle, hanging past her shoulders, no bangs, held straight to either side by a hidden network of bobby pins. She also wore heels, something she hadn't done in more than a year. After wearing them for so long (another one of Anthony's rules), she had to laugh at how the first few steps made her feel like a wobbly baby deer.

"Remember," Dan said as they sat waiting at the table. "Let me do the talking, and when it comes time for you to answer questions, be absolutely honest. Don't try to leave anything out or tell any half-truths. Lawyers typically don't ask questions they don't already know the answer to. If things get heated, or if Anthony lies, *do not* speak directly to him. Resist the urge. Let him have his say. If there's something we need to clarify or call him out on, we can do it later. Got it?"

She did, especially since he'd already gone over it twice during their 45-minute car ride over the mountains and into the city. During that time, they also discussed Anthony's phone call. After considering it carefully, Dan told her they should refrain from mentioning anything to the judge. The lack of proof meant bringing it up would likely only result in a useless back-and-forth.

Dan seemed to have done nothing but think about the case for the past week. He knew the facts better than she did.

Their main point of emphasis was going to be the drug test, the results of which had been sent directly to the judge. Dan wanted to show that she was not only a fit mother, but that the entire proceeding should be dismissed as an attempt to libel her. He noted that making the latter point would also be the first step in suing Anthony for damages later on.

After about ten minutes sitting in the conference room, the door opened. In walked Anthony. He looked Cristina's way, grinned, and then turned to stare straight forward as he took a seat. Her eyes went immediately to the side of his head. A large scar had left a blank spot in his otherwise perfect, light-brown hair.

Gone was the spacey look he'd carried with him during their divorce case and his criminal trial. In its place was the sharp, cocky glare she'd always found both attractive and obnoxious. He wore a sharp grey suit, red tie, and the gold Rolex his father bought him for his twenty-first birthday.

Sitting down next to Anthony – but only after dusting the chair off with a silk handkerchief – was Walden Chester III, Esq. A tall, thin man with a full head of immaculately styled grey hair. His suit was navy, the tie a bold yellow. He displayed a similar cockiness to Anthony's, but hid it well under a calm demeanor and a near-constant politician smile.

Walden Chester III neatly folded his hands on the table. Anthony did the same. Neither of them said a word.

The silence broke only when the judge entered, prompting them all to stand.

Judge Peterson was a short, nearly-bald white man with thick, round glasses that were exactly the same shape as his head. He wore a flowing black robe. It did little to hide the girth of his belly. He introduced himself, shook hands with everyone in the room, and told them to sit.

He placed a large folder with a string wrapped around it on the table. Cristina thought he looked like a teacher about to hand back assignments. He unwound the binding and removed several documents, stacking the papers on the table in front of him. Topping the pile was a previously-sealed envelope that had been cut open.

"Hello, everyone," he began. "Welcome to family court. Both of you have been here before." He peered sternly over his glasses at Cristina, then at Anthony. "So I won't waste your time with a lot of banter. Basically, we're here because Mr. Stevens is making the case that the circumstances of Ms. Rodriguez's custody of daughter, Anise, should be revisited."

He cleared his throat and continued, "When I first saw this case on my docket, I must admit to having been a bit perturbed by it, given the fact that you, Mr. Stevens, are an abuser." The judge stared at Anthony, who didn't react. "However, given the results of this test." He held the envelope in the air. "I'm now *gravely* concerned for the wellbeing of your daughter, Ms. Rodriguez."

Cristina snuck a glance at Dan after he visibly shifted in his chair.

The judge slid a stapled stack of papers from the envelope. He scratched a small patch of hair on the side of his head.

"Positive for methamphetamine," he said plainly, flipping the paper over and holding it up for Cristina to see. "What do you have to say for yourself, Ms. Rodriguez?"

She wanted to scream. Not just because the judge's words felt like a slap in the face. No, she was angry. At Anthony, whose balls she desperately wanted to slice open. And at herself for being so stupid. She knew exactly what had happened.

The chocolates. It had to be. You ate them and you were up all night. Enjoying the hell out of it, too. Weren't you Cristina? Cleaning the house. Doing art. You know what? I bet if you really thought hard about the whole thing, you'd have to admit that a part of you knew, didn't you? But you just kept on eating

those damn things anyway. Didn't you? Then you felt
sick. That wasn't the flu at all. That was a damn
comedown.

All she could do was picture herself leaping over the
desk and wrapping her fingers around Anthony's
throat.

"Ms. Rodriguez," the judge repeated. "Do you have
anything to say?"

"I didn't take any drugs," she said, biting her bottom lip, trying to stay calm. "At least not willingly. On
Sunday night, a box of chocolates was delivered to my
house without a name on it. I thought they were from
my boyfriend, so I ate them. I spent the next two days
awake, and then felt what I can now recognize as with-
drawal."

"And you didn't report this?" Walden Chester III
asked, speaking to her as though she was the lowest
form of scum on the planet. "You received this 'alleged'
box of drug-laced chocolates and didn't say *anything*
to *anyone* about it?"

She looked at Dan. He nodded, still looking slightly
worried, though less so than a few seconds earlier.

Cristina said, "I didn't realize what was happening.
I've had trouble sleeping before. And when I started
feeling sick, I honestly thought it was the flu." She
tightened her jaw, raised her chin into the air, and kept
talking. "Judge Peterson, Your Honor, I am *not* on
drugs. Not anymore. I've been clean for more than a
year, and I've worked *really* hard to stay that way. I go
to meetings regularly and work with a sponsor. I—"

"—When was the last time you attended a 12-step
meeting, Ms. Rodriguez?" asked Walden Chester III.

Her head slumped a bit.

"About a month ago."

"A month?" The slick lawyer raised his hands in

forced disbelief. "Does that sound like 'regular' attendance to you?"

"No. I guess not. But I've been in a new place. I just haven't gotten settled in yet. Before I moved, though, I was going almost every day."

The lawyer looked at her skeptically. "OK, Ms. Rodriguez, if you say so. And how would you explain these?"

Walden Chester III removed several photographs from his briefcase and placed them onto the table. The pictures were of her at the drum circle, holding a joint in her hand, laughing and swaying her body like some stoned hippy.

Cristina was mortified.

She told him, "Someone handed me that. I was just passing it on. I swear. I *did not* smoke it."

Her voice had cracked. She opened the bottle of water in front of her and gulped half of it down.

"Your Honor," Dan said. "Given that the test does not show any evidence of marijuana use, assuming of course that *is* marijuana in the photograph and not simply tobacco, it seems obvious that this piece of evidence is immaterial to these proceedings."

Walden Chester III tried to ask Cristina another question, but the judge held up a hand to stop him.

"That's enough. This isn't a courtroom, and you aren't cross examining her. I'll ask the questions here, thank you very much." Once it was clear who was in charge, he straightened his robe and continued. "Now, normally I'd say you're lying to me, Ms. Rodriguez. But given what I've read in the case file about the way Mr. Stevens conducted himself in your previous relationship, I'm inclined to give you some benefit of the doubt."

He paused and looked around the room, as if to make sure everyone was following along.

Then, he asked, "Ms. Rodriguez, are you still in possession of these chocolates?"

"Yes," she said. "There are a few left. I threw them in the trashcan when I started feeling sick, but they're still in there."

"Good. Then I'm going to send you home with a court officer who will collect them." He turned to Anthony, who'd lost most of his cocky demeanor. "And, Mr. Stevens, if I discover that what she's saying is true, you aren't going to be able to buy your way out of trouble this time."

"Your Honor," Walden Chester III said. "This is all quite speculative. We'd like to move to suspend custody of the daughter until this matter is resolved. Sir, my client is in fear for his daughter's life. All he wants is to protect her."

"I'm sure." The judge sat back in his chair and again scratched the puff of hair on the side of his head. "You think I haven't seen it all, counselor? You think I haven't seen the way men in this system get away with murder? Sometimes literally." He let out a long sigh. "I've been doing this for three decades now, and trust me when I say I *have* seen it all. And I for one am damn glad that the times are finally changing so these sick sons-of-bitches can't keep getting away with it. Now, unless you want me to completely dismiss this proceeding right now, I suggest you rethink your last comment and withdraw it."

For the first time since he sat down, Anthony's expensive attorney stopped smiling. He looked like someone had just slapped him in the face.

Cristina bit the inside of her cheek to keep from smiling.

Judge Peterson began collecting his things and added, "Thank you ladies and gentlemen. If need be, we'll reconvene this matter pending investigation into the questionable confections. For now, all custody matters pertaining to this case will remain unchanged. Ms. Rodriguez, please see the clerk. She'll assign an officer to escort you home. Until then, you aren't to leave the building."

They all stood again when the judge did.

Cristina remained stone-faced as Anthony walked out. He was now obviously upset. For just the slightest moment, he shot a piercing stare her way. It was likely imperceptible to anyone else in the room, but in that short period of time, his face contorted with vengeful spite. The look of a spoiled child who has been told no. She hated to admit it, but that glare still frightened her, like a kid whose father has come home drunk on Friday night looking for someone to take out the week's accumulated anger on.

42

In the clerk's office, Cristina and Dan sat waiting for an officer. They were told it would be "just a little while." In reality, more than two hours went by before a short female cop came out wearing a pantsuit.

In a formal police tone, the woman introduced herself as Detective Washburn, an investigator for the family court, specializing in cases of domestic abuse. It was her job to examine the crime scene and collect any available evidence. In particular, the alleged chocolates, which she said would be tested – both for the presence of methamphetamine, but also for fingerprints or any other indication of where they may have come from. Once everything had been processed, it would be up to Judge Peterson as to how the case would proceed.

Dan told Cristina he would meet her at the house.

The two women walked through a series of hallways and into a secure garage, where they got into an unmarked police cruiser.

Although Cristina had on dress clothes and was sitting in the front seat, hearing the crackle of the police radio brought back memories of getting busted as a teenager. She suddenly remembered the feeling of her aching shoulder after it had been almost ripped out of its socket by an overzealous cop who "didn't appreciate the attitude" Cristina had shown him. She could almost taste the coppery blood dripping from her lip after she'd been tossed into the back of his car, hands cuffed behind her, face slammed into the hard-plastic seat.

It was a strange feeling to have the cops on her side for once. At least, she *hoped* they would be. It was hard to believe that her future, and the future of her daughter, rested on a few small pieces of chocolate sitting near the top of her kitchen trashcan.

The ride to Pleasure Point began with Officer Washburn gathering some information about Cristina and her relationship with Anthony. For the most part, the questions she asked weren't unpleasant, and at times her tone was even sympathetic.

How old was Cristina?

How about her daughter?

How long were she and Anthony married?

And so forth.

All those were easy to answer.

What wasn't so simple to talk about was *how* the two had met. Cristina had worked hard to block out that part of her past. It was, after all, the darkest period of her entire life. But, as buried as Cristina thought the memories were, they returned to her in perfect, vivid detail as soon as she began to talk.

43

Cristina had been staying in the same place for about three months, which was an eternity as far as living in squats went. The spot wasn't too bad either, all things considered. At one point in time, it must have been some kind of an office building. There were still rows of abandoned cubicles set up. Most of them were now moldy and chewed by rats, but they at least offered some semblance of privacy.

There were about ten regulars, half of them guys and half of them gals, made up of a wide range of ages. The youngest was a 14-year-old named Cassandra, who everyone called "Shadow." On any given night, this core group was joined by somewhere between ten and twenty other "randoms" – people who stayed for a day or two and then moved on.

What brought them all together was a love of needles. There was plenty of sharing syringes happening, but luckily Cristina was never dumb or desperate enough to stoop that low. By that point in her life, she already knew of at least one person – an ex-boyfriend everyone called Muerto – who'd ended up with HIV that way. So she always went to the needle exchange to get fresh rigs whenever she needed them.

The space smelled like most squats. A ripe combination of sweat, mildew, and highly-concentrated piss. There were a few dirty mattresses, mostly used as a space for people to pass out after they got high. The regulars each had a "room," which was really just one of the cubicles, where they stored clothes and other belongings.

Not that anyone had much.

The vibe was pretty mellow, for the most part. There was some moody bickering, especially between one couple who got into it almost every night, mostly about who was cheating on who. But, all-in-all, people sort of looked out for one another.

In so much as anyone can trust an active junky.

The living situation worked as long as the drugs stayed flowing.

To that end, there was a certain arrangement at the squat, one Cristina couldn't remember having ever been spoken out loud. Nonetheless, it existed. The guys were in charge of making sure no one came in and jacked the place or otherwise started trouble. They also sometimes stole stuff that could be easily pawned. Things like cellphones and copper piping.

The girls were the real moneymakers, though.

Of course, employment options are rather limited when you're shooting heroin and meth into your body all day, every day.

Really, there were only two choices: robbing and prostitution.

A couple of the girls were really good at the first line of work. They would put on their best clothes, take the bus downtown, and find either a tourist or some other clueless-looking guy in a suit. Once they identified a mark, the girl (or girls if they decided to work in a group) would follow him until he was alone.

Next, she approached the guy and casually began to flirt. It usually didn't take long before she could get him alone in a bathroom or a car or whatever.

Then, out came the knife.

Any kind of struggle was rare, if the mark had been chosen wisely. It's amazing what the sight of a blade a few inches from a guy's manhood can do. If the girl *hadn't* chosen a good target though – usually because she was jonesing so hard she forgot about being cautious – the guy might try to fight. Then it became a choice between using the knife or flat-out running.

Cristina didn't particularly like robbing people. She wasn't afraid of defending herself, but she hated the idea of having to be purposefully violent.

Besides, she'd long-since become comfortable trading her body for what she needed. It was easy for her to slip into a state of mind that allowed her not to care what a trick did to her. After a while, and with enough dope in her system, it was all the same anyway. Wherever he wanted to stick it. Whatever he wanted her to do. None of it really made a difference.

On top of that, even as a full-blown junky, she still looked pretty good, which allowed her to make more money than the girls who had sores and rashes all over themselves. At least once she figured out the game.

But she didn't start off making that much.

At first, her approach was simple: pick a street corner wearing a short skirt and wait to get picked up. It usually didn't take long.

Once in a car, she told the trick to drive around to an alley she used. There, they got into the back seat, or she would wedge herself between two garbage dumpsters and take it from behind.

She almost never had to get totally naked. It was simple enough to hike up her skirt and be ready to go. Panties were nothing but a waste of time. Once the guy was done – usually no more than five or ten minutes – she took his cash and went back around the corner to find the next customer.

During that time, she had to do a dozen or more

guys to earn enough cash so she could stay high for a few days. Sometimes she could make that much last up to a week, depending on how many people she decided to share her stash with. But never any longer. Dope was really her only expense. She never had much of an appetite. And when she did eat, her diet consisted mainly of forcing herself to eat a McDouble, or a bag of Fritos from the liquor store. The only time she ate normally was when someone had weed. It was the only thing that gave her an appetite. That was rare, though. Most of the people she spent time around treated smoking pot like a joke and a waste of money.

With the right mindset and enough dope, working the streets was easy cash.

But not always.

Every once in a while, some guy drove off without paying. Surprisingly though, most of the tricks were pretty good about it. And Cristina came to look upon those who weren't as a cost of doing business.

Not that she would let them go willingly. She wasn't above getting crazy, even if she only had to actually cut someone once. A little scratch on the hand, really. The jerk coughed the cash up quick, too.

On top of the cheapskates, she had more than a few men who thought it was fun to rough her up. But by that time, getting hit was something she'd become numb to. So she usually just let it happen, knowing that struggling would only make it worse.

But the real threat turning tricks on street corners wasn't the abusers or the guys who decided they no longer wanted to pay for the load they just got rid of.

What Cristina feared most were the pimps. The first time one of them caught an independent girl working one of "their" corners, she would be lucky if she got away with just a warning. More likely they would beat her ass, and probably take a taste of her for good measure. The second time, she was likely to wind up with a bullet in her head, tossed in the dumpster to be taken away with the rest of the trash.

Eventually, Cristina realized she didn't need to work the street anymore. Even though she'd been shooting meth and heroin for a couple years at that point, she was still a young, curvy Latina with a pretty face and a smoking body.

Maybe it was the Fritos.

After having to hide in a dumpster one day to avoid a pimp with a baseball bat, she decided to steal a couple of nice cocktail dresses from the mall so she could start working the bars downtown.

These places were mostly filled with bankers, managers of tech startups, that kind of thing. Big shots at their day jobs, these guys were interested in surprisingly similar fantasies. They loved having a little brown-skinned girl spank them and tell them they were worthless. They wanted her to fuck them up the ass with a black rubber-cock, while they screamed about how scared they were and what bad little boys they'd been.

To Cristina it was kind of weird, but they paid well. And it sure beat getting rammed up against an alley wall that still stank of drunken vomit, or worrying about a pimp rolling up on her with a shotgun because she was on "his" corner.

It was in one such high-end bar that she met Anthony.

He was by himself, sitting in a booth drinking Jameson straight. He was much more attractive than the typical guy she approached. So much so that, for the first time in longer than she could remember, she actually felt turned on. He had a slim, fit physique. Full head of hair. Confident, almost cocky smile. Gorgeous blue eyes.

Everything about him screamed success.

They started talking and he treated her well, like a gentleman, even when he found out she wasn't hitting on him just for the fun of it.

After a few drinks, they went back to his condo, which wasn't too far from the bar. They did thick lines of coke and soaked his silk sheets with sweat. She even came, something that hadn't happened in years.

Before putting Cristina in a cab, he told her he wanted to make it a regular thing. He even gave her an extra cellphone he had sitting in a desk drawer, saying she could use it for whatever she wanted, as long as she picked up his calls.

After a week, she still hadn't heard from him. She was contemplating trading the phone to her dealer for a bag when it finally rang.

He said he wanted to meet her. Not just for sex, though. He wanted dinner. And a movie. Or whatever else she wanted to do.

In other words, he wanted to take her on a date.

She was really apprehensive about the whole thing. If this guy was looking for a girlfriend, she knew he was going to be pretty disappointed. At that point in her life, the only boyfriend she needed had a pointy metal tip, one she used to inject liquid-heaven into her veins. But she figured she might as well take the guy for whatever she could while his interest was there.

To her surprise, she actually had a pretty good time. They went to a nice Italian restaurant and had ice cream afterward. They didn't even have actual sex. Just lines of coke in his car before she gave him a blow-job. Then he dropped her off at the bus stop with a purse full of cash.

The next day, he called again.

And the day after that.

He always paid her. More than she asked, too. Enough money that she could afford a room away from the squat *and* a steady flow of dope. She didn't even have to bother with any other tricks.

They always ended the night with some kind of sex. After which she would go back to her dingy, pay-by-the-week motel, get high all night, and draw in her sketchpad while she waited for his next call.

Soon, she was having a hard time figuring out where the fantasy ended and her feelings began. What's more, she started to feel like she didn't *want* to know.

One night, they'd just finished having sex. Great sex, as usual. And instead of calling her a cab or grabbing his coat so he could drop her off, he handed her a small plastic bag from Rite Aid. She figured it was lube or condoms. But when she dug into it, she saw that it wasn't either of those things.

It was a toothbrush.

Part of her wanted to run and hide behind the emotional wall she'd spent so much energy building against the pain and hardship of life. But another strange, almost foreign piece of herself wanted to jump into his arms. Tell him that she loved him.

She stood there dumfounded, holding the sealed toothbrush package in her hand.

Without a word, she turned, walked into the bathroom, brushed her teeth, and crawled into bed to snuggle with a man for the first time in her life.

With her arms wrapped around him, cheek on his chest, she experienced a feeling she hadn't known for a long, long time.

She felt . . . human.

After that, the idea of shooting dope every day seemed disgusting.

It wasn't easy, but she kicked the habit. Not by going clean, but by replacing the heroin and meth with drugs Anthony liked to do. Mainly alcohol and cocaine, with a fair amount of ecstasy thrown in when they went to go see one of his DJ friends spin records.

For the next few months, Anthony treated her like a queen.

She moved her stuff in, and when he saw how little she had, he decided to take her on the first plane flight of her life. First class, all the way to New York City.

They shopped at stores she only knew from movies. Saks Fifth Avenue, Barney's, Bloomingdale's. He not only bought her expensive clothes, but the people who worked in those places treated Cristina like she belonged. They pampered her. Showed her how to do her makeup exactly the way she wanted it. She'd never felt more beautiful.

On the second day of their trip, Anthony bought her a diamond necklace at Tiffany's, one that sparkled like his eyes. When he put it on her, she felt like some kind of princess.

They went to dinner at restaurants whose names she couldn't even pronounce, where they ate meals that cost more than Tío Alberto made in a month of landscaping.

A few months later, out of the blue, Anthony asked Cristina to marry him. The proposal came with the biggest diamond ring she'd ever seen. She said yes without hesitation. Not only did it feel like she'd won some sort of lottery, but her heart was genuinely bursting with love for this man who treated her like a sacred treasure.

Overwhelmed with happiness and with big dreams for their future, she told him she wanted a huge wedding. The one she dreamed of as a little girl. The dream she'd completely forgotten about as she grew into a woman.

That was the first time she saw him upset.

His face changed as soon as the words came out of her mouth. Gone was his praise and worship. In its place, the kind of frustration one might show an unruly child. He demanded to know if she expected him to meet *every* desire she had, no matter how big. He lectured her on respect, and the need for her to understand "the way things are going to be from now on."

Looking back, of course, it was a big red flag that should have told her exactly what was to come. But she ignored it. Blinded by what she thought was love, and, more than she cared to admit, by the fact he was her ticket out of the ghetto.

On top of her heart's confusion, Cristina and Anthony usually did coke and drank from the time he got home until they finally went to sleep. *If* they went to sleep. Every single day. Her mind was in a constant fog.

She had no one around to help her sort through her problems. No friends. No parents. She hadn't talked to her uncle or grandmother in years.

So, without much internal debate, she went along with Anthony's plan of taking a weeklong trip to Las Vegas.

After 72 hours of partying in club after club, casino after casino, the two ended up in a makeshift chapel on the outskirts of the city. They were married by a man dressed as Dean Martin, but only after a frightening incident where Anthony raged at the poor guy, threatening to come back with a crowbar if Dino looked at Cristina's tits one more time.

The next two days were a blur.

One memory she would never forget though was spending time with a few other girls. High-class hookers with fake everything. It was actually a lot of fun, until Anthony couldn't get it up, which was unsurprising after five days of living on nothing but cocaine, ecstasy, and alcohol.

He started breaking stuff in the hotel room, yelling about how the women he'd hired were "nothing but dirty lesbians and a waste of his hard-earned dollars."

He threw a lamp against the TV. Then the TV against the wall.

At one point, he choked one of the girls so hard her lips turned blue.

Cristina had to scream in his face before he let her go.

Their trip to Vegas came to an abrupt end. They gathered their things in a hurry and caught a taxi to the airport, before the girls' employer could come looking for them.

Anthony's behavior didn't improve when they got home.

Instead of treating Cristina like a queen, he started acting like she was his slave.

He monitored her at all times, demanding that she keep a GPS tracking-app for her phone turned on whenever she was outside the apartment. If she did something as simple as make an unscheduled stop at the nail salon, her phone soon rang. On the other end would be Anthony, going berserk, wanting to know where she was and what she was doing.

When Cristina was home, he had an entire methodology for torturing her when she did anything he didn't like.

The first step was to take away her coke supply and her cigarettes. Before long, she'd be begging him to forgive her for whatever imaginary offense he thought she was guilty of.

Anything to get her fix back.

When she was totally weakened by fear, he would

literally hold her captive. He installed electronic locks on the doors and could seal the whole condo whenever he wanted, all with the click of a small remote he kept on his keychain.

And when *that* didn't satisfy his need for control, he just plain hit her.

She would never forget the first time.

They'd actually been having a good day. The sun was shining. They ate a nice breakfast at a local dive called the Mini Gourmet, and Anthony had promised to drive her up to wine country later that afternoon.

When they came home to pack a few things, he was smiling at her like he had when they first met.

But for some reason he decided to pick up her phone and go through the recent calls. He saw one from "Tío" and went ape-shit. He threw the little flip-phone across the room at her, almost splitting her forehead open with it. Luckily, she managed to duck at the last second.

After the phone exploded into about a thousand pieces against the wall, she tried to explain that the call was from her uncle, the one who'd basically been like a father to her when she was growing up. She'd decided to reconnect with him and her grandmother after so long away.

That only made things worse. Anthony started screaming about how *he* was her family now. He called her "a ghetto bitch" from "a family of dirty wetbacks that hadn't done shit for her."

Were *they* the ones who put her in designer clothes?

Had *they* taken her out to restaurants and bought her $500 bottles of wine?

No, *they* were the ones washing dishes in those restaurants.

They were nothing but dirty scum, whose purpose

was to serve the people who did the *real* work in society.

He ended his little speech by saying that if she really wanted to go back to "eating rice and beans," she was more than welcome to do so.

By the time he was done, his face had turned so red and twisted, it reminded Cristina of an evil clown she once saw in a carnival House of Horrors.

When she started crying, he backhanded her across the face.

At first she was shocked. It wasn't the first time a man had hit her. Far from it. But somehow it had been the worst. Anthony was supposed to be in love with her.

When she tasted the blood leaking from her split lip, a part of her brain said to dig her long, perfectly-manicured French-tip nails into his eye sockets.

He must have seen the anger in her eyes. For a moment, she could sense fear.

But it disappeared as soon as she made the regrettable decision to turn her eyes downward, just for a moment, like a dog frightened into obedience. In that instant, he felt power. And instead of showing mercy, he clenched his fist and punched her, just once, as hard as he could in the ribs.

For a week, it hurt every time she took a breath.

Each time he saw her wince, he said something like, "I hate that you made me do this to you, but hopefully it taught you an important lesson about how the world really works."

From then on, every time she didn't fight back, every time she didn't say something, every time she was out of the house and didn't take the opportunity to run as far away as she could, he grew bolder.

He soon started bending her over his knee like a child, slapping her backside with his favorite studded belt when he didn't get his way. At first, it was only for specific things, like if she forgot to pick up his dry cleaning. Then it became a kind of game to him. He was always purposefully vague about what he wanted her to do. That way he could respond to whatever choice she made by punishing her for it.

Eventually, the abuse became a daily routine. Her legs and backside and lower back started to develop blisters from the metal studs on the belt, sores that would fester and pop and ooze blood. Where the wounds did manage to heal, thick scars formed. After a while, they looked like the kind left on the backs of slaves in the south before the Civil War.

Anthony once saw Cristina staring at the marks in the mirror. He threatened to kill her if she ever told anyone. It was her own damn fault, he said. If she listened and did what a good wife was supposed to, instead of acting like some street-whore all the time, he wouldn't have to hurt her.

She tried to do her best to please him. But on more than one occasion, he almost killed her anyway.

One night, they'd done a ton of blow. Cristina even managed to score a bag of heroin by trading some expensive clothes for it, since she didn't have any cash of her own. Anthony, of course, didn't know. He was never shy about telling her how little he thought of "junky lowlifes."

She was in the bathroom cooking up and having trouble with it. After so many years of sticking herself, it was hard to find a vein, and she didn't dare shoot into her arms, for fear that Anthony would find out. It turned out not to matter. She was about to poke the needle into her leg, hoping he wouldn't notice it among the other bruises, when he kicked in the door.

"Oh, I knew it," he said, before proceeding to call her every hurtful name he seemed to know, everything from "dumb bitch" to "junky whore" to "hopeless cunt."

He said that if she wanted to kill herself, he would be more than happy to help speed up the process.

Grabbing ahold of her thick hair, he dragged her from the bathroom and onto the 20th-floor balcony of their condo. He wrapped his arms around her chest and hoisted her over the edge, telling her that if she screamed he would drop her and tell everyone she jumped. As hard as she tried to stay still, she couldn't help but squirm and kick her legs. Her body needed to escape from danger, like a fish out of water.

"Please," she pleaded, trying to keep her sobs as quiet as she could. "Please don't kill me, baby."

He held her there for what seemed like hours, but in reality was likely only a minute or two. A couple of times, he unclasped his hands, letting her drop a few inches before grabbing her again and hauling her up. She looked up and saw, not the psychotic grin he often had when beating her with the belt, but a blank stare that was colder than death.

"Are you ever going to do that shit again?" he asked finally, in a voice as lifeless as his eyes.

"No," she answered through the tears. "No. No. No. Never."

"Do you promise?"

"Yes, yes, yes. I promise. I swear, I won't ever do it again. I'm sorry I'm such a bad person. Please give me another chance, Anthony. Please don't kill me."

Without another word, he dragged her back onto the balcony and into the bedroom.

He threw her onto the bed.

He raped her again and again and again.

Only hours later, when the sun mercifully peeked in through the window, did he finally stop. By that time, she was bleeding and in so much pain.

After he slept and his head was a bit clearer, there had been fear in his eyes, as if even he knew that he'd finally taken things too far. He wouldn't let her out of the house for several days, presumably afraid she would say something. She wasn't allowed to go see a doctor, even when she kept throwing up in the days that followed.

That is, until three weeks later, when she missed her period.

He held her tightly by the arm as they walked down to Rite Aid to buy a pregnancy test. She threw up all over the condo's bathroom when she saw the pink plus-sign appear.

Even then, he drove her to the OB/GYN himself, making sure not to let her out of his sight. He was fidgety and nervous as they entered the parking garage at the doctor's office, no doubt worried they would discover the damage he'd done to her.

As it turned out, the doctor didn't examine her that day, but they did administer a test. And any hope she had of getting away from Anthony vanished when the nurse came in, a huge smile on her face, confirming that Cristina was indeed pregnant.

Anthony had no problem producing an enthusiastic smile that would have made any politician jealous. He hugged her and kissed her in front of the nurse, although she half-figured he would now try to beat her until the baby died. She hated to admit it, but at the time, part of her hoped he would.

A surprising thing happened, though. He started being nice again.

On the way home from the doctor, he pulled into a Safeway parking lot and ran inside. Ten minutes later, he came out with what must have been the biggest bouquet of flowers they had. An explosion of beautiful colors and scents filled the car as he handed it to her.

She cried, and honestly couldn't have said whether the tears came from wanting to believe that he'd had a change of heart, or from the fear that it was all a ruse to get her inside the condo so he could finish what he'd started that night on the balcony.

But in the days, weeks, and months following the news of the pregnancy, he continued to treat her well. Like a queen again. Like he had when they first met.

While Anthony continued to drink and do blow, he cut way back. And Cristina was almost completely sober while she was pregnant. For the first time in years.

The world was clearer than it had been in a long time.

He brought her flowers almost every day, often with her favorite hand-made chocolate-covered cherries. Once there was a pair of diamond earrings. Another time a bracelet.

She thought things might go bad again when they found out the baby was a girl. Anthony had been set on having a boy. But the kindness continued. As Cristina got bigger, he even started doing the dishes and helping with all the things she normally did around the house.

Despite the flowers and the jewelry, and as much as she wanted to believe his supportive smiles, Cristina always felt deep-down that it was all an act. In the back of her mind, she continued to devise ways to get away from him. But no matter how much energy she put toward plotting an escape, she always came back to the same conclusion.

What the fuck else was she going to do?

Go to the cops?

She hadn't exactly had the best of luck with them in the past, and she figured they would probably lock her up for child endangerment or something. Her baby would end up in foster care. Parentless, just like Cristina was.

She also knew that, if she did take off, Anthony would search for her. She would need to get as far away as possible. Maybe Mexico. But she didn't speak more than a few phrases of Spanish. And besides, what would she do down there? Go back to turning tricks?

It was hopeless. She had only two choices. Suck it up and go on with life, or suicide. And maybe those two options were the same, since she knew it was only a matter of time before he really did kill her.

Feeling overwhelmed, Cristina decided to do the only thing she'd ever been good at. She kept putting one foot in front of the other, hoping for the best.

Soon after Anise was born, Anthony went back to his old ways.

He hated the sound of the baby crying, to the point he sometimes walked around with his hands cupped over his ears, yelling for Cristina to make it stop. Usually she could. But sometimes babies cry for no reason. She tried to tell him that, but he acted like she was making Anise cry on purpose.

On one such occasion, the baby had been wailing for hours. Anthony was snorting a lot of coke, a habit he and Cristina both returned to in full-force after Anise was born. He was amped up and pacing around, mumbling about how he had so much work to get done.

Cristina started to fear that he would do something to her. Or, even worse, to the baby. She kept picturing that night on the balcony and swore, then and there, that if he *ever* tried to do anything to hurt Anise, she would kill him, even if it meant giving her own life.

She was sitting on the sofa. The baby was in her crib, finally beginning to settle down. In Anthony's eyes, however, it was already too late. He undid his belt — *the* belt — with a psychotic calm. The deadness washed over his eyes.

"Cristina," he said. "I thought that baby would have taught you how to be a better woman. I really hoped having our daughter in the house was going to transform you into the person we both know you can be if you choose to."

Her mind tried with infinite desire to hold back the tears, knowing it would only provoke him. They came anyway.

"I'm sorry," she cried. "I'll try to do better, baby. I'll try to be better. Just please, don't hurt me. Please, Anthony."

"It's for your own good."

During the next five years, he beat her almost every day.

The scars on her body were torn off and reformed over and over again, becoming thicker and thicker each time. And with every passing day, her resolve to do anything about it grew weaker.

When Anise was old enough to be aware of her surroundings, Anthony was always sure to wait until the girl was sleeping before he took Cristina into the other room, for what he'd come to call her "treatments."

Over the course of those years, everything good that was inside Cristina died. Every ounce of self. Every bit of desire to be something and to leave a mark on the world. All of it was dead. Killed by a man who said he loved her.

The only thing leftover was an empty shell of a person. And despite getting dressed up every day, desperately holding on to her external beauty, she went through her daily routines in a daze, trying to be as robotic and predictable as possible, knowing that perfection was her only salvation from more pain.

Part of her hoped he would just lose it one night and hold her over the balcony again. Only, next time she wouldn't plead for her life. She would tell him to let go. Beg him to do it.

There were times when she fantasized ways of ending it all herself.

She imagined filling up the bathtub and using one of Anthony's straight razors to slit her wrists from top to bottom, letting her blood cloud the steamy water.

Sometimes she pictured using his belt to hang herself. There would be poetic irony in that, at least. After all, it was the object she feared most in the entire world. More than all the guns and knives and nuclear bombs combined. She couldn't even bring herself to go near it, unless she was picking it up off the floor, and then only so it wouldn't get used on her.

Most of all though, she dreamed of scoring a fat bag of heroin and injecting herself with the biggest, thickest charge the needle would hold. She could watch the world drift off into oblivion as the angels kissed her soul.

But she always came back to thinking about her smiling little girl looking up at her as if the world was a perfect place.

Anise was an oasis in a desert of misery.

And, ultimately, it was the strength she found in her daughter's love that allowed Cristina to finally fight back. To say no. To leave the world of torment and pain and suffering behind. To seek out a better life.

When she grabbed that fire poker and cracked Anthony's head open with it, there was no doubt in her mind she was trying to kill him. Not because she necessarily wanted to see him dead, but because she couldn't picture him ever leaving her alone unless he was.

Now that he'd proven her right by trying to sabotage everything she'd worked so hard for, Cristina couldn't help but regret that she'd failed.

44

Officer Washburn hadn't spoken since Cristina began her story.

"I'm so sorry you had to go through that," she said now.

"Don't be," Cristina responded, feeling surprisingly good for having just relived the worst moments of her life. "If anything, it's my fault. For staying so long and being a victi—"

"—No, Cristina. The only person to blame for what happened is him. You shouldn't ever think otherwise. I'm sorry we weren't there to protect you then, but we're here now, OK? And you need to know that."

Cristina wanted to believe her, but wasn't finding it particularly easy.

"Thanks," she said anyway.

But going over the story really had given Cristina a renewed sense of courage and determination. It reminded her of how much she had to lose.

As the unmarked Crown Victoria passed into Pleasure Point, Cristina smelled the already familiar and comforting brine of the ocean. It made her think of Casey, and of sea lions. Of playing in the sand with Anise.

"Quite a view," Washburn said as the car ascended the sweeping hillside road toward the house.

Soon the car was under the thick canopy of pine and redwood. Then turning toward the driveway. The tires crunched gravel, then silenced when they hit the softer dirt of the courtyard.

Parked in front of the house was Cristina's Honda – old and beat-up, but still hers. At least for now. She pictured it being towed by the cops, taken away along with everything else she had.

They parked and got out.

Cristina unlocked the door to the house. As soon as she opened it, there was a crash from down the hallway. Followed by the swoosh of the sliding glass door.

Washburn bent at the waist, pulling up her pant leg to reveal a small-caliber revolver strapped to her right ankle. She removed it from its holster, checked it, and pointed the barrel down the hallway. She touched a hand to Cristina's shoulder, moving her aside so she could sneak toward the kitchen.

After confirming the room was secure, Washburn lowered the gun and beckoned for Cristina to follow.

Both their eyes went to the garbage can. It lay tipped over in the middle of the floor. Cristina hurried toward it. The box of chocolates was gone.

"Don't touch anything please, ma'am," Washburn said with authority, craning her neck to look out the back door. "Where does this lead to?"

"There's a hiking path through the trees."

They heard the cracking sound of a branch breaking somewhere up the path.

Washburn flinched. "Shit. OK. Stay here."

Gun in hand, she ran into the woods.

For ten agonizing minutes, Cristina stood in the kitchen, stunned and not wanting to move. She pictured Washburn holding hands with Anise as the two walked toward a police car, the little girl with a sad, questioning look on her face as she carried her stuffed octopus and a backpack full of clothes.

Tears, tinted black by Cristina's eye makeup,

dripped from her cheeks and onto the floor. She felt powerless in a world void of any real justice. There was no such thing as fairness. The bad guys won too often. It had always been that way, and it always would be. What was the point of even trying?

She heard a rustle of branches. A tall, slender man with his hands behind his back appeared, pushed through the trees by the much smaller Washburn. Cristina recognized him immediately as the guy from the pier and the drum circle.

Through the trees behind them came another figure. A short, portly man with a beard.

Jack.

He had on the same too-tight shorts he'd worn when he and Cristina hiked together. His powerful legs looked almost silly in comparison to his hefty gut. He carried a long stick in one hand, and a serious look of concern on his face.

He soon noticed Cristina standing just inside her back door, cheeks smeared black like a sweaty baseball player.

"Oh, dear," he said, taking her into his arms. "What's the matter? Everything is going to be OK."

"Th-th-they're going to t-take Anise away from me, Jack. But I didn't do anything."

"OK, OK. Everything is going to be OK."

He held her until Washburn returned.

"Don't worry," the cop said, putting a hand on Cristina's back. "We've got this guy good. He had the chocolates in his backpack. And he's already going to town about how Anthony was the one who put him up to it. According to the business card I found in his wallet, his name's Alan Wayfield. He's some kind of Private Detective, although I'm pretty sure after this he'll be lucky if he can land a job working security at the mall."

She smiled and extended her hand toward Jack.

"I'm not sure where you came from, but thanks for the assist, Mr. . . ."

"Jack. You can call me Jack. And it's no problem. Only, can someone please explain what's going on here? I was walking back from my other place and had, pardon the TMI, stopped to take a leak. All of a sudden I hear shouting. I didn't know *what* was going on. But I crouched down in the bushes. And from there, I saw our friend who now has the metal bracelets on making his way up the path. I could tell just by looking at him that he was up to no good. So I stayed real quiet and, right when he was about to pass me, I stuck out my trusty old walking stick, like this, boop." He made the motion to illustrate his point. "And down he went – SMACK! – into a rock. I almost felt sorry for him. Then I sat on his head."

Cristina's sniffling cry half-turned into a laugh, and although Washburn tried to contain herself, she couldn't help but do the same.

"He's not kidding," Washburn said. "I came running up, all out of breath from that damn hill, and there's my new friend Jack, sitting on this guy who's underneath him wiggling like a bug."

Cristina leapt at Jack and kissed him on the corner of the mouth.

His cheeks immediately turned bright red.

"Well, whoa. Wow. Holy moly. If I knew I'd get this kind of attention, I'd spend all my time sitting on people."

Cristina went upstairs to get a tissue and clean up. She was still incredibly shaken, but her sense of relief was immense. It was finally over, she thought. Surely they would arrest Anthony now. And this time, not even his hoity-toity lawyer could get him off. He was done.

Washburn called in additional officers to check the

kitchen and the hiking trail. Dan showed up while the evidence team was there and made sure everything was done properly. They didn't find anything else. But they already had what they needed, especially with Anthony's henchman apparently willing to spill his guts.

Before getting into her car, Washburn assured Cristina she would do everything within her power to make sure both Wayfield *and* Anthony went away for a long, long time.

Jack had gone back to his house, but returned after the cops left. He brought with him two roast beef sandwiches, some Lay's potato chips, and a couple bottles of ginger ale.

"You can have both the sandwiches if you want," he said. "I figure you're probably famished after all this excitement."

Choked up at the gesture, she again embraced him, this time reaching her arms around his broad chest in as strong a hug as she was capable of.

He didn't blush this time. Now he looked more like a proud father.

She said, "Thanks for everything, Jack. I realize we only met a little while ago, but I want you to know, you're one of the kindest men I've ever met in my life. I wish there were more people like you in the world."

"I'm not that special. I think I'm just the kind of person who likes to root for the underdog. The little guy never seems to win enough in this world, and if there's anything I can do to make that happen, I try my damnedest to do it."

"I'm serious," she said, trying not to tear up. "If there's anything I can ever do to repay you, please let me know. Anything, Jack. I owe you."

He looked at her and smiled.

He said, "You just keep raising that beautiful little girl of yours the right way. I have a feeling she's going to do some pretty important things with her life. So you show her how to be a good person and how to take care of others. That would be more than enough for me."

On cue, Aba's car came crunching up the driveway with Tío Alberto behind the wheel. Cristina ran toward it, barely able to let them come to a complete stop before she opened the door.

Anise had fallen asleep on the way and sat hunched over in her car seat, peaceful and serene.

Cristina beamed happy eyes at her uncle. He returned a loving gaze in his soft, yet strongly masculine, way.

Anise awoke for a moment when Cristina lifted her, just long enough to see whose arms she was in. The little girl's lips curled into a smile before she lowered her head down onto her mother's shoulder and went back to sleep.

LOSS

45

Cristina and Anise had been in their new house for almost six months.

Summer was winding down. There were fewer tourists in Pleasure Point now, and the sunsets were coming earlier and earlier each day.

Anthony had been arrested after it was determined that the chocolates Cristina received were indeed injected with small doses of methamphetamine. But for reasons beyond her comprehension, he'd been released on bond and remained free, albeit on court-ordered house arrest, pending a trial that seemed to keep getting pushed back.

Shortly after Anthony was arrested, Dan filed a suit in civil court claiming physical and emotional damages. He said it was likely they would collect a significant monetary sum, but warned that such a proceeding probably wouldn't even begin until after the criminal trial was resolved.

Nonetheless, there was a peace in Cristina's heart like she'd never known.

The dreams had stopped. Whatever spirit – real or imagined – that had been delivering them seemed to have moved on. She wasn't sure why, and didn't really care.

The only thing that mattered now was finally getting a chance to settle into her new life. And with Anise there full-time, mother and daughter embraced every breathtaking moment of the Pleasure Point summer.

They went to *The Wharf* at least twice a week, always making sure to ride Pinky the horse each time they were there. They also went to the beach. Hiked. Ate delicious dinners at Jack's house. Watched countless beautiful sunsets. And sometimes went to the drum circle on Sunday evenings, standing upwind, of course, to avoid what Anise called "that funny smelling stuff."

One weekend in late June, Tío Alberto came over and they all got their hands (and faces and clothes and shoes) dirty cleaning up the backyard. When the work was done, what had been an overgrown jungle was transformed into a nice little garden. Nothing crazy, but Cristina and Anise were both quite proud of their collection of tomatoes, zucchini, rosemary, thyme, and cilantro.

On top of all the wonderful time spent with Anise, Cristina was falling madly in love with Casey. Despite everything she'd been through in the past, which she described to him in detail one day while they sat together on the beach, he somehow managed to unlock her heart, making her feel as though she'd never been hurt before.

He treated her like she'd always dreamed of being treated. He didn't have much money, so he couldn't buy her things like Anthony had. But he did something much better. He treated her like an equal partner. Like a human being. He took interest in who she was as a person. Not just her body or her mind, or even her soul. He saw her as a unique package of individual parts, appreciating each one as a special gift to the world.

When she was with him and Anise, Cristina felt whole. He was so patient and kind with her daughter, always treating her as if she was his own child. Cristina loved watching the two together. Their laughter perfectly harmonized in her ear, like some flawless symphony of happiness.

Yes, things were going great.

Cristina even managed to stop smoking cigarettes. And after about a month spent hacking up disgusting globs of yellow goo in the shower each morning, her lungs felt better than they had since she was a kid.

She finally connected with Michelle again, too. Her friend and 12-step sponsor was crucial in helping Cristina get through the aftermath of unknowingly getting high.

But their relationship somehow wasn't the same. It seemed to belong in the past.

Not that she wanted to give up doing recovery work. Not in the slightest. That journey had, after all, saved her life and made her current happy reality possible.

Finding some new groups to attend was on her list of things to get done, eventually, once she found time for it. God knows Jordan and Dan were always trying to get her to go to one meeting or another. Especially since the three of them (plus Anise) had made Sunday evening dinner at the Venus Café a regular thing. But, for now, Cristina was focused on figuring out what she wanted to do with her life.

To that end, she took a part-time job working behind the counter at an art supply store a few days a week. Katlyn from *Bula's* had a little sister, Jacklyn, who babysat Anise while Cristina was there.

The store was called *Artifacts,* and it was just a few doors down from Casey's shop. There wasn't much money in it – she only made minimum wage. But working there gave her a sense of purpose that she really enjoyed. It was her first time ever having what most people would consider a "real" job.

Plus, being in that environment, smelling the paints and the chalks and the paper, got her interested in doing art again. Even if she had to admit that it was, at first, a little weird trying to do it sober.

The store also did classes, which were free for employees and their family.

Shortly after starting her job, she signed up for "Oil Painting the Sea," mostly because "Finger Painting for Kiddos" happened at the same time, one room away.

After their classes, Cristina and Anise usually walked over to see Casey at *Bula's*, or to *The Wharf* so they could ride the carousel and win a stuffed animal or two.

By the time summer was nearing its end, Anise's collection of plush critters had grown large enough to fill the top of her Minnie Mouse dresser and extend down the base of the wall.

In addition to all her old favorites, now there were aquatic creatures of every kind: a sea lion, a sea elephant, a sea turtle, a sea anemone, a sea star, a seahorse, a seagull, the octopus Cristina won for her the first time they went to *The Wharf*, a jellyfish, a walrus, a squid, a tuna who talked when you squeezed him, a dolphin, a whale, and a great white shark (he was all the way in the corner because his face was kind of scary).

Anise was getting ready to start a new school year. First grade. Cristina didn't know if she was ready for her baby to be so grown up. Kindergarten had been more-or-less a glorified babysitter. Now Anise would have homework every night, a holiday play in December, and all kinds of other big-kid activities.

All of which reminded Cristina to focus on the things that mattered most.

She wasn't sure what was going to happen with Anthony. But despite all the fear he put her through over the years, she now felt more safe than ever. The police were monitoring him, and Officer Washburn had made it her personal mission to call Cristina at least once a week to remind her of that fact.

Of course, that knowledge didn't keep Cristina from sleeping with her knife under her pillow. At least when Casey wasn't there. And lately those lonely lights had become rare. So much so, she was thinking of asking him to move in.

Besides the fact she loved him and felt safe with him around, she also hated the idea of him sleeping on that old cot in the back of the store. She knew he didn't mind it, at least that's what he said. But on the nights he wasn't with her, she would stay awake staring at the ceiling, thinking about him surrounded by boxes of shoes and surfboards and piles of unfolded t-shirts. She really didn't know what he did there, but she always pictured him sitting on the edge of the cot, eating a burrito by himself, listening to music as he tried to block out the loneliness.

In reality, he probably spent most of his time figuring out how to pay the bills.

Pleasure Point's Development Association – made up of what Casey called "rich jerkoff developers who didn't give a shit about the history or culture of the town" – had been trying to get rid of him since shortly after the store opened. As soon as they realized he wasn't going to deck *Bula's* out in their cheesy Pleasure Point merchandise.

Casey came over upset one night, talking about how the Development Association's efforts were getting bolder. Now they wanted to raise the rent so high he wouldn't be able to afford to renew his lease when it came up later in the year.

She asked him why they were doing it.

He said he really didn't know, except he'd heard

they wanted to put in some kind of visitor's center in the space where the shop was. Part of a bigger expansion project. He added that anyone looking for information about Pleasure Point – surfing or otherwise – was probably better off going to *Bula's* than anywhere else in town.

Cristina heard her new boss at *Artifacts* complain that the Development Association was trying to do the same thing to her as well. And *her* place had been open since the 70's.

Cristina hated the idea of losing her new job. She really liked it, even if the pay wasn't great.

There was definitely a lot more to life than money, anyway. All she really needed was a house, her family, and a sense of purpose.

For the first time, she felt like she had all those things.

Unfortunately, as had happened on so many occasions during Cristina's relatively short life, the time when the sun shined brightest turned out to be the moment just before the storm moved in.

46

"What do you mean they aren't going to renew it?" Casey asked into the phone, having excused himself from dinner halfway through his plate of spaghetti and meatballs.

He paced up and down the hallway.

The call was from a real estate agent who'd been negotiating with the Development Association on a new lease for *Bula's*.

Casey added, "You've got to be shitting me."

Anise gasped from her place at the table.

"Mamma," she whispered. "Casey said a bad word."

"I know, chica. It's OK. He's an adult. Just eat your food, OK? We have to get you into a bath and ready for your big day tomorrow."

"Aww," Anise said as she twirled pasta with her fork. Over the past few months, she'd become a lot more talkative at the table. "I want to go to my old school. All my friends are there."

"I know, baby." Cristina was trying to listen to what Casey was saying, but he'd gone upstairs. All she could hear now was a buzzing noise coming through the ceiling when he spoke. She continued, "Anise, you're going to make lots of new friends. Now, I want you to be a good girl and finish your dinner."

The ceiling-buzz increased in volume, and then a single word rang out, yelled loud enough to be heard perfectly well.

"FUCK!"

"Mamma," Anise said thoughtfully, no longer interested in Casey's choice of language. "What if no one
likes me?"

"Chica, that's not going to happen. You're the
sweetest, prettiest, loveliest, wonderfulist girl in the
whole-wide-world, and everyone is going to love you."
She added, "As long as you're a good girl and do what
your teacher tells you."

Anise thought about that for a while, still looking
into her spaghetti.

Footsteps down the stairs.

Cristina didn't know what to expect. Up to that moment, the strongest anger she'd seen from Casey had
been when he yelled at a group of kids driving by the
beach – they were so busy snapping pictures with their
phones, they almost ran into an old woman who was
crossing the street. Casey had let them have it.

"Anise," Cristina said. "If you aren't going to eat, I
want you to go upstairs and get ready for your bath."

"OK, mamma," Anise answered, looking relieved.

As she passed Casey in the hallway, she initiated
what had become their usual greeting.

"Hello, walrus."

"Hello, dandelion."

Cristina had no idea where they'd come up with that
one, but she smiled every time she heard it. Especially
now, because she at least knew he wasn't going to fly
into some fit of rage. Not that she could imagine him
capable of it. But she'd once thought the same thing
about Anthony, too.

Casey walked into the kitchen looking completely
dejected.

"Aw, come here, baby," Cristina said, pulling him
down toward her and kissing him softly on the lips.

"What's up?"

He sat in the chair next to her, but didn't turn her way. Instead, he seemed to be searching for the answer to her question somewhere on the blank wall.

"Babe?" she said, a little worried.

He finally met her eyes.

"Huh?" he said.

"What happened?"

Sounding a bit like he was explaining the situation to himself, he proceeded to tell her about the phone conversation.

The real estate agent had informed Casey that, despite the fact he was willing to pay almost 20 percent more in rent than before, the Development Association was refusing to renew his lease.

"They never wanted to," he told her. "Even my real estate guy says so. All they want to do is corporatize the whole area down by the beach. I'm not sure why I thought I could do anything about it. The rich and powerful always win in this world. Always."

Beginning the night of their first date, Cristina had seen that Casey wasn't afraid to share his feelings with someone he trusted. It was one of the many things she loved about him. But he wasn't the kind of guy who cried.

Until now.

"My store is everything, Cristina. Everything. I put all I had left toward making it work. Not just money, but my whole soul. I'm nothing without it."

She stood and then straddled him in his chair, pulling his head into the firm softness of her breasts, holding it there.

"That's not true," she said. "That's not true at all. First off, you have us. I love you. Anise loves you. No store, or anything else, is going to change that. Second, just because those greedy assholes won this round, that doesn't mean it's a done deal. There has to be something we can do."

"There's nothing. It's all over."

47

Cristina was starting to enjoy having a lawyer as a friend. And Danny Dee seemed more than happy to embrace any excuse to take on the powerful and corrupt.

She called him and explained what had happened with Casey. He said he would be delighted to help, and that he thought there was a good chance a judge would grant an injunction against the eviction, given the fact it sounded like the Development Association wasn't negotiating in good faith.

"It might take a few weeks," Dan said. "But I'd postpone the going-out-of-business sale for now."

Casey was thankful for the help, but it wasn't enough to get him out of the deep funk he'd fallen into.

Cristina started to worry. Over the next couple of days, he hardly ate. His strong, confident demeanor became buried under a droopy sadness.

He kept going on about how unfair the world is.

"It doesn't matter if you're the hardest working person in the world. If you don't come from money, all you're ever going to get is the shaft. The deck is stacked against the little guy, Cristina. Always has been and always will be."

She tried to cheer him up with a blow job, but he didn't even seem interested.

"I'm sorry," he told her with a distant sadness in his

eyes as he sat on the edge of her bed. "I think I need to go be alone so I can figure some things out."

She unsuccessfully begged him to stay, worried that he might do something irrational.

She didn't know what, exactly.

Except, didn't she?

Yes, with all her heart, she was sure he was going to relapse.

The last thing she did before going to sleep was send him a text saying that she loved him, and she hoped he would keep himself safe.

48

That night the dreams returned.

Again, it began with her in bed. After a moment for her eyes to adjust to the dark, she almost screamed at the sight of little Annie Stewart standing in the doorway.

Cristina caught her breath and realized that Annie appeared to be much more solid than the ghostly image she'd witnessed in the hallway. But somehow the girl still lacked color and definition. And when Cristina moved her head, Annie and her polka dot nightgown faded like a hologram.

The girl's eyes drooped sadly toward the stuffed hippo dangling in her hand.

DON'T TRUST HIM.

Those words, whispered by an unknown voice, echoed in Cristina's mind.

Annie's eyes darted around the room. A kid trying to make sense of an overwhelming situation.

Cristina sensed that Annie wanted her to follow.

As Cristina stood and walked that way, the girl turned and disappeared into the hallway, leaving a faint wispy remnant of blue smoke trailing behind, like someone walking through a dense fog.

Cristina made it to the door just in time to see the trail of smoke disappear down the steps. It crossed her mind to check on Anise, but she no longer seemed in control of her movements. As in the previous dreams, she felt compelled forward by some powerful, unseen force.

She made her way down the stairs, hearing them creak with each soft step. The smoke led into the hall closet, through the miniature doorway in the back wall. Cristina crawled into it, finding herself first enveloped by white light, then falling in the dark.

She expected to come out by the red cabin.

But this time was different.

When the world came to life, Annie stood next to her, still in the same polka dot nightgown, still with her stuffed hippo. But no longer ghostly, now appearing as real and solid as Cristina herself.

As if confirming her own reality, Annie reached up and took hold of Cristina's hand.

Cristina looked down at frightened eyes.

The two were in some kind of abandoned building. It didn't seem like any place Cristina had been before. From what she could see through the darkness, the place had once been a storage warehouse. There were empty crates and pallets strewn across the floor, rotted out as if they'd been there for a long time.

Windows near the high ceiling allowed a few sunrays to cut a path of light through the otherwise dark room. It was impossible to tell what waited for them beyond.

Cristina recognized instantly the rank odors of urine, feces, and mold, reminding her of pretty much every squat she'd ever spent time in.

The scent of rotted dreams.

Mixed almost delicately into the background was the crisp tartness of salt in the air.

At first, it felt like they were alone. But as Annie tugged on Cristina's hand, moving her across the room, strange noises faintly echoed from somewhere in the depths of the building. Sounds that were either squawking birds or the wails of a dying human.

With the girl pulling her along, Cristina stepped over countless pieces of debris and garbage, and an occasional puddle of dark liquid, until they came to a doorway. She sensed something horrible on the other side. But Annie continued forward, her hand gripping so tightly that Cristina wasn't sure she *could* let go.

Covering the doorway was a piece of black cloth. She heard a hissing sound coming from the other side, reminding her of the handheld blowtorches she used to use to cook heroin. She slid the cloth aside and saw that a gas-powered lantern dangled from a nail in one corner, illuminating half the room, leaving the other half in darkness.

Bathed in the lantern's yellow glow was the dirtiest mattress Cristina had ever seen. Its surface was blotted and stained with countless unknown liquids. Most of the splotches looked black under the harsh light, but Cristina guessed the majority of them to be either urine, vomit, or blood. Scattered around the mattress were dozens of used hypodermic syringes, their sharp tips caked with dried, milky redness. Mixed into the debris was a scattering of vials and baggies and blackened pieces of tinfoil.

As they walked closer, Cristina could see tiny bugs scurrying among the goo and the garbage.

She wanted to turn and run, but couldn't.

Annie's hand gripped her now with so much force it hurt.

The mattress felt like it wanted to reach out and grab Cristina. She imagined herself being held down on it, her body soaked in a wetness teeming with Hepatitis and HIV.

Thankfully, Annie pulled her past and continued into a hallway lit only by a single high window. A focused shaft of light ran the length of the long corridor. Across a sea of random articles of clothing and garbage was another doorway, this one with an actual metal door.

A new wave of intense, primal fear rose from the pit of Cristina's stomach, settling into her chest and spine. She wanted to vomit. Her bladder tingled to the point she was afraid she might wet herself.

About halfway across the room, she tried to plant her feet. Her body wouldn't respond. And the small girl seemed to possess a supernatural strength.

They reached the door, and Annie once more looked up with frightened eyes.

Silently, she pointed to the doorknob.

Cristina tried to speak. She couldn't even open her mouth. All she managed was a few warbled murmurs through sealed lips, a noise that sounded like a radio playing in another room.

Annie again pointed to the door. Her tiny eyebrows creased.

Cristina woke up.

Her bedroom was dark. The feeling of impending doom lingered in the air. She felt her own forehead, expecting to find sweat pouring off her face. Instead, there was a cold chill. All the usual elasticity of her youthful skin had disappeared, replaced by the deadness of a raw piece of chicken.

Leaping out of bed, she barely noticed the plastic crunch under her foot as she rushed into the hallway and toward Anise's room. In the glow of the girl's nightlight, it was difficult to tell whether the lump in the bed was indeed her daughter, or if the blankets had perhaps been ruffled in some kind of a struggle. Before she made it to the bed, she stopped.

Listening to the peaceful sound of Anise snoring, Cristina's lungs released a breath she didn't know she'd been holding.

The sense of dread receded like a crashing wave. Then hit her again. Even harder this time. A pulsing nervousness deep in her chest. Something bad was going to happen. She just knew it.

The sensation dropped into her stomach. She ran toward the bathroom.

A waterfall of Aba's tamales, half-digested from earlier in the evening, went spewing from her mouth and into the sink. In the grey moonlight, the liquid reminded her of the ooze she saw soaked into the diseased mattress.

Hands trembling, she turned on the water and stepped back, unable to look elsewhere as the clear water swirled away the contents of her stomach.

With her back against the wall, she slid to the floor, wiping her mouth and feeling tears rush down her cheeks. She tried to remain silent as the onslaught of sadness and worry and doubt overwhelmed her, but the intense emotions were impossible to hold in.

It felt like the end of the world.

The dream had left her completely empty, as if someone cut a bottomless hole inside of her. There were only two things she could compare it to. The intense desire for a fix when coming down from heroin, and the hopeless longing for death she felt when she contemplated suicide as a means of escaping Anthony's torture.

If she'd been alone in that moment, there's no telling what might have happened. What she might have done to free herself from the shadow of infinite sadness the dream had cast upon her.

The only thing that snapped her out of it was the quiet whisper of Anise's voice coming from the hallway.

"Mamma?"

Cristina lifted her head from between her knees and looked at her daughter, dressed in a polka dot nightgown. Not quite the same as Annie's, but close enough to seem like more than a coincidence.

The girl walked up to her mother and hugged her with the gentleness only a child knows.

"It's OK, mamma. It's OK. Everything will be alright."

Her daughter's love made Cristina cry even harder.

After a long time, she finally found the strength to stand, hoisting Anise in her arms as she did. Together, they made their way down the hallway and sat on the edge of Cristina's bed.

Directly across the room, illuminated by the grey light of the moon, she could see marks on the mirror attached to her dresser.

Writing.

With Anise still in her arms, Cristina cautiously stood and walked toward it.

Plastic crunched under her foot.

She saw now what she'd stepped on when she bolted into the hallway.

A tube of crimson lipstick.

Scrawled onto the mirror were three words.

DON'T TRUST HIM.

49

Cristina managed to sleep at least a few hours with Anise cuddled next to her.

When she awoke, the writing on the mirror was gonc. And just as before, the entire thing felt like a dream, harder and harder to remember with each passing moment.

The only part that didn't fade one bit was the sinking feeling in her gut that something bad was about to happen. A concern that only deepened when she looked at her phone and saw Casey hadn't returned any of her texts.

She immediately called him twice. The phone went straight to voicemail both times.

There were plenty of reasons why she shouldn't panic. Maybe he was surfing. Maybe he just needed a little space to clear his head. If so, her pushing him probably wasn't going to make him feel any better.

But something told her that wasn't it. She kept picturing him sad and alone, crying as he contemplated sticking a needle in his arm to dull the pain.

After dropping Anise off at school, Cristina drove directly to *Bula's*.

Lindsay, the blond cashier, said Casey hadn't been there when she came in at eight to open the store.

He most likely wasn't out surfing, though. His favorite board still leaned against the wall near his cot, right next to the framed picture of he and Cristina riding the wooden roller coaster at *The Wharf* on their first date.

Casey's duffle bag full of belongings, which he usually kept neat and orderly under his bed, was open, the clothes and most of its other contents poured out onto the floor.

Was he looking for something?

"His Harley isn't in the back alley where he usually parks it," Lindsay told her. "I also found this."

She handed over a note written on a small piece of paper:

> *Dear whoever,*
>
> *In case you're concerned since I'm not at the store, I just need to take care of a few things. Don't worry about me.*
>
> *-Casey*

"There's a little more on the back," Lindsay added.

> *Cristina,*
>
> *If you came by the store, seriously, don't worry. I'm fine.*
>
> *-C*

Part of her wanted to feel relief. More of her felt like he was full of shit, if only because it was exactly the kind of smile-and-lie she herself would have pulled back in the day.

She told Lindsay to have Casey call her as soon as he showed up, even though she was certain he wouldn't.

Standing on the curb outside the store, Cristina

paused, considering what to do. She really wanted a cigarette.

Offshore, the fog had partially burned away to reveal what would no doubt be another perfectly sunny day in paradise. She barely noticed.

Her panic simmered into a warm anger. At Casey for quitting on himself when he most needed to be strong. And at herself for giving up her heart to him so easily, allowing herself to be hurt again.

Then she caught herself.

Is that what love is? Being there only when it's convenient?

No, Cristina.

You don't even know what he's doing and you've already written him off. Maybe he needs help. And even if he did relapse, that doesn't mean he's gone forever.

How many times in the past six months have you felt like using?

A few at least.

Stop being so damn judgmental.

Despite her best effort to stay positive, she couldn't help but feel betrayed.

50

Cristina drove to all of Casey's favorite surf spots, hoping he was just trying out a new board somewhere. She asked around, but couldn't find anyone who'd seen him.

Finally, just before giving up, she was approached by a man with burned-out red eyes and a tic that caused him to jerk his head toward his right shoulder every few seconds. He stood way closer than Cristina was comfortable with, and spoke so fast it was obvious his words were having a hard time keeping up with his brain.

He asked, "Casey Peters the one you lookin' for, hot stuff?"

His breath smelled like battery acid.

Before she could answer, he continued, "Yah. Yah. Everyone knows that guy. I seen him. Seen him this morning. Tell you about it for a stogie."

"Sorry, I don't smoke."

He looked disappointed and then smiled. The lustiness in his eyes made Cristina sure he was about to ask her for a kiss, or something even worse. The idea of putting her lips on him made her want to throw up. His mouth was covered in cold sores from the bottom of his nose to the tip of his chin. She could barely look at him.

Thankfully, all he wanted was a dollar.

"Sure," Cristina said with relief as she pulled out her wallet, at the same time patting her back pocket to make sure her knife was there.

But he didn't go after her. He just stared off into nothing for a while, perhaps wondering how he could get a few more bucks out of her, or maybe just trying to grasp onto some sense of reality.

Either way, he snapped out of his trance to tell her that he saw Casey riding his motorcycle about an hour earlier.

"One of them big rumblers," he added.

"Where?"

"Out by the old concrete factory."

"In the neighborhood with all the abandoned buildings?"

"That's the one!" He held up a finger and smiled a near-toothless grin.

Cristina suddenly felt really sorry for him.

He continued, "Perkins Town is what a lot of people call it." He looked her up and down, as if really noticing her for the first time. "Might not be too good a place for a pretty girl like you."

This time he sounded more protective than crude. She could see, somewhere in his heart, a real desire to help her. Despite his mouth bumps, his bad breath, his constant twitch, and the way he kept scratching at his scabby arms, he was still a human being.

She pulled out a five-dollar bill and gave it to him.

"Get some food," she said.

"You bet!" he responded, snatching the money from her hand and limping away before she changed her mind.

With her worst fears confirmed, Cristina sat in the car and cried. She tried calling Casey twice more, only to hear the deep, cool tone of his voice as he asked her to leave a message.

51

Not knowing what else to do, Cristina headed toward Perkins Town.

The entire way, she couldn't stop thinking of the two junkies who approached her car the day Anise was with her. Their black, sunken eyes. She imagined Casey huddled together with the two walking corpses, all sharing a spoon as they cooked up.

The fog hadn't broken on this side of town, leaving the whole area shrouded in mist as she pulled her Civic onto what once must have been a cute little downtown strip.

Several store signs still hung in place over doorways.

Henry's Market.

Twice Bitten Secondhand Clothing.

The Paper Crane Stationery Shop.

There were more. But most were either dangling in the air, or had already fallen onto the dirt-caked sidewalk.

Many of the buildings had collapsed walls, their crumbling rubble spilling out onto the sidewalk and into the streets.

The whole area looked like a warzone.

Cristina had squatted in lots of neighborhoods, but she couldn't remember ever seeing one that looked this thoroughly forgotten by the rest of the world.

At the same time, more people were around than before. A sordid hive of dispossessed bodies, crawling in and out of buildings like roaches. Some of them turned bulging, paranoid eyes toward her as she drove down the street, but most simply staggered about like zombies in an old horror movie. A few others crawled on all fours, hands sweeping along the sidewalk, searching the ground for something to smoke or snort.

Cristina recalled plenty of instances living in squats when there was no dope around and no money to buy more. People developed something she could only now describe as insanity. They would imagine that different things could get you high. Someone would start with a "what if . . ." And before you knew it, the whole group was trying to smoke plaster or brick or Ajax, or whatever else was around and fit into a pipe or onto a piece of tinfoil.

The memory made Cristina shiver. She suddenly felt more than a bit afraid.

But she figured she'd be OK if she didn't stop.

No sooner had the thought crossed her mind when she felt a – THUD – from underneath the wheel of the Civic. The front end skipped into the air, then fell to the ground. The back end did the same. Her heart shifted itself into what felt like its highest setting – faster than when she speed-walked the hill behind her house to keep up with Jack.

Please let the tire not be flat.

Barely able to breath, she eased her foot back onto the gas pedal.

The car kept moving forward. It seemed OK. In the rearview mirror, she saw the culprit: a chunk of concrete that had either fallen or been thrown into the road.

The day darkened further. Enough that Cristina turned on her headlights.

She clicked the windshield wipers into action against the fog. The tops of the buildings were covered, shrinking the neighborhood, like a mouth trying to eat her.

The little downtown strip was coming to an end, giving way to the single-family homes she'd seen on her first visit. And still no sign of Casey.

She was about to turn around for another pass – sure that he was somewhere on this main street – when she happened to glance down an alley and saw, just barely through the grey soup, a glint from the Harley's chrome fork.

Cristina slammed on the brakes, skidding the car to a stop. She pumped the steering wheel toward the alley and pulled the car in, parking behind Casey's bike.

The headlights illuminated what she saw was a short dead-end. The light and noise startled two huge rats who were rummaging through a pile of loose trash. They both looked up at her for a moment, decided she wasn't a threat, and went back to work.

First gripping her knife into her hand, Cristina opened the car door and stepped out into the alley's dank air. She barely avoided stepping in a pile of rather fresh-looking feces, and tried to tell herself it was the work of a feral dog. Somehow she knew better.

Across the alley from the bike was a single metal door marked *Employees Only*.

An incredibly vocal part of her mind – the logical part – told her to simply get back in the car and drive away. But an even more forceful piece of her knew that Casey was somewhere inside, perhaps in trouble. If she was going to help him, she had to put aside her fear.

With a deep breath of garbage-tainted air, she tried the knob and it turned. She thought maybe it was bolted. It didn't budge when she pulled. But with one foot against the wall, she managed to apply enough force to pop it open.

The hinges cackled like an old witch.

The sound gave her chills, but that was nothing compared to the searing fear that burned through her body when she saw what was inside.

For a moment, all she could do was stand there, completely paralyzed.

It was the exact same room she'd seen after going through the portal in her dream the night before. Down to the smallest detail.

The dim light coming through the high windows.

The pallets and debris.

The sour odor of piss and shit and mold.

Across the darkened room, she saw the outline of a door, knowing that its path was blocked by a black curtain, and beyond . . . she couldn't think of *that*. Not if she wanted any hope of going through with her search.

Before charging into the building, she went back to her car and dug out a tiny LED penlight she kept in the center console. She tested it and was grateful to find that it worked.

Behind her, the door slammed shut. She jumped fully into the car, flipping open her knife as she spun around to see who was coming at her.

It was only the wind.

The door creaked once more when she reopened it.

Again, she stared into her dream as it dared her forward.

She entered the building and half-expected Annie's sad, blue eyes to come floating out from the shadows. It was hard to decide whether she would welcome the sight, or run back to the car screaming.

It was a choice she didn't have to make, because the only difference between the dream from last night and her current reality was the fact that she was now totally alone.

Her small flashlight barely penetrated the murky darkness. The quiet of the building was broken only by the dead echo of her flats shuffling across the concrete, and those muffled, scream-like noises.

Using a technique Michelle once taught her for stressful situations, Cristina tried to replace her fear with something that made her happy.

She chose Anise's smiling face going around the carousel at *The Wharf*.

The mental trick worked and her heartbeat slowed.

She reached the black curtain, hearing the hiss of a lantern beyond it. With one hand, she slowly pulled the fabric aside.

The mattress was there, along with its collection of dark stains. And the piles of used hypos, vials, foil, and other trash. But, like with most bad dreams, reality wasn't nearly as frightening, especially to someone who'd seen this side of life before. Awake, Cristina clearly grasped that the patches of blood and urine and who-knows-what-else were disgusting, no doubt, but they weren't going to jump off the mattress and grab her. That's not the way things worked in the real world.

For good measure, she pointed her dim flashlight toward the darkened section of the room. Seeing nothing but broken bottles of booze and discarded fast food containers, she moved on.

As in her dream, the next room was illuminated only by a single beam of light cutting down the center of a long hallway.

Before she could bring her flashlight up to examine the walls, the tiny device died.

"Fuck!"

The sound of her voice stirred something in the dark.

Whatever it was settled.

Is someone watching me?

She almost wished Annie *would* appear. At least then she could pull Cristina along with the inhuman strength she'd shown in the dream. But she wasn't there. No one was. And, thankfully, neither was the paralyzing fear and sadness Cristina had experienced before.

All her energy was now focused on what condition she was going to find Casey in.

She stood in front of the metal door that Annie had pointed to.

Its knob turned easily.

She pulled, producing another long, creaky squeak.

When she saw what was beyond, a thousand dark memories rushed into Cristina's mind.

52

In the years Cristina spent living on the streets, she saw many places where junkies came together to writhe in their collective filth and shared misery.

None were as horrible as what she now saw before her.

The floor was crammed with bodies, at least in the parts of the room she could see. Light from two of the high windows crisscrossed, casting rays of diffuse grey toward the center, leaving everything else in darkness.

Most of the sickly-looking people lay sprawled out on the floor like corpses, or on bare mattresses, the siblings of the one in the lantern room. Complete with the same revolting wet blotches. The same collection of used needles and filth surrounding them.

Miniature glass vials crunched beneath Cristina's shoes like tiny seashells.

There was little coherent conversation, but the room was far from quiet. Sounds drifted from the darkness. Sorrowful moans. The murmured babble of people talking to themselves. The clawing of overgrown fingernails on cloth and skin. Every so often, a fearful scream broke out, sounding as if the person making it was being tortured.

Cristina's overworked mind recalled the joy she felt when Anthony had asked her to marry him. The pain of kicking heroin. Part of her ability to do so driven by the prospect of never again having to step foot into this kind of hell.

Yet, there in that room, she was surprised to find some deeply hidden part of herself that was tempted to join these forgotten members of humanity. She wondered if, perhaps, that was why she was there.

Did part of her *want* to find Casey relapsed?

She could suddenly see herself in his arms on one of the filthy mattresses, snuggling close as he pricked her skin with a needle.

At that exact moment, a hand reached from the shadows and touched the back of her shoulder. Her first instinct was to go for her knife. She produced the blade and flipped it open without hesitation. Before she could plunge it into the dark, she heard a familiar voice.

"Wait, it's OK. It's me!"

"Casey?"

He stepped out of the dark, his hard, handsome face sitting atop the two interlocking roses that embraced one another up the length of his neck.

"What are you doing here?" he asked with real concern.

"What are *you* doing here?" she echoed.

He looked clearheaded, although a bit nervous, moving his head from side to side, trying to keep an eye on everything all at once.

"Well," he said. "It's a little bit of a long story. And, if you don't mind, I really don't like being in here, especially now that I have to watch out for you."

"I can take care of myself," she responded, trying to sound mad, but in her heart relieved that Casey was both okay and seemingly still clean.

The trademark smirk crossed his face and he continued, "The short of it is, a kid I mentor relapsed. I've been trying to find him."

Cristina's relief turned into guilt and shame.

"I'm so sorry, Casey," she said as she hugged him. "I thought you were—."

"—Getting high?" He pushed her back to arm's length, still looking around like some paranoid bank robber. "Yah, well I kind of thought you might. Look, that doesn't make me happy, but it doesn't surprise me either. In fact, it's partially my fault. I know it wasn't very respectful of me to just run off. So get that worried look off your face. I still love you. But I'd really like to get you, myself, and hopefully this kid Jeremy out of here as soon as possible."

Cristina managed a weak smile.

"What can I do?" she asked.

"*You* can stay right next to me. Someone Jeremy knows said he'd be in here. I've checked most of the place out, but there's still one corner I need to look in." He pointed. "If he's not there, my guess is he's probably moved on."

Casey grabbed her hand and they walked toward the darkest section of the room. Cristina noticed for the first time that he was carrying a police-grade Maglite. He flicked it on and directed the powerful beam forward.

At least a dozen people were huddled together in the corner, all in varying states of awareness. Casey swept the light from one person's face to the next. Most of the sunken, burned-out eyes barely reacted, sending back only empty stares. A few turned away or tried to block the light with their arms.

When the beam crossed the face of a young man, one who looked less decrepit and emaciated than those around him, he at first looked stunned.

Then he bolted.

"That's him!" Casey said.

He pulled Cristina along as he chased the kid toward a metal door on the opposite side of the room. The door was either locked or blocked somehow. Either way, the kid was unable to open it. There was nowhere else to go.

"Jeremy, stop!" Casey yelled, his voice harsh. Then he softened. "It's me, Casey. I'm here to help, OK?"

Jeremy didn't turn around at first. He stood with his back to them, staring at the door with his shoulders slumped in defeat. As they inched closer, Cristina heard him sniffling. She stopped a few steps short. Casey tried to pull her forward, but she gave him a look that said to go ahead.

He nodded.

Casey put his hands on Jeremy's shoulders, leaning in to say something Cristina couldn't hear.

"No!" Jeremy shouted. "I'm not going back."

Casey said something again, a long something. Jeremy turned around. The flashlight no longer showed his face, but Cristina could hear him crying. The quivering sound of a little boy lost in the dark.

They made quick introductions, but Jeremy hardly seemed to notice through his tears.

"Let's get the fuck out of here," Casey said.

In the company of the two others, the place seemed less scary. More sad now than anything. She thought of all the people she'd met in places like this. Some of them scumbags to the core, but most were kids whose biggest crimes had been having bad genes and no one to guide them through the troubled waters of life.

The three made their way out of the needle den, down the long hallway, past the mattress in the lantern room. Cristina stayed as far away from it as she could.

When they entered the last room, the weight of the building felt immense, like it wanted to trap them. The closer they came to the door leading outside, the more

Cristina felt sure they were about to discover someone had locked it.

But Casey pushed it open with considerably less effort than it had taken her.

The screech of the hinges was just as bad, however. Jeremy cringed at the sound.

Then the smell of rotting garbage hit him in the face. He vomited up whatever it was he had in his stomach. From the looks of it, Cristina guessed some kind of malt liquor.

Jeremy then flopped an arm over his brow to block out what little sun was penetrating the fog and the alley walls.

Casey laughed.

"Drugs are fun, huh kid?" he said, slapping him on the back.

Now that they were in better light, Cristina could see that "kid" was indeed the right word to describe Jeremy. He couldn't have been more than fifteen. If that. He stood six-feet-tall and weighed about 140. His gaunt face had piercings in the lip and through the right nostril. There was a mark under his eye that was either dirt or a poorly done tattoo. His nest of greasy brown hair was tucked under a *Bula's Surf Shop* trucker hat.

In response to Casey's comment, Jeremy raised his right arm and extended his middle finger.

"Look!" Casey said to Cristina. "He's feeling better already."

53

They loaded Jeremy into the backseat of Cristina's car, on top of a beach towel from the trunk. He was snoring before she could get the door closed, and didn't as much as twitch at the deafening roar produced when Casey fired up his Harley.

Cristina followed the motorcycle down the street, past the strip of abandoned stores. Again, she watched the denizens of Perkins Town scurry about like insects, moving from one impossibly important task to the next.

She tried to picture what the area must have been like before the cement plant closed. Jack had made it sound like a strong community of blue-collar workers. She was amazed by the devastation caused by one business's decision to pack up and move.

She let go a sigh of relief as they rolled out of the neighborhood, coming to a stop at the T-junction in front of the creepy mansion. She never wanted to come back this way again.

In front of her, Casey's strong back flexed and dipped under his leather jacket as he maneuvered the Harley into town.

In the rearview mirror, she saw Jeremy, face surprisingly peaceful, still wearing his hat, the brim knocked sideways when he collapsed.

Cristina didn't know where they were going, but

wasn't surprised when Casey pulled into the parking lot of *Surf City Donuts*. Having gained five pounds since quitting smoking, she was very much aware that sugar could be a surprisingly effective substitute for drugs, even the hard ones.

They parked. Casey snapped off his helmet before walking over to the car. His face was brighter than it had been the day before, bringing Cristina a new wave of guilt. She suddenly realized that, despite what might be happening with the shop, he hadn't gone back to old habits. He was choosing instead to focus on new ones. He'd left her house because he didn't want to sit around wallowing in his own misery, worrying about things he had no power to change.

He told her as much while the two leaned on the hood of her car, woofing down apple fritters and bear claws while Jeremy continued to sleep. The misty coolness of the lifting fog felt wonderfully fresh after being in the abandoned building. But Cristina didn't think she would stop smelling that acrid urine stench for a long time.

The back door of the Civic popped open. Jeremy sat on the edge of the seat, feet resting on the asphalt. He scratched his arms and looked dazed, but surprisingly more alert than he had been. Casey handed him a glazed donut, which he waved away. Casey insisted, and the younger man finally had a bite, washing it down with a few healthy gulps of orange juice.

"So tell me what happened," Casey said.

Jeremy looked at Cristina with apprehension, then shrugged and started talking anyway.

It had all gone to shit a few days earlier, he said, his voice worn and raspy. A friend brought over a bottle of Oxy he'd stolen from his aunt's medicine cabinet. It had crossed Jeremy's mind to call Casey, but by the time the friend had the pills crunched up into dust and carved into perfect little lines, the thought had passed. He and his buddy snorted a pill each, and Jeremy knew right away that he was off to the races.

"Bro, I told myself it would only be for a night, and only the Oxy. But once I had that evil little tingle going inside me, I wasn't going to stop anywhere short of heaven."

So he'd made his way to "the PT" (as he referred to Perkins Town), hoping to score a sack. His plan had still been to do only enough to feel the thrill, then check into the drug clinic for detox.

The thought of coming down made Jeremy scratch harder at the little bumps on his skin. Casey told him to have another drink of juice. It helped a little, but Cristina knew that it wouldn't be long before the poor kid really started jonesing.

Jeremy continued, "I actually didn't have any money. I wanted to steal some shit on the way over there, but I couldn't find anything worth jacking." He looked at Cristina again, this time with shame in his eyes. "I figured I'd be trading some ass for a taste. But it turned out I didn't need to. Some dude in that warehouse you found me in was handing out free samples like it was the fucking grocery store. He had needles and spoons and everything. All in a little package with this weird book inside."

"A book?" Casey asked. "Like showing you how to use it?"

"Nah, dude. Some crazy shit. I don't even know, really. I looked at it for a second, but it wasn't really my priority, know what I mean? I think I still have it though." He stood for a moment, reaching clumsy hands into each of the pockets of his cargo pants, then the back one for a second time. He brought out a small book that reminded Cristina of the miniature bible they give you in motels. He handed it to Casey, sat back down, and said, "I kept it just 'cause I thought it was a damn trip."

After one look at the book, Casey's mood changed. He was now obviously upset.

He asked, "What did the guy look like who was handing these out?"

Jeremy held his hands to his temples and shook his head.

"Damn, dude. I don't know. Bald. Shaved head. Hella tatts. Kinda like you, bro, I guess. But honestly it was crazy dark, and I barely even looked at him. All I really cared about was the fact he wanted to give me a vial with a decent amount of shit, and he didn't want no blow job or nothing for it. He did say something kinda weird when he handed it to me, though."

"What?" Casey asked.

"I don't know, dude. Something freaky, like out of a movie."

"What was it, Jeremy? It's important."

The kid looked up from behind his fingers and saw how serious Casey was. He strained to remember. His hands began to shake. He set them on his knees and rocked back and forth. Cristina knew he was trying – consciously or not – to stop the small tremors from turning into a full-body earthquake.

She said, "We should probably get him to a doctor, Casey."

He ignored her, flipping through the book.

"What did he say?" he asked again, without looking up.

Jeremy started rocking himself harder. He dug his fingers under his hat, tugging at the greasy hair underneath.

"It was some biblical shit, dude. The guy said something like, 'a new world is upon us, my friend. Soon the innocent will be slaughtered and a new day will dawn.'

He was a fuckin' kook, bro. Probably higher than I was."

Jeremy laughed.

Casey didn't.

"Alright, kid. Let's get you to detox. You're never doing dope again, right?"

"Nah, man. Never."

Casey smiled, the sad grin of a person who has heard himself tell the same lie.

54

After dropping off Jeremy at Pleasure Point's busy drug clinic, Cristina and Casey went back to her house.

They took turns in the shower, then together flopped onto the couch.

It was barely noon, but both were exhausted.

"I'm sorry," Cristina told him once more as she curled her feet onto the couch and snuggled against his chest. "I feel like a horrible person."

Casey shrugged.

"Forget about it, OK? Seriously, it's not even a thing."

"OK," she said, smiling to herself. "You're one amazing man, Casey Peters."

His only response was to run his fingers through her thick black hair.

After a yawn, Cristina asked what the deal had been with the book.

"Jeremy seemed pretty freaked out by it, don't you think?" she asked.

Casey stopped stroking her head. His muscles stiffened.

He asked, "Do you remember that group I told you about the night of our first date? The one I got wrapped up with when I was doping on the streets?"

Cristina, of course, did remember. Although she felt a bit awkward about it.

They'd discussed a lot of things since they met. She'd pretty much told him her entire life story. And he'd shared more about his. But after that night on the pier, they'd never again discussed *New Horizon*. And she'd definitely never told him about her research into the subject.

It wasn't that she'd purposefully kept it from him. Not exactly. But since he'd never made an effort to bring it up, neither had she.

She decided to continue playing dumb.

"*New Horizon,* right?"

"Right," he said. "I thought they were long gone from Pleasure Point, given that the guy in charge got locked up. He killed some cops a few years back. Right about the time I got clean. It was pretty gruesome, too. He burned them alive in their car."

Cristina nodded against his chest.

"Mmm-hmm," she said.

Casey continued, "But it looks like maybe there's some kind of a revival going on. That book is an updated version of what they called 'The Handbook.' It's like their bible. Basically it spells out all the group's bullshit in language that makes it sound like a way out to a vulnerable kid like Jeremy."

Cristina sat up.

"Can I take a look at it?" she asked.

He hesitated, but removed the booklet from his jacket and handed it to her anyway.

He said, "Their biggest belief is this idea that the world is messed up beyond repair, and it's going to take some kind of monumental shift in human perception to change things."

Cristina's face showed she didn't think that sounded too far off.

"Right," he said, answering her unspoken statement. "That part is what gets people to listen. Of course, according to these assholes, the transformation is only going to happen through two means. Drugs and blood. The drugs part is sort of obvious, and I think that side exists mostly just as a means to an end. A way to finance putting out propaganda like that book. Plus, the money allows the real die-hards to live out their sick fantasies about changing the world. Honestly, I never really bought into all that. I mostly just wanted to kill myself with dope. But I heard rumors there was . . ." He pointed to the book. ". . . or maybe I should say *is* a core group of people who go up into the mountains and do all kinds of weird stuff. I'm talking things like sacrifices. And I don't mean just animals either. I heard they once—"

Cristina was crying.

Casey wrapped his arms around her.

"Babe, what's wrong?" he asked. "It's OK. Everything's OK. We don't have to talk about it. I shouldn't have been so graphic. It messes with me too, even after all this time."

"N-no. I want to hear it, actually." She gathered herself. "It's just that . . . there's something I haven't told you about the house, and about what happened here with the little girl who died."

Casey's eyebrow twitched, but he said nothing.

She went on, "It's not that I wanted to hide it or anything. I just didn't want you to worry is all." She looked into his eyes. "I talked to a guy from the FBI who told me that these *New Horizon* people might have had some connection to the girl's death."

"Really?"

"Yah," she said, trying hard to gauge his non-reaction. "He didn't tell me much, except that they *could* have been involved, and that the stepfather who they say killed that poor little girl was either a member, or he had nothing to do with it at all, and in that case must have been setup to make it look like he did."

"Wow," Casey responded. He considered something for a moment. "Cristina, I'm not gonna lie, that really freaks me out." He took back the book and waved it. "This group is no joke. What I was going to say before is that there are a few real sickos involved. I never met them. But from what I heard, they really believe in all this end-of-the-world stuff. And I have no doubt they'd be willing to kill for it. If there's some connection to the house . . . you're sure your FBI buddy didn't say anything else?"

"Only that he seemed to think whoever killed the girl might have gotten away with it. And if they did, they probably were either dead or in jail now, since people like that don't usually stop. But he also said they could be waiting for the right time to strike again."

"That's what I'm afraid of, Cristina. That's exactly what I'm afraid of."

55

Cristina was at work later that week, feeling in a rut.

The sun had already gone down by the time Officer Washburn called to let her know Anthony hadn't shown up for his scheduled court appearance that day. His lawyer was there, but Judge Peterson had specifically ordered Anthony himself to attend the hearing, so he could answer questions about his involvement with the chocolates.

"I don't want to alarm you, Cristina, but we just went to Anthony's house. He wasn't there. And his ankle tracker had been removed and bypassed to send out a signal as if it was still in working order. We talked to the doorman at his building. He saw him get into a cab earlier today with several pieces of luggage. When he asked Anthony where he was headed, he apparently looked distraught and mumbled something about taking what's his and going far away."

Panic.

"Cristina," Washburn said after a moment. "Where's Anise?"

"At home with the babysitter."

There was a pause. And then Washburn's calm, authoritative cop-voice said, "Cristina, I'm sure she's fine. But I want you to call the house. Tell the babysitter to lock the doors. Don't let anyone in. I'm going to get the PPPD out to check on them. I suggest you head there, too."

Cristina was already gathering her things as she finished the call. Within seconds, she told her boss what was going on and headed out the door.

She was soon in the car, racing toward home as fast as the old Honda would go. With one hand on the steering wheel, she called the house and got no answer. She tried the babysitter's cellphone.

Nothing.

She wanted to scream.

A long red-light stopped her. Her heart raced. Her face was hot, even after she rolled down the window to let in the cool, foggy air.

As she stared at the car in front of her, wishing she could somehow drive over it, she thought of her neighbor with the big truck, whom she still hadn't seen since they drove past one another the day after she moved in.

Then Jack's face popped into her mind. She tried his house number and he picked up after a few rings.

"Domino's Pizza," he said.

"Jack!"

"Cristina? Is that you? Hey, I was thinking maybe this weekend we could—"

"—Jack, listen. I need you to go check on Anise. Her dad might be coming to take her. I'm on my way, and there should be some cops there soon, too. But until they show up, can you go make sure her and the babysitter are alright? I just tried calling and didn't get an answer."

"Shit. OK. OK."

He hung up without another word.

The light turned green and she gunned it past the person in front of her, who ended up making a right turn anyway. She flipped him off as she sped by.

Her car was pushing up the big hill when Jack called

back.

He sounded worried.

"Cristina?"

"Yah, Jack. What's up?"

"Um, there are a few lights on at your house, but I rang the doorbell and knocked, and no one answered. I tried the door, but it was locked."

"Dammit," Cristina said, trying to think. "OK, I'll be there in two minutes."

She slammed the accelerator all the way to the floor. It didn't do much good going up the steep hill. But as soon as she hit the flat section under the trees, she was flying through turns so fast she almost ran off the road. The tires screeched when she turned the steering wheel toward the driveway. The back end fishtailed left and then right on the gravel, but she managed to get it under control. A thick cloud of dust trailed the car as it skidded to a stop in front of the house.

Cristina only glanced toward Jack as she ran past him toward the front door.

On the porch, she fumbled her keys. They went flying into the thorny rose bush under the window.

"Goddamn it!" she yelled, trying unsuccessfully to fish them out.

Instead, she picked up what looked like a rock and slid the secret compartment open, revealing a spare key.

By then, Jack was standing behind her, bushy eyebrows furrowed.

She slipped the key into the lock, turned it, and slammed the door open. Before entering, she slipped her knife from her back pocket and into her palm.

"Anise!? Anise!? Jacklyn? Is anyone here?"

There was no answer, but Cristina heard sounds coming from upstairs. She bolted immediately for the second floor.

Climbing the last few steps, she heard a shriek from behind the closed bathroom door.

Her adrenaline shot through the roof.

But she soon realized that the sound hadn't been one of fear or pain. She inched toward the bathroom and heard more noises. Giggles. She also heard the tinny sound of music playing in the background.

Cristina pushed open the door.

"Mamma!" Anise said from behind a face full of frothy bubbles. "I have a beard!"

"Hey, Cristina," Jacklyn said nonchalantly. "You're home early. We're just finishing up with bath time and are about to put on our PJs. Huh, Anise?"

Cristina was not amused.

"I was trying to call and no one answered."

"Oh, yah. Sorry. I had some beats going on my phone. I guess it automatically shuts off the ringer. You aren't mad are you?"

Cristina *was* mad, and it took all her energy not to scream at the poor teenager, who hadn't really done anything wrong.

"Everything OK?" Jack said from the top of the stairs. He walked up, smiling when he saw that it was. "Oh, good. Everyone seems to be in fine condition. But what's that horrible noise? It sounds like aliens trying to communicate through a bunch of random sounds."

"Dubstep, man," Jacklyn said, adding a swirly little dance move for emphasis.

Cristina couldn't believe she'd ever been that young.

56

Casey arrived just after Jacklyn's sister came by to pick her up.

Cristina felt so much better with him there.

A friendly but serious male cop was now parked near the bottom of the driveway. He said he would stay there as long as he could, then gave Cristina his card in case she needed to call.

Jack kindly offered to cook dinner.

An hour later, they were sitting at the kitchen table, digging into juicy pork chops, crisp green beans, and sweet potatoes so creamy they didn't even need butter.

"You're so amazing, Jack," Cristina said.

"Yah, this is pretty damn good," Casey agreed.

Jack sat stroking his grey beard, a little red-faced and a lot happy. He sipped a glass of wine, the last of a bottle he'd brought. To their comments, he waved one hand and bowed his head.

"You guys are too kind," he said. "Alas, I'm but your humble servant."

The guys did the dishes while Cristina tucked Anise into bed.

Cristina checked the windows for a third time.

"Mamma?"

"What is it, baby?"

"Is Jack Santa Claus?"

Cristina burst into laughter. It felt good after the

tension of the evening.

"No, chica. He just looks a little like him, that's all. What story do you want to read tonight?"

They picked out *Where the Wild Things Are* and read it together. Anise sounded out some of the words. Cristina handled the rest. When they finished story time, she kissed her daughter on the forehead and told her she loved her more than anything in the world.

"Love you too, mamma."

Anise smiled and then rolled over, her favorite stuffed octopus tucked under her arm.

Back downstairs, Cristina thanked Jack for all his help, and for being such a great neighbor. She also told him what Anise said about him looking like Santa Claus, which reddened his cheeks even more than the wine.

He said, "I believe he and I are distant cousins of some sort."

Then he put both hands on Cristina's shoulders and added, "I'm only a stone's throw away. You call me any time if you need anything at all. Don't trust those cops to watch out for you, either."

He shook hands with Casey and said, "Take good care of these girls. I've grown quite fond of them."

"I will, Jack," Casey said. "Thanks again."

57

After checking on Anise one last time, Cristina finally allowed herself to brush her teeth and crawl into bed with Casey. He was still above the blankets, wearing only a pair of boxer briefs. His tattooed body looked like a statue as he sat with one hand resting behind his head, the other thumbing through the latest edition of *Surfer* magazine.

"She's going to be fine," he said without looking up. "We're right down the hall. Everything is locked. You've got that knife of yours. And me. We've got the cops close by. And Jack watching out his window, I'm sure. Anthony would be pretty dumb to try anything."

Cristina jumped out of bed and walked to the window. She cracked open the blinds and saw nothing but the blackness of the backyard and the woods.

"I hope you're right," she said. "I don't think you quite understand what a psycho he is though. I wouldn't be surprised if he showed up here in the middle of the night with a can of gasoline and set the whole place on fire. Just to hurt me."

Casey put down his magazine, sat up, and pulled her into bed, wrapping her curvy body into his arms.

"I know what you went through with him. But you don't have to worry, Cristina. Everything will be OK. I promise."

He kissed her neck and caressed the edge of her ear.

His hand traced its way down her spine to the small of her back, resting at the edge of her scars.

For a moment she relaxed, giving herself over to his touch.

Then she moved to get up again, saying, "I'm just going to check on her *once* more."

"No."

He grabbed her before she could stand, bringing her down to a sitting position on the bed. "You can't let him win by scaring you so bad you're jumping at your own shadow."

She wanted to agree. It was so unfair that Anthony could still cause her this kind of pain and sorrow.

"I guess you're right. It's just . . ."

"What?" he asked patiently. "What is it? You can tell me."

"Well, it's kind of morbid. But I guess I just really don't know what the hell I would do if I lost Anise." She felt a sting in her eyes. Without looking at him, she grabbed one of Casey's hands and squeezed it. "All I know is that, when the judge took those test results out of that envelope and said I was positive for meth, my first thought was . . . it was that . . . if they took her away, I was going to kill myself."

She turned to him, expecting to see judgement or anger in his eyes.

There was neither.

Instead, he took her by the shoulders and gently lowered her onto the bed. His blue eyes made her feel whole. He smiled his crooked grin and kissed her. First her nose. Then her lips. Her chin. Her neck. He slid her shirt up over her head and moved his lips down to her naked breasts. First the left nipple, then the right. The sides. The sensitive skin underneath. His stubble had grown a few days and was soft against her stomach as he kissed the skin below her belly button. It tickled wonderfully when he reached the sensitive spot just below her hipbone. She thrust upward in anticipation. His fingers slipped under the red cloth of her panties, slowly pulling them down her legs. He then pressed his lips against the inside of her knee and worked his way down her thigh. One soft kiss at a time.

Soon, her mind and body were in ecstasy, forgetting all the frustrations of the world, if only for a little while.

58

That night, their love was sensual and slow. There was no rush. No pressure of feeling like they needed to squeeze every ounce of joy out of the experience. There was only each other, and the unspoken faith that tomorrow would bring another chance.

Despite all the craziness, all the fear that somewhere out there her psychopath ex-husband might be plotting his revenge, Cristina felt like she, Casey, and Anise, were a unit.

A family.

That's why it seemed only natural to use that moment to finally ask Casey if he would move in.

Her only fear was that he might get scared. Say no.

In her mind, she'd built up an entire scenario in which she asked him and he laughed at her, before walking out of her life altogether. It wasn't rational, and she figured love never really was, but it was what she felt.

With their two naked bodies still intertwined, connected, him on top, eyes locked, little bursts of pleasure shooting through both their bodies, she finally worked up the courage.

"Move in with me, Casey," she said.

His always hard-to-read face gave her nothing for a few horribly tense moments.

Then he smiled. Not just the grin, either. He seemed

happily caught off-guard.

"Alright," he said casually, rolling onto his back.

"Alright?"

She laughed and hit him with a pillow.

59

Before going to sleep, Cristina checked Anise once more, smiling at the way her daughter's mouth rested half-open, a drop of drool working its way down her cheek.

Although she rarely did so, Cristina popped a couple of Benadryl to help her sleep. When she took it, she usually didn't dream, and she didn't think her nerves could stand another trip to the closet, the woods, or any abandoned buildings.

She just wanted to rest.

By the time she returned to her . . . to *their* room, Casey was snoring. She pulled her hair back into a ponytail and crawled over him, onto her side of the bed.

Despite everything, she felt safer than she had in years.

60

The morning sun peeked through the blinds that Cristina had forgotten to close, sending a piercing beam directly into her face. The light blinded her when she opened her eyes. Sleepy hands waved to block it.

Beside her, Casey was still snoring. Not a deep, rumbling bear-noise. More like the sound of a distant motorboat. It was actually kind of cute.

With care not to wake him, she quietly climbed over his body and out of bed. She closed the blinds, and then checked herself out in the mirror, smiling at the puffiness of her sleepy face, feeling wonderful about life.

Before going downstairs to start breakfast, she peeked into Anise's room and saw her daughter lumped under the blankets.

Cristina's feet lightly pattered down the stairs and toward the kitchen.

The bright sunlight coming through the sliding glass door seemed saturated with positive energy.

It was going to be a great day.

She gathered what she needed to make pancakes from scratch, being careful not to make any more noise than she had to. Eggs, milk, butter, and real maple syrup from the refrigerator. Flour from the pantry. Plates and cups from the cabinet. Silverware from the drawer.

The metal mixing-bowl was the hardest part. After Anise had used it for Cheerios, Cristina started storing the bowl on a higher shelf. She could now barely reach it herself.

Just when she thought she had it in her grasp, the bowl slipped from her fingers and tumbled toward the kitchen counter – BANG! – and then to the floor – BANG! BANG! BANG! The bowl rolled on its edge, coming to rest with the open side down, spinning a few times in a swirl of sound that lessened with each rotation.

"Whoops," she said out loud with a slightly evil laugh. "'Time to get up I guess."

When the batter was mixed, the pan hot and ready, Cristina walked to the bottom of the stairs.

"Breakfast time you lazy bums!"

She was taking off the first golden-brown pancake when she heard heavy footsteps plodding down the stairs.

"Hey handsome," she told Casey as he walked into the kitchen and kissed her with half-open eyes.

"Coffee," he said. "Must have coffee."

She poured him a cup and kissed him again. He held her close.

Looking lovingly into his eyes, she said, "Your breath stinks."

Casey blew a stream of hot air into her face and she wiggled away.

He stuck out his tongue.

"Where's the princess?" he asked, setting his steaming cup on the counter and leaning in to smell the pancakes.

"Probably snoring away still," Cristina said. "Another thing you two have in common, by the way."

Casey grinned and said, "Mamma's feeling feisty this morning."

"Rawr." She clawed the air with her hand and then kissed him on the tip of his nose. "Why don't you go wake her up for me."

He saluted. "Yes ma'am." Then turned to go.

"And brush your teeth!" she added as his feet thudded back up the stairs.

"Never!"

Cristina flipped another pancake onto a plate, then poured a big circle of batter for a face and two small ones for ears. She was about to add chocolate chips for the eyes, nose, and mouth when she heard Casey yell.

"CRISTINA!"

His voice told her something definitely wasn't right.

She turned off the stove and went running down the hallway and up the stairs.

"What?" she yelled on her way into Anise's room. "What is it?"

"She's gone."

A hurricane of emotions hit Cristina. Confusion, sadness, loss, furious anger, all wrapped into a storm that pounded her so hard she could barely breathe. If Casey hadn't been there, she probably would have passed out and hit the floor like dead weight. As it was, he barely got her to sit on the edge of Anise's bed, next to the lump under the blankets she now knew was only the girl's pillow.

"OK," he said. "Let's not panic. First, we need to look outside. Maybe she just wandered."

"Yah," Cristina responded blankly. "Yah, maybe."

But she knew that wasn't it. Since the second day they'd been in the house, when Cristina questioned Anise about going outside without permission, her daughter hadn't done it again. She was a good girl and didn't need to be told more than once.

No, she was gone. And *he* took her.

She was going to fucking kill him this time.

61

There was no sign of Anise outside. No evidence of forced entry. No footprints leading away from the house. No note. Nothing valuable had been taken. The only other thing missing was the stuffed octopus Anise loved so much. The doors were all still locked.

The girl had simply vanished.

Cristina told all this to a fat, uniformed cop as they sat in the living room. He slowly wrote everything down in a little blue notebook, not seeming to be in any particular hurry.

"You want me to get you some tea or something, pal?" Casey finally said.

The cop looked up as if to politely decline, then realized the heavily-tattooed man pacing the room was being sarcastic.

He responded, "Sir, I need to get the details correct so we can figure out what happened. The last thing we want to do is rush off in the wrong direction."

For a moment, Casey looked ready to tear the man's head off.

"Right," Cristina interrupted, taking some of the tension out of the air. "We're just really worried is all. We'd like to get out looking for her as soon as possible."

After hanging up with 9-1-1, Cristina had called everyone she knew. First her uncle, who was now on his way with Aba. Then Officer Washburn, who said she would do everything she could to help. Then Jack. He didn't answer, probably because he was still sleeping off the bottle of wine he drank. She left a message. Then Dan. He was on his way with Jordan. Cristina had been debating calling Agent Canfield when the uniformed cop knocked at the door.

"Well," the officer said in his slow voice, "our man down at the bottom of the hill didn't see anyone come up the driveway." He paused. Cristina could have sworn he was fighting off a yawn. "We'll have additional officers here in a few minutes. And a detective. We can start looking around more then. But first, let's try to get our ducks in a row, shall we? Now, you say that you think the father did this?"

"Yes."

Cristina explained the situation with Anthony. By the time she was done, Jordan and Dan were at the front door.

"Sorry it took us so long," Jordan said, though it had only been about thirty minutes. Still, the sentiment made Cristina feel supported.

Dan was in his disheveled street clothes.

The cop looked at him with more than a hint of disgust.

Cristina cringed.

"OK," she said, standing. "I'm no detective, but if your guy was watching the driveway all night, chances are that Anthony went out the backdoor and up the trail."

"Right," the cop said, tapping his pencil against his teeth. "Only, the officer wasn't there the *whole* night. He did have to leave for a call around 3 AM. He was gone for about an hour."

"Oh, for fuck's sake," Casey blurted out. "So then, for all we know, Anise could be hundreds of miles away by now."

The cop didn't have an immediate answer and Casey threw up his hands.

"OK," he said, springing into action. "You and you." Pointing to Jordan and Dan. "Let's hit the trail and see if we can find anything. We'll go as far as the quarry and then reevaluate from there."

They were out the door before the cop could protest.

The officer flipped through his notepad, snorting dismissively.

He asked, "Anything or anyone else you think we should look into, Ms. Rodriguez?"

He was now staring at her chest. She hadn't yet changed out of the thin shirt she slept in. The one that showed her dark nipples.

Clenching her breasts with her forearms, she had to fight off an urge to punch him in his face.

Noticing he was caught, the cop looked back at his notes.

"Yah," Cristina said. "The guy next door maybe. I haven't seen him around in months. I think he's been living out in the forest or something. But he seems like kind of a nut-job."

"Do you know his name?"

She had to think for a minute, and then remembered.

"Rick Atkins."

The cop wrote it down and closed the notebook. He stood, pulling his heavy belt over his gut.

"Well, I guess I'll go see if he's home."

He said something into the radio on his shoulder as he walked out.

Cristina was alone. Not just in the living room, but in her heart. In the world. She felt empty inside. A sense of loss deeper than anything she'd ever experienced.

If something bad happened to her sweet, beautiful daughter, she didn't think she could live.

Her eyes drifted toward the hallway closet as she began to cry.

62

The weathered detective who showed up a few minutes later was serious. His face stern, almost angry. The front door was cracked open and he walked into the house like he'd been there before.

Cristina was still in tears.

"Hello, Ms. Rodriguez," he said. "I'm Tony Myers, a detective with the PPPD. Can I get you something? Water maybe?"

She couldn't answer, still fighting to regain her composure.

He went into the kitchen and came back with a glass of water and some tissues. Cristina blew her nose and wiped the corners of her eyes.

The detective sat patiently across from her.

After a few moments, Cristina calmed herself enough to take a few sips.

"I'm sorry," she said.

He looked at her, a deep sincerity in his eyes. "Don't be. You don't need to be sorry for anything. We're going to find your daughter, OK?"

"OK. I just feel so helpless."

"You're doing great, Ms. Rodriguez. Do you feel up to having a little conversation with me?"

"Yes," she said, drawing on the inner-strength she'd inherited from her grandmother. "I'm OK. I'll do whatever you need. I want to do *something*. And, please, call me Cristina."

"OK, Cristina." He took out a pen and a small note-book. "And I'm Tony. Now, the patrol officer who was here gave me the basic details on the phone a few minutes ago, but I'd like to go over it all one more time with you, if that's OK."

Clenching the wad of tissues in her hand, she again described everything she knew, which felt to her like hardly anything at all. But at least she managed to make it through without breaking into tears.

At one point, the street cop returned and said nei-ther of the neighbors appeared to be home. He leaned toward the detective and whispered something into his ear.

Detective Tony nodded before telling him to call in a forensics team.

"I want the whole area swept. Fine-tooth comb. We're not going through the same bullshit again. And if the Chief or anyone else pushes back, have them call me directly. I'll threaten to resign if I have to. But we're not going to play any political games."

The uniformed officer shrugged as if he didn't really care much about all that, then went back outside to talk on the radio.

Cristina told the detective that her friends and boy-friend were already in the woods searching.

On cue, they heard the sliding glass door swoosh open.

"Cristina, come help," Casey said from the kitchen.

She and Detective Tony looked at each other before hurrying down the hallway, where they encountered the surprising sight of Jack. One of his arms was slumped over Casey's shoulder, the other over Dan's. His face and hair were crusted with dried blood. When he tried to look at Cristina, his eyes wobbled inside their sockets.

"What happened?" Tony asked.

Casey spoke while they carried Jack into the living room and set him onto the couch.

"We were about to turn back when we heard him moaning for help. He looks pretty bad, but I think he'll be OK. I'm not sure if he fell, or if someone did this to him. He hasn't really said anything." Casey got on his knees, eyelevel with the older man. "Are you OK, Jack? Can you tell us what happened? I think he hit his head."

Tony yelled outside for the street cop to call an ambulance.

Jack blinked his eyes distantly. His voice was grave and weak.

"I saw them," he said.

"Saw who, Jack?" Cristina asked frantically. "Anise? Anthony?"

He weakly nodded and said, "I saw her on the trail with a man I hadn't seen before . . . he was holding her under his arm. She didn't seem happy about it. I tried to stop him, Cristina. But he hit me over the head with something hard and I went down." He held a hand to his skull and winced. "I'm so sorry I couldn't get her back for you."

She knelt down and wiped his face with a wet towel. In addition to the coppery smell of blood, Jack stank like someone who'd been exerting himself heavily.

Fear, she thought. *That's what fear smells like.*

She said, "It's going to be OK, Jack. We're going to get her back."

"The search team is already being deployed," Tony said from behind. "Don't worry, we know what to do." And then, almost to himself, "I've spent a lot of time in these woods."

63

The world seemed to be both standing still and moving at a million miles a minute.

By noon, there were more than fifty law enforcement officials on the scene. About a dozen of them were combing the house and the surrounding property. The others had disappeared into the woods. Some with dogs. At least two helicopters were in the air. Every so often one zoomed overhead, although Cristina doubted they could see anything through the thick tree canopy.

Tío Alberto and Casey tried to console Cristina. Even Aba sat next to her on the couch, patting her back. Nothing any of them said or did made her feel any better. All she could do was stare at the clock, watching the minutes tick by, while her emotions oscillated between sadness and rage.

She was mad at the entire world, including Casey, who she yelled at more than once to get the hell out of her face and go find Anise. But she could tell he was afraid to leave her side. After the third such outburst, Tío Alberto suggested he and Casey go get some food for everyone. It was going to be a long day and they needed their energy.

Around 1 PM, a white Channel 7 News van made its way up the driveway and parked in front of the house. The cop who'd taken Cristina's statement earlier blocked them from coming into the yard.

Aba stumbled her cancer-weakened body out onto the front step. She raised an arthritic fist into the air and yelled at the news crew to "get the fuck off the property" or she was going to "kick the living shit out of every last one of them."

Regardless of the warning, the male reporter went live from close enough that Cristina could hear him through the window. He gave a short, vague report about the search for a "yet unnamed girl." But without much else to add, he spent most of his airtime rehashing the case from four years earlier.

The crew tried to hang around after the broadcast, but finally ended up leaving when the cop threatened to arrest them for trespassing.

Holding a takeout bag from In-N-Out, Casey walked in the door and told Cristina that the van was still parked at the bottom of the driveway.

"They stood in front of the car and yelled questions at us when we drove in. It was kind of crazy. I wanted to get out and smash that damn camera."

Cristina didn't touch her burger.

Officer Washburn called around 3 PM and said they'd located the cab driver who picked up Anthony from his building. Not much had come from it. Anthony had been dropped off near his office, but the cabbie drove away before he could see where his passenger went from there.

At 4 PM, Pleasure Point's Chief of Police, Walt Blunderberg, called to say they were going to hold a press conference at the main station for the 6 o'clock news. They wanted Cristina there so she could make a plea for Anise's return. The broadcast would also include the girl's picture, which he assured her was already being distributed to every law enforcement agency in the state, including the FBI, who were monitoring the situation but had not yet been brought in as part of the investigation.

He then updated her on the status of the PPPD search, adding little to what she already knew. The police were systematically covering the mountain trails in all directions, but there were several points in which Anthony could have conceivably gotten off the trail and into a vehicle.

"There are a lot of small little towns and communities as you get deeper into the woods, Ms. Rodriguez. All pretty secluded, and most of the people out there stick to themselves. On the plus side, everyone knows everyone, so there's a good chance an unknown vehicle or person would draw attention. But, Ms. Rodriguez, I won't lie to you. Your ex-husband had a good head start. It's possible he could have found an exit point."

If that was indeed the case, he added, their best bet was going to be roadblocks, which had been established all over the county.

"We'll find your daughter, Ms. Rodriguez."

Cristina was quickly getting sick of hearing people tell her that.

At 5:30 PM, an unmarked Crown Victoria arrived to take Cristina from her house to the police station. Casey sat next to her in the backseat, holding her hand and telling her everything was going to be OK.

On the phone, Detective Tony said that since Anthony was probably doing this to hurt her, it would be a good idea for Cristina to show as much strength as possible.

"It might take the wind out of his sails," he said. "Right now, he's probably tired and confused. Looking for a reason to give up."

Cristina didn't say anything, but she knew Anthony

wouldn't quit until he had what he wanted. And what he wanted was to punish her.

Still, she went along with what the police were doing, including reluctantly agreeing to read a prepared statement. She practiced it on the way to the station, finishing her third pass as they arrived.

At least five different news vans were parked near the steps leading up to the main entrance. Long poles topped with satellite dishes extended from their roofs, ready for live broadcast. Reporters stood in front of the building, going over lines, fixing their hair, and vying with one another for the best camera angles.

Unnoticed in the chaos, the Crown Victoria entered through a secure parking lot.

Inside, bright neon lights glowed over rows of cubicles. Cristina and Casey were shown to Detective Tony's desk by a pleasant but hurried secretary.

A few minutes later, Tony arrived carrying a paper cup of coffee, looking preoccupied, but calm and in control.

"OK, you ready to do this?" he asked, tidying the mess of papers on his desk as they talked.

"Yes," Cristina said, doing her best to keep her voice steady. "I only have one question."

"Shoot."

"In the statement, there's this section about Anise's kidnapping being part of a domestic dispute between Anthony and me." She pointed to the line in the text. "Do I have to say that? I mean, the way the statement is worded makes it sound like we're still married or something. Like we had some argument and he decided to drive off with our daughter. That's obviously not right. Anthony's a criminal, Tony. A psychopath. There's a reason he's not even allowed near Anise. Or me."

Tony took the piece of paper from her and read it as

if he'd never seen it before, shaking his head at parts.

"These guys are unbelievable," he said as he picked up a red pen and crossed the section out. "Sweetheart, you don't have to say anything you don't want to."

He looked around for a second, seeming almost paranoid.

He said, "I was hoping we wouldn't have to have this conversation, but it looks inevitable."

"What is?" she asked.

"You have to understand something, Cristina, and I'm going to be frank with you, because I don't want any of this to distract from the serious work we have left to do in order to find your daughter. And we *are* going to find her." He scratched his chin. "But the fact of the matter is, the longer the search for Anise goes on, the more attention the case is going to get. Already, I've been told that the national news organizations have reporters on their way here."

"That's a good thing," she said. "Isn't it?"

He paused, considering his words carefully.

"Let's just say that the mayor and his friends at the Development Association will be eager to keep things as clean and quiet as possible. More than anything, it looks like they're already particularly interested in limiting speculation regarding a connection between your case and the last investigation."

"I just want my little girl back," Cristina said. "I don't give a shit about any of your politics."

Detective Tony looked a little hurt.

"I'm sorry," she said, putting her hand on his.

He nodded.

"Don't be. You have every right to be pissed. If it makes you feel any better, I am too. As an investigator, the last thing I want is for anyone to restrict the flow of information. All I'm interested in is the truth."

A woman walked up to them wearing a pantsuit and

holding a clipboard.

"We're ready for you guys," she said, smiling way too much given the gravity of what was happening.

They walked down a long hallway while Pantsuit cheerfully explained how the press conference would work. First the Mayor would speak. Then the Chief, who would provide the public with an update on the investigation, as well as information on how the community might help. Last but not least, Cristina would read her statement. After that, the Mayor and the Chief would field questions from reporters.

Pantsuit asked if Cristina needed anything clarified.

"No," she said without emotion. "Everything is *quite* clear."

When they exited the building, Cristina was assaulted by the clicks of cameras and the sound of questions being shouted. So many people were there now, it was hard to understand what any individual was saying. Worse still, the sun was low in the sky and shining directly onto the steps, preventing her from seeing clearly into the crowd.

A tall, balding man in a blue suit limply shook her hand. He offered an empty smile but said nothing. She assumed he was the Mayor, but she'd never seen him before in her life. Chief Blunderberg also shook her hand, albeit more firmly. Dressed in full regalia, he looked official. He offered his condolences and again assured her they would find Anise.

Both men were a foot taller than Cristina. She felt dwarfed.

The scene overwhelmed her senses, to the point she could barely hear what the Mayor said. From what she did manage to process, his words seemed to follow the basic format Detective Tony had predicted. Three times, he called Anise's disappearance an "abduction grown from a domestic dispute."

By the time Chief Blunderberg took the mic, her head had cleared enough to follow a little more closely. He too used the same "abduction grown from a domestic dispute" line, and then also made several assurances that there was absolutely no wider threat to the community. Eventually the Chief did describe what Anise looked like, and asked anyone with information to call the PPPD.

Cristina saw clearly now that this whole performance was as much about making themselves and Pleasure Point look good as it was about the search for Anise.

When it was her turn to speak, Cristina stood at the podium and considered the paper with the statement. As much as she appreciated everyone's efforts, she wasn't going to play their games. Without another thought, she crumpled the sheet of office stationery in her hand.

She glanced toward the edge of the steps and saw Pantsuit looking somewhat mortified. Tony stood next to her, smiling.

"OK," Cristina began. "I'll make this quick, because what I really want to be doing is looking for my daughter. Her name is Anise and she's the most precious thing in the world to me. Her father took her. He's a *fucking* psycho. And if I find him, I'm going to cut his *fucking* balls off. Since I don't want to go to prison, I hope all of you out there will help the police find him before that happens. Even though he deserves it. And, again, thanks for all your help."

Reporters shouted questions and cameras clicked. But Cristina quickly turned and walked past the Mayor and his tough-on-crime scowl, past the Chief and his overgrown mustache, and past Pantsuit, who Cristina guessed was about five seconds away from having a heart attack.

Following her through the doors of the station was Detective Tony, covering a laugh with his hands.

"That was amazing," he said when they were safely back inside. "I've been wanting to say something like that for twenty years. I think you're my new hero."

Cristina moved her lips in the motion of a smile, but her eyes showed only sadness and frustrated anger. Tony asked if she wanted to get out of there and get back to her house, before the shit really started flying.

She nodded her head, but said first there was a phone call she needed to make.

64

Special Agent Jim Canfield answered on the first ring.

"Nice speech, Cristina," he said.

"You were watching?"

"You bet. Watching closely, in fact. I see the Mayor and old Chief Blunderberg are up to their same public relations mission."

"Yah, I guess so." She honestly didn't have any available energy for vendettas or grudges or territory disputes or anything else. So she simply asked, "Do you have a way to help? I haven't heard any useful updates from the cops, and I'm starting to think that's because they don't have a clue about what's going on."

Canfield didn't respond at first, sounding like he might be going into another room.

Finally, he said, "Cristina, I want to assist you. I really do." A pause. The same careful consideration of words as their last phone call. "But until I get the go-ahead, my hands are tied. I want to ask you something, though."

"What?" she asked, more than a bit disappointed.

"Are you sure it was your ex?"

The question caught her off-guard.

"Yes. Why wouldn't it be?"

"I'm not saying he didn't do it. Like I told you when we spoke before, asking a lot of annoying questions is just what we FBI guys do."

"Who else could it be?"

Long pause.

"You're right. There's not really anyone else, is there?"

"Do you know something you aren't telling me? Please don't hold back if you do. I need to find my baby."

This time his response was immediate.

"No. I'm sorry I said anything. Really, I wish there was more that I could do. But, like I said, I can't do much besides watch on TV until I get the OK from the powers-that-be. I promise, though, if and when that happens, you'll be the first to know. OK?"

"What needs to happen for you guys to get involved?" Cristina asked. "Does my little girl have to die?"

She was trying not to sound angry. Canfield had daughters, and she wouldn't have called him if she didn't think he really cared.

"No," he said with patience. "We either need to make the case that the PD isn't able or willing to do everything they can, or we need to be asked. The second option is a lot easier, and a lot faster. If you can get one of the local brass to put in a formal request, I can be on scene in an hour with the full force of the federal government behind me."

"That's it?"

"Yep, that's it. But, as you've already seen, the people in charge there in Pleasure Point have other interests as well."

"Fuck that," she said. He laughed for the first time she could remember. She added, "I'm going to make it happen."

"Good luck. I'll be standing by."

65

On the ride back to Cristina's house, Detective Tony opened up about his involvement with the search for Annie Stewart.

He talked about how frustrating it had been to hear his bosses order all resources put behind the search, only to have them simultaneously undermine that effort by downplaying the severity of the case to the public. He added that there had been multiple pieces of evidence the investigative team was ordered not to discuss publicly.

One was a copy of the *New Horizon* handbook, which had been found a short distance from where Annie's body was recovered in the quarry.

Another was a phone call that came into the station. To Tony himself, in fact. The caller, who used a voice scrambler, went on about how corrupt the world is. How nothing can change until everything does. That kind of thing.

"Basically all the same garbage found in that handbook."

But it was the last thirty seconds of the diatribe that really hit Tony. The caller stopped talking in sentences, and instead kept repeating, in a deadly voice that still haunted him to this day, the same phrase over and over again.

"The blood of the innocent will wash away our sins."

After finishing the recollection, Tony's tough demeanor was visibly shaken.

So was Cristina's.

He said, "I don't say all this to scare you. Any more than I'm sure you already are. All I want to do is make the point again that it's my sincere belief all this playing politics stuff really hurt the investigative team's ability to do our job. And I want you to know that I'm willing to put my own ass on the line to help make sure that doesn't happen again."

66

Cristina couldn't bring herself to eat that night.

Most of the cops had left. But Casey, Tío Alberto, and Aba were all still there.

Everyone was exhausted.

Cristina and Casey had joined the search team once they returned home from the news conference. A few hours past sunset, Casey had to practically drag her back inside so she could get some rest.

There was still nothing to report.

Except for Jack's sighting of Anthony and Anise on the trail, there wasn't a single clue indicating where they'd gone.

Cristina tried all evening to get the Mayor or Chief Blunderberg on the phone so she could convince them to ask for the FBI's assistance. Every time she called, however, they were "in a meeting" or "on a call" or had "just stepped out."

Cristina herself stopped answering the phone after the 20th or so reporter called and asked the same set of questions. She hated to be uncooperative, but each of those conversations was a painful reminder of the fact that the only thing she knew for certain was Anise had been fine when Cristina went to bed, and in the morning she was gone.

That was it.

That was all.

Over and over again, she asked herself how Anthony could have made it into the house without them knowing.

It all made zero sense.

Casey finally convinced her to try sleeping for a few hours. Cristina had vowed not to do so until Anise was found, but she also knew that she would soon be useless if she didn't get at least *some* rest.

In bed, she tried to apologize for being mean to him earlier in the day. He wouldn't even let her finish the sentence, instead reassuring her that he would do anything she needed.

He held her tightly in his strong arms until she drifted off to sleep.

67

The unseen force led her from the bedroom, down the stairs, toward the closet door. She crawled on her hands and knees through the small opening in the back wall, into the blazing light, not knowing exactly where she would end up.

The red cabin in the woods.

She was alone, except for the old car standing guard in the front yard. It welcomed her with its rusted smile. Dead pine needles crunched softly under her foot, muffling the sound of her steps and making her feel like she was floating.

The wind started to blow, beginning as a slow breeze and quickly increasing. The air seemed unnaturally cold – an icy chill that penetrated Cristina's bones, reminding her of winter nights spent sleeping in abandoned buildings.

Soon, needles and leaves and branches were being thrown about by the swirling wind.

With hands covering her face, Cristina made her way up the house's unpainted steps, onto its wooden porch. She stared at the door. It was red, too. Darker than the house itself. The color of dried blood.

Although she felt fearful of this place, her hand reached toward the door without being called upon. The knob was as cold as the wind. She turned it and pulled.

Inside, with the door closed, the small living room was silent. The air felt stagnant and damp. A single low-watt bulb burned from the ceiling, casting its yellow glow across a room that was bare except for a cold fireplace and an ancient rocking chair.

The walls seemed to whisper, though Cristina couldn't understand their words.

A pitch-black hallway led away from the front room. She walked toward the darkness. As she came to the edge of the light, a small hand appeared from the black and grabbed her wrist.

Cristina tried to scream but couldn't. Her lungs were being squeezed, to the point she could hardly breathe.

A face emerged from the shadows.

Annie.

The little girl looked up at Cristina with her sad, scared eyes. She clutched her stuffed hippo tightly against her chest, while letting go of Cristina's wrist and bringing a single finger to her lips. Message delivered, the pressure in Cristina's chest subsided. Annie again reached out, this time taking hold of Cristina's hand and guiding her forward into the darkness.

The two walked down the hallway. Cristina felt claustrophobic in the black silence. The walls seemed only a few inches away, like being trapped alive in a coffin. There was an odd sense of relief when the quiet was broken by a scream from somewhere deeper in the house.

Until Cristina realized it came from Anise.

68

"I know where she is," Cristina gasped as she awoke into a state of full awareness.

It was just past dawn.

"What?" Casey asked from next to her, trying to make himself alert. "Where? How?"

"My dream. I know where she is."

Casey blinked several times, but couldn't find anything to say.

She told him, "I know you probably think I'm crazy. But when you went to find Jeremy in that abandoned building, I dreamed about it the night before. That's how I knew where you were going to be. And ever since I moved in here, something has been trying to warn me."

She reached toward the nightstand for her phone and found Detective Tony's contact information. She called.

"Babe," Casey said as the phone rang. "I want to find her, too. More than anything. But a dream?"

"Yes, a dream."

The phone continued to ring.

"Hello?" Tony answered, sounding tired but awake.

"It's Cristina."

"Yah, I know. Hey, they've taken me off the case. Well, put me on desk duty at least. Said I wasn't handling the witnesses well enough. Can you believe that?"

She ignored him and said, "I think I know where Anise is."

He perked up.

"What? Where? How?"

"I'm pretty sure she's in a red house, somewhere in the mountains. The place has an old car sitting in the front yard. And there are pine needles all over the ground."

"And what makes you think that?"

"A dream."

"A dream?"

"Yes, a dream. Look, I know it sounds crazy. But you said yourself there are lots of places up there. Maybe Anthony rented a house or something and is hiding out until the coast is clear."

"Cristina—"

"—Do you guys have something better?" she snapped, having never been so sure of anything in her life.

"Well, no. But what I was going to say is that there are probably dozens of houses up in those mountains that look exactly like the one you're describing. It's going to take some time."

"I'm telling you, she's there. I know it. I'm going to drive around myself if I have to."

"No, it's not safe. If Anthony's doing this to get at you, the last thing I want happening is for you to show up there and give him two hostages."

He was probably right, and she was glad to hear it sounded like he actually believed her.

He added, "I can guarantee you the bosses aren't going to let me put the idea out to the public that there could be a crazed man on the loose somewhere in the mountains above Pleasure Point. Especially not based off of a dream. But I can take your description and drive around myself. See if I can find anything. Would that work for you? Hell, I don't have anything better to do."

"Yes. I'd be very grateful. Casey will go, too." She looked at him and he nodded. "If he finds something, he'll call you, OK?"

"Alright, Cristina. I think we might be wasting our time but—"

"—We're not," she said. "And when you find the place, because you will, I want you to call Jim Canfield from the FBI. He's ready to help."

She gave him the number.

Then said, "And Tony?"

"Yah, I'm still here."

"Thanks."

"You bet. We're going to get her back, Cristina. I promise."

Casey was already getting dressed.

They went downstairs.

Tío Alberto told Cristina he needed to take Aba to the doctor.

"Sorry, mija," her grandmother said, kissing her on the cheek. "I don't feel so good. You know I want to find that baby more than anyone. But I gotta get my treatment."

"Don't worry, Aba. I know. And we're going to find her."

For the first time in the past 24 hours, Cristina actually started to believe it.

69

Cristina sat alone in the living room.

The morning was brisk, a cool breeze blowing off the ocean.

There were no signs of any cops out the big front window.

They must all be out searching.

Across the courtyard, she saw Jack sitting on his porch. His body language suggested he still felt awful. She dialed his number and watched him pull the phone from his jacket pocket.

"Hello?"

"Hey, Jack. Want to come by for some coffee and breakfast? I could use the company."

"Oh, I don't know. I'm feeling a little whooped, you know. But OK. I think I can trot this bruised body over to enjoy the company of a beautiful woman."

They ended the call and she put on a pot of coffee.

A minute later, he was knocking at the door.

"You know, you don't have to knock, Jack," she said, trying to add some cheer to his dejected face. "You're pretty much family after what you did."

He waved off the compliment as she helped him inside. "Oh, you mean letting myself almost get decapitated? Yah, great move, wasn't it?"

They walked into the kitchen.

She offered to take his jacket for him but he declined.

"Don't worry, Jack," she said. "We're going to find her. I think I know where she is now."

She went about making eggs and pouring coffee.

Jack asked, "Oh yah? Where's that?"

She told him about the dream and the red house.

Something shifted in his face. Worry or surprise, she didn't know. Everyone was treating her dream like it was crazy, and she supposed she couldn't blame them. But that didn't change the fact she believed it.

"I know it sounds cuckoo," she added. "But I really feel in my heart that if we find the house I saw, we'll find Anise too." She turned his way. "You've lived here your whole life, any ideas?"

He seemed lost in thought.

Probably still dazed from the blow to his head.

He snapped out of it and said, "Oh, wow. That sounds like a million places up in the hills. I wouldn't even know where to start."

"That's what the detective said, but I was able to talk him and Casey into scouting it out anyway."

"Oh, that's good. Any luck?"

"They've only been out for a little while but—"

Her phone rang.

She said, "Maybe this is one of them."

She answered, and was a little surprised to hear Officer Washburn on the other end.

"Cristina, we found Anthony."

"What!?"

Relief drenched her entire being.

She said, "Is Anise OK? Where were they?"

Jack raised his eyebrows toward her.

She gave him a thumbs up.

"Cristina," Washburn said. "Anthony was trying to cross the Mexico border when an agent recognized him and took him into custody."

A pause.

She continued, "Cristina, Anise wasn't with him. He says he has no idea where she is. He didn't even know she was gone."

"What? That lying bastard!"

She turned away so Jack wouldn't see the tears rushing into her eyes.

"Cristina, he could be lying. But those border guys are good. They know how to get information out of people, and the agent I spoke with said he was ninety-nine percent sure Anthony was telling the truth."

"How can that be? If it wasn't him, then who took my baby?"

"Don't worry, Cristina. We're going to get her back. Don't lose faith. Something will come up. I'll be in touch soon."

As she ended the call, Cristina's entire world went black.

70

Her eyes blinked open.

Her head pounded with a deep, throbbing pain.

An intense beam of light blinded her vision. She tried to block it with her hands and realized her wrists were restrained by cold metal. It didn't take long for her to recognize the feeling of handcuffs, one pair below each hand, their other ends secured to a solid metal pipe.

Her legs were tied together with rope.

She wasn't going anywhere.

Her brain tried to piece together what had happened.

At first, she assumed the stress must have caused her to pass out, and this was all just another dream. But it felt too real. For one, her body was sore all over, like it had been dragged. And then there was the painful dryness in her throat. She could never remember feeling thirsty in a dream, but her mouth now felt like she'd been chewing on sand.

A metallic clang drew her attention away from the pain for a moment, though the light was too bright for her to see anything but a black curtain of shadows beyond it.

Another clang.

"Hello?" she said into the light. "Is someone there?"

The words sounded stupid to her ears. If there *was*

someone out there in the dark, she guessed it wasn't anyone she should be particularly eager to interact with.

Still, what else was she going to do?

Suddenly, she became aware of how quiet it was. She guessed maybe she was underground. It smelled that way. Musty and dank, like the Cave Train ride at the amusement park. There was the slightest hint of something else, too. Cinnamon maybe.

It was hard to be sure of anything, though. Her senses were clouded by the hammering in her brain.

She thought she heard a whisper of footsteps

"Hello?" she said again, imagining someone flying out from the shadows at any second.

There was nothing.

Except . . . for a moment, what could have been the faint sound of breathing.

In and out.

In and out.

In and out.

Again, she moved her head to see around the bright light. Her eyes sent back only orange and red spots over the blackness.

She tried to free herself from the handcuffs by sliding her hands through them. No luck. The cuffs were closed so tight that her palms had swollen to the point of pain.

It struck her that she had no idea how long she'd been there.

An hour?

A week?

Next, she tested the pipe. Pulling. Tugging. Picking up her bound feet, forcing the metal to support the weight of her small frame, hoping it would be enough to pull the pipe free from the wall. But she could only hold the position for a few moments before her wrists screamed at her, sending her feet back onto the ground.

A laugh from the dark. Familiar, but her disorientated mind couldn't quite place it.

"You'll break your wrists before you break that pipe."

It took a moment, but the sound of the voice brought with it a memory of smelling something toxic. Feeling rough cloth on her face. Dropping her phone. And then blacking out in her kitchen.

"Jack?"

"I know. I know." He stepped out from the edge of the shadows so his face was half-illuminated, like someone telling a scary story around a campfire. "Sorry to disappoint you. I'd so been hoping you wouldn't figure things out, even if I knew that somehow you would. You're a pretty sharp cookie, just like Amanda was." He shook his head thoughtfully at the mention of his former neighbor. He added, "I thought I did a great job, too. I even hit myself over the head with a rock. Talk about method acting!" He chuckled at his own joke and then sighed. "Not that any of it matters now. We're almost done. Almost done."

"Where's Anise, Jack?" She was raging inside. If she got out of the handcuffs, even for a second, she was going to make her best attempt to kill him. And with that thought, she rubbed her backside against the cold, concrete wall, surprised to feel the lump of her pocket knife still there.

"Oh, she's upstairs," he said. "All ready to go."

"Go where?"

"A new world, of course. One without so much pain." He smiled. "And not only will *she* go. But the sacrifice of her innocence will bring a whole new start to life as we know it."

"What are you talking about, Jack?"

"Her blood will allow us all to finally travel toward a new horizon. One of light and joy. Peace and prosperity. A brotherhood of mankind. It will be her gift to you, and to the world."

"You're fucking crazy."

"Yes, indeed," he agreed. "Of course, they said the same thing about Jesus Christ before they put him on the crucifix. And about Lincoln before they shot him. And Gandhi. And Martin Luther King. And John Lennon. And—"

"—Those men didn't kill little innocent children."

"Oh, you'd be surprised. I mean, Gandhi was reported to have slept naked with little girls."

That image made Cristina again struggle to free herself.

"Don't worry," he said. "I'm not *that* kind of monster. No, in fact, that's part of the beauty of Anise's gift to us. Once she gives her life, child molesters and their ilk will disappear from the earth forever. Along with all the other evil people: murderers, rapists, lawyers."

He laughed his hearty belly-laugh.

"You really believe that shit, Jack? You really think killing my baby is going to make all the bad people of the world disappear?"

His face turned thoughtful for a moment.

"Yes. Yes, I do. I know it didn't quite work with Annie. A pity really. And a waste. She was such a beautiful child. But I think the problem was location. I should have given her to the sea, so that the essence of her innocence could spread across the whole world. Yes, I'm certain that was the problem."

"So you killed Annie?"

"Oh yes. And her stepfather. Her poor mother, too, when she figured it out. You women are really much smarter than us men. I had to make it look like a suicide. And I wanted to do the same with you, the hanging that is. What a good story it would have been. But there just wasn't any time. So, here we are."

He held up a small bag that looked like a shaving kit. From it, he removed a glass syringe filled with an amber liquid, which Cristina instantly recognized as enough heroin to kill someone ten times her size.

He tossed the bag aside and added, "That's why we're going to make it look like a mother's grief drove you back to your old ways."

He stepped toward her and she kicked her bound legs into the air.

"Now, now, Cristina. I thought we were friends."

"You're a fucking lunatic."

"No," he told her sternly. "I'm your friend. And, you know what? I can prove it to you."

He lowered the needle. His face distorted into a kind of cartoon evil that didn't look human. Using his free hand, he rotated the light.

Without the heat of the lamp, the coolness of the room washed over Cristina's face and body.

The focused beam came to rest on the far corner. It took her a moment to blink her eyes into focus and make sense of what she saw. Then she knew where the smell of cinnamon had come from.

A badly decomposed body.

The face of this person – by the size of the corpse she guessed it had to be a man – was twisted and literally falling apart. Small pieces of blackened flesh had separated and peeled away from the rest of the skin, curling up like hangnails. There didn't appear to be any hair on the head.

Cristina's stomach turned and she dry heaved, causing a fresh stir of laughter from the darkness.

"You know who *that* is?" Jack asked, sounding excited. "Do you? Do you?"

"No, Jack. Please, I don't want to look at it."

"You won't guess?"

"No. I'm not playing any fucking games."

"Oh, you're no fun. And after what I did for you? Well, I'll tell you who it is anyway. *That* is our friendly neighbor, Rick. Or, as you like to call him, Mr. Psycho. I love that name, by the way. It fits him perfectly. Needless to say, I certainly didn't appreciate at all how he treated you. To be honest, I never liked the guy much in the first place. Funny story, I actually tried to set *him* up to take the fall for Annie. But he was a slick talker I guess, and the cops didn't fall for it. That's why I had to pin it on the stepfather."

She screamed, "You're a fucking psycho! Let me go!"

He turned the light back toward her face and then stepped forward, close enough that she could smell his stale breath. His face flared red with anger.

"I'm getting a little sick of your attitude."

Realizing he was close enough for her to kick out at him, he stepped back.

He added more calmly, "I don't understand why you're so upset, Cristina. I invite you to my nice little getaway in the woods. I make you feel at home." He raised the needle into the air and squirted a short stream of liquid from the tip. "And you treat me like, well, quite frankly, like a bitch."

Cristina heard a noise in the distance, she assumed from the main floor of the red cabin, which she figured had to be where they were.

It sounded like Anise crying.

"The baby is awake," Jack said. "Almost time to go then."

"Mamma!?" Anise yelled, sounding dazed. Maybe drugged.

"Chica! Baby! It's me! Everything's OK! I'm going to

get you out of here!"

"Tsk, tsk, Cristina. You shouldn't lie to your child. What kind of example is that setting for her?"

More crying from Anise.

"Well," Jack continued. "I must go save the world. Sorry we couldn't spend more time being friends. The revolution won't be the same without you."

He moved toward her.

Her eyes focused on the needle, but it was his sizable gut she was aiming for. When he was close enough, she wrapped her hands around the pipe and swung her feet into the air. Both heels slammed into his stomach, sending him reeling with a thick exhale of air.

The needle flew from his hands and disappeared into the darkness, followed by the sound of shattering glass.

She'd hoped he would fall close enough to her so she could stomp his skull in, but he managed to roll backward.

"You fucking bitch!" he said, again losing his composure. He regained it quickly, however, as he stood and laughed. "Oh, I'm going to make you pay for that, Cristina. Yes, I am."

His eyes were blank and deadly. Psychotic. Evil. Reminding Cristina of the way Anthony had looked as he dangled her off the balcony.

Jack continued, "I tried to make it easy on you. But now I'm going to make this last for days."

She spat toward him.

He clenched his fist, looking as though he wanted to make a charge at her.

Then he snarled like an injured dog and limped away, flicking a switch as he left, sending the entire room into pitch-blackness.

Again, she heard the shuffling of his footsteps. The clang of metal. Not knowing if she could still be heard or not, she yelled out, "Anise, mommy is going to get you. Don't be scared, baby!"

The sound of her voice echoed flatly, dying without an answer.

She was left alone in the dark.

Well, almost alone.

From the corner, where she knew the dead body of her former neighbor was slumped over itself, she heard the sound of tiny claws scratching along the concrete floor.

71

At some point, Cristina either passed out or fell asleep
She was dreaming.

This time, there was no waking up in her own bed.
No walking toward the closet door. No trip through a
tunnel of light. The force that had been with her, dragging her wherever it wanted, was strangely absent.

She found herself alone on a lifeless beach.

To her left was nothing but endless sand, stretching
for what seemed like a thousand miles. To her right,
the same.

No people. No animals. Not even a single seagull.

Behind her, the sand continued into the distance,
without as much as a single dry bush. Only sand. Forever.

In front of her was the ocean. Though, if it weren't
for the salty scent, Cristina might have thought it to be
the shore of a lake. The water lay eerily flat. Not one
wave crashed onto the beach. Nor did any whitecaps
ripple in the dead, windless air.

Even the sun felt cold.

Some instinctive part of her realized that it wasn't
just the beach that was dead, but the entire world. It
existed, but without love or hate, happiness or joy.

It was just . . . empty.

Cristina felt a small hand grasp her own.

Annie.

This time she was smiling, like the happy little girl Cristina was sure she was before Jack robbed her of life.

Together, the two walked toward the water.

They looked into its black and bottomless depths.

Cristina stared at her own reflection. She didn't look anything like herself. The woman peering back at her was older. Worn out. Sad. Her skin and body still lived, but only as a shell. Inside, she was as empty as the world Cristina now stood in.

Beyond this image, with some sense beyond sight, she could see an outline of herself, held unconscious by pain in the dark basement of Jack's mountain cabin.

"Wake up, Cristina!" she shouted toward the water, surprised to find that her voice even worked.

"WAKE UP, CRISTINA!" she repeated with every bit of energy she could muster.

Annie squeezed her hand.

Cristina saw the little girl smiling again.

Annie released her hand and began to wave.

The dead world flickered.

Annie's hand continued moving back and forth in the air as she and her polka dots and her hippo faded.

Cristina returned to the basement, where she heard the same metal clang as when Jack had departed. She waited for the bright light to reappear in front of her, readying her strength for another attack.

Footsteps. Yet, she swore it sounded like more than one set.

An intense beam from a flashlight cut through the dark. It moved along the wall and came to a stop on Rick Atkin's rotting corpse.

And then a familiar voice.

"Jesus Christ. What the fuck is that?"

"Casey!" she shouted.

The beam jumped toward her, blinding her for a moment before falling to her feet.

"Cristina?!" he said. And then, in the other direction, "I found her!"

More footsteps and another flashlight.

The beams danced together.

"Are you OK?" Casey asked.

Someone grabbed her wrist. She heard the click of a key turning in the handcuffs. Felt the stinging pain of blood rushing back into her fingers. Then again on the other hand.

Meanwhile, Casey struggled to untie the rope from her ankles.

"In my pocket," she said to him. "My knife."

He reached behind her and pulled out the blade.

"Get me out of here," she said as he freed her.

They moved through the basement, out a thick metal door.

From there, an iron staircase spiraled up through an opening in the floor. Detective Tony ducked to avoid hitting his head.

The trapdoor came out into a small, sparse bedroom, not much bigger than a closet. Just large enough to fit a twin bed with an ominous set of leather straps.

A single bulb burned above.

"He took her, Casey," she said as they walked through a hallway, into the fireplace room.

She noticed through the window that it was already dark, the moonlight reflecting off the top of the old car in the front yard.

"Jack took her," she repeated.

"I know," he said.

"You do?"

"Yes," a voice said from behind. Cristina thought it sounded familiar, but when she turned to see who it belonged to, she didn't recognize the fit, grey-haired man in the navy suit.

"Special Agent Jim Canfield," he said, extending his hand. "Cristina, as soon as it was clear Anthony wasn't the guy, I was almost certain it had to be Jack."

"You *knew?*" Her voice was heated and confused. "And you didn't tell us?"

"We didn't know, exactly. As I told you before, we always had another suspect in the original case, but we've also been trying to pin down Jack as the founder of *New Horizon* for going on three decades now. We were never sure of anything until today. Until right now, actually."

"What? Stop lying to me."

Canfield held up his hands. "I promise you, I'll give you all the details later. But the short of it is, until your boyfriend discovered you missing and called us, we weren't able to pin anything but suspicion on Jack. Casey told me about the red house in the mountains, which we knew about. But it's too secluded for us to monitor. So it wasn't until I walked into that room and saw the kid's bed with the straps that I really knew for certain."

Cristina was overwhelmed with emotion.

She wanted to be mad, but there was no time for it.

"OK, fine," she said instead. "But we have to find him before he hurts Anise. He's crazy. He thinks killing her is going to begin some new world of peace and prosperity."

"Right," Canfield said. "Do you have any idea where he might have taken her?

"I think I know," she realized. "How far is it to my house?"

"About fifteen minutes or so by road," Tony said. "Why? Is it close to there?"

"Very close. I just hope we can get there first."

72

"Now they're saying backup is delayed," Detective Tony told the others, visibly frustrated as they pulled the car up the gravel driveway. "So we're on our own for at least another fifteen or twenty minutes. Maybe more."

"If Jack's walking, it'll take him hours to get here, right?" Cristina asked.

Tony checked the clip of his pistol and answered, "I don't think he's walking. There were fresh tire tracks leading from that cabin. Looked like an ATV to me. So he could be here any minute now. Honestly, I don't think we have time to wait. We need to be ready to get Anise safe. And we need to be careful about how we approach him. I'm afraid if he sees cops he'll hurt her."

Cristina said, "OK, well what are we going to do?"

They spent about five minutes discussing it, with Agent Canfield doing most of the talking.

Afterward, he asked, "Everyone clear?"

They all nodded their heads while listening to the crescendoing buzz of an ATV coming from the woods.

"OK, there's our target," Canfield said. "Everyone into place."

***

As Cristina descended the wooden steps, she watched

the incoming fog clutch at the moon with its wispy fingers. In the last bit of light, she could just make out Jack approaching the rocky pathway from the beach side, the same way the two of them had come on their hike together. He seemed rushed and didn't look up. She doubted he would have seen her anyway against the dark rock.

Tucked under his arm was Anise.

Cristina fought the urge to yell out to her.

Waves crashed against the path's protective rock outcropping, each sounding angrier and more vengeful than the last.

A hundred yards away was the circular platform of tide pools she and Jack had stood on together. That's where Cristina wanted to be, certain it was his destination as well.

All she had to do was get there.

It had been hard enough when she first traversed the path in clear daylight. Now, in the dead of night, racing against time, and with a rapidly thickening fog all around her, she was more frightened than she'd ever been in her entire life.

Mostly she was afraid that she wouldn't be fast enough, strong enough, good enough, to do her part. Afraid that Anise would pay for her shortcomings. She inhaled a deep breath of wet, salty air and tried to clear her head, which still throbbed in pain along with the rest of her body.

None of that mattered.

The love she had for her daughter put her beyond pain.

Beyond fear.

Beyond stopping.

That sense of confidence was tested immediately, however, when, with her first step onto the wet rock, she slipped. Her hand instinctively reached toward the cliff wall to steady herself. Instead of rock, her out-stretched fingers found the hard shell of a crab. She nearly screamed, but managed to pull back the sound, knowing it could cost Anise her life. But she went down hard, badly bruising her shoulder and already sore ribs.

For a brief moment, she lay there wanting to cry.

She quickly replaced that thought with an image of Anise's sweet face traveling in circles around the carousel atop her pink horse. It gave her the strength she needed to push herself back up.

Continuing on, she gently stepped from jagged rock to jagged rock, reminding herself as she did to stay slow and steady.

The path was now completely covered in fog. She no longer had any way of knowing how Jack was progressing toward the tide pools. And given that he'd been so much more surefooted than she was when they walked the route together, it was obvious he had the advantage.

She wondered if Canfield would even be able to get a shot.

What if he couldn't? What was she going to do then?

Whatever it takes, she told herself.

Although she was filled with plenty of doubts, there was one thing she was certain about. She would gladly give her own life to save her daughter.

By the time she made it to the tide pools, the fog had condensed into some of the thickest she'd seen since moving to Pleasure Point. It was difficult to even see her hand as she planted it on the next rock.

There was no way Canfield would be able to shoot from where she'd left him, perched with a rifle on the cliffside. She was on her own, at least for the time being.

Nearby but unseen, wave after wave thundered like

the steps of a marching giant.

She pulled herself up onto the tide pool platform. The fog was thick enough that Jack could have been five feet away and she wouldn't have known it.

She listened, but heard only the deafening waves.

Continuing on hands and knees to avoid falling, she made her way forward, navigating around small pools filled with anemones and other creatures.

A spray of icy saltwater poured down on top of her, soaking her clothes and hair.

She heard Anise cry out from somewhere in the foggy darkness.

"I want to go home!"

"Quiet!" Jack told her.

Between the waves and the blanket of clouds, it was difficult to tell which direction their voices were coming from, but she crawled toward where she thought they might be.

The rock platform hadn't seemed all that large the first time Cristina walked out onto it, but it now felt endless.

After several painful movements across sharp rock, she heard Jack's voice again. At first, she thought he was talking to Anise, then realized it sounded more like he was talking to himself. And it wasn't English. He appeared to be incanting some kind of evil-sounding ritual in a language she didn't recognize.

His voice was deep and gravelly, reminding Cristina of someone from one of the shows Tío Alberto liked to watch about people being exorcised from demonic possession.

She continued crawling forward, inch by inch.

With her focus on pinpointing where Jack's strange words were coming from, she accidentally thrust her hand into one of the pools, splashing water loudly.

His voice stopped.

"Who's there?" he said, sounding startled, and then regaining the same psychotic chill he'd shown in the basement. "Is that you, Cristina? It is, isn't it? Come to see your little girl off?"

She could feel her heart beating in her chest, ticking off seconds in the darkness.

A wave shook the rocks.

Without warning, Jack jumped out of the fog and onto her back.

Her face slammed into the rock, barely missing a sharp point that could have easily impaled her skull. As it was, the impact made her see sparks.

Then Jack's stout body was smothering her.

With each breath, she took in less air. Fear and panic grabbed hold. Fear that she would pass out and never see Anise again. Fear that Jack would throw them both into the ocean to drown.

She imagined hearing Anise flailing her arms in the water, splashing unseen but close by, screaming for her mother to help, and Cristina being unable to do anything as the two either floated apart or were broken against the rocks.

The vision gave way as Jack's strong hands took hold of her hair, once more slamming her face into the rock. Another set of bright flashes, followed by a shocking sense of awareness as he lifted her head and thrust it into a pool of frigid water.

The sticky tentacles of a sea anemone latched onto her face. A hermit crab, trapped between the rock and her ear, wiggled as it tried to get free.

She felt the vibration of the waves through the rock.

The cold, salty water began to overcome her, creeping into her nostrils and mouth. Her brain begged for oxygen. Her arms waved desperately, trying to find something to latch onto.

Then, in a brief moment of clarity, she stretched her

arm, trying to reach the back pocket of her jeans. Her fingers came close, only an inch or two away. She could feel the top edge of the pocket's seam. But as hard as she tried, she couldn't seem to slip her fingers into the opening.

The last of her strength was fading. In the next few seconds, her brain would shut down. She could feel terror turning into a smooth, drifting calmness. An acceptance of the situation.

With one final effort, she reached the knife, grasping it with the tips of her fingers. A hold so slight she nearly lost it.

With precision gained from practicing for years in the corners of dark drug squats, Cristina used one smooth motion to slide open the knife and flip the blade so it faced upward. Without hesitation, she thrust the sharp steel toward where she imagined Jack's face to be, managing to hit him directly in the center of his left eye.

He screamed and fell on his side.

Cristina's lungs gasped in a greedy breath as she lifted her head from the water.

The waves continued to explode around them.

"You fucking bitch!" he said, writhing on the ground next to her, grasping the air in a vain attempt to pull the knife from his eye. Blood ran down his face and soaked into his beard, then trickled into a pool of water, clouding the anemones in darkness.

Cristina took a few more desperate breaths and finally rolled over. She looked around, trying to gain her bearings. Listening for any sign of her daughter.

"Anise!?" she weakly shouted. "Chica, are you there?"

A wave filled the air with its fury. As the sound subsided, Cristina heard nothing but Jack whimpering, his brain cavity no doubt slowly filling with blood.

She worried the victory would be worthless.

Where was Anise?

She once more felt overcome by fear and pain and loss.

Her mind returned to the shores of that dead ocean in a dead land.

A future without Anise.

Another wave hit. Behind its dying echo, she heard the end of a trailing cry.

"mma . . ." it said, and then started again. "Mamma!"

"Anise!"

The sound had been close.

Cristina stumbled toward it through the fog.

At that moment, Jack's hand reached up and grabbed her ankle, throwing her off-balance and slamming her back down onto the rocks.

"Please help me, mamma!" Anise yelled. "The water's going to get me."

Jack's hand held tight.

Cristina struggled, but he somehow continued to maintain an inhuman strength that refused to let go.

Then she stopped trying to get away.

Instead, she calmly turned and saw his face looking back at her. The knife still protruding from his eye socket. His beard now completely soaked in blood. Lips pulled back in a twisted, evil smile. Tongue lolled out of his mouth, it too dripping blood.

With patient precision, she leaned forward, expecting him to lash out at any moment. But he simply stared with his one good eye, grinning as if he'd won.

Then he spoke, blood gurgling from his mouth along with his words.

"You'll never get out. The waves are too high already. They'll take you and Anise and . . . the new world will finally be born."

As if reinforcing his prediction, the strongest wave yet crashed against the rocks.

For another moment, she stared into Jack's face. A part of her felt sorry for him. For his loss of sanity. That part of her could understand how someone could look at the world they lived in and believe in the presence of evil. In the necessity of some supernatural force to come along and defeat it, whatever the cost may be.

Then, she wrapped her fingers around the handle of the blade and slowly pulled it from his eye socket. Blood poured out, covering the damaged white orb before gushing down his face and onto her hand.

Jack's body spasmed, but his grip held.

Cristina pressed the point of the blade against his throat and pushed. She felt the steel penetrate the thickness of his windpipe, enter an open space, and then poke into the other side. She twisted the knife, trying to do as much damage as possible.

Jack gasped.

He finally let go.

She bounded away while he twitched and fought for air, grabbing at his neck and the knife.

"Anise?!" she shouted. "Anise!"

When there was no response, Cristina was sure the last wave had taken her.

But a second later, hope returned. She spotted her daughter lying unconscious and soaking wet on the rock. The wave had indeed hit her, but by sheer luck her foot had lodged itself in a crevice, holding her in place and preventing her from being pulled into the backwash.

As Cristina tried to free her daughter, another wave crashed. The surge of water covered them both and receded, pulling Cristina along with it.

She tried to hold onto the rock, but soon felt her

grip slipping.

There was nothing she could do now.

She had tried her best and failed.

Then a hand grabbed her wrist. Thinking it was Jack, somehow still alive, she tried to fight it off, even as the ocean refused to stop pulling her in the other direction.

The sea wanted her badly.

For a moment, she nearly let it take her.

EPILOGUE

A Summer BBQ

The Fourth of July, a beautiful summer day in Pleasure Point, California.

It had been almost nine months since Cristina nearly lost everything she ever cared about, including her own life.

Thankfully, when the fog had become too dense to execute their original plan of taking Jack out with a rifle shot, both Casey and Detective Tony rushed toward the tide pools.

If Casey hadn't grabbed Cristina's arm at that exact moment, if he hadn't held on with all his immense strength as she fought to escsape, she surely would have been swept away.

As it was, they almost all drowned trying to return to higher ground. The rising tide had almost completely flooded the path before they reached the safety of the stairs. But, in what they all later agreed was some version of a miracle, the water ebbed just enough to clear a temporary path for them.

Anise, who'd hit her head hard against the rock, didn't seem to remember anything that had happened.

For that, Cristina was grateful.

It made moving on with life a lot easier.

Not that anyone ever gets over an experience like the one they all went through. But, as with every other challenge Cristina had faced in life, she knew that the key was to never quit. She just had to keep putting one foot in front of the other.

A lot had happened since that day.

In the spring, Casey asked her to marry him. He proposed at the end of the pier. She pretended to think hard about it, just to mess with him, but then answered with an emphatic yes as she jumped into his arms. They weren't sure when they would do it, or where. And they didn't feel in any rush to decide. As long as they were together – the three of them – life would work out.

That's not to say everything had been perfect.

Casey ended up losing *Bula's Surf Shop*.

With a team of high-priced lawyers, the Pleasure Point Development Association sued and countersued until they got a judge that saw things their way. Casey was given a month to vacate. Cristina's boss at the art store, too.

The whole area was going to be torn down, including *The Wharf* amusement park. The Development Association planned to build condos alongside a beachside mall, complete with a Target and an Applebee's.

Casey and Cristina didn't talk much about the shop anymore. Doing so just made him sad. He would end up going on about how horrible it was that the culture of an entire town could be wiped away in the name of almighty profit. And, in the end, dwelling on it wasn't going to change anything anyway.

They were thinking of moving to Fiji, or maybe Aruba. Some place with a slower pace of life, and people who were interested in actually enjoying it.

Besides, they didn't need money.

Although he'd been unable to save the store, the talented Danny Dee *had* secured for Cristina a settlement of $10 million from Anthony, more-or-less securing them for life. On top of that sum, the majority of Anthony's other assets – totaling almost $50 million – were being put into a trust fund that would be available to Anise when she turned 25.

Dan refused to take even a single penny for his efforts.

As for Anthony, he'd finally run into the wrong man in Judge Peterson. Despite endless motions and appeals, Peterson sentenced him to the maximum sentence of ten years in San Quentin.

By the time he got out, Cristina, Casey, and Anise would be thousands of miles away, living a peaceful, happy life.

Of course, she would miss Tío Alberto, and was hoping to get him to come live wherever they decided to settle. But she doubted she could pry him away from his church community and his work. She'd given him a million dollars to keep for himself, and he still woke up and mowed lawns every day of the week except Sunday.

Aba had passed away. She died peacefully in her sleep just after Christmas, a couple weeks after getting the chance to see Anise play an elf in her school play. Cristina was sad at first. But part of her also felt like her grandmother had been, in a way, happy to be done with what was a difficult journey through life.

The hardest part about her death was explaining things to Anise. Ultimately, Cristina ended up telling her that Aba had gone to live in the world we go to when we dream. After an endless stream of questions, Anise was eventually satisfied with that answer.

Before deciding where to move, the three of them were going to spend the summer traveling.

"Weighing their options," as Casey put it.

To say goodbye, they invited all the people they cared about over for a BBQ, and to watch the fireworks if the fog didn't come in.

The guest list turned out to be relatively small. Cristina, Casey, Anise, and Tío Alberto, of course. Dan and Jordan were there. As were the ex-employees of *Bula's Surf Shop*, and Jacklyn (who turned out to be a great babysitter). Rounding out the attendees were a few surfing buddies of Casey's, including the long-haired, one-of-a-kind Jerry "Hound Dog" Parker, who brought over his collection of roman candles and almost lit the hillside on fire. Jeremy (nine months clean) made it. Along with Cristina's ex-boss, Detective Tony, and even Officer Washburn.

And, of course, Michelle. She was the life of the party, telling joke after joke, until the entire group was gasping for breath. She and Cristina had really reconnected, a bond that was crucial in helping Cristina recover from the trauma of everything that had happened. Despite the distance between them, the two talked every day, got together at least once a week for coffee, and on weekends for meetings.

There was, perhaps, no one Cristina would miss more.

When the burgers had all been eaten, the fireworks watched, and the goodbyes said, Cristina put Anise to bed in their Pleasure Point home for one of the last times.

Afterward, she told Casey she was bummed Agent Canfield couldn't make it, saying that if it hadn't been for him, neither Anise nor herself would be breathing.

"Did you invite him?" Casey asked.

"Yah, he didn't respond. I hope everything's OK."

"I'm sure he's just hella busy. I imagine the FBI keeps you on your toes."

Cristina brushed her teeth and was about to head back into the bedroom when she checked her phone – a flashy new one she'd just picked up. It had all the bells and whistles, although she hardly ever used any of them, except the camera for taking pictures of Anise.

The phone flashed with an email alert and she flicked down on the screen to check it.

From: Special Agent James R. Canfield, Federal Bureau of Investigation

To: Cristina Rodriguez

Dear Cristina,

Sorry I couldn't make the party. They have me stationed in Texas hunting down drug smugglers. It's too hot, but other than that I can't complain.

Thought you might like to see this memo I submitted to the file we have on Jack. In particular, the bio section.

I could get in big trouble for showing you this, so please keep it to yourself. But I thought it might help give you some closure.

Good luck in the future.

And take care of that little girl of yours. She's a cutie pie.

Best,
Jim

Cristina clicked open the attachment.

It was a formal memo, beginning with a bunch of technical jargon about how the information was gathered, a timeline, a part about how the suspect died (including mention of the fact his killer had been found to be acting in self-defense). All followed by a paragraph stating that no body had been recovered, the remains having presumably been washed out to sea.

She skimmed past most of this to the section marked *Suspect Biography*.

As she read through it, she learned that Jack Benning was born Jonathan Krauser. He spent thirty years living a double life. As a teacher of history and civics, and as the founder and invisible leader of the *New Horizon* cult.

Her jaw dropped a little when she read the next part.

Earlier in life, Jack had been John, a teacher happily married with two young daughters. His wife and both girls were killed when the old apartment building the family lived in collapsed. John was away at a teaching seminar when it happened. Apparently, many warnings had been made, by John and others, about the structural integrity of the building. All of which the landlord – a shady development company – had done nothing about.

Following the collapse, John spent several years trying to find a legal means of holding the company responsible, ultimately to no avail. Sometime in his mid-thirties, John gave up, apparently lost his mind, and formed what would become *New Horizon*.

A few years later, when the group started to attract attention, he faked his own death and started a new life under the name Jack Benning. After that, his influence on the organization was known only to a small leadership circle. The day-to-day activities were, and likely still are, run by this secretive body of dedicated adherents.

The rest of the memo was information Cristina already knew. An explanation of his role in the first murders, as well as in almost killing Anise and herself. All stuff she really had no interest in reliving.

After reading the email, she put away her phone and sat on the edge of the stairs, crying softly in the dark. She tried to imagine how she would react if the same injustice had been done to her. What Casey would do in that situation. What anyone would do. She really didn't know. All she could do was recall the countless times in her life when she'd seen a system that was supposed to provide opportunities for people, instead end up doing the complete opposite.

After finishing her tears, Cristina checked on Anise one last time. At first glance, all she saw when she peeked into the room was a lump of something under the blankets. She couldn't help but remember back to that horrible day. The memory made her heart race. It continued to beat faster and faster, until she took the few steps over to the bed and saw Anise was indeed there, clutching a stuffed animal.

Cristina kissed her daughter on the forehead and was about to turn for the door, when she suddenly realized what the little girl was holding.

Not a sea creature. Not one of the Disney characters she loved so much.

Wrapped tightly in Anise's arms was a stuffed animal Cristina had seen before, although never in real life. She smiled at the sight of the hippo, kissed her daughter once more, and headed off to sleep.

Like This Book?

Please leave a review on Amazon and Goodreads

Sign up to receive alerts about new releases from Jake Parent (and that's the only thing that gets sent to this list): http://eepurl.com/bXzepr

Purchase Jake Parent's debut novel, *Only the Devil Tells the Truth*, from Amazon

About The Author

Jake Parent is the author of *Cristina*, a new psychological suspense novel. His first book, *Only the Devil Tells the Truth*, was a #1 Amazon Bestseller. His influences include Charles Bukowski, Stephen King, Maya Angelou, John Steinbeck, Honoré de Balzac, Ella Fitzgerald, John Sanford, Jimi Hendrix, Ernest Hemingway, Greg Graffin, Pablo Picasso, Rickey Henderson, and Mac Dre. He grew up in San Jose, CA but now lives in the Washington, DC area.

For more information, visit www.jakedparent.com.

Made in the USA
Middletown, DE
11 July 2016